FORTUNE'S FOOL

FORTUNE CHRONICLES 3

KATHLEEN MCCLURE
KELLEY MCKINNON

MORE OUTRAGEOUS FICTION

<u>THE FORTUNE CHRONICLES</u>

Soldier of Fortune

Fortune's Fallen

Outrageous Fortune

Change of Fortune

Fortune's Fool

<u>THE ZODIAC FILES - with L. Gene Brown</u>

The Gemini Hustle

The Libra Gambit

PUBLISHED BY OUTRAGEOUS FICTION

Edited by Lori Diederich
Cover by Youness Elh

ISBNs:
978-1-947842-12-0 (eBook)
978-1-947842-41-0 (Paperback)

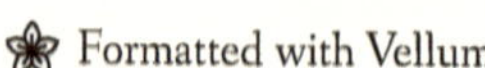 Formatted with Vellum

Thank you for continuing to choose The Fortune Chronicles.

If you are enjoying the journey, please consider leaving an honest review for each book. For individual creators like me, your feedback is the best way to help other fans of quirky science fantasy discover our worlds.

And for more outrageous fiction, including new stories, exclusive content, and our reader community, scan the QR code below to follow our Outrageous Crew on Ream. It's free, easy, and the best way to delve into our fantastical worlds!

Happy reading,

Kathleen

https://reamstories.com/outrageouscrew

For Connor

O ! I am fortune's fool!

— WILLIAM SHAKESPEARE

CHAPTER 1

Lower Cadbury-Outer 9th District
Nike City, Avon
United Colonies of Fortune
April 18, 1449 After Landing

His long coat whipping in the spring winds, Gideon Quinn came to a stop before a ramshackle building in Lower Cadbury.

Because the afternoon suns were shining with unusual vigor, he had to squint up at the faded sign nailed over the building's entrance.

"A Fine Mess," he read aloud, then grinned at the reptilian snort from the draco on his right shoulder. "Yeah, not much to look at," he agreed, giving Elvis a soothing scritch under his chin. "But we've seen worse."

A second snort indicated Elvis wasn't sure they had.

Since Elvis might be right, Gideon checked the lay of the collapsable baton under his left sleeve.

The baton, fondly named Lulu, had been created as payment for Gideon's first official job as a private facilitator.

Iliana, the client in question, was a designer of small devices and weapons.

She also, as Gideon learned after closing the case, brewed a mean cup of tea.

Assured his weapon of choice was locked and loaded in the spring holster designed by a friend, Gideon hauled the creaking door open and entered A Fine Mess, where he took a moment to allow his vision to adjust to the dim interior, then another to appreciate truth in advertising.

Taking in the odors of cheap booze and stale sweat, he continued into the pub, where flickering overheads failed to soften scorched walls pocked by gaping shutters.

The furniture he passed was of the "found on a curb" design, and the clientele draped in clothes as threadbare as their faces were worn.

But as he wound through the tables, Gideon overheard the same easy rumbles of conversation he'd expect in any other tavern, and a rattle of dice drew his eyes to a game of Colonists of Mercedes, where the last roll netted a player three beds of crystal, which she immediately used to build an airship.

By this time there were more than a few speculative gazes tracking his path, as well as a non-zero number of hands reaching for what might be concealed weapons.

Accustomed to this level of suspicion, Gideon clicked his tongue and murmured, *"High road."*

At the prompt, Elvis, his talons rasping against the pauldron on which he rested, leapt up, and with a single flap of his wings settled on the smoke stained rafters.

As often occurred when Gideon deployed Elvis, a series of gasps and sighs followed in the draco's wake, easing the overall tension in the room.

Or, most of the tension, as Gideon noted a fellow holding down a table at the rear of the pub who didn't seem the least interested in the draco, but was more than ready to meet Gideon's gaze.

A dagger of sunlight slashed through a nearby shutter to spark off the blood red studs in the man's ears, and highlighting a deep scar running down one side of his deep umber face.

And while there was nothing overtly threatening about the man, he sat with the kind of readiness Gideon associated with a natural fighter.

Curious, but as the bear dog in a waterman's clothing wasn't the reason Gideon had come to A Fine Mess, he offered a nod of greeting-slash-neutrality.

The bear dog's lip twitched, but he offered a reciprocal nod, and Gideon continued on to the bar where an individual with a neat goatee and a memory of hair ringing his scalp stood wiping a glass.

Easing up alongside a skeletal figure half a head shorter than himself, Gideon aimed his attention to the trio on his right, all half a head taller. "Rolf," he greeted the nearest giant. "Ulf, Freya." He tapped his heart in a quick Corps salute for the Stolichnayan triplets who, after an unfortunate first meeting, had proven to be both solid allies and good friends.

"Good day, Gideon," Ulf replied, as all three raised their glasses in greeting.

"What are you guys doing here?" he asked, glancing at the diminished bottle they shared. "I thought you'd all found work at the meat-growing plant."

Rolf shifted, clearly uncomfortable. "We did have this job, but—"

"There was a problem with Rolf mixing the makings of the poultry with the makings of the pork," Freya cut in, throwing her brother a disgusted look.

"Oh," Gideon said, while someone at a nearby table made a retching noise. He turned to Rolf. "*Why?*"

"I was thinking it would make the recipe for Chicken Tolstoy easier. No need to wrap the chicken bits around the ham bits, yes?"

"No," Freya said.

"Here, here," called one of the Colonists of Mercedes players.

"Gotta go with Freya on this one," Gideon agreed.

"So did the manager of the plant." Rolf sighed into his booze.

"So, the manager fired all of you?" Gideon asked.

"Not quite," Ulf said.

"First, they are only firing Rolf," Freya began.

"But then Ulf tried to prove how it was maybe not such a bad idea," Rolf joined in.

"By mixing the pork into the aurochs," Freya picked up the thread again.

"Like kebobs," Ulf explained.

The bartender paused mid-swipe of his glass. "Seriously?"

"Okay, so no meat processing for you," Gideon said to Ulf and Rolf. "Or cooking, I think." Then he focused on Freya. "Did you get the boot, too?"

"No one gives me the boot," that young woman said with a sniff. "I quit, in solidarity with my idiot brothers."

"Way to stick it to the Man."

"But the meat-plant manager is non-binary," Ulf told Gideon.

Some things, Gideon thought, weren't worth explaining. "It's a Fordian thing," he said. "Anyway, sorry about the jobs."

"There will be other jobs." Freya asserted calmly. "But where is Mia?" She leaned forward as Ulf poured more liquor into all their glasses. "She is still your apprentice, no?"

"She is still my apprentice, yes. But she's an apprentice with a geography lesson to finish, so she's back at the office."

"And are you liking the place on Doyle Street?" Rolf asked.

"I think it'll suit," Gideon said. "Mia and Jinna both like it a lot."

"Doyle . . . " A drinker at one of the nearby tables mused over the street name while the hook which replaced his right hand tapped the table. "Ain't that the street what burned to ashes when that morph house went up in flames?"

"Nah, you're thinking of Baudelaire Street," another patron intoned through a beard so thick, it could serve as a scarf.

"Not Baudelaire, neither," a third opined. "'Twas Byron."

"Morph houses are always catching fire on Byron," the barkeep tossed in.

"Aye, Doyle's a nice little spot," a woman from the Mercedes table agreed. "If you don't mind living off the crystal grid. And there's a nice bookshop down t'end of the street," she added, taking a drag from her pipe.

"Doyle isn't very populated," Gideon regained hold of the conversation and aimed it at the triplets. "But the cross streets, Cornwell and Butler, have a lot of traffic, so Jinna's confident the tea shop will do well."

"Mama was impressed that you and Jinna would be going into partnership together, you with your facilitating and Jinna with her cookery," Freya said.

"Speaking of, how goes the facilitating?"

At Ulf's question, Gideon felt a jerk of motion from the skeletal man at his left. "It's interesting," he determined, focusing on the triplets.

"As interesting as vat-grown Chicken Tolstoy?" Freya asked.

"Nothing will ever be that interesting," Gideon determined. "But with the facilitating, the biggest issue is while there are plenty who need my services, most of them aren't what you'd call rolling in starbucks."

"But how are you being paid?"

"In trade, for the most part," Gideon told Rolf. "Curtains, dishes, some bits of furniture. One of our clients is an engraver, and he paid up by making a sign for the office."

A sign he hadn't yet hung, he recalled with a twinge of guilt. *I'll get to it,* he told himself.

You keep saying that, his self said back. *And yet . . .*

"And lots of foodstuffs," he continued, drowning out the internal commentary. "Lots. Enough that Jinna's been able to test an apiary's worth of recipes for MacGuffin's. That's what she's naming the shop."

"We know," Rolf said with a quick grin. "We visited Jinna last week, and she let us taste her Man in the High Cassoulet."

"That's pretty good," Gideon admitted. "But you haven't lived until you've tried her Penne from Heaven."

The bartender made a choking sound.

"And is Jinna well?" Freya asked.

"Good. She's . . . good."

"When we see her last, she is looking, ah—" Rolf made a mounding gesture over his stomach.

"Ready to pop," Ulf filled in.

"She's pretty eager to get MacGuffin's up and running before the baby gets here," Gideon said.

"We could help," Ulf suggested. "Since we are not at the meat-growing plant."

"Sure," Gideon said. "Just, you know, don't mention the Chicken Tolstoy."

At which point a gentle clearing of a throat had him turning to face the bartender.

"Sorry to interrupt," he said to Gideon, "but did you plan to order a drink?"

"Do I look suicidal?"

"That's just hurtful," the bartender replied over Ulf's bark of a laugh.

Freya leaned forward on her elbows. "Gideon must have learned about the pool."

"Can't say that I have," Gideon replied.

"There is no pool," the bartender said.

"Yes, there is," Ulf asserted, slapping his hand on the bar with a meat-like thud. "I know this because we started it." He lifted his hand from the bar with a sucking sound as his skin pulled free from whatever substance coated the surface. "We three," he waved the sticky palm at his siblings, "are making book on how many drinks of Msr Martin Soong's booze it would take to put a person in hospital."

All across the room, Gideon heard glasses thudding and chairs creaking as bodies turned towards the bar.

"And how is the pool going?" he asked into the fresh silence.

"Not so good," Freya admitted.

"We three are the only ones to enter," Ulf explained.

"And since we are seeing no one keeling over . . . " Rolf added.

"Perhaps we find something else to be betting on," Freya concluded.

"Good plan," Gideon offered as all three clinked glasses and downed their theoretically hazardous liquor.

While the Ohmdahls played Stoli roulette with their beverages, the bartender, presumably Msr Martin Soong, let out a long-suffering sigh, then addressed Gideon. "If you haven't come for a drink, then why, may I ask, are you here?"

"I'm looking for someone," Gideon told him. "A guy named Jer Hardcastle."

Martin's angular brows angled more. "Have you ever heard that ancient Earth ditty? The one about the place where everyone knows your name?"

"Sure." Just hearing Martin describe the song started up an

echo in Gideon's head. "A guy in my company used to sing it. Until the rest of us made him stop."

"Yes. Well. My point is, this place is the opposite of the place in that song. Most people here don't want anyone to know their name."

"Never say it, Martin!" the woman from the Mercedes table called.

Martin grimaced a smile, then leaned closer to quietly add, "I'd be happier if none of them knew my name, so I'm afraid I don't know this Hardrook."

"Castle. Hardcastle," Gideon corrected.

"Rook, castle, pawn . . ." Martin straightened. "Whoever he is, I can't help you."

Which was when Elvis let out a low-throated keen, drawing Gideon's attention to the skeletal man at his left, and the metallic gleam of a stiletto, already in motion.

CHAPTER 2

THREE DISTRICTS AND SEVERAL WORLDS AWAY FROM A Fine Mess, Colonel Saeng Tenjin poured a second cup of tea while his aunt read the letter he'd brought to her attention.

As she continued to study the smudged and fragmented sheet of paper, Saeng sipped his tea and studied the office, which was as spare and utilitarian as ever, nothing in the decor indicating its occupant was head of the research and development division, much less a member of the company's founding family.

The only nod to comfort was her choice of Fujian oolong tea, which she served on the low slab of her oak desk, to which Saeng and Yuko had retired after the initial rounds of "You look wells", "How is the business-slash-your-mother?", and a firm, "Where is this new wife I've heard so little about?" from Yuko.

Only after promises of another visit, one that included said new wife, did Saeng present Yuko with the reason for his visit, a letter written near to ten years ago.

Still reading said letter, Yuko let out a small *tch*, and Saeng watched her eyes dart back up the page, as if rereading the latest paragraph to be sure she'd read what she thought she'd read.

Saeng didn't have to guess which paragraph had caused such a reaction; his aunt had no doubt reached the section describing the author's experiments with live crystal.

It was hard to imagine any sane person attaching electrodes to the crystals that powered Fortune, but not being a man of science, Saeng waited for Yuko to set the letter aside before asking, "What do you think?"

She didn't answer right off, but first picked up the tea she'd let go cold. "I don't know what to think." She sipped the tea, grimaced, and returned the cup to the desk with the faintest *clink*.

"But is it possible?" he asked. "To perform such an experiment and—"

"And not end up splattered over the landscape?" Yuko cut in. "Anything is possible, but even if one were to survive the attempt, what would be the point of the experiment?" She shook her head. "To be honest, I'm shocked to see this letter addressed to Amaya—Dr. Hidalgo," she said, tapping the name of the letter's intended recipient. "I can't imagine a scientist of Amaya's stature corresponding with what appears to be a madwoman."

"A mad Midasian," Saeng pointed out, "during the war."

"A very military outlook."

Saeng tipped his head and pointed to the rank insignia on his collar.

"Yes, yes." She waved a dismissive hand. "But what the military never grasps is that scientific growth does not occur in a vacuum. If a boffin wishes to pursue a new line of experimentation, or produces a fresh hypothesis, she will more than likely bounce her ideas off her fellows, Colonial or not."

"So it's possible this Midasian boffin and Amaya Hidalgo were bouncing ideas off one another," Saeng said.

"That seems most likely. Or, it would, if the idea weren't so patently insane."

"Unless they were not discussing science at all."

Yuko, in the act of lifting the teapot, shot him a look. "What else could they be discussing?"

"It is possible the letter isn't a letter, but a coded message."

"Whatever for?" She freshened the tea in both cups and set the pot down over the brazier.

"The letter was written in wartime," he pointed out. "And names a Midasian officer, as well as a time—the author wrote of the spring floods," he referred to a section of the note, "and a location."

"A very general location," she countered.

"If the message is cyphered, the key would deliver more specifics. Unless the author really did perform the experiment she wrote of, which is why I wanted your take." He indicated the letter. "Is there any good reason for this Dr. Tabak to have performed such a test?"

Yuko's hand rose in a vague gesture. "There isn't enough detail for me to draw any conclusions. Was there any further correspondence?"

Saeng shook his head. "We only have this because one of our airships discovered the wreckage of a blockade runner at the eastern reach of Dyar's Canyon. Signs indicate it crashed in an electrical storm back in thirty-nine."

"How could you know when it crashed? Of course, the date on the letter," Yuko answered her own question. She sighed and lifted her cup. "Well, now the war is over, is there any chance of reaching out to this Dr. Tabak personally?"

"There might have been," Saeng replied, "if Nour Tabak hadn't been arrested on charges of treason shortly after writing this letter. She died a year later, in Fort Ducati."

"Oh. How horrid." Yuko frowned at the letter. "But how did

you learn of her death?" she asked, looking up. "I can't imagine the Midasians would have shared the information."

"We had a man inside the fort when she died. An old mission," he explained. "And classified."

"Naturally."

"Since we couldn't speak with her, it seemed best to seek out the addressee, Dr. Hidalgo. It was helpful to find she was a Tenjin employee."

"Was," Yuko agreed. "And I'd have been happy to introduce you to her, had Dr. Hidalgo not died . . . in fourteen thirty-nine." She lifted her cup and studied his face. "But you already knew that."

Saeng's head dipped in acknowledgment. "A bad year for boffins."

"It was a bad year for many, myself included," Yuko noted, glancing down a the letter. "Amaya was more than a colleague. She was my friend."

"I'm sorry," Saeng said, meaning it. "More sorry to bring this all back, but I have to ask; do you recall anything from that time? Anything in Hidalgo's behavior to hint at her involvement with the Midasian?"

Yuko, who'd been lifting her cup, suddenly set it down. "I see." She tapped the desk before her. "I see," she said again. "You and your CO are worried I, or Tenjin Corporation, might also be involved."

"Personally, not in the least," he assured. "And officially . . . " He hesitated, but this was, after all, family. "Officially, I haven't yet brought this information to my CO. I wanted to get a better understanding of the matter before I flagged the letter for a full inquiry."

"Is that wise?" Yuko asked. "Not that I don't appreciate your circumspection, but—well, you've never been one for breaking rules."

"I'm not breaking any now. Any number of documents come through our offices, and only a fraction lead to useful intelligence. This wouldn't be the only case I've investigated, only to discover it wasn't a case at all."

"If you're certain," she said, with obvious concern.

"Thus far, there is no indication that any current member of the Tenjin Corporation is or was engaged in an act of espionage. But this letter indicates Hidalgo and Tabak were engaged in correspondence. It may even be possible this correspondence was related to both women's deaths."

"Amaya was murdered in a crime of passion," Yuko stated flatly. "Unless you believe her spouse was also a Midasian spy?"

Stranger things have happened, he thought, recalling the recent unmasking of an actual Midasian spy in Nike City. But all he said was, "I couldn't speculate on the husband's motives. I can only try to discover the truth with the information I have."

"So, you bring me a letter from one dead scientist to another dead scientist . . . hoping for what?"

"I was hoping you'd have access to Amaya Hidalgo's papers."

"All Amaya's work at Tenjin is proprietary—classified, in terms you'd understand."

He'd seen that coming and had a ready answer. "Of course. But if you, personally, were to look into it?"

"And what would I be looking for?"

"Anything out of the ordinary. Anything like the key to a code, or any indication her work was making it into enemy hands."

"I thought you didn't suspect treason?"

"I don't," he said. "But even the most innocent can be duped by enemy operatives."

"Even if she were, there's nothing to be gained from her now. She's gone, and the war is over."

"The armies are stood down," he agreed, "but espionage knows no treaties."

"I wish I could argue with that," she admitted with a hint of chagrin, "but espionage is an issue for us, as well; we recently lost a freelance prototype before it even reached our offices."

"I hadn't heard."

"It was kept quiet. I didn't even tell your mother," she explained. "And while the project itself was scrapped, the board of directors opted to make a change in security." Her eyes glittered with dark humor as she added, "As you've no doubt seen."

"Black Chiral," he said, recalling the ebony-clad figures patrolling the compound.

Black Chiral Security was a private defense organization—mercenaries by any other name—formed in the last years of the war. Once hostilities ceased, Black Chiral's founders adapted by branching into the private sector, taking over security operations for ristos and businesses such as Tenjin throughout the colonies.

"Given our mutual understanding of security issues," he said to his aunt, "will you at least look into Dr. Hidalgo's papers?"

"Like a bear dog with a mammoth bone," she muttered, but her rueful shrug told him he'd won. "I will look, but after over a decade, I can't make any promises."

"Understood."

She shook her head, then rose, fluidly unfolding herself from the cushion on which she'd been resting. "This will likely take some time." She gestured him back as he, too, began to rise. "I hope your commander can spare you."

"I'm on leave at the moment." Saeng felt his cheeks warm. "Something of a belated honeymoon, actually."

Her expression blanked. "Do you mean to tell me you're neglecting your wife on a decade-old wild dodo chase?"

"She's chasing a lead of her own," he explained, clearing his throat. "She enjoys a good mystery."

"And your mother complains about how many hours I work. You have more Tenjin in you than you realize," Yuko noted before turning to leave the room, the soft drape of her lab coat wafting like a cloak.

Left alone, Saeng used the two-way snugged to his belt to radio his wife, letting her know he'd be longer than expected.

She responded with the information she'd tracked down the former colonel who'd shared Nour Tabak's cell at the time of her death.

With great reluctance, he agreed to meet her at the man's place of business.

After he signed off, he tried to relax with his tea, but his eyes fell on the letter.

Perhaps digging into a tragic, decade-old mystery wasn't the usual way for newlyweds to spend their honeymoon, but Saeng and his wife had come together through tragedy and mystery, so it seemed only apt they continue as they'd begun.

Thinking this, he picked up the faded words written by one doomed boffin to another.

What were you two involved in?

With luck, Yuko would be able to uncover the answer to that question, and Saeng could radio his wife with the news there was no longer any need to visit Gideon Quinn.

CHAPTER 3

Spinning from the bar, Gideon shot his left hand out to catch the skeleton's wrist, twisting it counterclockwise so his opponent had the choice of bending with the force or dislocating his elbow.

The skeleton bent, letting out a guttural, "*Owowowowow,*" as Gideon liberated the stiletto and passed it to Martin, who dropped it behind the bar.

At last, Gideon released the man's bony wrist and slung an arm over the equally bony shoulders. "Jer Hardcastle, I presume?"

"Yes. Fine." The shoulders poked up and down in an irritable shrug. "I'm Hardcastle. What's it to you?"

"Well—" Gideon began.

"That was not so nice," Ulf cut in, his baleful glower echoed in both his siblings' eyes.

Gideon, still holding Hardcastle in place, felt the first stirrings of worry since walking into the pub.

He knew from experience that the triplets functioned like a semi-coordinated avalanche; slow to get moving, but once they did, impossible to stop.

"It's okay," he said, holding up his free hand. "In fact, everything's crystal and comb. Isn't that right, Jer?" Gideon emphasized the question by leaning a little more heavily on Jer's shoulder.

It didn't seem possible, but the man's mashed potato skin paled further.

Clearing his throat, Jer aimed his muddy brown eyes at the triplets. "Yes. Of course. A simple misunderstanding. All cleared up. Completely. Keeper's oath," he added, as the wall of Ohmdahls continued to loom.

"See?" Gideon said. "We're all good here." He patted Jer on the shoulder, hard enough to make him whimper. "Nothing to worry about."

The three Ohmdahls hovered a moment longer before Rolf muttered a quiet, "Not my fjord, not my puffin," before the three returned to their places at the bar.

Then the rest of the pub's guests—who had gone silent at the appearance of Jer's stiletto—creaked back to the business of drinking, gaming, and griping.

"Listen," Jer began.

"Where is it?" Gideon asked at the same time.

"What?" Jer asked back, his Adam's apple bobbing above his collar. "Where is what?"

"The object Mikkel sold you this morning."

"Mikkel?" Jer pursed his thin lips and shook his head, straightening the hat his set-to with Gideon had tipped off-center. "I don't know any Mikkel."

"You sure about that? Because Mikkel knows you. Sends his regards, by the way." As he spoke, Gideon reached into a pocket and produced a rusty switchblade with the words "Propurty of Mkkl Kran" etched on the hilt.

Jer inspected the knife, and as Gideon watched, his entire

demeanor changed from bewildered innocence to bland acceptance. "And how is Msr Crane doing?"

"Breathing," Gideon told him as he dropped Mikkel's knife into Martin's waiting hand. "But he won't be needing your services for the foreseeable future. Where," he asked again, "is it?"

Jer let out a frustrated huff. "Listen, even if Mikkel and I did conduct some business this morning, why would you care?"

Gideon's head tilted slightly. "Why wouldn't I?"

Jer glanced up to where Elvis was seated on the rafter, tail and tongue lashing before asking, "You are Gideon Quinn, are you not?"

It seems his reputation had preceded him. "Last I looked. Why?"

"So, buzz on the street is you were a dodger yourself, back in the day. Even did a spell in the nick." Jer gestured towards the tattooed number on Gideon's right hand, a souvenir from his time in the Morton Barrens. "Being as you've dipped a toe into the shadow trade some yourself, surely you don't begrudge the rest of us pocketing our share of the comb."

"You're right," Gideon said. "For the most part, I don't. You, or Mikkel, or any one of the outgrown dodgers in this town want to steal from the ristos or rob Tenjin Corporation blind, I won't hold the door open, but I won't interfere. That said," Gideon continued, "there are a few activities on the shadow side that don't sit well with me. Such activities include, but are not exclusive to, stealing from the Corps; grifting a keeper; laying hands on non-combatants—kids in particular," he clarified, "that one will absolutely put me in a bad mood."

At that statement, a few murmurs of approval rose from the audience.

"And lastly," Gideon concluded, "profiting off the misery of others."

"All perfectly understandable," Jer said, hands rising, palms out in a little wave. "Perfectly. But I don't see what those activities have to do with what Mikkel sold me." Then he added a muttered, "Allegedly,"

"It has everything to do with what Mikkel sold you," Gideon replied, "because Mikkel stole it from the Vin-Cielo flat while Cora Vin-Cielo took the kids to Yousafzai hospice to say goodbye to their father. And in case you weren't paying attention, that would fall under the heading of 'profiting from the misery of others.'"

"Heard Vittorio didn't last the night," the pipe-smoking patron offered.

"This is true," Freya said with a soft sigh. "We heard it from our mama, who heard it from Tiago Hama, who heard it from Rachel Vin."

Throughout the pub, hands touched foreheads and hearts in sympathy.

"Mama means to visit later," Ulf threw in.

"She's making her kissel," Rolf added.

"Everyone loves Mama's kissel," Freya declared.

"Mikkel did not do right if he stole from a grieving family," Ulf concluded.

"I didn't know," Jer said, the Adam's apple bobbing again. "You understand, people in my line—people who move merchandise—we don't ask for provenance."

"Friendly piece of advice?" Gideon gave a not very friendly smile. "Start asking. *After* you return Cora Vin-Cielo's property." He held out his right hand.

"Of course," Jer agreed, and after the slightest hesitation, reached into his coat and withdrew the property in question. But as Gideon reached for it, Jer's fingers tightened, and he clutched it to his chest. "The thing of it is," he said, licking his lips, "I already paid Mikkel, and I believe it only fair that I recoup my loss."

"That's one way of looking at it," Gideon said, considering. "Another way of looking at it is, by giving me that relic and accepting your losses, you'll be doing a kindness to a grieving woman . . . and retaining the use of all your limbs."

"That is a very compelling point of view," Jer said, though it took him another few seconds before he closed his eyes and dropped the relic into Gideon's waiting hand.

"The Vin-Cielos thank you." Gideon gave Jer's shoulder a bolstering pat before tossing a wave to Martin and tapping a salute at the Ohmdahls, all three of whom raised their glasses in a toast.

He tucked the recovered relic into his oversized ammo pocket and headed for the exit while Elvis dropped from the rafters to settle on Gideon's shoulder.

They'd just reached the door when it swung open, causing Gideon to freeze, as did the woman in the doorway, and for the space of a few heartbeats they stood on either side of the threshold, staring at one another, allowing Gideon time to take in the tumble of black curls, the warm brown of a heart-shaped face, and the deeper brown eyes that displayed an appealing curiosity.

Then she edged past him, just close enough for the oilskin of her coat to brush his hand as she continued into the pub.

Gideon breathed in the vanilla and water scent of her, turned to watch her cross the room and take a seat at the same table as the large, silent waterman with the carnelian earrings, who now gave Gideon a look one didn't need a sensitive to read.

Dipping his head in acknowledgment of the warning, Gideon turned and stepped out of the building, letting the door groan to a close on the population of A Fine Mess, where no one wanted to know your name.

He made it all of five steps from the door before a shadow leapt at him from atop the pile of brick.

CHAPTER 4

Spinning to face this newest threat, Gideon triggered the spring that shot Lulu into his hand while Elvis spread his wings, prepared to take flight.

Then the leaping shadow landed lightly on the broken pavement and tossed her russet hood back to ask, "Why do you care if anyone steals from the Corps?"

"Mia." Gideon grimaced and gave a very Elvis-like hiss while Elvis himself flapped his wings and gave a trill of greeting to Gideon's apprentice, who grinned at the draco as she shoved her hands in her coat pockets.

The coat was new, and large for the diminutive dodger, but, as Jinna had pointed out, little dodgers grew into big dodgers, plus Mia had gone swarm over the color.

She'd gone just as swarm over the pauldron buckled over her coat's right shoulder—a smaller version of the one Gideon wore—which was dyed a deep green, and had a stylized draco etched on the arm piece, in the same place Gideon's held the two suns of the Infantry.

Like Gideon's baton, the pauldron had been payment for one

of his cases; in this instance, a leatherworker who'd been losing shipments of pineapple leather and who also, Gideon discovered on closing the case, enjoyed sharing a pot of tea of an evening.

"So, why do you care if anyone steals from the Corps?"

"You heard that?" Gideon collapsed Lulu back into her holster and glanced back at the pub's gaping shutters. "Were you eavesdropping?"

"I wasn't eavesdropping," she replied. "There weren't no eaves involved. And I didn't drop nothing. I just listened at the window, like."

"So, yes," he said, starting to walk. "You were eavesdropping."

"Why do they call it that?" she asked, trotting along at his side.

"I have no idea," he replied. "I just know I have mixed feelings about the fact you're doing it."

"Why?"

"Because it's bad manners, but it's excellent facilitating."

Mia's brown eyes rolled as she trailed him around the slumping remains of another building decimated by an Adian air assault a couple years' back.

"So . . ." Mia's breathless voice drew his attention to the fact she was taking three steps for each of his one.

"So, what?" he asked, slowing his pace.

"Sooo, why *do* you care if anyone steals from the Corps?" she asked.

"I have a better question," he countered. "Why are you here in Lower Cadbury when you're supposed to be working on your geography lesson?"

"Oh, that." She made a pfft sound and waved her hand. "Finished."

Gideon paused in the middle of the street. "And if Keeper

Thalia stops by tonight and asks to see how your lessons are going, you'll be able to show her a completed assignment?"

"Fine, it's mostly finished," she amended, scuffing the pavement with a boot as new as her coat.

"How mostly?" Gideon asked. "Mostly, like you mostly made your bed this morning? Or mostly, like you mostly washed the dishes last night?"

"How do you know how my bed looks when it's up in Jinna's flat?"

"I know, because I'm not your only guardian." Thank the Keepers; in particular, the aforementioned Thalia, who'd done the needful to see he and Jinna were granted the right to share Mia's fostering.

"Jinna ratted me out?"

"Jinna mentioned that ex-dodgers have a sketchy idea of what a made bed looks like, compared to, say, an ex-sergeant of the Corps, such as herself. So," he persisted, "does the geography homework look more like the bed or the dishes?"

"Like the dishes."

He waited.

She rolled her eyes and continued. "I filled in the names of the Dole and Campbell archipelagos, and Hollywood, which according to the book ain't a proper island but more like a small continent," she added, though Gideon was almost certain the text hadn't said "ain't." "Plus all the Coalfart—Coalition states," she automatically corrected herself at his narrowed gaze. "And I got most of their cities done."

"Not bad," he admitted. "And what about your darning?"

Mia's nose wrinkled in the way it always did when he brought up the homely task of darning socks.

"I know it's not as glamorous as the book work," he said, "but just you try humping twenty kilometers through an Adian jungle in a poorly darned sock, then you'll know true misery."

"Did you go uphill both ways?" Mia asked.

He offered her a bland stare.

"Maybe I thought about working on the socks," she tried next, "but then I figured, as your apprentice, I should be on the streets, keeping an eye out, watching your seven, making sure you don't come home dead."

"Your sacrifice is duly noted," Gideon said as they continued on their way. "But Elvis had me covered this time."

At the sound of his name, the draco commenced rubbing his head against Gideon's cheek. His scales rasped against the stubble of beard, which Elvis must have enjoyed, given the rumbling Gideon felt all the way to his teeth.

He glanced over as they passed a building that had retained both floors and most of its glass, where the flicker of movement behind one window indicated at least one soul was occupying the relic.

"But really," Mia broke the silence, "why do you care if anyone steals from the Corps?"

The kid was like a draco with a desert viper. "Why do you care that I care if anyone steals from the Corps?" he asked back.

"I care because ain't they the ones what—"

"Aren't. *Aren't* they the ones," he corrected as they turned right at the next corner.

"Aren't they the ones what stuck you in the nick?" Mia asked.

"Technically," he admitted.

"So technically, the Corps done you up, proper," she pointed out. "Seems to me if someone was stealing from 'em, you'd let 'em take their rotten comb and be done with it. For certain sure you don't owe them nothing."

"I don't owe them *anything*, and it's complicated."

"Because?" she prompted.

"Because the Corps isn't just General Rand or the court that

convicted me for his crimes. The Corps is soldiers and aeronauts and medics and sailors. It's Jinna, and Rory and his crew,"
he continued, referring to the crew of the airship *Errant*, all of
whom had suffered because of the events at Nasa, which had
cost Gideon half his company and six years of his life. "It's
everyone who ever put on a uniform and took the oath."

"So, it's like a family," Mia said after a beat.

"I guess it is." Gideon glanced at Mia as she kept pace with
him and noted her expression had gone thoughtful.

Thoughtful was good.

Thoughtful meant she might not ask another question for at
least half a block.

"So, what did Mikkel steal from the Vin-Cielo's, anyway?"

Or a quarter of a block.

"I'm not sure." He pulled the item from his ammo pocket
and held it up.

It was a disk of some sort, made of a hard, lightweight plastic
only ever found in relics from Earth.

The entire thing was pink, with the variance in shade that
indicated fading over the centuries, and it featured an inward-
curving edge around the circumference, as well as a grooved
pattern on the convex side that was pleasing to the touch.

Gideon flipped it once. Then he flipped it again because it
was eminently flippable.

"Maybe it was a plate?" he suggested, holding it flat, like a
tray.

Mia studied it doubtfully, then tilted her head under to read
the lettering molded in the center on the convex side. "Says here
it's a frisbee," she said, straightening. "Does that mean it's for
serving frisbees?"

"But what's a frisbee?"

They both looked at the pink circle as they turned onto Jaffa
Street, where most of the buildings were still in one piece.

"Could be a frisbee's another sort of naan," Mia offered. "Or a fish? Or an Old Earth fruit?"

"We may never know." Gideon flipped the thing sideways, then, on a whim, tossed it into the air, where it spun a few times on the vertical, causing Elvis to sit up on his hind legs and let loose with the low thrum that was his hunting growl.

"Oy!" Mia protested as the disk began its descent. "That's no way to treat a relic."

"Sorry." Gideon caught the thing in his left hand and clutched it to his chest. "Down, boy." He soothed Elvis back into a crouch.

Probably the frisbee plate could survive a fall, but it'd be suspicious if it turned up with teeth marks.

"Do you think Cora will sell it?" Mia asked.

Gideon glanced at the disk, recalling Cora Vin-Cielo, and the practical set of her jaw and the grieving, haunted eyes. "I doubt it."

Which had Mia making another *pfft*. "Can't think why not. Old as it is? And made of plastic? She could be swimming in crystal and comb."

"Probably," Gideon agreed. "But it's more likely she'll hang on to it, and pass it down to the oldest, who will pass it down to her oldest, and so on, and so on, until Fortune stops spinning."

"Why do people put so much pollen in all this old stuff?" she asked as they reached the stairs leading up to the building the Vin-Cielos shared with their friend, Tiago Hama. "Most of it don't even—"

"Doesn't even."

"Doesn't even have a use. I mean, I get some of them tools, because they're tools, right? But this?" She flapped her hands at the disk. "This is just a *thing*."

"To us it's a thing," Gideon said, holding it up so the

sunslight passing through lent a rosy glow to Mia's upturned face. "To other people, I guess it's something else."

"Like what?"

"Like . . . continuity," he suggested after a pause to think. "It's not the frisbee plate that matters, it's the frisbee plate's connection to their past, to Vittorio, that they care about."

"Maybe," she said with a sigh before reaching out to touch the frisbee plate. "I suppose you can't get much more past than Earth, can you?"

"Suppose not," he agreed, then jerked his head towards the stairs. "Come on. Let's go return Vittorio's history to his family."

***

At the same time Mia was accosting Gideon outside A Fine Mess, the man with the carnelian earrings waited for his daughter to join him.

"Why did you warn him off?" she asked, settling into the table's other chair. "I rather liked his looks."

The man shook his head. "That one would be more trouble than he's worth." He let his eyes traverse the pub before allowing them to return to hers. "And didn't you already have a fish on the line?"

"I did, but . . ."

"But what?" he asked as she trailed off.

She met his questioning gaze. "There are family issues."

"Pity," he said. "But you're right. Best to let that draco fly."

He thought he caught a flash of relief in her expression, but then it was gone so quickly, perhaps he'd imagined it?

He hoped so.

"Anyone else catch your eye?" he asked.

"Only the tall drink of water at the door." Her lips quirked in a smile that went some way towards reassuring him. "You're sure he'd be too much trouble?"

"Gideon Quinn," he recalled the name at the same time Jer Hardcastle thumped his empty glass on the bar and turned to leave. "Calls himself a private facilitator. Got an office up on Doyle, along with a partner and an apprentice."

"What in comb is a private facilitator?" she asked.

"Swarmed if I know." He focused on his daughter again. "So, since your lad's off limits, you've lowered yourself to joining your poor old dad for a drink?"

She gave the bottle a pointed look. "I love you, but no. Wex radio'd the *Yemaya*." She reached into her pocket and drew out a folded bit of paper, waiting until he accepted it before adding, "He used your arena name."

"He thinks he's making a point," he said, reading the message.

Olalekan

Tenjin Peninsula

1530 Hours

+ 4

"Typical." Lekan folded the paper, shoved it into his pocket. "I have to go."

"I could come along," she offered. "He asked for four more."

He considered it. Of all their crew, there was no one he trusted more than his daughter, but—

"Best not," he decided. "In case whatever Wex has planned goes swarm, I'll need you to take command."

"Father—"

"Daughter—" he echoed her tone. "Who else could I count on to come to my rescue?"

Her eyes narrowed, but she didn't argue. Which was good,

because if he were to reach Wex's stated destination in time, he had to fly.

"While I'm dealing with this," he said as he rose, "why don't you spend a little time here?" He flicked his eyes to the Ohmdahl triplets, still at the bar, then back to her. "Maybe you'll find yourself some company."

She angled her chair and glanced at the Ohmdahls. "I like the long-haired one."

"I'll send Miguel and Xian along." He leaned over, dropping a kiss on her windblown curls. "Should the need arise."

"If the need arises, you should probably send more than just Miguel and Xian."

"I'll see what I can do. Make some friends," he said. "And whatever you do, don't drink the whiskey."

"Wouldn't dream of it."

Content that his girl would do her part, Lekan's mind shifted to Wex Jihan, the one man on Fortune with any claim to his loyalty, and the one most likely to make sure he remembered it.

He had no idea what task Wex had in mind, but sure as the suns rose in the east, it would be an ugly business.

As he stepped into the broken sunsshine, he had to admit, that gave them something else in common.

CHAPTER 5

If he'd had his way, Gideon would have dropped the frisbee and left.

But once Cora returned the relic to its place of honor over the mantel, she pressed him and Mia to stay for tea and a plate of the copious amounts of food provided by the others who'd come for the grieving.

He might have refused the invitation, but Mia was hungry.

Then again, Mia was always hungry.

And beyond his apprentice's bottomless appetite, he hadn't been able to deny the quiet desperation woven through Cora's request, which told him more clearly than words how, in this moment, she needed other people, other voices, to fill the space Vittorio had occupied.

It was an emptiness Gideon understood, so he accepted the invitation and, once his plate and cup were filled, found a bit of wall between two windows to lean on.

Mia followed, crouching at his side and absorbing—he could think of no other way to describe the way the dodger made food disappear—her cake.

Then she absorbed his cake.

While she did, Gideon sipped his hyacinth tea and scanned the room until he found Elvis, who'd abandoned his perch on Gideon's shoulder the second they entered the flat.

The draco was curled on the lap of Cora and Vittorio's middle child, a dark-eyed girl of six or so, as she sat in front of the fireplace.

Both child and draco appeared comfortable with this arrangement, so he took another sip of the bright, tart tea and focused on the rest of the somber party.

The discussions were mostly subdued, words of comfort interspersed with sniffles and the occasional shimmer of laughter as someone recounted an amusing tale of the deceased.

Since he had never met Vittorio, Gideon had nothing to offer, and was wondering how much longer they needed to stay when the door of the flat opened to reveal Sonja Ohmdahl—Rolf, Ulf, and Freya's mother.

The surprisingly petite Ohmdahl matriarch came bearing the kissel Freya had mentioned in the pub, which she immediately traded for an armful of the youngest Vin-Cielo, a child of indeterminate gender who came in general toddler size.

With Sonja providing emotional reinforcements, Gideon felt better about making an escape, and he was about to nudge Mia into motion when he heard his name.

Turning to his right, he saw Tiago Hama making a beeline from the flat's kitchen, wearing a faded brown coat, a worn satchel, and an expression of concern.

At his approach, Mia set Gideon's plate to one side and rose to share a grin and an elbow bump with the young man she and Gideon had first met shortly after Gideon's arrival in Nike.

Since that day, Tiago and Mia had become as close as siblings, sharing a taste for biscuits, a passion for space opera, and a lack of patience with the older generation . . . particularly in the persons of Gideon and Tiago's father, Detective Sergeant Ishan Hama.

"Tiago." Gideon raised his cup in a toast of greeting. "I didn't know you were here."

"I was in the back room, packing up the medicines and such, so Cora wouldn't have to."

Now that the kid was closer, Gideon noted a pallor under the golden-tanned skin, along with the shadow of a beard and dark circles under his eyes.

"Oy!" Mia gave Tiago another elbow thump. "You look like a bloke on a three-day bender at the end of his fourth day."

"Umm," Tiago said, looking confused.

"What Mia means to say is, you look as if you could use some rest."

"Oh, well, yes," Tiago agreed. "I was at the hospital last night with Cora and the children, plus I'm on first shift for a fortnight, and then there were lectures, and some patients in the neighborhood. It has been a busy week," he concluded.

"Ever hear of burnout?" Gideon asked. "Also . . . " he paused and glanced at Mia. "Give it back."

"What?" Tiago looked confused. "Give what back?"

"Mia?" Gideon held out his hand, palm open, and waggled his fingers in the girl's direction.

She hunched her shoulders, then sighed, then opened her right hand, in which she held the wax-sealed vial she'd dipped from Tiago's satchel during the second elbow bump.

She was in the process of dropping the vial into Gideon's waiting hand when Tiago snatched it back with a gutter curse that had both Gideon and Mia's brows raising.

"I wasn't gonna keep it," Mia said, visibly affronted. "Just trying to keep nimble, is all."

"Commendable," Gideon said to her, "but—"

"Not with medicines," Tiago cut in sternly. "And especially

not with this." As he spoke, he held up the flask, balanced between his thumb and forefinger, checking for damage.

Both Gideon and Mia joined him in studying the bottle, which was the length and breadth of Gideon's thumb, and filled with a deep purple liquid.

"What is it?" Mia asked, her eyes narrowed as she peered at the contents, which moved in a thick, syrupy way as Tiago examined the bottle.

"My final exam for pharmacology," Tiago explained, his dark eyes showing a perfect mix of pride and concern.

"Oh, yeah?" Gideon grinned. "What sort of pharmacology? Because with your dad being a copper and all . . . "

"Not that kind." Tiago gave the tube one last perusal, then lowered his hand and wrapped his fingers around it again. "My professor asked everyone in the lecture to create a drug based on a particular potion from Earth's ancient literature, using native Fortune flora. Plants," he added, before Mia could ask what flora meant.

She frowned over that. "But aren't Fortune's plants the same as the ones on Earth?" she asked. "Seein' as Fortune was seeded from Earth stock and the like, before the First Landers—you know—landed?"

Gideon felt a stab of pride that, for once, she didn't say "ain't."

"Seeded, yes," Tiago agreed, visibly appreciating the question. "But, while the seeds of life on Fortune came from Earth, when those seeds took root here, the differences in gravity, atmosphere, even sunlight, caused them to evolve further.

"There are many boffins who speculate every bit of life on Fortune, from the smallest microbe to the largest kraken, has mutated to a certain extent since it first took root. The theory would explain, for instance, why we have such large beavers, upwards of seven feet long, when most of the Earth records had them averaging at three feet."

"I've heard the same about dracos, but in reverse." Gideon indicated Elvis, across the room. "How they were all massive and could breathe fire."

"Glad that didn't take," Mia said, also looking at Elvis.

Tiago smiled. "The theory also accounts for why no one on Fortune has ever been able to grow a coffee plant."

"I still think they made coffee up." Mia sniffed. "But I get it. You had to use what we got on Fortune to make the same sort of potion what they might have used back in the day on Earth." Now she jerked her chin at the vial. "So, what's yours do, then?"

"If it works properly, this drug should slow the heartbeat and respiration of the person who takes it."

Mia's eyes widened. "Why would you want to do that?"

"Ideally, to halt tachycardia," Tiago said. "But it may also prove helpful during surgery. With the correct dosage, this potion should even simulate death. Certainly, the source material Professor Basil provided indicates it is possible."

Gideon looked up. "Source material?"

"The play Professor Basil chose, the one featuring the potion."

"Wait." Mia leaned in, eyes eager now. "Did your prof pick this potion out of *Star Trek: The Musical*? You know, the bit where it looks like Spock killed his captain, but he didn't kill him, see, because their mate Bones had this potion that only made it look like the captain was dead?"

"Are there any plays you haven't seen?" Gideon asked.

"I worked the Circus a lot of nights," she said. "It's good dipping territory."

Since Gideon had dipped more than a few wallets along Miyazaki Way in Turing, he couldn't argue.

"Still, as entertaining as *Star Trek* is, the potion Bones gave

Kirk before the final duet was not the source," Tiago said. "Professor Basil has us using *Romeo and Juliet*."

"Seriously?" Gideon, shocked, looked from Tiago to the vial in his hand, and back.

"I know that one, too," Mia said. "It ended—"

"Badly," Gideon inserted.

"Why wouldn't your prof want the one from *Star Trek*?" Mia asked.

"Instead of the one that killed two kids?" Gideon added.

"First . . ." Tiago focused on Mia. "Even though *Star Trek* had a happier ending, the potion involved was not based on any existing plant life. The potion Friar Laurence gives to Juliet in the play, however, was based on real herbs that grew on Earth in that time period, and analogues of which exist on Fortune today.

"And second," he took a breath and turned to Gideon, "because the potion we're mimicking from Shakespeare's play did not kill anyone. It did exactly what it was supposed to do, which was make Juliet appear as if she'd died. Romeo later killed himself with an actual poison, and Juliet killed herself with Romeo's dagger.

"And technically," he continued, speaking now to both Gideon and Mia, "one could suggest it wasn't even the poison and dagger that killed the young lovers at all, but the hatred of their two families that did the deed."

"Nah." Now Mia shook her head, sending her curls to bouncing in syncopation. "It was that Friar Laurence what done for Romeo and Juliet."

Both men looked down, speechless.

"It's obvious, ain't it?" Mia asked. "Every single thing what went wrong with them kids was because Laurence told 'em to do it. Which just goes to show," she added, with the sagacity of youth, "you should never put your trust in a fry cook when it comes to matters of the heart."

Gideon and Tiago continued to study Mia for a beat, then looked at one another.

"There's something to be said for that interpretation," Gideon offered.

"No doubt," Tiago agreed, tucking the vial into his coat's inner pocket. "But, as much as I enjoy discussing theatre and the arcana of ancient medicines, I was hoping to ask you a favor. Professionally, that is."

"Ask away." Gideon set his empty cup on the windowsill and waited.

"Keep in mind, I'm not sure there's anything you can do, but . . . " Tiago paused, sighed, and offered a slight shrug, forcing him to hitch his satchel back up onto his shoulder before continuing, "The thing is, I've been losing patients."

CHAPTER 6

Back at the Tenjin compound, Saeng closed the book he'd been reading as his aunt returned to her office, this time in the company of one of the Black Chiral mercenaries.

"Forgive me; that took longer than even I expected," she said, then glanced at the book. "But I see you still carry something to read wherever you go."

"It's proven a useful habit," Saeng admitted, laying the book next to his sword.

"Obviously," Yuko agreed, then took a sheet of paper from the woman at her side. "I only wish I could say your wait was worth it." She offered him the paper. "I can't say I wasn't expecting something of the sort, but I had hoped."

So had Saeng, but as he read the report, he discovered Amaya Hidalgo's projects and papers had all been removed to off-site storage in late 1445, where they were subsequently lost in the Adian air assault of '47.

"Is that usual?" he asked, handing the paper back. "Moving research off-site?"

"More than you'd think. We only have so much space; why clog the files with projects that will never be finished or have become obsolete? She is truly gone now," she murmured, tracing the lines of text on the note with one finger.

"I'm sorry to have brought all this back," he said, feeling a tug of guilt. "If there had been anyone else to ask—"

"I understand," she said, shaking her head and tucking the note into her lab coat pocket. "I might be able to make more inquiries—discreetly—if you left the letter here," Yuko said, then glanced at the Black Chiral officer. "Thank you, Skellig, that will be all."

"Director." The woman turned to the door.

"I can't give you the original," Saeng said as Skellig pulled open the door. "But I don't believe anyone would take issue if I made another copy."

"Another copy?" Yuko asked.

"My wife has the first," he explained as the door closed behind Skellig.

"He's on the move."

Outside the Tenjin compound, Lekan watched Wex Jihan pocket his binoculars and drop from the branch of a plum tree. A short burl of a man, he landed with surprising grace. "You and your men made it just in time," he observed, brushing a few petals from his uniform jacket.

Lekan grunted, then looked over the grove, where two of his men crouched behind a thick stand of the blossoming trees. Both had a good grip on one end of the rope they and their two crewmates—now stationed on the other side of the path—had just finished covering with mulch and dirt.

In the gusting wind, the deep pink petals that perfumed the orchard were already drifting down to cover the disturbed earth.

The *thrum* of an approaching motorcycle had Lekan raising

a hand, and all four of his crew dropped flat to the damp earth, their muted clothing blending admirably with the landscape.

Seconds later the target appeared, sweeping around the curve.

Goggles covered the man's eyes, and his black hair streamed behind him. The rank insignia on his Corps long coat gleamed in a brief glimmer of sunslight, causing Lekan's spine to straighten as his lips spread in a feral grin.

And then his men were yanking on the rope, and the cycle, just crossing the buried line, flipped up, throwing its rider from his seat.

But the target was both agile and quick; even as the cycle reared, he flung himself in the opposite direction, landing with a damp thud on the path, where he continued to roll to his feet.

Lekan, however, was also agile and quick, and bounded down the path, taking even his own men by surprise.

"No killing!" Wex called, following on Lekan's heels.

No promises, Lekan thought, as the target ripped his goggles away with one hand and drew his sword with the other, ready to take on all comers.

Lekan, coming up short on the path, drew his shooter, checked the load, aimed, and fired.

"Wait—" Wex protested, rushing forward. "Wait," he said again, skidding to a halt over the slick carpet of last year's fallen leaves.

Then Wex and Lekan watched the target spin, sword still at the ready, his left hand rising to pluck the fletching protruding from the side of his neck. He took a step towards Lekan, but his sword was already dipping as he studied the small dart.

"Interesting," Wex murmured.

Then the dart fell, the point burying itself in the loam just as the target's legs gave way and he, too, dropped onto the petal-strewn path.

Lekan's men waited, and only at his gesture did they converge on the target.

"You know," Wex offered into the fresh silence, "you could do quite well for yourself, if you ever decided to take a position with my employers."

"I work for no one," Lekan said.

Wex glanced over. "I rather think you're working for me."

"What I'm doing for you is repaying a favor." Lekan's eyes fixed on the deep green of the target's coat. "Though this time, repaying it is also a pleasure."

On the road, the four men made quick work of stripping the target's sword, ring, radio, and anything else of value they could find.

"I need any papers he's carrying," Wex said.

"You heard the man." Lekan holstered his weapon.

"New toy?" Wex asked, glancing at the shooter.

Lekan gave a grunt of assent. "Got it off an Adian." He didn't say how, and Wex didn't inquire. "And no, you can't have it."

"I wasn't going to ask."

"Yes, you were."

"Yes, I was," Wex admitted before turning to retrieve the waxed envelope one of Lekan's crew discovered.

"What do you want us to do with him?" Lekan asked.

"Anything you like, as long as you don't kill him," Wex replied, tucking the letter into his pocket. "You'll find a crystal-batt van at the southern border of the orchard for your use, for as long as you stay in the city. Just make sure there's no blood inside when you return it."

Lekan nodded, then asked, "Who is he, anyway?"

"Saeng Tenjin," Wex said as both men studied the colonel. His face was pale, his hair spread in a black web over the dark earth, and fuchsia petals stained his coat like drops of blood.

"And now he's nobody," Lekan murmured.

CHAPTER 7

Mia's eyebrows shot up at Tiago's statement. "Losing patients?" she echoed.

"I don't think that's the kind of thing a doctor wants to admit," Gideon said in an undertone.

"'Specially not at a grieving," Mia added.

"Not that kind of lost." Tiago waved the air with one hand, but he did angle himself away from the rest of the mourners. "What I mean is, I'm losing them. As in, they're missing. Absent. Not where they're supposed to be."

"How many people are we talking?" Gideon asked, his voice still low, but with an edge Mia was beginning to recognize as the start of a job.

"Three, that I know of."

"Did you mention any of this to your father?"

"Yesterday," Tiago replied tightly, "and he told me a body had to be missing a full 84 hours before they could be considered officially missing—"

"That is the dumbest rule," Mia huffed.

"Exactly," Tiago agreed. "And then he pointed out that the

sort of people who settle in Lower Cadbury don't settle for long."

"Oy," Mia began, bristling.

"Tell me about your missing patients," Gideon cut in with a warning glance in her direction.

"The first, George, is a former POW," Tiago said as Mia huffed. "He was taken prisoner at the first battle of Asgard, liberated after the second. He settled into Lower Cadbury a few months back, after being released from hospital."

Gideon nodded. "And you assume he's missing, why?"

"He wasn't home when I stopped at his flop."

"Well—"

"And none of the others in his shelter had seen him since the day before."

Mia looked up as Gideon took a breath, then released it. But he didn't say anything. His expression reminded her of the time Elvis knocked over the lamp in Jinna's flat, but more so.

"I know what you're thinking," Tiago said.

"I don't," Mia said.

"It's—" Gideon began.

"He thinks George topped himself," Tiago told her, ignoring Gideon's warning hiss.

"Oh." She thought about that. "*Ohhh.*"

"And I won't say it's impossible," Tiago continued, focusing again on Gideon, "except that Lupe and Meki have gone missing as well."

Mia watched Gideon do that thing with his jaw that said he was trying to be patient. "And Lupe and Meki would be?"

"Lupe is a woman who recently relocated from Sewlal."

"Where's Sewlal?" Mia asked.

"Allianza, settlement south of Santiago," Gideon told Mia. "You haven't covered that one yet."

"Lupe came to Nike looking for a new start, and found a

few thousand others with the same idea," Tiago explained. "After a time, the starbucks ran out, and she ended up here in Lower Cadbury."

"How did you meet Lupe?"

"Remember that rash of influenza went round last month?"

Mia, who'd caught it, made a little *ack* noise.

"We remember," Gideon assured.

"It hit Lower Cadbury hard," Tiago said. "I treated Lupe and worked it out with the others in her building to check in on her. They've all gotten friendly since, and it was her downstairs neighbor who came to me with the news she'd disappeared."

"When was this?"

"I can't say for certain. Bakbibi, the neighbor who contacted me, recently got a job, so she hasn't been around the flat much. At first, she figured they were simply missing each other, but when she—Bakbibi—came into her first week's pay, she wanted to treat Lupe to a meal. Except Lupe wasn't home. So Bakbibi checked the next morning, and again that evening, after work."

"Still no Lupe?" Mia guessed.

"Still no Lupe," Tiago affirmed.

"And there's no way she just left?" Gideon asked. "Could be she got a job offer herself, or decided to call it and go back home."

"Not without saying goodbye. And not without her belongings, which are still in the flat. Not much, I'll grant you, but if she did leave, she didn't even take a toothbrush."

"Odd." Gideon admitted. "And what about the last patient?"

"That would be Meki," Tiago said, his golden skin darkening slightly. "I might have stretched the part about her being a patient, given she's quite . . . healthy."

Gideon's brow rose, but he said nothing.

"She's also in the way of being a refugee; from Domino," Tiago concluded.

"And when you say 'in the way of being a refugee,' do you mean what I think you mean?"

Mia opened her mouth.

"You have covered this one," Gideon told her before she could ask what was going on. "Remember? Those whopping two paragraphs on Domino."

"Yeah." She remembered it mostly because Gideon had been pretty vocal about the sparsity of text on the Coalition States. "It said Domino is one of the Adian coastal cities."

"And?" he prompted.

She closed her eyes, remembering. "It's connected to the northern continent by an isthmus, supplies most of the Coalition's sugar, and it's known for keeping with the Adian practice of slavery, and . . . Oh."

"Exactly." Gideon turned his attention back to Tiago. "So?" he asked. "Is this Meki what I think she is?"

"Not being a sensitive, I don't know what you think she is."

"Tiago . . . " Gideon shook his head and shifted his position, so both he and the younger man had their backs to the rest of the guests. "Listen," he continued, "I won't say I'm keeping up with every line item of the peace treaty, but even I know the whole slavery issue is murky as the Amazon mountains during storm season. Murky enough, if anyone in the brass figures out there's an escaped—that there's an Adian refugee—in Nike, and that you're connected to her . . . "

"It could become an international issue," Tiago completed the thought Gideon left hanging. "As the son of a copper, I understand the ramifications."

"No, you don't," Gideon replied, his expression icy enough to have Mia shifting from foot to foot with nerves. "We just put paid to a decades' old war, and no one in the brass or the parliament is going to risk starting another one over what a *former* enemy state does inside its own borders."

"I understand that, but—"

"But," Gideon cut Tiago off. "Suppose someone figures out this woman is what you're carefully not saying she is. And that someone reports it to the authorities? If that happens, the best-case scenario is she'll be returned to Adia. Worst case? She does another runner and gets away before she can be sent back."

"How is that the worst case?" Mia asked.

"It's the worst case," Gideon explained, keeping his gaze on Tiago, "because if she does get away, Adia would be within its rights to request recompense. In kind."

"What?" The question burst from Mia's lips in a squeak.

"Do you truly believe it would come to that?" Tiago asked. "That the entire Coalition would take arms over a single individual?"

"Do you want to risk they wouldn't?" Gideon asked in his turn. "Anyway," he continued on an exhalation, "it may not matter."

"How so?" Tiago asked.

"You say she's missing," Gideon replied. "It's just as likely she already moved on. If she's smart, she'll be halfway to Hollywood."

"Perhaps she will, someday," Tiago said. "But not yet."

"Why?"

Tiago didn't answer right off.

"Tiago?" Mia's hand came to rest on the student's elbow, this time out of genuine concern, rather than attempting a dip.

He sighed. "I don't believe she's left the city because she left her things in my flat."

"Your flat? *Your* flat?"

"Yes, I—"

Gideon held up a finger before Tiago could say anything

more. Then he stalked all the way into the kitchen and turned to where she could no longer see him.

She looked at Tiago, who looked at her.

As they stood in an uncomfortable silence, Elvis decamped from his position by the fire and flew across the room to settle on Mia's shoulder, his tail circling her throat like a bronze necklace just as Gideon returned.

Tiago began to speak.

"Don't." Gideon held up a hand. "Just. Don't." He took a breath, let it out. "Let's start by going to your flat. I want to look at her things. Meki's personals."

That gave Tiago a start. "Why?"

"Something she left behind might point to where she's gone."

Tiago's expression eased, and Mia felt her own chest loosen.

Even Elvis seemed to relax, curling around the back of her neck so his head was under her left ear.

"Don't get your hopes up," Gideon continued. "Searching for someone in her position—there are a lot of questions I can't ask without raising more questions I can't afford to answer."

"Maybe you can't ask—"

"Listen to me." Gideon's hand gripped the young man's shoulder. "This isn't anything like what you're used to. This is politics, and nothing—no shadow trade, no street hustle, no local corruption—can shine a crystal on the kind of filth that lives in politics. So, you expect me to help, you have to do two things. First, you show me what this woman left in your place. And second . . . you will forget we ever talked about this. Don't look for her. Don't ask about her. Don't get involved. Promise me," he urged, giving the shoulder he held a little shake. "Promise me you'll stay out of it."

Tiago's dark eyes went kind of hollow, but rather than challenge Gideon, he asked, "And Lupe? And George?"

"I'll ask around for both, but with George—you know as well as I do—"

"He did *not* kill himself," Tiago said with a certainty Mia admired.

She watched Gideon's eyes darken, but he released his grip on Tiago's shoulder.

"Well." Tiago stepped back. "We should say goodbye to Cora."

Mia and Gideon both turned their attention to the widow, standing by the fire, one hand stroking her daughter's hair, the other holding on to the teapot as if her life depended on it. "I guess we should."

As the two men joined Cora to say their farewells, Mia scritched Elvis on the chin and wondered if Gideon noticed Tiago had never promised to stay out of it.

Tiago's place was as sparsely furnished as the first time Gideon had seen it, though the student had added a few more books to the pomegranate crates he used as shelving.

Mia, Elvis still clutching her shoulder, made a beeline for those shelves as soon as she walked in the door.

By the time Tiago had hung his jacket and satchel on a hook, she was curled in an oversized chair near the living room window, poring over what looked to be an acupuncture textbook.

"When did you meet Meki?" he asked Tiago.

"We met three . . . no, four days ago."

"So, not long," Gideon observed.

"Longer than a dance in Red Crystal Alley," Tiago countered.

"Or a cuppa with Pandora," Mia supplied, still studying the book.

"Who's Pandora?" Tiago asked.

"A—"

"One of our clients," Mia overrode Gideon's response, peering over the book. "She's always asking Gideon over to her place for a cup of tea."

"She's sociable," Gideon said.

"Is that so?" Tiago asked.

Gideon rubbed his jaw. "I'm a big fan of tea."

"He doesn't know me and Jinna cracked his 'tea' code weeks ago," Mia supplied.

"I do now," Gideon told her, and was rewarded with a grin before she turned her eyes back to the page. "So, four days," he said to Tiago, crossing the living area and passing the kitchen to peek into the nook of a bedroom. "And where did you meet her?"

"I ran into her." Tiago trailed after Gideon. "Literally. I wasn't watching where I was going and slammed into her outside the old marketplace where George lives. I'd been tending a nasty case of carbuncles, there was seepage—"

"Don't need the details," Gideon interrupted.

"Right. Well. I ran into her, and one thing led to another, and while we were talking, I learned she was searching for a place to sleep so, I, ah . . . I brought her home."

"I hope you offered her dinner first."

"Dinner, and I slept on the chair." Tiago jerked his chin over to where Mia was curled, Elvis stretching down from her shoulder as if he, too, were reading. "At least, for the first night," he admitted quietly.

Gideon suppressed a sigh. "And the last time you saw her?"

"That would have been yesterday morning. I left her here, having tea. Actual tea," Tiago said over Mia's snort. "This was when I stopped at the precinct to speak to my father about George and Lupe. After, I went to my lecture and by the time I came home, she was gone. But she left her things," he added, indicating a knotted parcel of fabric.

Gideon crouched beside the little bundle and began unknotting the nubby bit of scarf, which was embroidered with a rose pattern common in Allianza.

Inside the scarf, he found a wide-toothed comb, a bag of soap chips, toothpowder and toothbrush. He hesitated over a pair of well-worn gauntlets of the type used for labor, or combat, before pulling out the few articles of clothing.

Gideon showed no delicacy in searching the undergarments as carefully as the shirt and trousers.

"You search like a copper," Tiago noted.

"Most soldiers do," Gideon said. "There's always a chance to find some ammo, supplies, enemy dispatches, plans for upgraded canon..." He paused as he found a pouch filled with Adian rubiks, hefting it so that the squared coins inside jingled merrily. "Not your average 'carrying around' money."

"She is from a Coalition state," Tiago reminded him, all the while staring at the clothes strewn over the floor.

Gideon thought it unlikely an escaped slave would have that much cash on hand, but he said nothing as he put Meki's belongings back into the bundle, wrapped it up and, after a moment's thought, buried it deep inside the pallet, where only a determined search would find it.

Then he rose and joined Tiago in the doorway, so they were side to side, with Gideon facing the living area while Tiago continued to study the bedroom. "You didn't say you were in love with her," he murmured.

"It's not like that." Tiago shook his head. "As you said, she's on the run; may always be on the run, so . . . It's not like that."

Gideon glanced at the younger man, who was staring at the rumpled bedclothes, and wondered if Tiago knew he was lying.

After leaving Tiago's place, Gideon, Mia, and Elvis headed to the dockside marketplace where George, the first of the missing patients, had been squatting.

Neither the docks nor the market were in use, having been abandoned after the '47 air raid made Lower Cadbury the next thing to a ghost town.

As they paused in front of the partially roofed market, Elvis, who'd flown most of the way, glided in to land on Gideon's shoulder, his wings gleaming as the setting suns pierced the clouds. The river sighed in the distance, and a loose roof tile rattled in the wind.

"What was that?" he asked, indicating what had been a single story building but was now a few walls with no roof.

"Some sort of storage, I think," she said with a shrug, then turned towards the shadowed maze of the market. As they neared, he drew a hand torch from its pocket and flicked it on.

"This used to be a stable before it was a market," Mia told him as they followed the narrow trail of Gideon's light. "They kept horses and camels, a few alpacas, like that."

"Impressive," Gideon said.

"There was a spice merchant in that stall." She gestured to a heap of blackened timber and tumbled bricks, some of which had been formed into a circle, and in the middle of the circle was a pile of charred wood.

The air smelled of smoke and damp.

Mia stared at the space a moment longer before moving on.

Gideon moved with her, thinking once again how little he knew of her life before they'd met. Who her parents were, if she'd had any siblings—or if she could pick her home out of the skeletal spires that had once been buildings—he couldn't say.

More, he found he couldn't ask.

He had questioned Jinna, but her knowledge of Mia's former life was as sketchy as his own.

"At first, I didn't want to push because she was skittish, what with her being a dodger and me not. Then I didn't want to ask because it might make her sad," Jinna had explained, laying a protective hand over the new life growing inside her. "I think we've all had enough sad."

Gideon couldn't disagree.

So now he followed Mia into the dark, and he listened as she pointed out the booth where the pineapple leather had been sold, and the honeycomb merchant's stall, and the smith's.

And any time one of the enclosures they passed turned out to be occupied, he set a protective hand on Mia's shoulder while Elvis let out a hiss of warning.

Finally they reached the shed three rows back and five stalls down, where Tiago said George had made his place.

There was no sign of George, but there was a neatly stowed infantry kit in one dusty corner, and a neatly made pallet in another.

Gideon ran his torch over the rest of the space, but he couldn't tell if it had been a day, a week, or a month since its tenant had last stopped in.

He handed the light to Mia and, as he had with Meki's belongings earlier, crouched next to George's infantry pack.

Inside, he found a mess kit, a pouch containing a razor in good condition, along with the requisite soap, brush, and bowl, and a bit of a broken mirror, wrapped in burlap.

There was one spare set of clothes, outer to under, all surprisingly clean, which made Gideon wonder where the homeless of Nike did their laundry.

Did they use the river? Was there a functioning washateria in the ruins?

He was turning to Mia, the question on his tongue when Elvis, who'd hopped up to one of the smoke-stained rafters on their arrival, let out the low keen of warning.

Almost on top of the draco's call, a shuffle of steps emerged from the corridor.

Gideon and Mia both rose and turned from George's stash, just in time to face the newcomer.

As they did, Gideon stepped forward, attempting to block Mia, but she was on to his ways and simply scooted around him, raising the torch to reveal a walking mountain of rags.

"That's George's stuff, that is," the mountain uttered, coming to a halt and bringing with it a stench so sour, Gideon's eyes teared and Mia slipped behind him, bravado abandoned in the face of the aggressively wafting odor.

"So I hear," Gideon said to the mountain, keeping his voice easy despite the sudden lack of breathable air.

"He was s'posed t'bring back some tea. George always brings the tea. We brings the veg. Wally brings in the tinned meat, right? And George brings the tea. Sometimes he brings cakes for afters." A bit of wet pink appeared between the cracked lips, and just as quickly disappeared. "But George never came, so there was no tea."

"I'm sorry to hear that," Gideon said. "A friend of George's —a friend not from around here—thought George might be in trouble."

"You mean Tiago? E's a good'un, that. But he's always tryin' t'get us into the warsh." The mountain shuddered, then one side heaved upwards in what Gideon took to be a shrug. "He came looking for George hisself, but had no luck. George's gone, he is. That's all there is to it."

"When did you last see him?" Gideon asked.

"Not since . . . " A hand, crusted with filth, appeared, and the fingers ticked. "Not since two days gone. That's when he last brought the tea. That's the day we found us a fine squash at the garden. George, he liked that. Said as he'd try for a pinch of cardamom, in case there were more squashes to be had. But he never came. Not yesterday, nor today, neither."

"So, George planned to be back?"

"It's what he said. But folks say things, don't they? An' folks hereabouts are leavin' all the time." The top of the mountain dipped, a foot wrapped in layers of tar-coated fabric shifted. "But we'll miss George's tea, right enough."

"I don't have any tea." Gideon was digging starbucks out of his pocket even as Mia's elbow nudged him in the ribs. "But maybe you could buy some?"

"Not the same." The figure stepped back, bits of fabric fluttering with the motion. "Not the same if it ain't from George."

"No." Gideon's hand, still holding the bills, dropped. "I guess not."

The pile of fabric paused, and the pitted eyes met Gideon's for a moment, then the head dipped, and the figure shuffled away.

"Keepers," Mia whispered.

Gideon turned, saw her dashing at her cheek with the torch hand, so that the light crossed his gaze, temporarily blinding him.

He stared up at the slat roof, and while he waited for the white blobs to stop dancing in his eyes, said, "We should head home."

"What about George?"

"We can come back tomorrow," he told her, then gave a click that drew Elvis from his perch. "If he still hasn't shown up, we'll try to retrace his steps, see where he went to get the tea. And there's Lupe to check on, too."

"And Meki?"
"And Meki."

<hr>

As Gideon and Mia made their way out of the market, another man drew back into the shadows.

The man's name was Petris, and he had been making a last sweep of the market when the soldier and his companion had arrived to check George's stall.

Then the stinking heap of rags showed up, and Petris had settled down to listen to their conversation, which proved interesting enough that, as soon as Gideon and Mia departed, Petris made his way straight back to the *Yemaya*.

Lekan would, he was sure, want to hear about this.

CHAPTER 8

THE JOURNEY HOME INVOLVED WALKING TO THE NEAREST operating tram station outside Lower Cadbury. Here they caught an uptown local to Cornwell Street.

The ride wasn't long, but sometime during the trip the earlier clouds massed together to create a soft evening rain.

Gideon, still stewing over Tiago's missing people, unfolded himself from the bench while Mia bounced off the tram and Elvis—who had again opted to fly—flapped down to land on her pauldron.

"I can't get over how little he weighs," she noted as the draco settled.

"It's the hollow bones," Gideon noted.

"I get how dracos are like birds, and all that," she replied. "But he looks more solid, is all." Then, because she was watching the draco and not where she was going, she took a long step off the curb when the walk curved onto Doyle Street. "Sorry," she said, as Elvis hissed his displeasure at being jolted.

The draco shook, then angled his head forward to let out a low-throated rumble, similar to a cat's purr, but with more of a trill.

Gideon followed Elvis's gaze to the tallest building on Doyle, which had the added whimsy of an attic with a dormer window overlooking the nature park on the other side of the street.

It wasn't a large preserve, filling just the one city block, but it was big enough to host a healthy grove of mixed trees and shrubs, which in turn provided homes for some of the local wildlife, including the owl already ghosting out of the trees.

All in all, it was a nice block, and the only complaint Gideon had was that Doyle Street wasn't as near the river as he might have liked.

As it was, his fascination with the near occasion of water often led to Gideon leaving his windows open when it rained, which caused Mia and Jinna to repeatedly rush into his office to slam the window closed, with dire warnings of leaks and damp rot.

Gideon would listen politely, wait for whoever was on water patrol that day to leave, and then crack the window open again.

He did, in deference to the dreaded leaks and rot, keep a few towels handy to catch any stray drops.

Tonight, however, the rain was barely a whisper of damp, swirling in the same breeze that had Gideon's coat dancing as he and Mia passed Words, Words, Words—the Doyle Street bookshop, just as the store's owner stepped out.

The bookseller, Tomaz Ang, was built like a gladiator and dressed like the tenor in a Fujian Night Opera. In fact, he was singing now, and as he finished locking the door, straightened and belted out the last, "sleep will come no more," like a challenge before turning to spy Gideon and Mia.

"Well, if it isn't Sweet Buns and Honey Bear," he said with a welcoming grin.

"Tomaz," Gideon nodded over Mia's delighted, "Oy!"

"And here's our Elvis." Tomaz bent down to the draco's level. "Give us a tune, there's a lad."

In response, Elvis arched up on his hind legs, stretched his neck to the fullest, and warbled out the last few notes of *Moons' Shadow*.

"Good boy," Tomaz said, and a visibly pleased Elvis resumed his crouch.

"How—?"

"When did you teach him that?" Mia cut off Gideon's query.

"I didn't." Tomaz adjusted the scarf he'd draped over one shoulder. "I just noticed him humming along with me from time to time whenever you come by the store."

Mia gaped. "But we only been coming for a few weeks."

"Most every day for a few weeks," Gideon reminded her. "And it's *we've* only been coming."

Tomaz laughed and, like everything else about him, the laugh was big, bright, and beautiful. "You know you're welcome anytime," he told Mia, then stepped back to better view the pair with his kohl-rimmed eyes. "So, have you facilitated any villains today?"

"Gideon got two, good and proper," Mia said. "And returned a frisbee plate to its rightful owner."

"Good for you," Tomaz said to Gideon. "But what on Fortune is a frisbee?"

"We're not sure," Gideon admitted. "But it wasn't what you'd call a tough job. Not when the thief has the strategic skills of a dodo and the fence fights like one."

Tomaz *tched* at Gideon. "Never downplay the wins, Sweet Buns. It's bad for business. Speaking of business," he added, "tell Jinna I said to use 'The Chosen One.'"

Gideon looked at Mia, who raised her brows and shook her head. "Okay."

"Brilliant. Now you'll have to excuse me; I'm off to the Shakespeare Circus."

"What's on tonight?" Gideon asked as all three began to walk up the street.

"Darling, with so many stages, what isn't?" Tomaz replied. "But tonight I'm going to see my latest beau; he's one of the Queen's Rogues."

"Never heard of them," Mia said.

"I think I have," Gideon said, but couldn't recall why.

"They've been touring forever," Tomaz explained. "But Shahrukh tells me they've got a new manager—or maybe it's an old manager who returned—and is pushing them to bigger venues. What's his name? Horatio something. Aldis? Alvion? Alfalfa?"

Hearing the name, Gideon remembered where he'd first heard of the Queen's Rogues. "Was it Alva?" he asked. "Horatio Alva?"

"That's it!" Tomaz clapped his hands together. "Do you know him?"

"We've met." Which, Gideon thought, was an understatement at best, as he and Horatio had served time together in the Barrens. They'd both been paroled on the same day, and last Gideon had seen of the grifter, Horatio had been heading towards an east bound riverboat.

"I'll be sure to give him your regards," Tomaz promised.

As he spoke, a rickshaw stopped at the corner of Butler to let off a fare. "And there's my ride," he said, waving a hand and letting out a whistle that had one of the forest's birds whistling back.

As Tomaz raced off, he waved at the owners of The Bitter Herb, who were just then stepping out of their store.

"Maria, Kinu." Gideon and Mia stopped in Tomaz's wake,

getting a whiff of cinnamon and cardamon as Kinu shut the door of the spice shop. "How was your day?"

"Oh, the usual." Kinu waved the hand not holding the key. "Just passing the thyme."

"Giving sage advice," Maria added.

Mia groaned.

"That almost hurt," Gideon said.

"It's a skill." Maria flipped her braid back and took Kinu's hand as her partner finished locking the door.

"You off to the milonga?" Mia asked, studying the frothy shawl wrapped around Maria's skirt.

A reasonable guess, Gideon figured, as the couple shared a passion for the argentango, as well as horrible puns.

"Not tonight. We're headed to Marlowe Street. There's a poetry jam at Here's One in Your Eye," Kinu said. In the street-light, her earrings glowed gold under the short crop of black hair, where already droplets of mist sparkled like crystal.

"But you have to expect at least a little music." Maria flirted her skirt so the shawl's red fringes danced like flames.

"Someday," Kinu said, eying Gideon, "you'll have to come to the milonga with us."

Gideon thought of the argentango, its intricate steps and subtle flicks of the leg. "I don't think so."

"I bet we'll get you on the floor before the second planting season."

"I'd take that bet, but I hear it's poor form to steal from the neighbors."

Kinu laughed and, with a wave, she and Maria headed off towards Cornwell, and the tram that would take them to Marlowe Street.

Gideon turned back towards their destination, one door up from The Bitter Herb, his eyes skimming the rest of the block, but there wasn't much to see, beyond a black van, gleaming with rain, parked on the street in front of Sally's Mech Repair. Which was odd, given that Sally's was almost never open.

Maybe Sally had taken the rare day on, he thought as his gaze slid back to 9 Doyle. "Light's on in the tea shop," he noted.

"So?" Mia asked.

"So, why would Jinna still be downstairs?" Most evenings, their partner would be settling into the third-floor flat she shared with Mia, reading, or working on the baby's room, or inflicting her knitting needles on yet another unsuspecting ball of yarn.

He looked up and saw a sliver of light slicing through a crack in the second-floor curtains, but not the third.

Since the second floor contained Gideon's office-slash-residence, and he was obviously not at home, this struck him as even more odd than the lights in the tea shop.

Because it did, he increased his pace towards the picture window, on which the words *MacGuffin's Tea and Pastries* had recently been painted.

Seeing nothing, he glanced at Mia, who'd come up even with him. "Stay behind me," he ordered as he stepped into the foyer, which smelled of paint and Jinna's preferred citrus cleanser. Since all was quiet, he turned to his right, and the half glass door leading to Jinna's shop.

The door had an echo of the window's sign painted on the glass, but it still allowed a decent view of the dining room and counter, and a sliver of kitchen, where a moving shadow caught his eye.

With a warning glance at Mia, he placed his right hand on the doorknob . . . then the shadow resolved itself into the shape of Jinna Pride, emerging from the kitchen's open arch with a dishcloth in her hand, and Rory McCabe, a close friend of Jinna's from their time in the Corps, at her heels.

Very close, Gideon recalled, as Rory drew Jinna into an embrace, which quickly became quite involved.

Gideon started to back away, but Mia slithered under his arm and shoved through the door while Elvis launched from her shoulder to buzz the young man's head. "Oy, Rory!" she greeted with a grin.

Rory didn't quite duck, but he did release his hold on a laughing Jinna. "Mia," he greeted her. "How's that baton holster working?" he asked Gideon.

"Works to spec," Gideon said. "And thanks."

"You could start a sideline," Jinna told Rory, flipping the cloth over her shoulder before looking at Gideon." Also, good timing."

"How so?" Gideon asked. "Oh, wait, before I forget. We passed Tomaz outside. He said to tell you, and I quote, 'The Chosen One,' whatever that means."

"Oh!" Jinna beamed. "Thanks. That's perfect."

"Okay," he said.

Rory, meanwhile leaned his arms on the counter. "I like your new place," he said to Mia, his voice rich with the burr of the Campbell Isles.

"It's Gideon and Jinna's place," Mia replied to Rory, resting her elbows on the counter across from him. "Even if Gideon ain't put up his sign yet."

"*Hasn't*, and I'll get to it."

"Ain't, hasn't, it's still not done," Mia said with the double whammy of a shrug *and* an eye roll. "How are we to get more clients, if no one knows we're here?"

"Speaking of clients . . ." Jinna tucked a lock of red-gold hair behind her ear and focused on Gideon, "you have one waiting in your office."

"A what? In my *what*?"

"She showed up about ten minutes ago," Jinna explained.

"Closer to twenty," Rory amended, clearing his throat.

"Oh." Jinna flushed. "Right."

"Do we know who she is?" Gideon asked.

"Not from around here," Jinna told him. "Her accent leans Fujian, and she's wearing a Corps long coat and a pair of truly excellent boots."

"You always notice the shoes," Rory commented.

"Shoes say a lot about a person," Jinna replied. "These shoes say she may have some starbucks to her name." She returned her attention to Gideon. "This might be the first case you make a profit on."

Gideon wasn't so sure about that, since the only Corps officer from Fuji he could imagine wanting to hire him would be Kimo Satsuke, the head of Special Operations.

Gideon and Satsuke had a complicated history, as she was the officer who'd presided over his court martial before, six years later, overturning his conviction.

I wonder what she wants, he thought.

"I wonder what she wants?" Mia asked, pushing off from the counter.

"Only one way to find out." He raised his hand and Elvis, ever attentive, launched himself from the counter, again buzzing Rory's tousled hair on the way to his favored perch on Gideon's pauldron.

"I'll be locking up after you," Jinna announced as Mia joined Gideon at the shop door. "We're going to Xanadu."

This announcement caused both Gideon and Mia to stop and regard the heavily pregnant woman.

"That sounds—exciting?" Gideon ventured, which was an understatement, given that half of the entertainment facility called Xanadu was a polished bamboo oval where people wearing wheeled skates went around and around and around— for fun.

The other half was less physically risky, but it was filled

with games of the sort traveling carnies used to sucker locals out of their hard-earned starbucks.

"Are you sure that's a good choice in you—are you sure that's what you want to do?" Rory amended quickly.

"*Good save*," Gideon murmured out of the side of his mouth.

Jinna's hands fisted on her hips. "You think I can't skate?"

"No. I just, I know I can't," Rory said.

"*Another good one*," Mia murmured back.

Jinna's eyes narrowed, then she smiled. "Then I guess it's lucky for you I'm in the mood for skee ball. And wasabi nuts—and lemon ice."

"Ack," Rory said.

"Have fun with that," Gideon offered as he and Mia backed out of the door into the foyer, leaving Rory to deal with Jinna's maternal cravings.

"How long do ya think it'll be before Jinna asks Rory to wed her?" Mia asked as they turned to the stairs.

"How do you know he won't ask her?" Gideon asked back, then grinned at Mia's snort. "Yeah," he agreed, "you're probably right. Anyway, as long as she sticks with MacGuffin's, I don't care who asks who to do what."

"What?"

"Never mind."

They climbed two more steps before Mia spoke again. "Why is she calling her place MacGuffin's, anyway?"

"No idea."

"Fine." Mia sighed weightily. "But do you even know who MacGuffin is, then?"

"Not who," he replied. "What."

"So, what's a MacGuffin?"

"A MacGuffin is a trope."

"And what's a trope?"

Now *he* sighed weightily. "A trope is a literary device."

"Right." She waited one whole step before asking, "And what's a literary device?"

"Ask Tomaz."

"He ain't here, is he?"

Gideon came to a halt just below the second-floor landing.

She came up alongside him. Her mouth opened.

He held up a "wait a minute" hand and, wishing Tomaz was here, sifted through his incomplete education to find examples that would satisfy her curiosity.

"Okay," he said, stepping up to the landing and turning to face her as she joined him. "So first off, a literary device isn't a device like a spanner, but it *is* a kind of tool that writers use to help tell stories. Like foreshadowing . . . which is a hint about something that'll happen later," he explained, as her expression foreshadowed the question. "Or metaphors. You know metaphors, right?"

"Is that the bit where Juliet's lips are pilgrims?" Mia asked, referring to the play they'd discussed earlier.

"Yes, exactly," he said, impressed. "Anyway," he continued, "those are a couple of tropes. There are also some others that are more like maps of where a story is supposed to go, and how it's supposed to get there."

He turned, crossed the landing, and grabbed hold of the cool brass knob of his office-slash-flat.

"Maps?"

"Kind of, yeah. There's one called the Hero's Journey, which is the deal in that space opera you're always humming."

"Gyro's Journey," Mia said, slapping her own forehead as she named one of Jinna's menu items. "*Now* I get it."

"That's just one of them," he said, and pushed the door open to reveal the flat's main room, unfurnished but for the scarred desk and a trio of foundling chairs. "There's also The

Hungry Corporation and The Unlikely Hero . . . and one really old one about people and refrigerators that I'm not going to explain because it'll give you nightmares."

As he spoke, his eyes tracked past the desk to the window, from which hung a heavy drape of midnight blue, which had been his payment after a job for a small textiles business.

But it wasn't the drapery he noticed now.

What he noticed now was the woman standing in front of the drape.

The first thing that struck him about her was that her hair was just as he remembered: black as onyx and straight as a hard rain. "And this," he finished calmly, as if his bones hadn't just turned to water.

"This?" Mia slid through the door. "This what?"

"This trope," he explained as the potential client—who was not, in fact, General Satsuke—turned from the window. "The Lost Queen."

CHAPTER 9

WHILE GIDEON WAS COMING FACE TO FACE WITH THE trope in his office, Tiago was staring out the window of his flat, hoping that any second he would spy Meki striding down the street.

"Don't look for her."

His face heated at the memory of Gideon's order, and he drew back from the cool window only to catch sight of his reflection in the glass. As always, he saw the bits of his late father in the shape of his eyes, the angle of his jaw.

But while it was Paulo's features imprinted on the mirrored face, the expression was all Ishan; that expression, a kind of fierce determination, was the same one his remaining father wore most every day on the job.

For a moment, Tiago considered that reflection.

Then, before he could think better, he abandoned his station at the window, crossed the flat, and yanked his coat from the hook.

The next Tiago knew, he was outside, with the light rain chilling his face, and his hands diving into his pockets in search of his gloves.

He didn't find any gloves, but he did find the vial Mia had lifted from his satchel earlier.

With a resigned grimace, he tucked the potion back into his coat's inner pocket and strode down the street, intent on finding his missing people.

Inside A Fine Mess, Rolf leaned on the bar and considered another drink.

He considered it with great care, given he was already quite drunk.

At his side, Freya and Ulf were making noises about heading home, with Freya postulating that if they started walking now, they'd be halfway sober by the time they got to their flat, and therefore half as likely to make their mother angry.

Which made sense to Rolf, but he wasn't ready to go.

He wasn't ready to be even halfway sober, and he most especially didn't want to face his mother, who would be disappointed to learn how Rolf lost his job in the meat-growing plant.

"Stupid job, anyway," he muttered, angling to lean his back against the bar.

From here he let his gaze wander until it caught on a table by the wall, occupied by a young lady with a face much softer than those of the others partaking of Martin's horrible liquor.

"Most of them are stupid jobs," Ulf said, in answer to Rolf's earlier complaint. "But work is work, yes?"

"No." Rolf met his brother's wavering gaze, so like his own. "Work is . . . work should be . . . should have . . . it should *matter*."

"You sound like father." Freya, a half jigger less sauced than her brothers, said softly.

"Father had some good thoughts."

"He had many good thoughts," Ulf agreed with Rolf's defensive statement. "But even he knew it is hard to live on ideas."

Come." Freya patted both brothers on the shoulders. "We should be getting home. And also be saving some starbucks for Mama to put into the pantry."

"Here." Rolf dug into his pocket and slapped his last remaining ten-star into his sister's palm. "Take this home."

"You are not coming?" Ulf asked.

"Not yet." Rolf's eyes slid towards the young woman, who was now watching him. "I follow. Later."

Freya and Ulf frowned, two sides of a coin, then followed Rolf's gaze, then let out dual chuckles.

"Luck to you." Freya gave him an encouraging punch to the shoulder. "And be a gentleman."

"Do you need protection?" Ulf asked.

Rolf shook his head at his siblings' blunt solicitousness. "What I need is for you to be going now."

Both Ulf and Freya grinned and lumbered through the tables, their hair glinting as they passed under the scatter of lamps.

As his siblings stepped out into the chill night, Rolf turned his attention back to the young lady, only to find she was no longer sitting at the table but sidling up to the bar to take Ulf's place.

He looked down and discovered her eyes to be a deeper brown than her skin, but just as warm, and when she smiled, a single dimple appeared.

"I don't know about you," she said, "but I hate to drink alone."

"It is the same for me," he said. "Plus, in the Mess, is best to drink with someone who knows first aid." He recalled the exhortation to be a gentleman and placed his hand over his heart before offering it, palm up. "I am Rolf."

"I'm pleased to meet you, Rolf." She returned the gesture before placing her hand in his and, while small, her palm had the calluses of one who knew the hilt of a sword. "I would be even more pleased to buy you a drink," she added.

"That is most kind." As he spoke, he made a drunken attempt at a bow.

He raised his head in time to see a shadow cooling those warm brown eyes, but it was soon gone. And then she was raising a finger to Martin, and Martin was filling their glasses.

And so he forgot about the shadow as they raised those glasses in a toast to new friends, and to not drinking alone.

CHAPTER 10

GIDEON TRIED TO SPEAK, BUT NOTHING CAME OUT AS THE woman stepped away from the window. She wore the Infantry coat, as Jinna had said, except where the pauldron bearing the gryphon of the Air Corps should have been buckled, only a few bruised plum blossoms stuck to the fabric.

She'd unbuttoned the coat, so it hung open over a civilian shirt and trousers and a brocade waistcoat of garnet. The garnet, he noted, was tooled in a dull gold thread that picked up the golden brown of her skin.

But the gun belt she wore was straight out of the Corps armory, as was the shooter holstered low on her right hip, and the gloves she'd yet to remove, despite the relative warmth of the flat.

The boots, as Jinna had suggested, were impressive.

Blue suede shoes, he thought, then looked up to see her watching him, her expression unreadable.

"Gideon," she said.

"Nice boots," he managed.

Her eyes dipped, rose. "They were a gift."

"Dani—"

"Oy!" Mia, her jaw dropping, darted forward to stand between the two adults. "This is Dani?" She turned from Gideon to their ostensible client. "You're Dani?"

"I am." Her expression shifted to a smile for the curious girl.

"Sorry," Gideon said, then paused to clear the rocks that seemed to have lodged in his throat. "Lieutenant Indani Solis—"

"Actually, it's Captain—it's Captain, now," Dani said, the brush of her Fujian accent softening the interruption. "And you would be Mia?" she asked.

"Yeah, that's me." Mia eased back a step. "How did you know?"

"I've been in touch with General Satsuke," Dani told her. "She was deeply impressed by you. Especially by how you helped Gideon with the Rand affair." Her head tilted and the rain-like hair whispered over her shoulders. "Is it true you drove to his rescue in a compost lorry?"

"True as a keeper's oath," Mia replied with a grin. "Kept him from drowning in a bathtub, too. Elvis helped with that bit." She jerked a thumb to where Elvis perched on Gideon's shoulder, following the proceedings intently.

"Elvis?" Dani eyed the draco as the hint of a smile danced over her lips. "It appears Gideon is fortunate in his partners."

"That's what I keep tellin' him," Mia agreed before stepping closer to Dani, visibly taking the woman's measure. "I thought you was dead."

"Oh?" Dani blinked.

"Mia," Gideon began.

"It was the way he never talks about you, see?" Mia said, ignoring him. "Only time he says your name is if he's dreaming like, and then he wakes up and I'm all, 'Who's Dani', and he's all, 'It's complicated,' and then he gets broody and moping about—"

"I do *not*—"

"—so naturally I figured you was—"

"*Were.*"

"—dead," Mia finished over Gideon's automatic correction.

"I see." Dani met Gideon's gaze. "You moped?"

"I think," he said, glancing at Mia, "now would be a good time to offer our guest some tea."

At that, Mia turned and goggled. "You don't waste much time, do you?"

"What?" And then he recalled the earlier discussion in Tiago's flat. "No. I mean *actual* tea," Gideon resisted—barely—the urge to slap himself in the forehead.

"Oh." Mia's brow scrunched in thought before she brightened. "I guess it makes sense, seeing as you'd want to catch up a bit before you went for the other sort."

"What other kind of tea is there?" Dani asked as Mia dashed out of the room.

"It's—"

"Complicated!" Mia called over her shoulder.

"That," Gideon said.

Dani didn't protest the offered tea, real or otherwise.

Not because she was thirsty, but because making tea removed Mia from the room.

She only hoped Gideon's partner in facilitating took her time. Although, from the sounds of cupboard doors slamming, Mia was rushing through the preparations in order not to miss anything exciting.

Privately, Dani thought the situation looked good for Mia, given thus far the only words to pass between the two adults had been Gideon's offer of a chair, and Dani's acceptance of same.

Once they'd each taken a seat on opposite sides of his desk, silence had fallen.

Worse than the silence, though, was the underlying tension; a tension so strained, she was sure a single wrong breath would snap it.

Only Elvis seemed at ease, slinking from the scratched pauldron on Gideon's coat, all the way down his arm and onto the desk.

Once there, he circled four times clockwise and three counterclockwise before lying down, pointed chin resting on taloned paws, tail curled close around his body and wings folded back to resting.

Finally, his eyes gradually shuttered, one lid at a time.

With some regret, Dani let the sleeping draco lie and turned to Gideon, only to discover his eyes were fixed on the curtained window, where she'd been waiting when he entered.

What he doubtless guessed, though he didn't ask, was if she'd been looking through those drapes, watching for him.

She had, of course.

While watching for Gideon, she'd also admired his view of the park, where the leaves were only now budding, and swaths of emerald moss carpeted the roots. Dani could easily imagine how, in a month's time, the park would burst with color and scent.

For now, however, it waited; a slice of unrealized potential.

Rather like Gideon's flat, which Dani had explored after her manners had lost a brief but intense war with her curiosity.

What she'd discovered was a series of rooms scrubbed to drill sergeant specifications and, with one exception, mostly empty.

No art or tapestries on the walls; no mementos on shelves (and no shelves); no rugs to soften the plank floors underfoot.

Not even a table in the dining nook.

Just as well, as she'd found little in the way of food in the kitchen.

The bath held a few towels, a brick of sandalwood soap, and a shaving kit he apparently hadn't used in a day or so.

The flat had two bedrooms, but one had apparently been designated a storage space, as it contained a virtual treasure trove of supplies. There were cleaning and building materials, piles of fabric, crates of dishes, glasses and cookware . . . all for the tea shop, she supposed.

Clever of Gideon, she'd thought, merging two utterly disparate businesses, and in so doing, giving Jinna Pride a foundation for her family-to-be.

As well as ensuring that he'd never have to cook for himself.

The second bedroom, she discovered on peering in, fulfilled its stated purpose by possessing an actual bed.

Or at least a mattress.

The thick pallet had no frame, resting instead on the bare floor, but it was neatly made under a coverlet woven in bleeding shades of blue, complimenting the midnight drapes billowing over the bedroom window.

She almost closed that window against the light rain that had begun, but thought better, knowing Gideon would remember he'd left it open.

Instead, she crouched to study the book he'd left on the floor next to a table lamp in need of a table.

A glance at the green cloth binding showed it to be a collection of stories by Ruby Farzan, one of Fortune's earliest writers, and her vivid descriptions of a world new in every possible way still held imaginations centuries later.

A scrap of leather marked his place.

Running her fingers over the binding, Dani could almost see Gideon reading, his back propped against the wall, book in one hand, and the little lamp at his side, pushing back the dark.

The sheet, she knew, would be tossed carelessly over long legs crossed at the ankle, and his eyes fixed on the page as if he weren't merely reading, but absorbing the words.

She'd seen him so, in the past, when she entered his quarters at Epsilon Base, or slipped into his command tent during those rare times her 'ship anchored near his company's bivouac.

And then his eyes would rise to meet hers, and then the book would fall to one side as she dropped her gun belt, and they would make the most of whatever brief time the war gave them.

It was after those memories, which struck like a blast of crystal det, that Dani ceased her explorations and returned to the office window, arriving in time to see Gideon and Mia turn onto Doyle. From there she'd watched them greet the owner of the bookshop, and then the women who ran The Bitter Herb.

At the time, she'd noted that he still walked with the same long, wolf-like lope.

Now, sitting on the opposite side of a desk in Gideon's office, she could see how he'd changed.

The man across from her was leaner than she remembered, and there were more angles in a face more deeply tanned. Hints of silver sheened his hair, and there was a new scar on his jaw.

Her eyes dipped to his right hand, where the number 66897 had been tattooed; a permanent reminder of a wrongful conviction.

At least his eyes hadn't changed or, if they had, they'd only become sharper than the day Gideon confessed to treason.

And though she had known down to her bones that his confession was a lie, she'd been powerless to stop him from making it.

And no point revisiting that flowerless meadow, Dani reminded herself, even as those sharp eyes turned to meet hers.

"I see you kept your coat," she said, wincing at the shallow observation.

The sharpness in his eyes receded to a faint glimmer, and the hint of a smile told her he'd caught both the wince, and its meaning. "It's a good coat," he said before asking, "Why are you here?"

It was the question she'd been waiting for, and the one she feared answering, so she delayed. "Maybe I wanted to see you." As she spoke, she started to tug her right glove free.

"I've been in the city for two months. Or didn't General Satsuke include that detail when you spoke?"

"She didn't, but I could point out, seeing as you've been in the city for two months, you could have contacted me." She dropped the right glove and turned her attention to the left.

"I tried," he admitted, staring at that fallen glove. "After things settled, I wrote a letter. I wrote a few, actually. I figured I could send them to your parents."

She paused in the act of loosening the fingers of the left glove. "My mother never mentioned my receiving any mail."

"I wrote them," he explained. "I never said I sent them."

"Ah."

"If I had sent one of those letters, would you have opened it?"

"Because you never opened mine?" she asked back. "Colonial Mail is tenacious," she continued as he gave a start, "even dealing with mails to the Barrens. Several months after I wrote you, the letter came back to Epsilon Base with the words, 'Refused, Return to Sender,' scrawled across the address."

His eyes darkened. "You know why I did that."

"Do I?" She returned her attention to the glove, now half-off, when his left hand snaked out to catch at her wrist, stalling the maneuver.

"Why," he asked again, "are you here? Because if it's for the apology I owe you—"

"It's not that," she interrupted, extricating her wrist. "I'm here because I need your help." Now, finally, she looked up, at the same time sliding her left glove free to display the bright, moon-silver ring as she added, "My husband needs your help."

For a space, there were no words, only a quiet so frigid and so deep she dared not breathe.

Then the kettle shrieked from the kitchen, shattering the ice of Gideon's expression.

Without a word, he rose from his chair and his boots thudded hollowly as he walked to the window. There he came to a halt and stood, staring at the deep blue fabric of the curtains, as if lost.

Dani held herself still as a new silence draped over the room in a sticky web.

One no doubt spun by the spiders disguised as nerves skittering up her spine.

CHAPTER II

GIDEON'S EYES MIGHT HAVE BEEN FOCUSED ON THE WEAVE of the drapes, but that didn't prevent him from sensing Dani's discomfort.

Since he wasn't ready to deal with her discomfort, he whipped back the curtain to stare out into the street, where a whisper of movement from below had him looking to see Jinna and Rory leaving the building.

While Jinna turned to lock the street door, Rory draped a shawl of forest green over her shoulders.

His hands lingered, brushing the wrap smooth until Jinna's left hand rose to rest on his right.

For a moment they remained so, her leaning against him, his head bent over hers.

Watching them, Gideon felt a disconcerting shift of memory, so instead of the young couple below, he was seeing himself and Dani on Epsilon Base outside the mess.

They were both wet and out of breath, having dashed through the rain from where the *Phalanx* hovered at anchor.

He'd been attempting to brush the excess water from her

hair when she reached up to hold his hand close, and had leaned into him, just as Jinna leaned into Rory now.

Gideon realized his breath had frozen in his chest, so he released it as he once again focused on the view below, where Rory and Jinna's hands were now linked over the swell of the child she carried.

A child fathered not by Rory, but by the best friend Rory and Jinna shared—and *that* was a story of its own—before Jinna tucked her hand in his arm and they started towards Butler at the same time a man turned from Butler onto Doyle, where he turned to peer into the window of the mech repair shop.

Then Jinna and Rory were rounding the corner and the man at Sally's straightened and continued on his way to Cornwell.

Gideon waited until the street was empty to speak. "I charge five starbucks a day," he said to the window. "Plus expenses."

He heard her rise from her chair, listened to the *thud* of her blue suede boots crossing to where he stood.

"Gideon . . ."

"Don't." His eyes, somehow, rose. Somehow met hers. Whatever she saw there, it was enough to hold her in place. "Just, don't."

Her breath huffed out, but she didn't say anything more.

Nor did she come any closer, choosing instead to lean a shoulder against the wall on the other side of the window.

"So," he said at last, forcing himself to face her, "you got married."

"Yes." Her hands slipped into her coat pockets, hiding the ring. "It's been close to seven years, Gideon."

"I'm aware how long it's been."

"It would have been a lot longer if I hadn't pushed General Satsuke to reopen your case."

Gideon's mouth opened, but nothing came out, not while her statement bounced around his skull, each echo spawning more echoes.

And around and through those echoes, he recalled the discussion he'd had with General Kimo Satsuke, shortly after she'd arranged his parole.

"*—one of my officers was chasing a ghost in the ranks—*"

His eyes narrowed as he recalled more of the conversation.

"*—as the months passed, we became aware of a continued hostile presence within the Corps.*"

A hostile presence that Gideon had ultimately discovered to be Celia Rand, AKA the Midasian spy Odile, AKA the reason Gideon had ended up with half a company dead and himself in the Barrens.

That interlude with Satsuke, and the events which had sprung from it, now wove through the echoes of Dani's statement, creating a dull buzz, blocking out everything until Mia's voice scythed through the internal murmuration.

"What did you do to him?"

"Nothing," he said, rousing himself to see that, yes, there was Mia, holding a battered tray on which sat a steaming pot wrapped in a tea towel, three cups, and the packet of biscuits Gideon had hidden (ineffectually, it appeared) at the back of the cutlery drawer.

"Not quite nothing," Dani countered.

Gideon grimaced. "It's complicated."

Mia shot him a disgusted glare over the steaming pot.

"I told him the truth," Dani explained in the face of that youthful affront and crossed back to where Mia was setting the tray down with a rattle. A wave of tea sloshed out of the spout to land near Elvis, who woke with a start and a throaty growl.

"Sorry, Elvis." Mia dabbed at the splash with the tea towel as she looked at Dani. "What truth?"

"The truth about how he got out of prison," Dani told her, then turned to Gideon. "You're welcome, by the way."

"About that . . ." He joined them at the desk. "What do you mean when you say you pushed Satsuke?"

"What do you mean, what do I mean?"

At Dani's snappish tone, Mia edged back from the table.

"I mean," Gideon said, "General Satsuke told me it was one of her officers trying to reopen the case."

"And?" Dani moved her gloves, still on the desk, a few inches to the left.

"*And?*" He came perilously close to a Mia-level eye roll as he pointed out, "*And* you aren't part of Special Operations. You're a jumper."

"Ooo, like Jagati," Mia said, referring to one of Rory's crewmates.

"*Was* a jumper," Dani corrected Gideon, then she moved the gloves a few inches to the right. "I transferred to Special Operations."

"When?" he asked, watching her fiddle with the gloves. Dani had never been a fiddler.

There was the slightest hesitation before she responded. "About a month after you were sent to the Barrens."

"Why?"

"Seriously?" Mia spun on Gideon before Dani could reply. "A person gives up her place inna corps so she can work on gettin' you outta the nick and you're asking why? I don't even like the quarterstar romances, and I can figure out the why."

"*Very* fortunate in your partners," Dani reiterated.

"All of which makes sense in a quarterstar romance kind of way," Gideon said, waving at Dani, "*if* she hadn't up and married someone else in the meantime."

"What?" Mia now spun on Dani.

"It's complicated," Dani insisted.

"UGH! Grown-ups!" Mia threw her hands up in the air and dropped into Gideon's abandoned chair, startling Elvis.

With an irate flick of the tongue, the draco launched himself into the air, flapping down to the floor before stalking to Gideon's bedroom with a reptilian grumble.

Gideon ignored both prepubescent judgment and draconian irritation and focused on Dani, which was a mistake because she was altogether too close and too real and too *her* and he'd thought—hoped—that finding her waiting in his office, just like the trope of the lost queen, meant . . .

He cut that thought off at the knees and met Dani's anxious gaze. "You said your husband needs help?"

Dani let out a huff of breath then glanced in the direction Elvis had fled, as if considering the merits of a similar retreat, but, at the last, she shook her head and met his gaze. "He does."

"Okay then, let's start with the basics." *Just like any other case,* he thought, and picked up the forgotten teapot.

"Basics?" Dani asked.

"Like, what kind of help?" He poured out for Mia. "And maybe, you know, his name?" He moved to the next cup and started to pour.

Dani didn't respond while that cup filled, nor when the tea streamed, fragrant and black, into the third cup.

Finally, as casually as he could manage, he asked, "Do I know the guy?"

"It's . . . it's Saeng."

Gideon looked up, forgetting the pot in his hand until Mia's sharp "Oy!" alerted him to the overrunning cup.

He put the pot back with a rattling *thud.* "I'm sorry," he said, tapping his ear. "I don't think I heard that right because it sounded like you said your husband's name is Saeng."

Mia, again mopping up the spilled tea, gave him a wary glance.

Dani's arms crossed over her chest, and her chin tilted a little further. "You know you heard correctly."

Gideon's hands dug into his coat pockets. "Saeng as in Saeng Tenjin?"

"Yes."

"Wait. Is that Tenjin like Tenjin Corporation? And Tenjin R&D? And Tenjin Colonial Air?" Mia asked.

Dani sighed. "Yes."

"Cor," Mia murmured, eyes wide as she reached for the biscuit packet.

"Family ties aside, this would also be the same Saeng who tried to get me discharged after the *Bounty* incident."

"Wait." Mia waved her biscuit as she asked, "What's the *Bounty*?"

"An Adian supply 'ship I liberated during the war," he replied.

"And then he crashed it," Dani added.

He turned to face her. "I like to think of it as an aggressive landing."

"On top of Epsilon Flight's admin building." She took a step towards him.

"No one was hurt," he asserted, taking a step towards her.

"Major Ranjeet lost her ficus."

"I got her a new one!"

By now they were so near each other, he could feel the warmth of her breath cross his cheek as she exhaled in frustration.

He could also see when she realized how close they were standing.

Their eyes met, and as one, they took a deliberate step away from one another.

"Saeng wasn't trying to get you discharged," Dani said at last. "The review board ordered him to investigate, and he did."

"I'd say he followed those orders pretty diligently. Digging up every ding on my record to make extra special sure the review board knew what a crap officer I was."

"He never thought that," Dani said. "He did his job, but he supported your actions. Most of them," she qualified. "He also stood for you after Nasa. He never believed you were guilty. Never."

He glared.

She glared back.

The packet crinkled as Mia grabbed another biscuit.

"Fine. Maybe that's true," Gideon finally conceded, dropping his gaze to the overfilled teacup. But he didn't have to like it. Or him.

A soft footstep was followed by the weight of Dani's hand on his shoulder. "He's a good man, Gideon."

He jerked free of her hand at the same time the squeak of his chair told him Mia had shifted to watch the scene unfold.

"Do you want me to leave?" Dani finally asked, though he could hear what the asking of it cost her.

Yes, he thought.

"No," he said. "But you could tell me what kind of help you think he needs."

"That's the thing." She stepped back. "I was hoping he could tell you, except I think he's missing. I mean, he is. Missing. That is."

Rolf slammed his glass down on the bar and tried to focus on the young lady in front of him, who had somehow become two young ladies.

Also, he couldn't feel his feet.

Had he lost them?

He peered at the floor, but there he found too many feet. "It might be I have had too much of Martin Soong's liquor," he slurred.

"You *are* looking a bit worse for wear." His companion's voice slammed into Rolf's skull like a wave.

"I feel very badly worn," he confessed.

"We should get you outside," she determined, and while Rolf thought that was a fine idea in theory, there remained the problem of too many feet.

"You all right there, Rolf?" Martin Soong's voice slid, asp-like, into Rolf's ear.

"Guess one of the Ohmdahls finally reached their limit," one of the other drinkers said with a laugh.

Normally, Rolf would have laughed too, but there was nothing normal about the way he felt now.

"Keepers," he mumbled. "Could I be having a sickness?"

A hand, small but strong, took hold of his arm. "I'm sure it's just this foul—this liquor. Let me help you outside," the young lady said. "The air will help, and my home is close. You can rest there."

"But I must contact my mother. She will worry. Very much worry."

"A short rest only, and perhaps some tea," she suggested.

"You are being very kind," he told her as she slid under his shoulder and helped him walk. "I don't meet so many nice ladies, you know."

He thought she mumbled something, and that something sounded like, "*You haven't met one now*," but that had to be the horrible drink talking.

While Rolf battled his own feet on the way out of A Fine Mess, Tiago was heading towards it.

He'd already searched every street in Lower Cadbury where people dared live and found no sign of Meki or the others.

The only place he'd yet to check was Martin Soong's pub.

And though he thought it unlikely he'd find Meki in the Mess, there was the chance one of Martin's patrons would have seen her, or George or Lupe.

He hoped that was the case, as even thinking of A Fine Mess had his throat thickening in anticipation of the fetid, booze-soaked air.

But it would be worth it, he thought.

As long as he found her—them—*her*, it would be worth any amount of trouble.

Lekan's daughter was a strong woman.

She had to be.

In her world, the weak didn't survive.

Even so, she was starting to falter under Rolf's teetering weight.

Hard to believe he was one of three such giants.

His poor mother, she thought.

And then thought it again, though for a different reason.

"I have never seen the world being sideways before," Rolf said, a moment before his knees buckled, taking her down with him.

"Swarming hornets," she cursed as her knees splashed onto the wet pavement.

At the same time, two figures separated themselves from the

deeper shadows, one medium height and thin, the other taller and thicker.

"About time," she said, squinting into the rain as Xian and Miguel joined her. "I might have been crushed."

Miguel eased in to take the bulk of Rolf's weight from the left. "We wanted to be sure no one followed you out."

Rolf grunted, raised his head, and blinked over at Miguel. "Ah, you are a good person to be helping."

"That's me." Miguel grinned. "Always willing to lend a hand."

With most of Rolf's weight shifted to Miguel, she straightened and patted Rolf's shoulder. "Not too long now, and you can rest."

"Hello?"

The voice that emerged from the dark was familiar.

It was also one she'd hoped never to hear again.

Internally, she cursed.

Externally, she tried to get Rolf and Miguel moving.

"Excuse me," the voice called again. "I wonder if you can help? I've been looking for someone, or several someones, and, oh! Hello, Rolf!"

"Tiago?" As Rolf spoke, he tried to straighten, overcompensated, and tipped backwards.

Tiago raced up to grab Rolf by the lapels. "Steady on."

"Sorry," Rolf said. "I am not well."

"I can see that." Tiago's teeth flashed in a smile for Miguel. "Lucky you have friends here to help you to . . . " He paused as his gaze slid in her direction. "Meki?"

"Meki?" Rolf echoed as Meki's eyes rose to meet Tiago's. "This is your name?"

"I don't understand." Tiago stepped back.

"No," she agreed at the same time Xian, cosh in hand, appeared behind the youth. "You don't."

Then the cosh struck Tiago with a sickening *thud*.

Rolf blinked into the rain as Tiago dropped to the rain-slicked ground. "I think Tiago is also not feeling so good."

CHAPTER 12

"Missing?" Mia echoed Dani's statement, forgetting the biscuit in her hand. "Was your husband in Lower Cadbury, too?"

"Like a Tenjin ever came within spitting distance of Lower Cadbury," Gideon said.

"Saeng was visiting his aunt, up on the Tenjin peninsula," Dani told Mia. "And that's reverse classism," she added to Gideon.

"Hey, if the class fits . . ."

"Do you have to be so snarky?"

"How long have you known me?"

Mia gaped. It was like watching a play.

Then Dani's expression went flat while Gideon's got all crooked, the way it did when he was sorry about something.

Sure enough, his next words were, "I'm sorry." Then his breath huffed out, and he appeared, to Mia, to be having a sort of chat inside his head. Finally, his eyes focused again on Dani. "So, the last time you saw Saeng would have been . . . ?"

"Earlier today, when he left the hotel."

"Hotel? I mean . . ." Gideon cleared his throat and his

expression got crookeder. "I figured you'd have been staying on Nike base."

"We're on leave," Dani said before adding, in a quick burst, "actually, we're on a belated honeymoon."

"Whoa!" Mia perked up and waved her hands. "If you're only just married, maybe Saeng, you know . . . " She made two walking fingers and trotted them through the air. " . . . scarped. Like in *The Risto's Dilemma*."

"Except that was a play," Gideon pointed out, though he sounded hopeful.

"And we've been married for over two months," Dani told Mia.

"Funny, that." Mia said. "Gideon got sprung from the Barrens two months back."

"Yeah, funny that," Gideon agreed.

Dani opened her mouth, then closed it.

"Right." Gideon grabbed the nearest cup of tea and tossed it back like it was something a lot stronger. "So, tell me about Saeng."

"Ahh—"

"You said he left the hotel this morning. What time?"

"Oh. Around twelve-hundred hours," she replied, after a moment's thought.

"So, sleeping in," Gideon observed.

If Dani noted Gideon's snark this time (and Mia didn't see how she could miss it), she didn't comment. "He was meeting Yuko, that's his aunt, for tea."

Gideon nodded. "And did you hear from him again?" he asked, falling into the pattern of questions that preceded every facilitation.

"Yes." Dani flipped her coat aside so they could see the radio hooked on the belt behind her shooter. "He radio'd to tell me the meeting was taking longer than expected. That was sometime after fourteen hundred."

"How did he travel? Do you know?"

"Cycle from the motor pool." Dani picked up the last remaining teacup.

Mia saw something flicker across the businesslike expression Gideon wore for clients.

So, apparently, did Dani.

"I've telephed Corps Medical at the base, and Yousafzai and Komnene hospitals," she told him. "The only cycle injury today was a female rickshaw driver, over in the tenth district."

"Did you—"

"Morgues too," she cut in shortly. "I even called the coppers."

"Too bad they won't call a bloke missing until they're gone over eighty-four hours," Mia groused.

"That is such a stupid rule," Dani complained.

"I *know!*" Mia agreed, slapping the desk. "We was just talking about it—"

"*Were,*" Gideon murmured.

"*Were* talking about it, because of our other case."

"Other case?" Dani looked at her.

"Yeah. In Lower Cadbury, see? That's why I figured your Saeng might have been down there. 'Cause it turns out our friend, Tiago, has got some missing folk, too."

"How odd." Dani set her tea down, having never tasted it.

"Not really." Gideon inserted himself into the conversation. "And I'm still not convinced Tiago's people are actually missing."

"Except they're not *there*." Mia popped out of the chair to face him.

"Fine. Yes." He set down his empty cup. "And if these hypothetically missing people were you, or Tiago, or Jinna, or the

Ohmdahls, I would call it odd. But these particular people? Not so much."

"You mean street people," Mia said, feeling her face grow hot. "People who don't matter."

"That's not what I said."

"It's what you meant."

"It's—okay, all I'm saying is Tiago's people each fit a particular pattern, and those patterns often include a body suddenly moving on, often without bothering to tell anyone."

"Tiago doesn't think that."

"Tiago's not thinking with his brain," Gideon muttered, but raised his hands in a "hear me out," gesture. "I mean, just look at the girlfriend."

"*Meki*," Mia corrected. "Her name is Meki."

"Assuming she gave Tiago her real name," he countered. "And real name or not, there's every reason to believe she scarped."

"If she scarped, why'd she leave her kit at Tiago's?"

"Maybe she didn't have time to come back for it."

"Why not?" Dani asked.

Both Gideon and Mia turned to where Dani stood, wearing her Corps coat, with her Corps shooter and radio.

And the Corps, Mia recalled from Gideon's earlier rant, might take issue with an escaped Adian slave running about the city.

"Trouble in her past," he said.

Mia had to admire how he managed to tell the truth without spilling the whole jar of honey.

Dani's eyes narrowed, but she appeared to accept the explanation.

"Anyway." Gideon turned back to Mia. "She could have scarped, or could be she's back at Tiago's place. But if this Meki really cares about Tiago, she'd have left. She'd have gone away to keep him safe."

Dani jerked at that, but Gideon kept his eyes on Mia.

"Then there's Lupe," he continued. "A recent immigrant, looking for work. Maybe she found that work? Hells, the meat-growing plant has three new openings. So, say she gets the job and just happens she's on the job when Tiago and the downstairs neighbor stop by."

Mia tapped her foot; ran the odds. "Fine," she said, accepting the theory. "But there's still George."

Gideon sighed. "You know what I think about George."

"I don't," Dani said.

"He thinks George done himself in," Mia explained. "But he won't say why he's so swarming sure of it."

"Shocking," Dani said, sounding anything but shocked.

He turned on Dani, but Mia, pleased to have an ally, kept going. "Especially when there's nothing Tiago said that makes George out to be, you know . . . " She lifted her hands to pull an imaginary noose tight around her neck, then straightened. "He's just going about his business, right? Until all of a sudden, he's not."

"Yes." Gideon snapped out the word as he spun back to face her. "Because that's how it works. Day after day, going about your business, until one day, you *can't*. So you don't."

"*Gideon*." Dani's voice was a low warning, though of what Mia couldn't tell.

All she knew was that suddenly Gideon and Dani were staring at each other and they were both tense in ways that made no sense to her, but she knew she didn't like it.

Then Gideon let out a breath and Dani relaxed and everything felt less . . . just less.

"You're right," Gideon said, then turned to Mia, adding a quiet, "I'm sorry."

"So, are we gonna keep looking for George?" she asked. "And the others?"

"Yes," Gideon said after a beat. "We will look for George, and Lupe and keepers help us, Meki."

Dani shifted.

"And we'll help you find Saeng," Gideon told her.

"Two cases." Mia plopped back into the chair, feeling oddly winded. "How we gonna manage that?"

"Not sure," he admitted. "But we can start by getting the rest of the vitals on this one. So . . . " He fixed his attention on Dani. "Saeng contacted you a little after fourteen hundred. How much later did he leave Tenjin?"

"His aunt said he left her office between fifteen and fifteen thirty hours."

"You spoke to her directly?" Gideon asked, and when Dani nodded, continued with, "Teleph or—"

"I went to Tenjin," she told him.

"Did she say where he was going next?"

"She didn't have to." Dani's fingers danced a beat over the desktop, then stopped. "I already knew. He was coming here— to speak with you."

Mia whistled. "Cheeky."

Dani almost laughed at Mia's comment, but Gideon was already asking, "Why on Fortune would Saeng want to see me?"

"For the same reason he wanted to visit his aunt."

"Yes, that makes sense," Gideon said. "Because the Tenjins and I have so much in common."

"Usually you wouldn't." She glanced at Mia. "Don't get angry, but this is genuinely a complicated issue."

Mia gave a resigned sigh but didn't protest.

"It's also a long story." Dani returned her attention to Gideon. "One that began ten years ago . . . in Ducati."

"You're right," he said with a shrug of seeming indifference. "It is an old story. So old, I find it hard to see how it could connect me to Saeng or his auntie."

"It doesn't," she said simply. "The connection comes from a letter written in thirty-nine and addressed to a Dr. Amaya Hidalgo. She worked for Tenjin R&D at the time. Except the letter never arrived at its destination."

"If it never showed up, how d'you know about it?" Mia asked.

"One of our airships discovered the letter, along with the rest of the contraband, inside a downed blockade runner," Dani explained. "The captain of the discovering airship turned all the papers over to Special Operations. This letter was damaged— the ink faded in some spots, the paper chewed away in others. Saeng kept the original, but I have a copy." She drew one of the brown envelopes used by the Corps from an inner pocket and turned it over in her hands.

"And?" Gideon asked, as she failed to hand it over.

"The thing is, the signature on the letter tells us it was written by a Midasian crystallographer." She looked up, met his expectant gaze. "Her name was Tabak. Nour Tabak."

Even as she spoke the name, Gideon's entire body rocked.

"Gideon . . . " Dani reached out to him while Mia, worry shooting from her eyes, again jumped from the chair.

But Gideon stepped away, warning them off with a single, sharp jerk of his head before turning to stalk out of the room.

As soon as the bedroom door slammed closed, Mia turned on Dani.

"That's the second time today he's walked out of a room like that," she said, her eyes accusing. "Why'd he do it this time?"

"He met Dr. Tabak ten years ago, on one of his missions," she said, which was *a* truth, but not the entire truth.

The entire truth was that the Ducati operation, which had brought Gideon and Nour Tabak together, had gone swarm soon after Gideon and his team stole a set of blueprints for a new crysto-plas cannon the Midasians were developing.

When their escape was compromised, Gideon had taken the role of decoy, so the rest of the team could get the blueprints to safety.

In the end he'd been captured and locked in a cell alongside a boffin named Nour Tabak, where a Midasian officer named Revin tortured both prisoners, taking each in turn, using their own pain and the pain of another in an attempt to break them.

From Gideon, the major's ambition was clear: he wanted the stolen plans.

From Tabak, Revin's desires were more opaque, at least to Gideon's pain-hazed memories.

But in the end, neither prisoner gave Revin what he wanted, so the mutual abuse continued until two of Gideon's company mounted a rescue.

They got Gideon out, but they were too late to save Dr. Tabak.

Standing inside the bedroom door he'd just slammed shut, Gideon didn't hear Mia's sharp question or Dani's soft response.

Nor did he catch the sigh of rain that slipped through the window he'd left open.

Instead, his ears rang with the echoes of those hours in the Ducati cell.

The crack of a whip.

The snapping of electricity.

Wet sounds. Tearing sounds.

Sounds a human throat should never make, but did.

A shudder racked his spine and woke him enough to take a deep breath, but the past was pungent as well as noisy, and all he smelled was sawdust and iron, burning and blood.

Unthinking, he crossed the room, flipped the curtain aside, and slammed the window shut, as if by closing the pane of glass he could lock out the fetid tide of memories called forth by the sounding of a dead boffin's name.

The window's *thud* was followed by a hiss from behind, and he twisted to see Elvis on the bed, rousing from sleep.

With a hiss of his own, Gideon turned from the irate draco to peer out into the night, just as he had earlier, when Dani first told him she was married.

Except this time, he wasn't taking a journey into his past.

He was trying to find a way out of it.

Trying so hard, he pressed his hand to the glass with enough force to sense the faint ripples in the glazing.

It wasn't much, but it was something; something tactile; something from the *now*, and he held to that, his eyes fixed on that pressing hand, on the ridges of bones, and on the number 66897 etched over the back.

He hadn't had those numbers in Ducati.

They'd come after.

Gideon released another shuddering breath and turned his eyes out, past the hand—and the numbers on it—to Doyle Street.

It made a picture, he thought, and he allowed his eyes to rest on the patter of drops dancing in the light of a streetlamp.

Soothed, his gaze drifted over the warm glow of that lamp, spreading in a circle that reached all the way to the park on the other side of the street.

And it was there, at the edge of that gilded circle of light, that he spied the two men huddled under one of the trees at the park's edge.

<hr />

"Why is Gideon smogged up about some boffin he met, back in the day?"

Mia's question had Dani shaking off the memory of Gideon returning from Ducati. "He's upset because she died."

"People die all the time," was Mia's pragmatic response.

"True, but—some deaths are worse than others."

"Why?" Mia asked. "How did she die?"

"Badly," Gideon said.

Dani and Mia turned to see him standing in the corridor's entrance, Elvis once again on his shoulder.

"And, no," he said as his gaze landed on Mia, "I'm not going to tell you about it. And neither is Dani."

"I wasn't planning to," Dani muttered.

"Why not?" Mia asked at the same time.

"Because it's ugly," he said as he strode past his apprentice to the window where he eased the curtain aside, making certain not to be seen as he peered outside.

Dani and Mia shared a glance, then looked at Gideon as he turned to Dani. "Is there a chance you're being followed?"

"Followed?" Dani echoed, joining Gideon at the window, where he eased back so she could slip in front of him.

"Under the maple," he said, peering over her head as she peeked through the scant gap in the drapes.

"I've got them," she said, then froze.

"What?" Gideon asked.

"I've seen that man before," she explained. "The short one on the right."

"He was outside, earlier," he said, "when Jinna and Rory headed out."

"And I saw him aboard the tram I caught from Riverside, near the Tenjin peninsula," Dani said.

"Tenjin," Gideon murmured, still staring out the window. "Bet that's no coincidence."

"Gideon doesn't believe in coincidence," Mia said as she slithered in front of Dani to peek outside.

"Neither do I," Dani told her as Elvis, still perched on Gideon's shoulder, made a rumbling noise.

"Neither does Elvis," Mia guessed.

"Looks like they're arguing," Dani said as the taller man waved at the flat and the shorter raised a cautioning hand.

"Looks like," Gideon agreed at the same time a sleek black van, the twin of the van parked in front of Sally's, turned from Cornwell Street.

Dani, Gideon, and Mia all watched as the van pulled to a halt in front of the two men.

"Now, that's weird," Gideon said as the two men exited the cab and all four moved out of sight behind the vehicle.

"What's weird?" Mia asked.

"I know one of those guys," he said. "I saw him earlier at A Fine Mess—a pub," he explained to Dani, "in Lower Cadbury."

She looked over her shoulder to meet his gaze. "Weird," she echoed.

"Bet that's not a coincidence, either," Mia offered.

CHAPTER 13

Outside, the man Dani had recognized looked at the man Gideon had recognized. "Lekan," he said, tipping his hat back to better see his sometime associate.

"Wex," Lekan replied. "What are you doing here?"

"Merlin and I are tying up a loose end," Wex replied with a dismissive flick of a hand. "And you?"

"Dealing with a troublesome private facilitator."

Wex frowned. "And what is a private facilitator?"

"Not sure, but I think it's something like a copper for hire," Lekan explained. "Anyway, this fellow, Gideon Quinn, was rousting a fence at A Fine Mess this afternoon," he continued, then indicated his companion. "Later on, Petris here overheard Quinn asking about a missing squatter down at the Lower Cadbury market."

"Interesting," Wex murmured. "And you suspect your facilitator is here?"

Lekan shrugged. "He said his office was on Doyle, and attached to a place called MacGuffin's."

"Even more interesting, given my loose end is in the same building," Wex noted.

Both men stepped to the rear of the van, edging out just far enough to view the structure in question, and spied a flicker of motion at one of the curtained windows.

"Now that makes me think we've been spotted," Wex said.

"Best get down to business before they teleph the coppers," Lekan agreed.

"Or the neighbors return home," Wex muttered, then glanced up to see Lekan's questioning look. "Turns out I've met one of the locals," he said.

"Not a friend?" Lekan guessed.

Wex recalled the last time he'd seen Rory McCabe, hanging from the struts in the *Kodiak*'s cargo bay while Wex administered a lashing. "No, not a friend," he said, angling to study the door of 9 Doyle. "So, how do you want to do this?"

Gideon watched the two men peer around the corner of the van, then slide back behind it.

"This would be a good time to teleph the police," Dani suggested.

"We're not on the teleph," Mia said, before Gideon could reply.

"Of course you're not."

"And what's that supposed to mean?" Gideon asked.

"I just wonder how you expect clients to find you. No teleph, no business sign—"

"Told ya'," Mia said.

"Not now," Gideon said to Mia. "And have you ever tried to get teleph service?" he asked Dani.

"No, but—"

"I was able to sign my life over to the Corps by checking a box," he told her. "But try to get one smogging tel installed, and you have to provide records of residence and employment for the past eight years, along with your family lineage all the way to the First Landers."

"I don't think it's that—"

"Someone's moving," Mia cut in.

Gideon and Dani both looked down to see two men were coming around the van to cross the street.

"Take the office door," Gideon said to Dani.

She went, dropping the envelope she still carried on Gideon's desk before flipping her coat back to draw her shooter and toggle the charger to active.

As she took her place, Gideon peered outside.

"I can't see the other two."

"Is that bad?" Mia asked.

"Not necessarily."

While Mia chewed at her lip, he tapped the side of his leg, gave Elvis a scritch, listened to the patter of rain.

"I have an idea," he said at last.

Dani, still at the door, glanced his way. "Did you know Special Operations has a file as thick as a mammoth's leg filled with your ideas?"

"It's been mentioned. In my defense, most of those ideas panned out."

"And some of them crashed."

"One airship." He held up his index finger. "Crash *one* airship, and it follows you around for life."

"What happened to that aggressive landing?"

Mia whistled. "Don't know if you're interested, but I'm pretty sure one of them's trying to pick the lock on the front door."

Gideon eased the curtain out and angled his head until he could spy the bent-over figure of a man directly below.

He laid a hand on Mia's shoulder. "Time for you to scarp."

"No swarming way!"

"Yes, swarming way. I need someone on lookout, in case—"

"Your idea crashes into the barracks?" Dani cut in.

"*I'm* supposed to be the snarky one," he told her. "But yes," he said to Mia. "We could use your eyes."

"Fine." She shrugged, a study in ill-temper. "Where?"

"The attic." He jerked his chin towards the door, then clucked at the draco on his shoulder. "You too, Elvis." He gestured to Mia as he added, "You watch our back. He watches yours."

The draco's tongue flicked once, then he leapt over to the girl's shoulder, talons digging into her pauldron as she darted out the door Dani held open.

Gideon listened to the receding thud of footsteps and then, a few moments later, the squeak of wood against wood, followed by more steps.

Another few seconds passed before a *snick* told Gideon that Mia was safe in the attic, with the hatch closed behind her.

"So," Dani said, closing the door, "what's this idea of yours?"

"Keep an eye out," he told her, by way of an answer. "I'll be right back."

Before she could protest, he ran to the back room, which held the bulk of his facilitation payments.

Flicking on the light, he moved a box of hardware, shuffled past a stack of wainscoting Jinna thought would work in the tea shop, and finally found what he wanted.

He raced back into the office, where Dani was at the window. She turned as he dropped the pile of braided curtain sashes onto the desk. "I never got around to pulling these out," he explained, finding the end of one sash and knotting it to the end of another.

Dani's cheek twitched. "Are you thinking what I think you're thinking?"

"Have I ever *not* been thinking what you think I'm thinking?"

"No," she admitted with a resigned sigh.

"It's a good thing you brought your gloves," he added, eying the nubby blue and brown fibers as he pulled the knot tight.

"Keepers," she hissed, still staring out the window. "Wouldn't it be simpler to wait for them to storm the place, then take them out here?"

"Simpler, yes." Gideon dumped the knotted mass on the desk. "But given I just bought this building, I'd prefer not to trash it in the first month."

Dani turned from the window. "*You* bought a building?"

"What about it?" He moved around to the side of the desk.

"Nothing." She crossed to the office door again, tilting her head to listen for any sound of movement.

"It didn't sound like nothing." He channeled his irritation at the question into shoving the desk closer to the window. As he pushed, cups rattled, and the teapot slid treacherously close to the edge, stopped only by the lump of Dani's gloves.

"I forgot how smogging heavy this thing is," he groused, giving the desk another shove, hard enough that Nour Tabak's letter slipped onto the floor.

"Here." Dani joined him. Putting their backs into it, they moved the massive piece of furniture until Gideon deemed it close enough to the window.

She grabbed her gloves and put them on. "I'll take that," she said, before Gideon could anchor the rope to one of the desk's legs.

He let the expert take the job and headed back to the window. "I can't see anyone," he said. "They might be hugging the wall, or they might be inside by now." He looked back to see Dani holding up the free end of the rope, waiting.

He reached through the drapes to unlatch the window, but he didn't open it.

"Take my place," he said, stepping aside. "Make sure whoever's out there can see you're watching."

She nodded and slid in to fill the space he'd left while he shot Lulu out of her holster and headed for the door.

"When do you want me to move?"

"No idea." He peered over his shoulder to see her standing at the window, one gloved hand at her shooter, the other holding the decorative rope. "Use your instincts." Then, as she met his gaze, added, "I trust you."

He heard her soft, "Better late than never," as he darted out of the flat, just in time to hear the telltale squeak of feet on the stairs.

Raising Lulu, Gideon swung around the corner of the landing to leap down and meet the incoming bruiser halfway up the stairs.

As he dropped, he swung Lulu to the right in a cheek-opening crack before bringing her back to slam the guy's wrist, sending his shooter clattering down the stairs.

Five seconds and three blows later—head, throat, and gut, respectively—the limp, bleeding bruiser followed the fallen shooter, with Gideon racing behind to discover Bruiser Two striding through the open door, cosh in hand and murder in his eyes.

Gideon continued to run, leaping over the inert heap of Bruiser One and lowering his shoulder to slam into Bruiser Two's gut, shoving the opposing body back out the door.

From this hunched over position, Gideon had the opportunity to notice both the size of B-2's boots (mammoth), and some torn-up bits of plum flower on the boot laces, before Bruiser Two's fists came down on Gideon's kidneys.

In the white-hot explosion that followed, Gideon's vision

blanked, but still he held fast to B-2's scratchy coat as he snapped Lulu straight up and into the giant's nethers.

As the wheezing B-2 folded over his favorite bits, Gideon fell-slash-staggered to a minimum viable upright position, whereupon he spun and slammed Lulu to the back of B-2's head, putting him out of his misery before stumbling back into the street, where he had all of two seconds to enjoy the quiet before Mia's voice exploded from above.

"Left!" she shouted, her voice pitched to carry.

He spun towards Cornwell.

"Your other left!" Mia shouted again, then quickly added, "I mean, right! *Your* right, *my* left . . . Sorry!"

Since her apology arrived at the same time as the rush of feet splashing across the pavers, Gideon didn't have time to send her a recriminating glare; but he thought about it.

Especially as every one of the approaching quartet was armed; two shooters and two crossbows, respectively.

Not the best odds, he decided, and, as they circled him, held his arms out at his sides, Lulu hanging by the tips of his fingers. "Guess you got me," he said to the fellow Dani identified as her stalker who, up close, put Gideon in mind of a tree stump with a mustache.

"So it would appear," the tree stump agreed, holding his shooter steady. "A pity I don't want you."

"That's just hurtful," Gideon said, while the tree stump flicked a finger at one of his cohorts.

At the prompt, Flunky One (she was too slim to merit Bruiser), leveled her shooter and headed towards the open door.

While she moved, Gideon scanned the street, trying to figure out how the tree stump had produced three more fighters. Then his eyes lit on the van still parked in front of Sally's. Its rear doors were open, and the quarterstar dropped.

"That's how," he murmured, meeting the tree stump's watchful gaze. "You brought a lot of muscle."

"I find it pays to have backup available at all times."

"It's a sound tactic," Gideon agreed, glancing to where Flunky One had passed the inert form of Bruiser Two to check the foyer.

"Merlin's down," she reported, stepping back, her shooter at the ready.

The stump's brows rose all the way to the dripping brim of his jauntily angled derby. "It appears Lekan was right when he said you were troublesome," he said to Gideon.

"Lekan?" Gideon echoed, while another of the flunkies, earning himself the moniker Flunky Two, yanked Lulu from his fingers. "Hey," Gideon protested. "Careful with her."

"Her?" F-2's lips pulled back in a sneer as he dropped Lulu into a puddle, then aimed his crossbow at Gideon's chest.

"Finish Solis," the tree stump ordered.

Flunky Three, who had yet to say a word, cocked his crossbow and jogged off to join Flunky One.

Gideon began a mental countdown.

Ten . . .

Nine . . .

Eight . . .

Seven . . .

On six, a blaze of plasma shot from the second story, landing next to F-3's left boot.

Gideon had to give credit where due because F-3 didn't waste time gawking at the smoking mess of a paver, but snapped his bow up and aimed for the window—in time for a second shot of plasma to score him in the thigh.

Dani's shots were enough distraction for Gideon to fling himself down, avoiding the tree stump's plasma shot *and* the arrow loosed by Flunky Two, which bounced off the unoccupied building next to MacGuffin's.

As he dove forward, a flash of motion above formed itself into Dani making an arcing leap from the window to rappel down the side of the building, accompanied by a raucous cheer from the dormer window, where Mia was watching.

Dani's boots splashed the pavement at the same time Gideon snapped up the fallen Lulu.

Then he was on his feet, knocking the gun from the tree stump's grip before turning to face F-2, now swinging his empty bow at Gideon's face, and his focus narrowed to the simple necessity of survival.

Bones jarred, knuckles tore, and Lulu reverberated as he blocked or landed blow after blow from two sides.

Gideon heard the plasma burst and fleshy *thuds* of Dani's engagement, and possibly a rickshaw passing over on Butler, but if anyone spied the action on Doyle, they didn't stop to investigate.

Then Gideon got close enough to F-2 to deliver the head-to-nose blow known commonly as the Epsilon Kiss, sending the man staggering back, eyes glazing over, blood spouting from his nose to mix with the steady fall of rain.

"Behind you!" Mia shouted. At the same time, Gideon felt the vibrating muzzle of a live shooter at the back of his skull, followed by the calm voice of the tree stump telling him to "Behave."

Gideon's response was to drop straight down, so the tree stump's fingers tightened on the trigger to send a blob of plasma through the space where Gideon's head had been, to graze the still-wavering F-2 along one ear.

"Bother," the tree stump said, barely audible over F-2's howl of pain, then yelped himself as Gideon shot a leg out to sweep the tree stump from his feet.

In the shadows of the park, Lekan watched as Quinn, then the woman, decimated Petris, Wex, and four other members of Wex's team, all while an enthusiastic waif leaned out of a dormer window above, playing lookout.

Originally, his task was to remain in hiding and, if needed, he would take Quinn out with a dart while Wex dealt with the woman he'd claimed was a loose end. But Quinn had exploded onto the street with such chaotic speed, Lekan had no opportunity to take the shot before Wex's people had him surrounded.

Then the woman had also erupted onto the scene, changing the dynamic once more.

Proof, he supposed, that even the most simple plans could go astray.

As he crept towards the street, Lekan figured he could take Quinn now, while the facilitator was focused on Wex.

But that left the woman and her shooter.

He could try to take them both.

If he could reload fast enough, he *could* take them both.

But even if he did, that would be two darts gone, and he had less than a dozen remaining, with no sure way to replace them.

Then the girl in the dormer shouted, "Behind the van!"

Gideon was dragging the tree stump in Dani's direction when he heard Mia's warning.

Still holding the other man by the collar, he turned towards the vehicle nearest the park when he heard a soft pop, which was followed by a softer cry, and that cry by the primordial shriek of a draco.

He looked up, saw Mia sliding from the window onto the slanted roof beneath.

At which point, there came another sound, more animal than human.

Later, Gideon would know the sound had come from his own throat, but in the now, his body was moving without any guidance from his brain, swinging Lulu into the tree stump's temple. He was racing for the flat before the man's head hit the pavers. "Dani!"

"The shooter's getting away," she said, starting for the park.

"The window's too small." He was pointing and running at once. "I need you. *She* needs you."

He didn't look, didn't have to, because her boots were splashing as she caught up with him, then overtook him, and they both raced into the building, leaping over the stirring lump of Merlin.

Some minutes later, Wex groaned and pressed a hand to the side of his head. He'd lost the hat at some point, so the rain was falling steadily on his face.

He was just contemplating how best to get to his feet when there came the heavy tread and heavier voice of one he knew.

"That could have gone better," Lekan said, before hauling a dazed and dizzy Wex to his feet.

CHAPTER 14

bare planks of a locked cell.

His legs were crossed, his hands rested on his thighs, and the Corps' long coat he still wore spread around him like a green rug.

The coat, like Saeng himself, was the worse for its recent travels—he didn't care to think too closely on what might have caused those stains—but for all that, both man and outerwear rested with apparent ease on the gently shifting deck.

Not, he thought, the drift and tug of an anchored airship, but the softer back and forth of a watercraft.

He caught no sense of forward motion, but recognized the occasional rebound as that of a vessel thudding against a dock.

From the muffled quality of the bulkhead's collisions, he suspected the deck on which he sat was below the waterline, which explained the lack of any portholes and, consequently, the lack of any chance of signaling for a rescue.

On first waking, he'd discovered that five of the eight cells on deck held prisoners, and hoped they could together make enough noise to be heard from shore.

It was a hope that proved futile, as Saeng also soon discovered that every one of his fellow captives was in what appeared to be a drugged stupor. Kept that way, he suspected, through the rations he'd seen delivered soon after he woke.

The trays, containing mounds of a lentil stew with hunks of bread, had been shoved through open sections at the bottom of each latticed cage.

As he'd watched, most of the slumping bodies stirred themselves to grab a hunk of the bread, down a few handfuls of the lentils or, at the least, slurp a ladle of water from the buckets hooked over crossbars of each cell.

Soon after this sluggish repast, each one of the prisoners slumped back to the deck, any which way, and fell again to sleep.

Thinking on that strange, silent dinner hour, Saeng opened his eyes to study his own tray, still untouched, while hunger rattled in his belly and thirst rasped at his throat.

Then he closed his eyes, and once again turned his thoughts to the act of breathing.

In for a count of ten

Out for five.

In for ten.

Out for five.

In for—*What on Fortune is that smell?*

He winced, shook himself, settled again.

In for ten.

Out for five.

In for ten.

Out for five.

In—*Smogging cold down here.*

Out.

In.

Out—*Dani must be worried sick.*

In—*Likely she went to Quinn for help.*

Saeng's eyes snapped open and the next breath came out in a huff as he unfolded himself to rise from the meditative pose that obviously wasn't working.

As he did, the rattle of keys and metallic *k-chunk* of an opening lock pulled his attention to the ladder at the forward end of the deck.

An echoing *clang* and the thick block of light slanting down told him the door to the hold was open.

Before the first boot clomped onto the stairs, Saeng was again sitting, legs crossed, eyes closed, hands resting loosely on his thighs.

Footsteps, accompanied by dragging *thuds*, sounded on the steps and continued down the aisle until they stopped in front of Saeng's cage.

"Not asleep yet?" a deep voice asked breathlessly. "Lucky we've brought you company."

Because he knew it was expected, Saeng opened his eyes.

Two of the five individuals on the other side of the bars he recognized from the earlier tray delivery and knew their names to be Miguel and Xian. Both stood in the center of the aisle while a woman he'd not seen before brought up the rear.

Miguel, the one who'd spoken, supported a big man with long blond hair and clouded blue eyes.

At Miguel's side, Xian hefted the limp body of another man slung over one shoulder.

Before Saeng could do more than identify a pair of worn shoes knocking against Xian's legs, the woman eased past him and Miguel, stopping at the cell to Saeng's left, at present occupied by only one other prisoner.

Her motions were swift and silent as a specter, which was fitting, given her skin was ghostly-pale, and her fair hair shorn so close to her scalp, he could see the scars of battle beneath.

But there was nothing ethereal about her agate-brown eyes, or the ridged muscles visible in the arms displayed by the rolled-up sleeves of her shirt, revealing the tattoo of a sinuous jaguarundi etched around her left wrist.

While he watched, she hefted a large ring on which hung a single, oversized key. This she fit into the door of the cell, from which a series of metallic *snicks* emerged before she hauled open the door with a scrape of metal on wood.

Despite the noise, the cell's current occupant continued to sleep off his latest meal while Miguel maneuvered his burden inside.

"We are at Meki's home now?" the blond man asked as he slumped up against the bars shared with Saeng's cell.

"Sure." Miguel lowered him to the deck. "This is Meki's home."

As Miguel spoke, Xian slid his semiconscious burden to the deck next to the blond giant.

"Tiago, my friend." The blond patted his companion's shoulder. "Be at peace. We can rest now. We are at Meki's place."

As he spoke, the cell door closed with a *clang*, and the key turned the lock home with the same percussive series with which it had opened.

"He is quite pretty," the woman commented, peering through the bars at the youth. "Meki has good taste."

"Lekan will be pleased," Xian said, rotating his shoulder.

"Where is Lekan, anyway?" Miguel asked as the woman started for the stairs. "Xian?" he turned to his crewmate.

Xian gave his neck a resounding *crack* before he answered. "Boss is dealing with a problem. Petris spied some Fordian called Quinn snooping around at the marketplace."

That got Saeng's attention.

"Thing is, Lekan had already come across a Gideon Quinn

at the pub," Xian continued, as he and Miguel followed the woman up the stairs. "Said he looked like trouble."

"Boss has a good eye for trouble," Miguel offered, then glanced back to where Saeng was watching, and gave him a wink. "Lucky for us, he also has good aim . . ."

Despite his best intentions, Saeng's anger over the ambush surfaced in a quick snarl, but Miguel missed it, having followed the others up the stairs.

Moments later, the door clanged shut, and he heard the dull *clunk* of a bar slamming into place.

"Lekan," he murmured. At least now he knew the name of the man who'd shot him.

He'd never before experienced anything like that sharp, percussive impact, nor the cold lassitude that followed.

He hoped never to experience it again.

With a last glance at the stairs, he unfolded himself and rose in one smooth motion.

Smooth, that is, until he reached his feet, where he stumbled and grasped the nearest crosshatch of bars, which happened to belong to the same wall he shared with the newcomers.

A soft snore, followed by a groan, had him fighting off the dizziness to note the giant had slipped into sleep, while the youth he'd called Tiago was coming more fully to life.

While the lad's eyes remained closed, one hand rose to probe at the back of his skull.

"Contusion, dizziness, but no nausea," a smooth, educated baritone emerged, belying the young man's bedraggled appearance. A heartbeat later, his lids eased open to reveal eyes of a deep brown. "Still," he continued, "there is the possibility of mild concussion."

"You're a doctor, then?" Saeng asked.

On hearing him, the young man started to rise, then rolled immediately back into a slump.

Saeng leaned his head against the chill metal. "Be easy."

"*Easy.*" The word came out as a cross between a cough and a bitter laugh. "You don't ask much." The brown eyes narrowed, then focused on Saeng, then Saeng's coat, with its rank insignia. "Colonel—?"

"Call me Saeng," Saeng replied wryly. "I doubt rank has much meaning here."

"Saeng," the youth echoed. "Well, Saeng, my giant friend here is called Rolf, and I am Tiago," he pointed to himself, then scooted carefully up so his back was against the bulkhead. "And I'm an intern at Yousafzai," he continued, turning his head from side to side, studying his surroundings. "I doubt that has much meaning here, either."

Then his gaze landed on the third occupant of his cell. "*George,*" he murmured, and then, "How did you get here?" Then he frowned. "And where is here?"

"At a guess?" Saeng gestured at their fellow prisoners. "I'd say we're aboard a slaver's ship."

"Slavers? Here? In Nike?" Tiago shook his head, then winced. "I didn't think slavers ever came this far west." Then his eyes darkened, and he looked away.

"And yet, here we are," Saeng pointed out easily. He lowered himself once again to the deck, where he leaned on the bars to address Tiago. "I don't suppose you happen to know a fellow by the name of Quinn, do you?"

CHAPTER 15

"—ISN'T SHE WAKING UP YET?"

Mia, deep inside a silver fog, thought that Gideon sounded upset.

"Give her time," Rory's voice murmured.

Rory? When had he come home?

And why was her shoulder so cold?

As if someone heard the question, something warm and damp pressed over the chill, but with the warmth came a hot, pulsing pain, echoed by a dull ache around her middle.

"You're hurting her!"

"It's the great whacking bruise from that dart that's hurting her." Rory's voice remained soft, but Mia was impressed by the allusteel beneath.

"She should be awake," Gideon insisted. "It's been at least two hours."

"And it can take that long to recover from a sedative," Rory said, still keeping his voice low. "Add to that, I've little doubt she took a dose meant for an adult."

"Someone should go for a doctor," Jinna's voice slid in. "Or Tiago. Or Tomaz."

But Tomaz is at the Circus, Mia thought.

"Tomaz is at the Circus," Gideon said, outside her head. "And no one's leaving here tonight."

"The street's still empty," Dani said, though she sounded farther away than the others.

"No one's leaving," Gideon echoed his earlier statement.

"Do you think they'll be back?" Jinna asked. "There was no one about when the rickshaw dropped us home."

"Maybe we should call the filth," Rory offered.

"We're not on the teleph yet," Jinna explained. "And also, a lot of the police don't like Gideon."

"Is that so?" Dani asked.

"The coppers don't like the idea of a civilian doing the job they're supposed to be doing," Gideon said. "And she should be waking up by now."

"M'wake," Mia mumbled, ordering her eyes to open, and what she saw when the lids raised enough to let anything in was Gideon's face, hovering over her own.

"How are you, then?" Rory asked, and her eyes shifted right to see he was on his knees next to her.

Gideon, meanwhile, was leaning over the back of the couch and, from the scales at her cheek, she guessed Elvis shared the pillow someone had placed under her head.

Her hand twitched atop the blanket drawn up over her chest—drawn up to her chest because her tunic was half-off.

Then the pillow moved, and the wedge of Elvis's head popped in front of Gideon's.

"What in smogging comb happened?" she asked.

Or that's what she meant to ask, but her mouth wasn't working yet, so what came out was more like, "*Whsmgpnd?*"

Elvis and Gideon's heads tilted at the same angle.

"Here," Rory said, holding up her head and pressing something cool and smooth to her lips. "Have some water."

She had some water and was sorry when Rory drew the glass away.

She gave her tongue a testing click, which Elvis returned, then tried again. "What happened?" she asked, enunciating carefully.

"This happened," Gideon said, straightening and holding up a tube-like object, all bright and silver, with fletching on one end and a needle on the other.

"What's that?" She started to sit up, but Rory's hand on her arm, the ache in her shoulder, and the swooshing in her head told her to stay put. "It looks like them plungers that keeper medic used on me and my mates after you rousted Ellison."

"Hypodermic needle," Rory tossed in. "For your vaccinations."

"They hurt," Mia said, remembering little Antonio's howls with a grimace. "But nothing like this."

"Probably has something to do with this needle being shot from a gun," Gideon said, letting his hand fall to his side before adding, "I've never seen anything like it."

"I have," Dani offered, crossing to the couch. She rested her hands on the sofa's back, next to Gideon, and offered Mia a smile.

"Where?"

"Keepers in the protected zones use darts like that to sedate wounded animals," Dani answered Gideon's question. "But they don't use shooters. They use blowguns."

"Oy, I've made those," Mia said. "But I only shot bits of paper."

"Those bits of paper were your maths studies," Jinna commented from the head of the couch, sweeping a hand over Mia's hair as she added, "I'll make tea."

"And I'll do a sweep of the block." As he spoke, Gideon pushed up from where he leaned.

"I'll go with you." Dani pushed up as well.

"Someone has to stay here," he told her.

"I'm here," Rory pointed out.

"Someone with a shooter," Gideon told him.

Dani met Gideon mid-room. "If it's not safe for anyone else to leave, why would it be safe for you?"

"Because I won't be alone." He clicked his tongue, and Elvis, after a last nuzzle of Mia's cheek, jumped from the pillow, flapped over to Gideon, and assumed his usual position.

"Stay here," he said to Dani. "I'll be back soon."

That was all he said out loud, but Mia sensed something more was being spoken through the look he shared with Dani, because her shoulders settled, and she stepped back, hands held up in a kind of surrender.

Then his gaze landed on Mia with an intensity that had her stomach hurting before he turned and walked out the door.

She more than half expected him to slam it, but it closed gently, with a quiet little *snick.*

Mia, with Rory and Dani, remained silent a moment, and then another, and another, before the telltale *thud* of footsteps said he was moving.

As soon as those steps receded, Mia turned to Dani. "Is he mad at me, then?"

"Oh." Immediately, everything about Dani softened and saddened. "No. He's not mad, he's—"

Scared boneless, Gideon thought as he emerged onto the deserted street where, despite his professed intention of sweeping the block for unfriendlies, he stopped just past the edge of the sidewalk and turned to study the lines of the building.

The rain had ceased, and there was no longer a small, rust-clad arm dangling over the edge of the dormer ledge, but the image had seared itself into his brain so, even as he stared up at the deeper shadows of the eaves, he could again see the limp hand and the flutter of hair telling him how close to the edge Mia had fallen.

Following hard on that thought was how, if Dani hadn't been here—Dani with her slender, jumper's build that could fit through the child-sized window—he wouldn't have been able to get to Mia.

And as he stared up at the roof of 9 Doyle, as his mind shook with the echo of Mia's fall, his vision wavered, and the view shifted in place as well as time, so he was looking up not at the copper roof of his new home, but at the graffiti-covered walls of a teleph tower, back in occupied Turing.

Rather than a damp night filled with clouds, the air was dry, and the sky purpling in the wake of the suns' setting.

And as his mind's eye watched, he once again saw the airship sailing placidly overhead while the canisters of plasma fell from the gondola's open bay doors.

Standing on cobbles shining with damp, Gideon again felt the concussion of one of those canisters rocking the tower ladder he'd been descending.

Again his breath caught, as it had when he fell from the ladder and again his eyes filled with the bloom of expanding plasma.

It should not have been beautiful, he thought, seeing it all again, but it was.

All that hungry plasma, rivaling the sunsset while it devoured the allusteel tower—and everyone in it.

Then Elvis crooned and flexed his wings, and Gideon blinked, and the past returned to the past, and he was no longer staring up at the tower, or even at the empty roof, but down at the pavement.

Looking at the ground, his eyes narrowed, and he recalled this was where he'd dropped Bruiser Two.

After staring a moment, he crouched to retrieve the bruised petals from where they'd fallen off of B-2's boots.

On rising, he clicked and pointed, and Elvis took wing towards Butler, scanning for trouble.

Gideon followed, pausing only once to study the ground in front of Sally's, where the first van had been parked.

Once he and Elvis confirmed Butler was empty of life, he strode down to Cornwell, walking along the park's edge.

Again he stopped, again crouched, this time where the man who'd shot Mia had been standing.

Finally, he stepped into the road, stopping when he reached the spot where he'd knocked Dani's stalker, the tree stump, to the ground.

The rain had ceased, but everything was still damp, so the dark stain of petals from the tree stump's hat had stuck to the pavers.

Crouching, he collected the blossoms, which still carried their spicy scent.

These he added to the petals already collected from B-2's landing spot, the parking space in front of Sally's, and the position Mia's attacker had held.

Then he glanced at the park, the slice of wilderness he'd visited almost daily since moving to Doyle Street.

And because he had, knew it held not a single plum tree.

Inside Jinna's flat, Mia was sitting up, sipping tea, with Jinna sitting next to her.

Dani, who'd shed her coat at some point, stood at the window, one hand on her shooter, watching the street, while Rory poured himself a cup at the heavy dining table that had been payment from another of Gideon's clients.

Mia's shoulder still ached fiercely, as did her stomach, or rather, the muscles around her stomach. When she asked about that, Jinna made a sound of distress and it was Rory who answered, "You tossed your biscuits before you fully woke."

"Oh." Mia looked at her tea. "Ewww."

"I've seen worse," he told her.

"I haven't," Jinna said.

At which point, the door opened and Gideon entered.

His gaze swept the room, lingered on Mia before he crossed to Dani, pausing next to where her abandoned coat was draped over one of the dining chairs. "What do you, a couple of toughs from Lower Cadbury, a handful of flunkies, and a tree stump with a mustache have in common?"

Her brow arched. "I have no idea. Is this a test?"

"Ha, and no. So, let's try this." Now Gideon held up one hand, opening it enough for Mia to see what appeared to be a clump of wet potpourri, like Kinu and Maria sold in their shop, then pointed to Dani's coat, where a few bruised petals stuck to the fabric. "Where have you been today that has plum trees?"

Gideon watched Dani's expression shift from dry irritation to blank confusion to narrow-eyed suspicion.

"Tenjin," she said. "The entire facility is surrounded by a plum orchard." She contemplated the crushed petals in his palm. "These came from the attackers?"

"Some were on the collar of Bruiser Two," he said.

"And which one was Bruiser Two?" Dani asked.

"The one who showed up with the man I saw in the Mess, who I think goes by the name Lekan—something the tree stump said," he explained to the others. "Anyway, there were also a few flowers stuck to Tree Stump's hat, and even more on the ground where the second van parked."

"So you're saying every one of the wasps who attacked us has been to Tenjin today?" Mia asked.

"There's more than one orchard in Nike," Jinna pointed out, before he could respond.

Gideon spared both his partners a glance, noting Mia's ashen pallor and Jinna's shadowed eyes.

"There are," he said, gentling his tone. "But not so many, and what are the odds that Dani, and Tree Stump, and the man we'll call Lekan, plus a gang of bruisers, all visited different orchards before deciding to lay siege to our building?"

"Not great," Jinna admitted, easing back to sip her tea.

"So let's assume the simplest solution is the right one, and both Lekan and Tree Stump—"

"Are you going to keep calling him that?" Dani asked.

"You got a better name?"

"I once knew a fellow who matched that description," Rory said, rubbing at the back of his neck. Jinna made a soft sound, and he dropped the hand, offering her a weak smile. "Ancient history. Any road, why would your Tree Stump and this Lekan chap and Dani here all be in Tenjin's orchard?"

"I was there looking for Saeng," Dani said.

Gideon waited, watched the quarterstar drop.

"And so were they," she said, turning back to face him. "That's what you're saying. You're saying they were at Tenjin because of Saeng."

"Yes."

She blinked, and her eyes emptied. "You think they killed him."

"No." He shook his head, squeezing the blossoms in his hand to a pulp. "No, I don't. I think they took him."

"Why?" Rory asked, stepping forward. "I'm sorry," he said to Dani, "but these are people who'd shoot a child—"

"I'm not—"

"Legally you are," Jinna patted Mia's leg to calm her.

Mia's expression remained perturbed, but she settled back into the cushions.

"Okay," Gideon pulled everyone's attention back in his direction. "While it's true that the people you and I tangled with tonight were out for blood, the one who shot Mia wasn't trying to kill her. He wanted to clear the way for his partners to escape."

"It worked," Dani said.

"And whatever he meant, Mia still might have died," Jinna pointed out.

"I know." All the way to his bones, he knew. "But listen, what did he shoot her with?" He drew the dart from his pocket, held it up. "A tranq. Tranqs aren't for killing, they're for calming a body down. And beyond that," he continued, "there's the fact I first spied this Lekan character in Lower Cadbury, where several people have gone missing. And while I still maintain there are any number of reasons that a person might disappear, there are far fewer reasons for them to be taken; and the most common, the most profitable reason, comes down to—"

"You must be joking," Rory cut in, setting his cup on the table with enough force to rattle the pot.

"Here?" Jinna almost rose from the couch, but the sheer effort had her falling back, one hand over the baby.

"Why?" Dani asked, hope and horror at war in her voice.

"What?" Mia topped off the round of astonished questions. "What's the reason?"

Gideon took a deep breath. "Not joking," he said to Rory.

"Yes, here," he added to Jinna. "And, I don't know," he told Dani. "In Saeng's case, especially, I don't know, *and* . . . " he turned, reluctantly, to Mia, " . . . the reason is they're slavers. I think they're slavers. I think they're taking people from Lower Cadbury to sell on the slave docks of Adia."

CHAPTER 16

It was near to oh-one-hundred hours, and Dani was pushing a soggy towel over Gideon's office floor.

The wet floor—along with the dripping sashes Dani had used as her jump line—had been waiting to greet her and Gideon on their return from Jinna's flat, but Dani found herself grateful for the mindless labor.

Especially as Gideon, who at present was wringing the sashes out in the bathroom, determined they couldn't take any action before the suns rose.

At that time, he and Dani would pay a visit to the Tenjin orchards, to search for any clues as to what had become of Saeng.

"Chances are, the rain washed away any trace," he'd admitted, standing in the middle of Jinna's living room and glowering into his tea while Elvis dozed on his shoulder. "But we have to try."

And while he and Dani searched the orchard, Mia, Jinna, and Rory would visit Detective Sergeant Hama at the ninth precinct.

"You said the coppers didn't like Gideon," Dani pointed out from the rocking chair to which she'd retired.

"D.S. Hama's different,' Mia explained. "He's a decent sort."

"And his son's a friend," Jinna added.

"Good lad," was Rory's summation.

"But the D.S. will be grumpy about us giving him more paperwork," Mia concluded with a face-splitting yawn.

At which point, Jinna insisted they call it a night.

Gideon's expression said he wanted to argue, but Dani watched him as he looked—*really* looked—at his partners.

"Right. You two should get some rest," he'd agreed, turning away from both so quickly, Dani knew he missed the hurt in Mia's expression. "I'll take first watch," he told Rory.

"*We'll* take first watch," Dani corrected, rising and grabbing her coat.

Gideon's scowl might have carried more weight if he hadn't had a snoring draco wrapped around his neck.

"Fine." He met Rory's amused gaze. "I'll wake you at oh-four-hundred."

Rory responded with a sigh and the Corps' salute of a tap to the heart.

Thinking of Rory, and being on watch, Dani left her mopping to check the Doyle Street window.

She lifted the damp curtain to see the streetlights dimming, their internal clocks counting down to the blackout shift required by Apian Law.

She hoped the owls, bats, and other nocturnal creatures appreciated the darkness, especially as the dimming lamps made it swarming hard to see to the end of the block.

Movement below had her eyes shooting from Butler Street to the alley between MacGuffin's and the empty store on its left.

"Gideon!" Her call was little more than a breath, but the

results were immediate. Before she'd parted the curtain again, she heard his boots thudding from the back of the flat.

"Two figures, approaching from Butler," she said as he neared, his shirt damp, and the sleeves rolled up to the elbow. He still had his baton, loaded in a sheathe buckled over his forearm, but was lacking a draco. "Where's Elvis?"

"Napping in the sink," Gideon replied, easing in close enough for her to see the shadows under his eyes.

"Tomaz," he said, and she watched the tension leach from his muscles as he tracked the pair below. "Coming home from the Circus. Wow," he added, prompting Dani to follow his gaze to the right, where Tomaz and the man she presumed was his date were now locked in a torrid embrace against the picture window of The Bitter Herb.

"Oh," she said, and cleared her throat. "Well."

Gideon gave the rest of the street a cursory study, let the curtain drop. "I think we can afford to give them a little privacy."

"Of course." Though Dani wasn't sure the pair downstairs would notice if the entire audience of the Circus had followed them home.

She looked up and saw Gideon watching her. "So, you've made friends with the neighbors," she noted.

"There aren't that many to know," he told her. "Unless you count the pangolins in the park."

"Will you miss them?" Dani heard herself ask.

"What?"

"Nothing." She shook her head, turned, and stooped to pick up the damp towel. "I should put this in the—somewhere." One hand under the dripping cloth, she started for the hall, but he was there, blocking her path.

"It didn't sound like nothing," he said. "What did you mean?"

Her breath escaped in a huff. "Nothing. Really. It was just words, falling out of my mouth. A thoughtless comment."

"It didn't sound thoughtless, either." He removed the towel from her hand and tossed it on the desk behind her, where it landed with a *splat*.

"You'll stain the wood," she protested.

"Have you *looked* at this thing?" he asked. "A water mark or two could only be an improvement."

She turned to study the desk, battered with time and use, and covered with splotches of ink and scratches, as well as the remains of their tea.

Further study showed one of the side-drawer pulls had broken in half, and the other was absent, leaving only the sharp tip of the screw that would have held the knob in place. "How do you not stab yourself?" And, before he could answer, asked, "Where did you get the desk, anyway?"

Gideon shifted, cleared his throat. "I facilitated an issue for a local author. She had this old desk."

"And did she ask you up for a cup of tea?"

"Maybe?" He pushed the biscuit package away from the wet towel.

"If you're worried I'll be angry that you've enjoyed a few cups of tea over the years, don't be."

"Why would I expect you to be angry? You've moved on. And traded up."

"What?"

"Nothing. Just words, falling out of my mouth. A thought-less comment."

Her breath caught in her chest as he threw her own excuse back at her.

He regarded her a moment, then walked back to the window to give the street another scan.

After a beat, she followed his example, crossing to the rear window, but when her boot slipped, she paused to retrieve the battered envelope she'd presented to Gideon hours ago, before the attack.

The copy of Nour Tabak's letter.

Clutching the envelope, she peered through the curtains and over to see a white owl sweeping overhead, silent as a ghost.

"Mine's clear," Gideon reported.

"This side is quiet," she replied.

So quiet, she wondered if they were the only ones left awake in all of Nike.

Then she recalled Tomaz, lost in the arms of his lover, and she wasn't prepared for the gut punch of Saeng's absence, or the following twist of Gideon's presence.

At last she turned, saw he was leaning against the opposite wall, his arms crossed over his chest.

Waiting.

"I did not trade up," she said. "I didn't even like Saeng, at first."

"And yet, here you are, married to him."

"Yes."

"Why?"

"Because he was there."

"Really? That's your base requirement?"

"Yes. It is. Because being there means he trusts *me* to be there, too. It means he loves me enough to risk losing me, and it means I wasn't alone when—" She paused, and her eyes dropped to the letter in her hand, the soft silver glow of her wedding band. "I wasn't alone," she concluded.

"Okay."

At that simple acceptance, she looked up, and he glanced away.

"What *did* you mean?" he asked again, studying his front door. "About missing them?"

"Is this how you facilitate issues?" she asked back. "By repeating the same question, over and over?"

His eyes slid back. "If the hive's productive . . ."

"Fine." She crossed back to the desk, slammed the letter on top, then faced him. "I meant, I wonder if you'll miss Mia, and Jinna, and lucky Tomaz, and whoever else you've come to care for, when you decide it's time to cut your line and run."

That had him straightening. "Who said I'm going to cut and run?"

"You did," she told him. "Every gesture, every glance, every word you've spoken since Mia woke up says you've already started sawing at the line." Then, as he drew a breath added, "Do you even care that you'll be breaking that child's heart when you push her away? Just like you pushed me away?"

His breath hitched and his jaw set. "I didn't—"

"Not that I shouldn't have expected it," she continued over him. "You made it obvious, early and often, that you're terrified of commitment."

"I'm not terrified of commitment."

"No?" she squared off with him. "What about your motto? How did it go? 'Never get comfortable, don't even make dinner plans, because if you do, life will just serve you up a dish of pain,'"

"I am *not* terrified of commitment," he reiterated, stepping closer. "I *am* terrified of how the people I commit to keep dying. So I have learned it's better for everyone if I don't. Commit."

For a moment, she stared. "Have you ever heard the term *post hoc ergo propter hoc*?"

He raised his hands, then let them fall. "Do I *look* like someone who's heard the term *post hoc* blah blah *hoc*? What is it, anyway? Another euphemism for tea? Because that first bit—"

"No," she said, stepping forward. "No. It's nothing to do with . . . tea."

He edged closer. "Is it like when an Ohmdahl puts vat chicken and vat ham together?"

"What? No!" She pressed her fingers to her eyes. "It means," she said, dropping her hands, "that correlation does not equal causation."

"And *blah, blah, blah.*" His arms shot out again.

"How about this? Believing that you loving someone causes them to die is a logical fallacy. It's like saying, every time I make a jump, someone dies."

"Except, most every time you jump, someone *does* die. Because you shoot them."

Dani felt a tickle of a laugh that may have been a precursor to hysteria. "Maybe that was a bad example?"

"You think?"

Which was when she realized, as they argued, they'd closed the distance between them. Gideon was so near she could feel the heat shimmering from his skin.

"I loved you," she said, as the tickle faded to a tremor of a different sort. "To the point of pain, I loved you."

"And I loved you," he replied. "Enough to push you away."

"Gideon—"

"Because," he cut in, "it's not a logical fallacy if it *keeps happening.* And it does. My family, Martine, half the 12ᵗʰ died at Nasa . . . Walsie, Nbo, Carver—Rand took them all, and he said he'd take you, too. He knew where the *Phalanx* was, and swore that if I didn't confess to treason, you wouldn't come back from the next jump."

Dani felt every part of her go cold. "Why didn't you tell me?"

"I couldn't risk it. I couldn't risk he'd find out. I couldn't risk losing one more person I loved."

"Except you did," she said.

"I did," he agreed, his voice rough. "But you're still *here*."

"I'm not talking about me."

"If you're worried about Mia—"

"I'm not talking about Mia, either."

"Then . . . who?"

She didn't answer right off, instead turned away from him, returning to the abused desk. "I never told you why I transferred to Special Operations," she said, once she had a little space.

"That's not—" he began, but when she glanced over her shoulder, he'd shoved his hands in his pockets and was glaring at the floor. "I figured Mia had that one pegged. You transferred to prove my innocence. To get me out."

"She was partly right." Dani's eyes fell back to the scarred wood. "After you went to prison, I couldn't go on not knowing what really happened at Nasa. But that wasn't the only reason." She turned to face Gideon, but kept her eyes on the curtains behind him. "I left the *Phalanx*—and the Air Corps—three weeks after you were sent down to the Barrens . . . after I discovered I was pregnant."

His head whipped up, but she continued to stare at the curtains as she continued. "I moved to Special Operations, where I'd be able to have the baby, and stay in the service. And while I was there, I looked into your case." And now she looked at him. "And Saeng looked into it with me," she said. "Without my asking. At first, he helped because he believed you were innocent. Later, he helped because he'd come to love me."

Gideon said nothing, just stood, still as a statue, his face— unreadable.

She looked away. "So we worked together throughout the pregnancy, on your case, and whatever else Satsuke assigned. And outside the job, Saeng was still there, making sure I ate right, slept enough, got to the prenatal appointments and drank all the right teas.

"And he was there on the day, late in my seventh month, when I lost her. Our daughter," she said. "You and I . . . we would have had a girl."

"Dani—" His hand rose, then dropped again.

"But here's the thing," she continued. "You never knew about her. You never even knew of the possibility of her, because you never opened the letter I sent to tell you I was pregnant. You never knew, never had the chance to love her," she said again, her voice thick with unshed tears, "but you lost her, anyway."

Gideon didn't know how long he stood frozen after Dani's last pronouncement.

It was only when he felt the faint prick of Elvis's talons on his shoulder—and when had *he* arrived?—that he became aware of the rush of air flowing in and out of his lungs, heard the *thud* of his heart as that stubborn organ continued to beat.

That was when his eyes finally slid back into focus and he found himself, once again, alone.

With a monumental effort, Gideon forced himself to turn, to raise the curtain, to look out the window, where he found the street empty of Tomaz—and anyone else.

A part of him noted this was a good thing.

He let the curtain drop, and, with the care of one recovering from a long, debilitating illness, went in search of Dani.

He found her in his bedroom, curled on top of his bed, asleep.

Not peacefully, he thought, noting the streaks of tears on her cheeks, the shooter she'd left close to hand.

Continuing to force muscles that seemed to have atrophied into motion, he spread the blue throw over her, then stepped out, closing the door behind him.

On his shoulder, Elvis crooned.

For once, the sound did nothing to soothe.

He continued to move from window to window until Elvis gave up and opted to curl up on the desk.

When the university bells chimed four, he took himself to Jinna's flat, where Rory opened the door at the first tap. His gold-brown hair stood up every which way, and there were lines on the side of his face from whatever he'd used as a pillow, but his eyes were alert, the set of his mouth grim.

Gideon left him to the watch and returned to his office, where he dragged his chair over to the desk.

As soon as he sat, Elvis slunk from the cold wood surface to drape himself over Gideon's lap, like a scaly blanket.

While the draco's breathing slowed, and his tail commenced the twitching that said he was dreaming, Gideon sat still, studied the blank wall before him, and again lost track of the passage of time.

He didn't sleep.

Couldn't.

But there was, in those quiet, lonely hours, a sort of null space, one in which he could sit and observe the facets of hurt—both his and Dani's—in the way a crystallographer might study the facets of a crystal.

And when the mournful call of an owl brought him back from that long contemplation, and he felt Elvis shift on his thigh, and Rory's footsteps from upstairs creaked towards Doyle again, Gideon understood what had to be done.

So he pulled open the side drawer, the one with half a knob on it, and drew out a sheet of paper from the stack within, along with the stub of a pencil.

He set the paper on an open space on the desk and, careful of Elvis, still stretched over his leg, scrawled the first words that came to mind.

When the pencil ceased moving, he held it over the page for another few seconds, as if there were more to be said, but in the end he shook his head and dropped it on top of the paper.

With care, he lifted the sleeping draco from his lap and, rising from the chair, placed him on top of the desk, next to the envelope holding Tabak's letter, and even now, even after the prior day's events, seeing that envelope brought on the same slick horror which always accompanied thoughts of Ducati.

Which made it only the more surprising to Gideon that he picked up the stained, wrinkled envelope.

For a time he stood, staring at the familiar brown paper, then the creak of footsteps above told him Rory was walking to the back window.

That meant Doyle was, for the moment, free from observation.

With one last stroke for Elvis and one last glance at the corridor leading to his bedroom, Gideon crossed to the door, picking up his coat from the guest chair where he'd dropped it so many hours ago.

If Rory held to pattern, he'd be looking out on the back side of the flat for another three minutes, allowing Gideon to speed down the stairs and into the early morning dark, where only a smattering of stars were visible through the remaining ink-blot clouds.

In that darkness, he jogged from Doyle to Butler, heading east for two full blocks before pausing to put on the coat.

And only then, as he slid his arms into the sleeves, did he realize he was still holding the smogging envelope.

"One ghost at a time," he muttered, shoving the letter into one of the coat's inner pockets, before he continued on his way.

Alone.

CHAPTER 17

Elvis winged through pre-dawn Nike, hard on Mother's trail.

And while his wings dipped rhythmically, and his focus remained fixed on the *bigmetalbox* Mother had boarded, his entire frame shivered with draconian ire.

Mother had left the nest without him.

Fortunately, Mother had forgotten the window in the water room, always left ajar for Elvis's particular use.

But still, Mother had left the nest, and without Elvis.

And not because he wanted Elvis to watch the little sister, or the bright mother, or even the *newswiftsharpdark* one who had caused Mother's scent to change.

He'd just . . . left.

That was not like Mother.

Not at all.

The sitting up through the *darksleeptime*, well, that *was* like Mother, a little.

He'd done that many times in their old nest, in the *hotdrycold* place of Elvis's hatching.

Those times, Mother would wake of a sudden, starting Elvis

from his own sleep, and, waking, sit and stare, or stand and pace the closed-in part of the nest.

Those wakings had most often been accompanied by Mother's hunting-scent.

Mother's hunting-scent was the first Elvis tasted, the day of Elvis's hatching, when Mother killed the viper that had, in its turn, killed Elvis's hatching mother.

But the scent Elvis tasted through this last long dark was unlike any of Mother's previous scents and tasted, to Elvis, like *coldstillemptyloss*.

It was that scent, that emptiness, that tugged at the draco's hindbrain as he flew, drawing him onwards into the first graying hints of sunsrise, just as it had drawn him to curl up on Mother's leg the *darksleeptime* before.

As he flew, he spied the skittering of a dinner on the ground below, followed by a swifter, more feral motion that told him one of the many furred hunters who lived in this *wetstonemetal* place had claimed that particular dinner as its own.

Just as well, because the *bigmetalbox* had turned, and was now rattling in the direction of the *movingwater*. As Elvis followed, the echo of Mother's *coldstillemptyloss* took on a new dimension, that of the *brighthotcopper* that told him Mother, too, was hunting.

Mother hunted quite a lot, but, unlike Elvis, he almost never hunted for dinner.

Mostly, Mother hunted other wingless dracos.

Then again, Elvis noticed the wingless dracos as a whole were always hunting for something.

Some hunted *stillcoldfood,* and some the shiny objects their species seemed to treasure.

Many hunted for mates, though not all the wingless ones mated for nesting purposes; and so far, Mother had brought none of his mates home to nest.

Elvis had also noticed how some of the wingless ones hunted for blood, which was not the same as hunting for dinner.

Mother had come to this *wetstonemetal* place hunting for blood . . . and found it. But that was many settings of the suns past, and Elvis hadn't sensed the blood hunt in Mother since.

More often, he hunted for something *clearsharplight*.

Elvis didn't think the *clearsharplight* as interesting as dinner, or even the shiny objects the other wingless ones hunted, but finding it left Mother (and therefore Elvis) with a sensation of openness that was also, and oddly, filling.

Swooping on an updraft, he saw that the *bigmetalbox* had stopped.

Coming to a perch on a greening metal roof, Elvis watched Mother step from the *bigmetalbox*.

He considered descending to take his accustomed place on Mother's shoulder.

But what if he did and Mother sent him away?

He had never disobeyed Mother . . . well, there was that one time, with the many-legged stinger inside the old nest, but afterwards, Mother had been very pleased by Elvis's quick work.

But there were no many-legged stingers here, so he remained aloft, where he could keep an eye on Mother without Mother knowing of his presence.

It was an action he'd never have considered back in their old nest, but he noted that the little sister did it *all the time*, and the behavior seemed to serve her, and Mother, quite well.

So for this once, he would be like the little sister, and keep a distant eye on Mother.

It said something of Gideon's state of mind that he didn't notice his winged shadow.

Back in his days of dodging, and later, as commander of the 12th Company, he'd never have overlooked a tail.

Except this wasn't back in the day, and he wasn't a dodger, or a soldier, or even a convict.

All he was now was the man who'd left Dani alone to face an unimaginable loss.

The loss which now sat in his heart, a tiny, cold fist of what could never be.

Which left him with only one course of action.

And, while that one action couldn't change the past—couldn't fill the hollow space—it could at least promise Dani a different future.

He could do his damn job, and find that uptight, walking rulebook she'd married.

So, he told himself, *stop moping, and do your damn job*.

I'm not moping, his self said back.

With a sneer for the other half of his inner dialogue, Gideon continued to walk into the first hints of sunsrise, making his quiet way to the edges of Nike's fourth district and from there to Riverside Drive which, true to its name, followed the curve of the Avon River.

As the sky pearled with the approaching dawn, he could just make out the airfield on the other side of the river, with the low humps of buildings and the faint outlines of airships hovering at high anchor, or snug to the ground, a hanging garden of transports of all sizes and vintages, from the sleekest passenger vessels to the oldest, most patched freighters.

He'd come to Nike on one of those patched freighters, searching for revenge.

What he'd found was so much more.

Mia . . . Jinna . . . Tiago and Ishan Hama . . .

The machinations of Celia Rand, and a city at war with itself—not to mention the Ohmdahls—

—You just mentioned them—

—Shut up—

—all of which had poked and prodded and driven him to seek more than a simple ending.

And because they had, he'd stayed, and taken on the role of private facilitator.

Turning from the air docks, and the memories of that first day in Avon's capital, he had to wonder, was it only a role?

Because if he'd truly accepted it—this job, this place, these people—wouldn't he be able to think of 9 Doyle Street as home instead of the flat, or the office, or Jinna's place?

Wouldn't he have, as Mia was always poking at him to do, hung up the damn business sign?

It's a good sign, he told himself.

It's a great sign, his self agreed, *but—*

Whatever he meant to tell himself was cut off as, from behind, he heard the low rumble of a vehicle coming up the road.

Since there was only one possible destination for anyone driving along this road—the Tenjin Compound was the literal end of Riverside Drive—Gideon figured it for an early delivery and ducked into the stand of plum trees at his left.

As soon as he was under the relative cover of the orchard which, even now, he noted, was thick with blossoms, he turned to watch the vehicle pass, and saw the man riding shotgun, who turned out to be the man from A Fine Mess.

Who was also the man who'd shot Mia.

Gideon was running before he could think.

Then he thought.

Wait, he said to himself as he ducked under a plum tree's low-hanging branch, *what are you doing?*

I have a plan, his self replied.

*If your plan involves getting into it with those wasps, think
again. You're outnumbered and outgunned.*

I know. Thing is, that's *the plan.*

Up ahead, the van angled left.

Gideon dodged between the trees.

His muscles hummed in pleasure at finally taking action.

Around him, early rising squirrels scattered, and a flock of
starlings took wing, their musical chirps scolding as they did.

Another flurry of chirps sounded from on high, and the
murmuration of starlings lost cohesion, but Gideon ignored the
avian discord because he could see the curving road ahead, a
pale line in the graying sky, and threw himself forward,
exploding out of the trees just as the van turned onto the drive.

He scrambled to a halt and faced the oncoming vehicle,
counting himself lucky the driver was able to stop before the
van plowed into him.

For a moment, the only sounds were the deepening hum of
the engines damping down, the creak of the van settling, and the
angry flutter of wings.

Then the passenger door creaked open, and Mia's assailant
emerged just as Tyche's rays made their first foray above the
eastern horizon, sparking against the man's carnelian earrings
and the shooter in his hand.

"So, you're Lekan?" Gideon asked.

The other man nodded. "And you're Gideon Quinn."

"Never would have marked you as a messenger service,"
Gideon noted, nodding at the van.

"And no one in their right mind would mistake you for a
boffin." Lekan gestured towards the shadow of Tenjin's central
tower, spearing over the orchards.

Both men held their positions for the space of a few heartbeats, then Gideon popped Lulu into his hand and sent her
flying.

Lekan, of course also moved, so the baton bounced off the van's hood, while Lekan's shooter spat its dart exactly where he'd aimed.

Gideon felt the sickening impact of the dart as it struck just below his collarbone.

He heard Elvis shriek from above and had time to think, *Not now! Not here!* He wondered how long it would take for the drugs to—and then his legs were buckling, and his knees slamming into the pebbled path, and he thought, *Ah, that long.*

After that, there was just enough time to tell himself: *this is a terrible plan.* And for himself to reply, *I know*—before the dart finished its work, and a silver-tinged darkness came, and Gideon fell so deep, not even his thoughts could follow.

Lekan holstered the dart gun and approached the fallen man.

From behind, he heard Petris jumping out of the van, then heard him curse, and turned to see Quinn's draco, still shrieking, sweep towards Petris, taloned feet extended.

Petris grabbed Quinn's fallen baton and braced, but the creature changed course with admirable agility, taking itself up and out of range.

"And here I was, only expecting you to drop off the van."

At the comment, Lekan turned to see Wex Jihan stepping out of the orchard, now dressed in the worn and faded clothes of a laborer.

He had, sometime over the past few hours, shaved his mustaches.

"I suppose Solis led him to investigate the compound," Wex speculated, studying Quinn. "But why dare such a foolish attack? He had to know the outcome the moment he spied you."

"I did shoot his daughter," Lekan pointed out.

Wex grunted. "Anger makes a poor strategist."

"I suppose you'll want us to dispose of him?"

"If you'd be so kind," Wex said. "I'll send someone to retrieve the van. Spare you another trip."

"Why don't you come along, take it back yourself?" Lekan asked.

"I have another assignment," Wex said, but didn't explain further, which was fine with Lekan, who gestured to Petris.

"Good luck at the market," Wex said as Petris heaved Quinn up and over his shoulder. "Who knows when we'll meet again?"

"Never, if I have my way." Lekan started for the vehicle, where Petris was already slamming the doors closed on their latest catch.

"You wound me," Wex called placidly after him.

"Not yet," Lekan replied, climbing into the cab.

Wex's laugh melded with the hum of the engines' catching, but Lekan had already dismissed the other man's amusement.

Something about Quinn's expression troubled him.

Not the initial anger, or the shock of the dart's striking—those were expected—but in those first sparking beams of dawn, Lekan was certain he'd spied something else.

Something calculating.

He recalled his first impression, back in A Fine Mess, that Quinn would prove more trouble than he was worth.

Then he considered the potential rubiks Quinn would bring in Domino, where the coliseum owners were always on the prowl for fresh blood.

At which point he supposed he'd have the opportunity to learn, to the last cube, exactly how much Gideon Quinn was worth.

Perhaps it was because his thoughts were filled with Quinn, and the weighing of risk versus profit, that Lekan missed the draco flying above, keeping pace with the vehicle.

CHAPTER 18

THE *SMALLMETALBOX* CARRYING MOTHER SWUNG BACK
towards the *movingwater* and Elvis, wings sweeping, caught
another gust muttering from the western *greatwater*, and let it
carry him high above the rooftops, only angling downwards
when the *smallmetalbox* rocked to a halt at the edge of a stretch
of *deadwood* that tasted of algae and rot.

He perched atop the remains of a ruined nest near the *dead-wood*, folded his wings, and peered into the shreds of mist
forming as the rising suns struck the wide expanse of
movingwater.

He sent a warning growl at one of the white-winged flyers
that ducked too close, and as the flyer flapped away, swung his
head back towards the *smallmetalbox*.

At the other end of the *deadwood*'s long path, there was one
of the floating nests Elvis often spied when Mother visited the
movingwater. As he watched, several wingless ones emerged
from the floating nest.

Some of the wingless ones clomped over the *deadwood* to
join those spilling out of the *smallmetalbox*.

After milling about in a disorganized talon, two of the new

wingless ones dragged Mother, still unmoving, out of the box, over the deadwood and into the floating nest, so Elvis couldn't see Mother anymore.

He danced from foot to foot to foot to foot.

Mother was in *so* much more trouble than usual.

A flutter of motion—and a familiar taste of refuse—pulled his attention to a partial nest, collapsing in on itself. Huddled in one corner was a mound of tattered scales.

Elvis's tongue told him he'd tasted the mound before.

But unless the mound had a talon of its own, it could be of no help to Elvis or Mother.

Turning back to the floating nest, he watched the remaining wingless ones converge on the *smallmetalbox* before one got inside.

While the *smallmetalbox* grumbled back to life, the others crossed the *deadwood*, returning to their floating nest.

Elvis hissed and, with one sharp keen, leapt from his perch and, working against the salty breeze, headed back to the nest.

<hr>

Mia woke to the aroma of griddle cakes and the muffled sounds of Rory and Jinna talking.

She didn't hear Gideon or Dani and wondered if they were in Gideon's place.

Or maybe they'd gone off looking for the bad guys, which would, she thought, be smogging cheeky of them.

Or maybe they'd gone full *Risto's Dilemma* and were even now enjoying a cuppa.

Or maybe—

Then her stomach grumbled, and she gave up on wondering what Gideon was up to.

She slipped from her bed—and she was still over the moons

that it was a *real* bed, with *real* sheets—stretched her spine, and wriggled her shoulders under the soft fabric of the pajamas Jinna had helped her shop for.

There was still an ache where the dart had struck, and she felt sure she could drink half the Avon she was that thirsty, but beyond those fiddly issues, she felt no other ill effects from her encounter with the dart.

She gave her curls a quick finger comb and changed into a clean set of clothes before heading straight to the kitchen, where Jinna was sliding a heaping platter of griddle cakes into the oven to keep warm.

"Are we feeding an army, then?" she asked as Jinna, with visible effort, straightened and closed the oven door.

"Between Gideon and Rory, we may as well be." Jinna turned back to the bacon she was cooking. "How are you feeling?"

"Almost perfect." Mia waved her arms to demonstrate, then winced because of the ache in her shoulder.

"I'd say don't try any climbing or heavy lifting for a spell," Jinna said, shifting bacon from the pan to drain.

Mia snagged a slice, flipping it from hand to hand until it cooled. When Jinna didn't tell her to wait until they sat down to eat, she asked, "How about you? I mean, are you all right?" she added as Jinna's eyes flashed her way. "It's just, you look a bit knackered, is all."

"Oh. Well. Busy night." Jinna summoned a smile. "That, and someone's decided sleeping is for other people." She patted her belly, which, under the soft drape of her tunic, moved.

"Oh." Mia crunched bacon and frowned at the shifting mound, then watched Jinna rub her back with her free hand. "Where's Rory?"

"In the living room. He's taking his shift on the watch seriously," she explained, focusing on the cooking bacon.

The idea they had to set a watch at all set the bruise on Mia's shoulder to throbbing. "I'll go make sure he stays awake," she said, nabbing another bit of bacon before swinging out of the kitchen.

"I saw that," Jinna called after.

She found Rory standing at the street-side window with a cup of tea in his hand and a grim expression on his face. At some point during the night, his shirt had come untucked, and his hair stood up in spikes as if he'd run his hands through it a few dozen times.

"How long have you been at that?" Mia asked him.

He blinked, looked back. "Only since oh-four-hundred. And not a sign of any action. Well, except for Kinu and Maria dancing their way from Cornwell back to their shop around half four."

"They love their argentango," Mia said, polishing off the bacon.

"They're good at it." He slurped tea, looked out the window again. "The only other thing I saw was Elvis, stretching his wings, close to sunrise." He looked at her. "How does he get out, anyway?"

"Gideon leaves the bathroom window open a crack, so Elvis can go when he, ah, has to go."

The brown eyes widened, and Rory's lips quirked. "Funny, I never gave much thought to that. I suppose it makes more sense than having a draco box."

"Rory . . ." Jinna appeared, a teapot in one hand, a pitcher of syrup in the other. "Now the suns are up, we're probably safe from an all-out assault. Why don't you go fetch the plates? And Mia," she added, crossing to the table they'd set up near the back window, "can you tell Gideon and Dani breakfast is ready?"

"I like how she makes it sound like she's asking when she's really giving orders," Mia said.

"She has a gift," Rory agreed.

"*She* is standing right here," Jinna pointed out.

"And the suns never rose upon a lovelier sight," the undaunted Rory replied.

Jinna's eyes narrowed, but her lips twitched. "Dishes," she said, then looked at Mia.

"I'm going, I'm going," she said, trotting to the door and down the stairs, but when she reached the door of Gideon's office, it was already swinging open to reveal Dani, looking a little rumpled and a lot furious.

"Jinna's made breakfast," Mia said, peering past Dani to find Gideon. "So the two of you can keep arguing over griddle cakes."

"Too late," Dani said, and held out a sheet of paper.

Mia took the rumpled missive without thinking, and though it took a bit of effort to read Gideon's left-handed scrawl, she got the gist quick enough.

"He *left?*" Her eyes fixed on the note, as if waiting for the words to reform themselves into something innocuous. Something like, "I've gone to Market Street for milk," or, "Noni asked me up to tea."

But no, the back-slanted letters continued to lie dead on the page to say, *I'll find him. I'm sorry.*

"He left," she said again, her stomach feeling heavy and empty at the same time.

"He does that," Dani said, her eyes dark with anger and worry, and something else Mia couldn't name.

"Why did he say he was sorry?" Mia asked, her own voice thick in her throat. "For leaving without telling me—us?"

"A little. I think a little," Dani said. "But that's not the main reason."

Mia looked up. "What is the main reason?"

For a moment, she was sure Dani wouldn't tell her, or would

say it was complicated, or private, or ugly, or any of the other reasons grown-ups used to avoid telling her the truth. But after letting out a long breath, Dani's head dipped in a nod and she met Mia's eyes and told her of the argument she and Gideon had had the night before.

"So really, it's my fault he's gone," Dani concluded, her expression calm but her voice wavering. "I should never have told him about the baby."

"Smog that," Mia told her, while sadness and anger and pity churned horribly inside her chest. "If you hadn't, it'd be just like how he never told you about smogging Rand."

Dani blinked. "I hadn't thought of that."

"You should. Just the way he should have thought—" But then the bell to the flat chimed, interrupting her.

At once, Dani's hand dropped to the shooter at her hip. "Do you often get visitors this early?"

"Not often." Mia swallowed.

Even as she spoke, they heard the chime for Jinna's flat sound upstairs.

"Whoever it is really wants in," Mia said, then brightened. "Maybe Gideon just forgot his key?"

"Maybe." But Dani didn't seem hopeful as she stepped past Mia to meet Rory, who was thudding down from Jinna's place.

"Mia," Rory began.

"Don't even *think* about telling me to stay here," she said, and, before he could, slipped between the two adults and down the stairs

She heard Rory's curse and Dani's sigh, but kept going until she reached the foyer, where the door was, in fact, locked. But there was also a crack in the glass that hadn't been there yesterday.

And on the other side of that cracked glass, she spied two out of three Ohmdahl triplets, and their mother.

Mia unlocked the door just as Dani and Rory clattered to a halt at the base of the stairs. "It's okay, they're friends," she said, pulling it open.

"Of a sort," Rory muttered, glaring at Ulf and Freya.

"I am sorry to be bothering you so early," Sonja Ohmdahl said as she entered, giving Dani and Rory a wary eye. "Only, I was hoping to find Gideon here."

"He's, ah, he's on a job," Mia said, glancing over to where Freya and Ulf stood, their expressions more worried than she'd ever seen. "Wait." She looked back at Sonja. "Where's Rolf?"

Sonja's expression went from concerned to bleak. "That is why we are coming here so early," she told Mia. "My son—my Rolf—he is missing."

Mia met Dani's gaze, then turned back to Sonja. "You'd better come inside."

At the same time, some blocks away, Tiago's father, D.S. Ishan Hama, was sitting in a tea shop favored by the coppers of the ninth precinct.

He poured his second cup of tea, added a dollop of cream, then pulled out his pocket watch, though he hardly needed the finely wrought hands to tell him his son was late.

He tucked the watch—a gift from his late husband—back in his waistcoat pocket and stared at the empty cup on the other side of the table.

The weekly breakfast was more than a meal; it was a family tradition, begun when Tiago was a child, and the table for two had been a table for three.

Now, even so many years after Paolo's death, Ishan and Tiago kept up the tradition, providing both a much-needed foundation and a sense of continuity.

Of course, there were times one of the two might need to cancel. Days Tiago had exams, or Ishan was working on an active case, for instance. But on those occasions, the busy party always left a message with Claude, who'd been working at The Copper Pot since Ishan was a constable.

As if on cue, Claude appeared at Ishan's elbow. "Still no sign of the lad?" Claude set a plate of scones and a bowl of mixed berries on the table and flicked a towel over his shoulder with enough vigor to set his great, gray mustaches to trembling.

"Must be an emergency at the hospital." Ishan forced a smile. "The life of an intern, eh?"

"Intern." Claude shook his head, and the mustaches set up a counterpoint. "Keepers preserve my ancient bones, but I remember you and Paolo bringing him in for a sup and a cup when he was but knee high to a sunsflower." The old waiter let out a gusty sigh which sent his mustaches to blowing outwards. "Where do the seasons go, my friend?"

"They fly, fast as dracos to the Amazons," Ishan capped the adage. But even as he spoke, his eyes and attention were returning to the street outside the window.

He turned back and found Claude dropping a check on the next table over, where Sergeant Tyree was just finishing her breakfast and the morning newspaper before reporting to the precinct.

"Claude," he said, drawing both the waiter's and the sergeant's attention. "Would you do me the favor of packing up the breakfast? If Tiago is working through the morning, at least we can see he gets a decent meal."

"Should I mark you down as taking some personal time?" Tyree asked from her table.

"Not necessary. I have a two-way on me. If anything happens, just radio through."

Tyree nodded and went back to reading her paper.

Ishan knew she'd be devouring the theatrical reviews, which should be covering the latest production of Crystal of Death, a popular melodrama in which her partner played the villain.

He knew this because, as with every time Sayyed was cast in a play, Tyree informed the entire precinct, posting flyers for the production on the community board, and making not terribly veiled references during roll call.

Ishan planned to take in the current production that night, thinking perhaps to ask Tiago to join him.

When Claude returned with the boxed-up meal, Ishan handed him some starbucks and bid farewell to the waiter and the sergeant.

As he stepped out of the shop and into the chill of morning, he struggled to convince himself Tiago was merely swamped at work, and not holding a grudge from his recent visit to the precinct.

Still, it couldn't hurt the cause of father-son relations if he were to follow through with the theatre invitation.

Likely it would help even more if he agreed to help Tiago search for the patients he believed had gone missing.

Bolstered by these plans, Ishan set the boxed meal in the basket of his motorcycle and set off to make things right with his son.

CHAPTER 19

Back in Jinna's flat, Dani positioned herself at the
Doyle street window, where she could keep a weather eye out
for Gideon.

"So, tell me about Rolf," Mia said, crossing her arms over her
chest and dipping her chin in what Dani recognized as a very
Gideon-like pose.

"We left him at A Fine Mess," Freya began, standing at ease
behind the sofa in which her mother perched, while Ulf
propped himself against the wall behind his mother and sister.

"Of all the places in all of Nike to get drunk, why go to the
Mess?" Rory asked, leaning on the back of the rocking chair
positioned next to Dani's window.

Jinna looked up from the tea she was pouring. "You've been
in a pub that wasn't The Frayed Rigging?"

"John used to be partial to it, before we bought the *Errant*,"
Rory explained. "And from the few times I joined him, I learned
that to drink Martin's booze is as close as a person can get to
drinking from a bact tank and live to tell about it."

"It is not quite that bad," Ulf said.

"Close," Freya murmured.

"But also cheap," Ulf added.

"So, you left your brother at the Mess," Mia prompted.

Ulf shuffled, visibly uncomfortable, as he glanced from Mia to his mother. "He wanted to stay and, ah, speak to a young lady who was also at the pub."

"And you don't think he could still be—talking to this young lady?" Rory posited.

"Maybe they're just having tea," Mia said.

Jinna coughed, and Dani bit the inside of her cheek and angled to study the street outside.

"Not without contacting me," Sonja replied to Rory, then turned to Mia. "My children always let me know if they are not coming home."

"Not a lot of telephs in Lower Cadbury, though," Rory offered.

"Not a lot of anything," Mia added.

"It wouldn't matter," Sonja insisted.

Dani shifted her attention from the Gideon-less street back to the crowded room. "Can you be sure? What if he'd had too much to drink? Or became ill?"

"I am telling you, it does not matter!" Sonja snapped, then shook her head and patted Freya's hand where it had come to rest on her shoulder.

"I'm sorry," Dani said.

"No." Sonja's head shook again, though it was a moment before she continued. "It is I who am sorry. It was a sensible question, and deserves an answer."

"Mama," Freya came around to sit next to her mother while Ulf stared over their heads, looking at nothing so far as Dani could tell.

"It is well," Sonja told her daughter, then looked at the waiting group. "To understand why I believe so strongly, you must first understand how it was in Kopernik, during the war."

"Border city," Rory noted.

"We heard it was bad," Jinna added.

Freya muttered a curse in her native tongue.

"Bad. Yes," Sonja agreed. "For over two years we lived with the enemy camped on our doorstep, which meant there could be no trade, no farming. No escape. By the second year of the siege, supplies dwindled, and sickness and cold took as many as the enemy plasma." She took a breath. "Scavenging became a way of living, by the end. And many times, a person would go out, seeking food or medicine—and they would not come back. My husband, their father . . . " She glanced over at her two children, "He did not come back."

The statement, delivered as a simple fact, left a small pocket of silence in its wake, and for a moment, no one moved.

"So, yes, very bad," Sonja echoed. "Bad enough that Rolf *knows* never to leave me wondering. He would tell me, as I would tell him. The only reason he has not contacted me is because he *cannot*."

There was another breath, two, before Dani broke the silence. "I'd say, given what we already know of the others gone missing—"

"Others?" Freya turned to Dani. "What others?"

"I got this one," Mia said. "You all know Tiago . . . "

"Of course," Ulf said, as Sonja nodded.

"Right, well, turns out Tiago's been noticing a few folks going missing from Lower Cadbury, and he asked Gideon and me to facilitate that, and then, when we came home, we found Dani here—"

Dani raised a hand in a vague wave.

"—whose husband is also missing."

"But not in Lower Cadbury," Dani pointed out.

"Which may not signify," Rory added, "given last night's attack."

Sonja gave a start. "*Attack?*"

"More of an ambush, I'd say," Mia determined.

"Whatever we call it," Dani said, "one of the opposing team was a man I'd seen earlier in the day on the tram I took from Tenjin R&D, where my husband was last seen."

Mia nodded. "And the other was a bloke Gideon first noticed at the Mess, yesterday."

"At the Mess," Ulf echoed.

"Where Rolf was last seen," Mia pointed out.

"And now we are speaking of Gideon," Ulf aimed his fierce eyes at Rory. "Where is he?"

"We think—" Mia began.

"He went to look for—" Dani said at the same time.

But before either could finish, a dark shadow came fluttering up to fill the window at Dani's side.

Sonja gasped, and she and Freya popped up from the sofa.

"*Elvis!*" Mia called out, springing from her spot to head for the window, which Dani was already unlatching.

As soon as she pulled it open, the draco came sweeping in on a chill gust of morning air. He flapped his way around the room twice before landing on Mia's shoulder, where he chittered madly and plucked at her hair.

"Easy, boy," Mia said, wincing.

"What's wrong with him?" Rory stepped closer.

"Can dracos get the frothing? The rabies?" Ulf asked.

"He's not mad," Mia said, trying to soothe the manic creature. "He's scared."

Dani stared at the draco. "It looks as if he wants you to do something."

At her statement, Elvis stopped yanking on Mia's hair and flew to the window that still stood open. Here he landed on the sill, shifting from foot to foot to foot to foot and focused first at Mia, then at Dani and, finally, at Jinna.

"It's Gideon," Mia said, staring hard at the draco. "Isn't it? You know where he is?"

At her question, Elvis stopped dancing and sat back on his haunches, raising his head to let out a low, sorrowful keen.

"Definitely Gideon," Jinna said, coming closer, then patted Mia's shoulder. "Better get your coat."

"Wait." Rory's head spun from Elvis to Jinna. "You're saying you think this flying reptile knows where Gideon is?"

Gideon's two partners looked at each other, then back to Rory. "Of course," Jinna said.

"He's helped me track Gideon before," Mia told him.

Rory shook his head, "'Tis just like the Saga of Lassie."

"*Pfft*," Mia flicked her hand as she dashed out of the room to fetch her jacket. "Elvis is smarter than any dog."

Dani believed her, and, while Rory didn't appear quite so convinced, a *look* from Jinna had him, also, fetching his coat.

"We should be going along, as well, yes?" Ulf said. "If you think Gideon might be searching for missing people, he may have found Rolf."

"That he might," Rory said, already slipping his arms into the battered Air Corps jacket hung on a rack near the door. "But given the attack last night, I'd as soon not leave Jinna alone here."

Jinna tossed him a genuinely filthy look but, luckily, the Ohmdahls missed it.

"Certainly." Sonja eyed the exceedingly pregnant young woman. "We will stay and keep Jinna company."

Dani, meanwhile, crouched in front of the draco, who angled his head to meet her eyes. "We'll find him," she told Elvis. "And when we do, I hope you'll make his life a smogging hell."

Elvis's response was a stretching of the wings and a dip of

the head that may have meant anything from, "*You got it, sister,*" to "*I have an itch.*"

But there was no doubt of his intention when Mia came rushing back, as he leapt to her shoulder, now safely covered in wool and leather, and aimed his head for the door.

"Well," Mia said, "what are we waiting for?"

"One second," Dani said, crossing to the table where the dart which had struck Mia still lay, exactly where Gideon had left it the night before, next to one of Jinna's napkins.

Dani wrapped the dart in the napkin and tucked it in her pocket.

"I think General Satsuke will want to know about this," she said to Jinna's questioning look.

"Good idea," Jinna agreed.

"Brilliant. Can we go *now?*" Mia asked, pulling open the door.

Rory grimaced, then turned to Jinna, who tapped her heart, then touched her lips, making him smile.

Dani followed him and closed the door on Ulf offering to help Jinna with the construction in the tea shop.

Downstairs, she followed Mia and Rory to the street.

"Right, then." Mia looked at Elvis, still gripping her shoulder with all four feet. "Where is he?"

With an eager thrum, the draco launched himself into the air, flying towards Cornwell.

Mia took off after him.

Rory and Dani shared a glance, then took off after Mia, both jogging at an easy pace to keep up with the young facilitator in training.

And then Rory spied a rickshaw emerging from Christie Street. "Hold up!" he shouted at both the driver and Mia, who quickly altered course to tumble into the slowing transport.

Before either adult could give directions, Mia was leaning

out of the cab and ordering the driver to "Follow that draco!"
with a great deal of relish.

To his credit, the driver didn't even blink, but put his motorcycle into gear and took off after the low-flying Elvis.

"How long have you been waiting to say that?" Dani asked
when Mia dropped back into the seat.

"Oh, only since Gideon and Elvis showed up in Nike."

"That's what I thought." Then Dani grabbed the side of the
cab as they took a turn at speed.

The driver continued to push his cycle to the limits to
keep up with the draco, and Dani couldn't help but be
impressed by how Elvis stayed over the streets as he made
his way steadily east and then south, even alighting on a
roof or lamppost any time their driver had to stop for
traffic.

For his part, the driver seemed to enjoy the challenge, not
even balking once their route took them from the more populated, and fare-friendly, streets of the inner city to the abandoned docks of Lower Cadbury.

The thrill of the chase turned, however, as Dani watched
Elvis back-wing to hover over a decrepit pier that stuck out into
the river like a rude finger.

"What's he doing?" Mia asked as the driver brought his
cycle to a rumbling halt at the foot of the pier.

Dani watched as Elvis flapped out over the water, and then
began to circle, as if hunting.

"I'm not following him into the water, if that's what he's
wanting," the driver said.

But Mia was already flying out of the cab, with Dani on her
heels.

"Just—wait here," she heard Rory say to the driver, leaping
out after them.

Dani shot him a look, which he understood because even as

she struck the decrepit dock, he was flying around to block Mia's forward progress.

"What are you doing?" Mia demanded as Elvis came to rest on one of the pilings.

"You're not to go out there," Rory said.

"But what about Gideon?" Mia's voice was an arrow, striking Dani in the shoulders. "What if he's—if he's—"

Whatever Mia said next was lost as Dani skidded to a halt at the end of the pier, and though her own heart was anything but easy, a glimpse at Elvis reassured her, for his attention was fixed not on the river's cloudy depths, but out and to the south.

In addition, he was focused, not frantic, as Dani expected he would be if Gideon were drowned.

Still, she had to look. Crouching, one gloved hand pressed against the slimed piling, she leaned out over the slowly rolling Avon.

She spied the lengths of moss growing on the pier drifting out, like a long green coat over the dark water.

Swallowing, she leaned further, and her eyes narrowed, and she closed her ears to Rory's voice as he tried to comfort Mia.

What she spied had her dropping to her knees so she could run her fingers over the edges of the pier, where something seemed to have rubbed away the accrued moss and slime of disuse, revealing the wood beneath in wide swaths.

Easing back on her heels, she turned her attention to the post on which Elvis sat, still staring to the south, and noted a winding line of exposed, clean wood.

The sort one might see if, say, someone wrapped a mooring rope around an old, mossy post.

A quick study of the second post showed it also denuded of the native gunk, with a few stray fibers she took to be hemp.

At last she wiped the muck from her glove onto a plank, then rose and turned towards the shore. "There was a boat," she called out, jerking her thumb at the piling on which Elvis rested. "A boat was moored here."

Mia spun around and Rory straightened, their expressions hopeful and cautious, respectively. Then Dani spied something —some*one*—else, emerging from the mists cloaking the shore.

The body passed the waiting rickshaw driver who, she noted, was waving his hand with a disgusted-sounding, "Oy there. Bathe much?"

Dani's hand moved to her shooter, and a cosh appeared in Rory's hand.

"No, wait," Mia said, patting Rory's arm, much as he'd been patting hers moments before. "I know him. Her. Them?" She huffed out a breath. "We've met. Oy there!" she called out in greeting.

"Have a care," Rory cautioned.

"Only thing you have to have a care for is your nose," Mia replied, before striding out to meet the mass of rags.

"You missed 'im," the mass said, the top of the heap angling down towards Mia.

"Who?" Mia asked, as Dani, with Rory, joined her. "Who'd we miss?"

"Your friend. The tall one from the Corps what came with you t'the market. They took 'im on their boat, they did."

"You're sure it was him?" Mia asked, her voice achingly hopeful.

The heap shifted again. "Reckon he weren't feeling too well, as they 'ad to carry him aboard, but it was 'im, right enough."

Despite the stench, Dani stepped closer. "How long—"

"Do you remember when the boat first showed up?" Mia cut in.

Something that might have been a hand wrapped in several layers of tattered cloth appeared and scratched at the general region of a shoulder. "Might be it came around about seven, eight days past," the heap said. "No more'n that though, as it was ten days ago, us an' George and Wally came out this way to try our hand at fishing."

"And how'd that go?" Rory asked, shrugging, as Dani and Mia both turned to stare. "Just being polite."

"We mostly pulled up bits of weed, but Wally has the touch, and caught us a nice Guinness salmon, so's we had a fine tea that day."

"But the boat," Dani prompted.

"Yeah, it was sometime after our fishin' day the boat showed. Us'n Wally an' George spied it, like I says, mebbe eight days past. So's we couldn't use the pier. Wally, he made to go out and try anyways, but a big fellow with lots of hair and earrings, told him to sod off."

"And the man with the earrings. Do you remember anything else about him?" Dani asked, sharing a glance with Mia.

"He was a big 'un, like I says. Hair in braids, skin darker'n your'n." The heap tipped Mia-wards. "Voice like thunder."

"Sounds like the man from last night," Dani offered.

"Did you see anyone else being carried onto that boat?" Mia asked.

"We doesn't have time to sit on the smogging river all day long now, does we?" The heap shuddered. "We has places to go, people to see an all that."

"Right. Sorry."

"So." Dani placed a hand on Mia's shoulder, "A boat docks at a pier in Lower Cadbury where very few are likely to see it."

"And soon after, a number of folk from the area start to go missing," Rory added.

"People no one would have noticed were gone, but for Tiago, and yourself—selves," Mia said to the heap.

"But, there's your husband," Rory said to Dani.

"The outlier," Dani agreed. "But for all that, it's looking as if

Gideon's theory was correct, that this man with the earrings, and his crew, have taken them all."

"Including Gideon," Mia threw in.

"And that's all well and good," Rory said, "but even if Gideon and the others *are* on the smogging boat, how are we to find it?"

"Oh," Mia said, her shoulders slumped.

Then she and Rory both turned Dani's way.

"No chance of getting a Corps vessel," she said, reading their expressions. "Until we have proof Saeng's on that ship, it's a civilian matter."

"And the coppers can't take the chase outside Nike, even if they believed us," Rory said.

The three looked at each other, then, as one, out at the river.

As they did, Elvis let out a keen Dani felt all the way to her bones. "There has to be something we can do," she said.

For a moment all was silent, then Elvis lifted off and circled back to land on Mia's shoulder, flicking a tongue at the rag heap, who flicked a tongue back.

"Maybe," Rory said, staring at the draco, "we'd be better off tracking Gideon by air. Am I right?" he asked Elvis.

"Is he talking to that there bird?" the rag heap asked.

"He's not a—" Mia began to respond, then shook her head. "Yeah, he's talking to the bird."

"And people say we're a nutter," the heap said, even as Elvis dipped his head in Rory's direction.

"Excepting we can't follow Elvis, and he can't take on a boat of people stealers all by himself," Mia pointed out.

"That's not what I was thinking," Rory said.

"You're thinking airship," Dani realized.

"That, yes."

"But the Corps is no more likely to lend us an airship than a sailing ship," she pointed out.

"And the *Errant*'s still out of town," Mia added. "Isn't she?"

"I know," Rory told Dani, then looked at Mia, "and yes, she is."

"OY!" the rickshaw driver, all but forgotten, called out. "Are you gonna stand about jawing all day long?"

"No!" Rory yelled back. "We'll be wanting a ride to Donne Street!"

"Donne Street?" Dani asked.

Rory nodded and gestured for them to follow. "As it happens, I know a fella' with an airship." His eyes went dark as they neared the rickshaw. "And he owes me a favor."

"Guess your tall friend give up on finding George, then?" the walking heap said, shuffling alongside the trio.

Dani paused at the rickshaw's cab, but it was Mia who replied.

"No," the girl said, daringly patting a filth-encrusted arm. "I think he found him."

CHAPTER 20

Gideon had, in his time, experienced many uncomfortable wakings, often preceded by just as many uncomfortable puttings-to-sleep.

Because of this, he'd become accustomed to assessing such wakings quickly, as, more often than not, the levels of discomfort would soon become much, much worse.

On this particular waking, what Gideon first noticed was the motion, a gentle rolling, accented by a sort of thrumming burr under his cheek.

It might have been pleasant, except for the second, third, and fourth things he noticed, beginning with the sick ache under his collarbone, followed by the temple-spiking headache, and rounding to a close with the wildly uncertain stomach.

"I think he is coming around!"

The voice, loud, stolid, and thick with Stoli, set those spikes in his temple shivering, and Gideon heard-slash-felt a small groan escape his lips.

"Definitely coming around." Another voice, this one youthful, Nikean, and worried, followed. "Best turn him to his side."

At the suggestion, someone's hands grabbed hold of Gideon's coat.

"Why is this?" the booming voice asked.

"So he doesn't—"

Gideon's uncertain stomach came to a decision, and he threw up.

"—aspirate," the younger voice concluded.

As his body ceased heaving its limited contents, Gideon's brain identified the young speaker to be Tiago.

"Hold fast, Quinn," a new, yet oddly familiar, voice chimed in.

Gideon, still wrestling with the uncertain stomach, opted not to speak, nor was he quite ready to open his eyes.

He managed to rustle up enough energy to push away from the sour smell of vomit, leaving him with a bouquet of too many humans in need of a bath.

And fish.

Fish?

Gah.

Pushing farther up and away, as if that might lead to some fresher air, his head thudded up against something—things—hard, flat, and metal. "Ouch."

"Mind the bars," the naggingly familiar voice spoke again.

Bars, Gideon thought. *That sounds—bad.*

While he thought this, the voice's owner helped him to a seated position, holding him steady against the aforementioned bars, as if afraid he'd tip over.

"Did he strike his head?" Tiago's voice flowed from behind Gideon. "I don't see any contusions or bleeding."

Gentle fingers probed Gideon's scalp.

"It's okay," Gideon said, reaching up to pat his own head—and missing. "No fight. Just the . . . " He held up his left hand, thumb up and forefinger out in imitation of a shooter.

The hand holding him steady moved from its rest on Gideon's shoulder, and cool, hardened fingers patted over his throat and neck before pulling open his coat and shirt to discover the puncture wound.

"*Ouch*," Gideon said again, to the back of his eyelids.

"Sorry." The offending hand withdrew. "Drugged," the voice continued. "I had a similar experience. Waking was—unpleasant."

Which Gideon thought to be an understatement.

And who do I know, he now asked himself, *with a flare for understatement?*

Ah, his self replied. *Of course.*

He opened his eyes. "Saeng," he greeted Dani's husband.

"Gideon." Saeng's head dipped in a nod that had his hair sliding forward.

Gideon wondered if he'd ever seen the other man's hair loose. Back in the day, it had always been so tightly braided. Gideon figured he lived with a perpetual headache. "So, you're alive, then?"

The brows, sharp as the edge of a sword, rose. "Disappointed?"

"No. Maybe. A little."

The two considered each other for a moment. "Where is Indani?" Saeng finally asked.

"*Dani* is fine." Gideon's rising irritation gave the lingering nausea an elbow shove to the side. "Was fine. She was asleep when I left her at my place."

"Asleep?" Saeng's eyes widened. "At *your* place?"

"Put some smoke on the hive." Gideon dismissed the simmering jealousy. "She got the bed, I got the desk. Which is exactly as much fun as it sounds."

"But you left her," Saeng said. "Again."

Gideon's already-shaky system turned to ice because, *of course,* Saeng would know the story.

"We are not getting into—that's none of your business."

"You think not?"

"Am I missing something?" Tiago asked.

"A few somethings," Gideon said, looking up to find the student hovering on the other side of the bars with Rolf—likely the source of the booming voice—at his side. "I think I'm missing a few somethings, too," he admitted.

"So you are." Saeng eased back on his heels, his expression colder than moments before. "Where would you like to start?"

Gideon tried, but no appropriate insults came forward. With a sigh for missed opportunities, he let his gaze shift past Saeng to the cage they shared.

It wasn't large; there was just enough room to pace roughly five steps from side to side, and about four steps from the cage door at his left to the bowed, windowless stretch of interlocking planks to his right.

It also lacked the basic amenities, like, say, beds. But from the odors rising from it, he assumed the hole drilled into the deck near the bulkhead stood for the privy.

Gideon studied the hole, just a hand's breadth from where he'd lost the contents of his stomach. "What's under there?" he asked.

"Bact-tanks," Saeng replied.

"So, no sneaking out that way, then."

"*Ach,*" was Rolf's summation of that idea.

Gideon could relate. The image of all that hungry bacteria—designed by Fortune's first landers to devour waste and leave nothing but clean water behind—teeming beneath the deck gave him a fresh set of chills.

"Okay," he said, then cast about, noting a bucket hanging

from the bars with a tin cup looped over one side. "Mind if I have some water?"

"I wouldn't," Tiago warned.

"Why?" Gideon squinted up at the kid.

"Drinking, or eating, anything aboard this ship is a bad idea," Saeng explained, then rose and gestured around the hold.

Curiosity won out over the remains of the drug in his system, and Gideon also rose, climbing his way to his feet, using the bars separating him and Saeng from Tiago and Rolf.

Once on his feet, and sure he'd stay that way, Gideon looked around.

It didn't take long to spy the huddled shapes of the other prisoners, apparently sleeping. His gaze fell on the slumbering prisoner in Tiago and Rolf's cell. He looked at Tiago.

"That's George," Tiago confirmed. He didn't add, *I told you so*, but it was implied.

Then again, George being here supported Gideon's own theory that Saeng's disappearance was linked to those in Lower Cadbury.

He looked at Saeng as the deck thrummed and continued its rolling motion.

"Ship?" he echoed Saeng's earlier statement.

"Mid-size, crystal-powered fishing vessel," Saeng confirmed. "One of the first Tenjin manufactured, back in thirty-eight."

"You know your boats." Rolf sounded impressed.

"Family business," Saeng said before he continued to explain. "The thing about this particular design?" He gestured towards the curved boards making up the bow. "It's rated for river *and* ocean sail, which may be a problem for us."

"A bigger problem than being locked in the hold of said mid-size fishing vessel?"

Saeng regarded Gideon coolly. "Yes, a bigger problem,

because as long as we're on the Avon, freedom is only as far as the riverbank. But once we hit the Oracle . . ."

"We'd be a long way from help," Gideon concluded. "I guess that means there's no time to waste," he said, and shoved himself, more or less directly, for the cell's locked door.

As the others watched, he crouched before the lock, trying to eyeball the make and style.

"I've already tried that," Saeng told him.

"Yeah? And I bet your squeaky-clean upbringing was real helpful with that."

"I suppose now I should apologize for my lack of a criminal past?"

"Plus," Gideon continued as if Saeng hadn't spoken, "unlike the rest of you, I was *trying* to get here. It's all part of the plan."

"Here?" Tiago asked.

"Plan?" Rolf echoed.

"What plan?" Saeng demanded.

"The plan to find you," he said to Saeng. "But not *here*, here. Fact is, I had no clue where you'd been taken, so when the opportunity presented itself, I improvised."

"You got yourself captured," Saeng concluded.

"That was the plan. Pretty brilliant, right?"

Saeng looked from Gideon to the bars and back. "Sheer genius."

"Hey." Gideon glanced back. "*I'm* supposed to be the sarcastic one, *you're* the one with the stick up his—"

"And how is the plan going so far?" Tiago cut in.

"Let's find out," Gideon said. He already knew both Lulu and her sheathe were gone, so he reached up under the collar of his coat. "Ha," he said, grinning as he drew out a curved bit of metal with a handle. Next, he sat on the deck to ease a small, flat bit of allusteel from between the sole and the heel of his boot.

"Cannot take the dodger out of the facilitator," Rolf observed.

"I should put that on my business card," Gideon said as he crouched before the lock.

"The thing is," Tiago said as Gideon probed the plug with the tension wrench, "even if we can unlock the cages, what then? Most of these people are too far gone to even set foot out of their cells."

"If even one of us were to make it out," Saeng responded, before Gideon could, "that one could get to the river, swim for the banks and raise the alarm. The river patrol would be on this ship like wasps on caterpillars."

"Gross, but, yes, that," Gideon agreed.

"I can't swim," Rolf inserted. "But I can knock heads together."

"I imagine you can," Saeng agreed.

While the other three huddled together over possible methods of escape—or of getting word out to the authorities—Gideon continued to work the lock.

After three different configurations failed to trip even one tumbler, he dug into the lining of his coat for a second pin.

He could try—

The rattle of metal, followed by the creak of an opening door, had him rising and stowing his tools even before Saeng let out a warning hiss.

With a speed that belied the lingering headache, Gideon settled himself against one side of the cage before the new arrival finished climbing down the stairs.

Moments later, a familiar figure stood directly in front of the door Gideon had been trying to open.

"You know," he said to Lekan, "if we keep meeting like this, people will start to talk."

"Quinn." Lekan's eyes narrowed, and he rested a hand on

the dart shooter he wore at his hip. "I see you have a sense of humor. Enjoy that. It won't last."

Gideon tilted his head. "Friend, I spent six years in Morton, and I'm still cracking wise."

"First, we are not friends, and second, you know nothing of what awaits you."

"But you do," Saeng offered, gesturing at the dark ink of the serpent wrapped around Lekan's left wrist. "That's an owner's mark. Several of the crew have similar tattoos," he added as Gideon turned his way.

"Meki has that mark," Tiago said, then flushed as Lekan turned his way.

"My daughter and I were both gladiators in the Domino arena," he said. "Until we escaped."

Which told Gideon everything he needed to know about the presumed-missing Meki. He glanced at Tiago with his own unspoken, *told you so,* before turning back to Lekan. "How did you get out?"

"Luck, and timing." Lekan replied to Gideon. "One of the other fighters took advantage of a Colonial attack on Domino during his bout. His actions opened the gate, literally."

"Interesting," Gideon said, his thoughts flashing to another escaped gladiator, and wondered if Eitan Fehr and Lekan knew one another.

Saeng, meanwhile, let out a soft *tch.* "You escaped slavery to become a slaver?"

"Actually, I can kind of see it," Gideon said before Lekan could respond. "Get out from under The Man, get a sailing ship, start selling other people to The Man. It's a circle of life kind of thing."

"Again with this *Man*," Rolf muttered.

Lekan's head tipped towards Gideon. "Very much so."

"Still, it'd be a challenging business, wouldn't it?" Gideon continued, leaning back on the bars. "Especially in the Colonies, where slavery is kind of frowned upon."

"Ah, yes, the ever-principled Colonies." Lekan's lips twitched to a sneer. "A pity that high-mindedness doesn't extend to the poor, the vagrant, the refugees."

As he spoke, his eyes turned to the collection of drugged prisoners in the starboard cells. Some were dressed in the next thing to rags, others were visibly ravaged by hunger. In the corner of one cell, Gideon spied a woman with ink-black hair, cloaked in one of the serapes popular in Allianza.

"Lupe." Tiago stepped up to the bars as he identified his other missing neighbor.

"She can't hear you," Lekan said. "One of the reasons we go after the type. They're too hungry to say no to a meal." Here he cast his gaze at the glop on the tray Saeng had left untouched.

"One of the reasons." Gideon latched on to that. "The other reason you choose them is they won't be missed."

Lekan's eyes rose to meet his. "It's a sound business practice."

"That it is," Gideon agreed before asking, "So why break the pattern now? I mean, maybe you figure Rolf here would be written off as having tipped over the docks in a drunken stupor, but then you've got *this* one." He jerked his chin at Tiago. "A medical student, with friends, patients—a family. And him?" he jerked his chin in Saeng's direction. "What you have here is an active officer in the Corps. And, as you might have guessed, his absence has been noticed."

"You've never heard of a target of opportunity?" Lekan asked.

"Sure I have," Gideon replied. "I've also heard of the smog of war. I don't know about you," he said, turning to Saeng, "but it's getting a mite smoggy down here."

"A regular lentil soup," Saeng agreed.

Lekan's gaze flicked to Saeng.

"Come on," Gideon prompted. "What difference does it make if you tell us now?"

Lekan's lip twitched. "What the hells," he said, and turned to point a finger at Rolf. "He was right about you. Anyone with family is a calculated risk, but the rubiks a bruiser such as yourself will bring on the block made it a risk worth taking." He turned the pointing finger to Tiago. "You were in the wrong place at the wrong time, and thanks to that, I'll be coddling my daughter's conscience for months."

Tiago gave a start, but Lekan had turned to Gideon. "You made yourself a target."

Gideon uncrossed his arms and held both hands up in a "What are you gonna do?" gesture.

Lekan actually smiled, then his eyes shifted to Saeng, but he said nothing.

"Well?" Saeng prompted. "What about me? Why am I here?"

"You . . . " Lekan paused. "You were a favor."

That surprised Gideon, and Saeng appeared just as shocked.

"A favor?" Saeng echoed, stepping forward. "For *who?*"

"The man who got me and my daughter out of Adia."

"And I bet that man looks like a tree stump and talks like a politician," Gideon said.

Saeng, however, was shaking his head. "Why?" he asked Lekan.

"Don't know. Didn't ask," Lekan said. "He did me a good turn, now I've done him one. Far as that's concerned, we're done. Now, if you'll excuse me, I've a course to plot." He turned, started for the forward ladder.

Gideon's hand slid into his pocket, reaching for the lock pick, when Lekan paused at the second port-side cell.

"Anything I need to know, Galen?"

At his question, a lonely pile of rags huddled in that cell unfolded and rose with a grace very unlike the poor, the vagrants, or the refugees Lekan hunted.

The woman who now faced Lekan was nearly as tall as he, with a warm mahogany complexion, but where Lekan sported that mass of braids, she'd opted to go in the other direction by shaving her hair to the scalp, and no one could miss the warrior's muscles beneath her ragged costume.

"They are plotting an escape," the ringer—Galen—reported. "The one called Quinn has a set of lock picks."

"Does he, now?" Lekan glanced at Gideon before pulling out a key—and not just any key, but a Kairos multi-quad-mech—which explained why Gideon's tools couldn't trip the tumblers.

It'd take two seasoned dodgers with at least four picks, working in tandem, to trip a Kairos quad-mech lock.

"A good third of our cargo are thieves," Lekan said, eying Gideon. "I'd be a rare fool if I hadn't prepared for the occasional dodger." And with that, he slid the key into Galen's cell door and flipped the toggle.

Even from three cells away, Gideon could make out the mechanized *whirr* of the key pins rotating, followed by the metallic *kerchunks* of the tumblers being tripped in the locksmith's programmed order.

"It didn't occur to you to tell me this was a Kairos multi?" Gideon muttered in Saeng's direction.

"As I pointed out, my criminal education is lacking."

"Say that again." Gideon turned back to find Galen had left her cell to stand in front of him.

"You'll toss the picks to Galen," Lekan ordered as he once again locked the cell door.

Gideon didn't move. "I will?"

"You will," Lekan replied, "unless you want him to suffer."

He pointed to Tiago, who stepped back a pace. "I can make his last hours of freedom a torment."

From his left, Gideon caught the low rumble that preceded an Ohmdahlanche. "You think you can get through him?" he asked, jerking a thumb in Rolf's direction.

"What do you think?"

"I think you haven't seen Rolf in action."

"I have seen enough in action," Lekáhn said, returning to Gideon's cell. "Which is why, even if I did not have this . . . " he placed a hand on the dart shooter. "I would still have a crew of twenty-five souls who will do whatever I say, even if what I say is to send a bolt through each of their hearts."

Rolf growled. Tiago paled.

Gideon drew the lock picks from his pocket, held them up, and tossed them out onto the deck at Galen's feet.

She crouched to retrieve them.

"And the coat," Lekan ordered.

"You want me to catch a cold before we hit the blocks?"

"The coat," Lekan confirmed, "or shall we test your resolve with the boy?"

"I'm not a—"

Gideon silenced Tiago with a *look*, and then, gritting his teeth, shrugged out of his coat, rolled it up, and shoved it through one of the squares of bars towards Galen.

She took it and, at Lekan's gesture, headed forward and up the ladder.

With a last scan of the hold, Lekan followed her.

For a time, no one spoke, and the only sounds were the creak of the bow, the thrum of the engines, and the whisper of water.

It was Saeng who finally broke the silence. "So," he began as he turned to face Gideon, "was that part of the plan, as well?"

CHAPTER 21

THE GUY RORY KNEW, DANI LEARNED, WAS ONE TARIQ EL Karim, a shadow trader the *Errant* crew had met two months prior.

"Are you sure El Karim is in Nike?" she asked, as the rickshaw jerked to a halt in front of a gate on Donne Street.

"He's here, right enough," Rory confirmed. "I had a drink with the *Al-Djinn*'s chief mechanic, day before yesterday, and he said they were to be moored in Nike for the better part of a fortnight." As he spoke, he climbed out of the cab and commenced patting his pockets in search of the fare.

Dani simply produced a five-star and handed it to the driver while Mia climbed out after Rory.

"You want me to wait?" the driver asked, tucking the five-star in his pocket.

"Maybe that's best," Rory said, glancing down the empty street, lined with gated houses. "I doubt this'll take long, one way or the other."

Refusing to think on the other, Dani climbed out of the cab while the driver pulled a flask from his side saddle.

With the fervent hope the flask held nothing stronger than tea, Dani followed the others across the street.

"This place is pure risto," Mia said, eyeing the red-tiled townhome. "You sure this Tariq fella's in the shadow trade?"

"He's in the trade . . . and a few other things." Rory shrugged, his leather jacket creaking, but didn't explain further.

"Whatever he does, it pays better than facilitating," Mia observed as they passed through the unlocked gate.

Dani, gazing over the apiary, the flower beds, and the outbuilding hulking in the morning sunslight, had to agree.

On reaching the door, she was bemused by the brass knocker designed to resemble a female djinn emerging from clouds of smoke. Her fiery hair looped around to form the rapper Rory now dropped in three loud, brassy clunks.

Seconds passed.

The door remained stubbornly closed.

"Maybe they're not home?" Mia suggested.

"Or still asleep," Dani offered.

"They're here," Rory said. "And if they're still asleep, I can think of one sure way to wake them." He reached into a pocket and drew out a wallet, which he opened to show a set of lock picks.

"Brilliant!" Mia said.

"Oh, now," Dani began, just as the door swept open.

Rory hopped back and stuffed the picks away, grinning at the ominous figure now standing at the threshold.

The man, who had to be Tariq, stood panther-still. His wavy black hair, just silvering, curled over amber eyes that glittered with annoyance, and his shirt, worn over flowing trousers, was open to the waist.

Oh dear, Dani thought.

"What?" Tariq asked, eyes latching on Rory.

"Are we interrupting something?" Rory asked.

"As a matter of fact, you are."

"I hope it's breakfast," Mia muttered.

Tariq's eyes narrowed at the young dodger, then further narrowed at the draco wrapped like a scarf around her throat. But it wasn't until his eyes fixed on Dani—or, rather, Dani's Corps long coat—that she saw the flicker of genuine anger, which he turned on Rory. "No," he said.

"What d'ye mean, 'no'?" Rory asked. "You don't even know what I've come to ask."

"I don't need to know." Tariq started to close the door.

"Tariq? Who is it?" A female voice came from inside the house, accompanied by a soft *tap-shuff, shuff, tap-shuff,* which was in its turn, followed by the arrival of a woman at Tariq's side, the short crutches she used explaining the tapping. Her pure black hair was a tumble of loose curls over her shoulders, and her shirt, unlike Tariq's, was fully buttoned.

This bit of modesty was offset by the fact that the shirt was *all* she wore.

The burgundy linen ended at a discreet mid-thigh, but it allowed Dani a view of legs that were long, golden, and thin to the point of emaciation.

"Oh. Rory!" The woman smiled, and her deep brown eyes warmed as they met the young mechanic's. "What a pleasant surprise."

"No, it isn't," Tariq said.

"Sameen." Rory grinned at the woman. "You're looking—spry," he offered as Tariq's glower escalated.

"It's been too long," Sameen said.

"No it hasn't," Tariq countered.

"Don't be rude." Sameen gave Tariq an elbow to the ribs.

It was barely a touch, but he stepped back from the doorway, allowing Sameen to come forward, where Dani could see a silver medallion lying bright against the fabric of her shirt.

"Now, Rory, who've you brought to visit?" she asked.

"He's brought the Corps," Tariq said, jerking his chin at Dani's uniform coat.

"Just one soldier. On leave," Dani pointed out. "And what happens on leave—"

"Stays on leave," Sameen capped the quote with a grin.

"Then, by all means, *leave*."

"Be*have*." This time Sameen's elbow to Tariq's ribs was more vigorous and had him wincing.

"*Delbar-am*," he murmured, but then Elvis's head appeared from the mass of Mia's hair.

"Is that a draco?" Sameen's eyes widened with delight.

"This is Elvis," Mia said. "He's my friend's draco. He's *really* hungry."

The draco let out a plaintive croon that had Sameen's eyes softening and Tariq's rolling.

"We'll just have to see about that, won't we?" Sameen maneuvered herself back a few steps, then sent her husband a *look* that had him sighing and pulling the door further open. "Please, be welcome," she invited. "We'd just started our breakfast when you knocked."

Mia didn't need to be asked twice and popped right in and Rory, grinning, followed, although Dani noted he kept as much distance between himself and Tariq as physically possible.

Inside, Sameen was already sharing her regrets that her son was off visiting his grandmother, as he'd have loved meeting Mia and Elvis.

"Sorry to interrupt your morning," she said to Tariq as she entered.

"Not half as sorry as I am," he said, closing the door behind her.

She noted the stairway curving up one side of the entry hall, while on either side of the foyer stood arched doors, both flung open.

Rory was tailing the others into the room on the left, so Dani, with Tariq looming behind, followed him into the homey comfort of a crackling fire and overstuffed furniture, all contained in a perfect octagon of a room.

One wall held the fireplace, and another, directly opposite the snapping flames, was made up mostly of curtained windows. There was just enough of a gap in the drapes to let in a sliver of sunslight, which bisected a ruthlessly organized slate-topped desk.

The remaining walls held built-in shelves and cabinets of gleaming wood filled with an impressive collection of books, as well as assorted document tubes and maps. There was also an eclectic selection of toy airships, water ships, cycles, and trams, along with a stuffed mammoth and draco, both lounging next to a spinning globe of Fortune.

One of the higher shelves boasted a broken arithmometer and an Air Corps cutlass.

Dani glanced at Sameen, already maneuvering herself into one of two chairs, upholstered in the same comfortably worn fabric as the sofa.

Both chairs angled away from the door to face a low table, upon which sat a small mountain of variously folded pieces of colored paper, a tall glass tea pot, and a tray bearing rounds of flatbreads, fruits, an assortment of meats and cheeses, and a selection of pastries.

On the far side of the table, Mia was already sitting on the large sofa. On her shoulder, Elvis raised his head, tasting the air with interest.

"Please, help yourselves," Sameen said, tucking her canes next to the chair. "Rory, you'll find the extra cups just under that shelf." She pointed to a cabinet built at the base of the book-shelves.

Rory followed her directions and found three clear glass cups, set in brass holders, to match the two already on the table.

"Now that we are all cozy," Tariq said, coming up at his wife's side, "what sort of trouble are you in, and how long will it be before you leave?"

"I apologize for my husband," Sameen said easily. "He can be a bear dog when his plans go awry."

"That would be an understatement," Rory commented as he poured out.

"It is hardly my fault your crew poked a hornet's nest last February," Tariq replied, even as he passed the cup Rory gave him to Sameen.

"I believe your mother poked that nest first," Sameen told her husband, blowing on the tea to cool it. "Either way," she said to Rory, "we're still grateful for your crew's assistance. Where is your crew, anyway? I so enjoyed chatting with Jagati."

"They've just gone off on a short run to Faraday." Rory handed a cup to Mia, who was gathering a small pile of the smoked aurochs for Elvis, who'd crawled his way down her arm to the table. "And Izaldine?" he asked while the draco tore into his breakfast. "What's he been at these days?"

"Besides visiting his nan? Growing like a weed," Sameen told him, sipping. "And he's taken to origami."

Everyone looked at the pile of folded bits of paper covering the table.

"He has more passion than skill at this point," Sameen explained.

"That's a likely airship he's made." Rory gestured to one of the more oblong shapes as he offered Tariq a cup.

"That is a leviathan," Tariq informed him, ignoring the cup

Rory held out and pulling a rust-colored blanket from the back of Sameen's chair.

Rory gave the cup to Dani while Tariq draped the soft throw over his wife's bare legs. Sameen raised her free hand to her husband's cheek in a gesture as well-worn as the library's furniture.

Dani took a sip of the bright mint tea and absolutely *did not* think of Saeng.

"Nice as all this is, and it's right brilliant," Mia said, "we've got us a mammoth-sized problem, and no mistake."

"I told you so," Tariq murmured, settling on the arm of Sameen's chair. "So, what does the *Errant*'s mechanic, Gideon Quinn's apprentice, and their unnamed officer want from me?"

"Captain Solis," Dani introduced herself. "But please, call me Dani."

"Charmed," Sameen said.

"Hmm," was Tariq's comment.

"How d'you know who I was?" Mia demanded, brows drawn in fierce suspicion.

Tariq turned her way. "My chief mechanic loves nothing more than a good gossip," he told her. "And in the past weeks, Nike has taken to buzzing about an ex-dodger, ex-soldier, ex-convict by the name of Gideon Quinn who, with his pet draco and undersized apprentice, wanders the streets, righting wrongs, helping the helpless . . . and in other ways convincing my son he wishes to become a private facilitator when he grows up."

"*Undersized?*" Mia challenged.

"Could be Izaldine's on to something there." Rory grinned.

"It is not even a real job," Tariq grumbled.

"*Tariq,*" Sameen said.

"Stay on course," Dani told Rory and Mia both.

"Right. Yes." Rory slurped his tea.

"Sorry," Mia said, then turned to Rory and Dani. "One of

you had best tell the tale," she said. "I'll just muddle it, and we don't have time for muddles."

Dani met Rory's gaze. "You do it," she told him, thinking Tariq might be more inclined to listen to Rory. "I'll fill in any gaps."

"At present, it is *all* a gap," Tariq reminded them.

"And I'll fill it," Rory told him, with some heat. "But 'tis a swarm of a problem, as Mia said, and we think it started with people going missing from Lower Cadbury."

And then, as Dani listened, Rory laid everything out for the couple, just as he'd heard it the night before, from Tiago Hama's approaching Gideon to Saeng's disappearance to the attack on 9 Doyle to the missing Rolf Ohmdahl.

Tariq said nothing, until Rory reached their dawn race to the empty dock, at which point he held up a hand. "Do you genuinely expect me to believe a *draco* showed you where to seek Quinn?"

"Elvis is crystal and comb when it comes to keeping track of Gideon." Mia brushed crumbs from her tunic as Elvis let out a growl.

"You are quite a smart one, aren't you?" Sameen told the draco, who responded with a little trill, and commenced grooming himself.

Tariq appeared unimpressed, but allowed Rory to finish the story, including their interview with the ragged individual who claimed to have seen Gideon loaded onto a boat.

"That is quite a story," Tariq said when Rory stopped and took a sip of tea. "It also sounds a job for the filth."

"Except the coppers' rules on missing people are smogged," Mia said.

"Plus the boat our witness spied Gideon boarding has already sailed," Dani added.

"So," Rory picked up the thread of the tale, "they'd be already out of the city coppers' jurisdiction."

"You need an airship," Sameen said quietly. "You need the *Al-Djinn*."

"Believe me, if the *Errant* were here," Rory said, raising his free hand.

"If the *Errant* were here, you would still need the *Al-Djinn*." Tariq dismissed Rory's statement with a gesture. "A boarding requires more than one jumper, and one jumper is all your crew affords."

"They'd have two," Dani stated. "With me, they'd have two."

Sameen's lips tilted in a small smile. "You've the look about you," she said.

Dani's hand tapped her heart, then gestured to the medallion hanging over Sameen's shirt. "One recognizes one."

"You're asking me to risk my 'ship, and my crew, to pursue a man we don't know. Two men," Tariq added, glancing at Dani.

"Three that we know of," Rory said.

"Probably more, with Tiago's missing mates," Mia added.

"Tariq," Sameen said.

"This is not what we do." He looked at his wife. "*Delbaram*, understand, if I use the *Al-Djinn* in a rescue operation, people will notice. The crew . . . and others . . . will take note."

"Surely, just this once," Sameen began.

"I've an idea on that," Rory said, sending Sameen a wink before turning to her husband. "You could consider it less a rescue operation, and more the first crack at a bit of non-Colonial weaponry."

"Weaponry?" Tariq echoed.

"Show him," Rory said to Dani.

"Rory . . . " She raised her brows at him, and he raised his back.

In for a quarterstar, she thought, and set her cup on the table and dug the dart, still wrapped in Jinna's napkin, out of her inner pocket. "This was used on Mia," she explained. "Last night, during the attack. We think the dart contains something like morph, but faster acting."

"A wicked sting it has," Mia agreed.

"Someone drugged you?" Sameen's eyes darkened. "What kind of wasp—"

"Not only drugged," Rory shook his head.

"Shot," Dani clarified.

Tariq said nothing, but held out a hand.

Dani, with only a moment's hesitation, dropped the dart, napkin and all, into the shadow trader's palm.

He parted the bit of cloth, eyes narrowing at the dart before lowering it for Sameen to see.

"It's rather like the darts Rangers use for injured wildlife," Sameen offered.

"Except this came out of a shooter," Dani told her. "Longer-barreled than the standard plasma repeater, and with thrice the range. That dart was fired from the ground, and struck Mia outside a third-story window, on the opposite side of the street, in the rain."

"That's impossible." Sameen shook her head. "A crossbow and a few plasma rifles, maybe, could make the shot you're describing."

"We saw it," Dani said.

"And I felt it," Mia added, rolling her shoulder.

"No need to say more," Tariq said. "We will help you track this boat."

Mia gaped. "You're saying a shooter's a good enough reason to lift off, but actual people ain't?"

"Yes."

"It is a good enough reason no one will question it," Sameen explained.

Tariq palmed the dart, then brought his wife's hand to his lips. "This is *not* the morning I had planned."

"We'll make it up when you get home."

He said nothing, but pressed his head to the top of hers for a moment, a moment in which Dani felt compelled to look anywhere else, so she focused on Elvis, as the draco had decided to investigate the nature of a pomegranate.

After the space of several breaths, movement at Dani's left had her eyes rising to find Tariq now on his feet. "We leave as soon as I've changed," he announced before sweeping from the room, a study in purpose and irritation.

"What about Jinna?" Mia asked, reaching for a pastry.

"Jinna," Sameen echoed, her face distant with thought. "I know that name."

"Jinna Pride," Rory reminded her. "She was involved in the matter from February."

"Oh, of course!" Sameen's smile bloomed again. "Lovely girl, and I should think due any day?"

"That she is, and most every other minute she's trying to talk the wee beggar out, as she's quite done with the carrying of it."

"I know the feeling," Sameen agreed, then she and Rory launched into a comparison of pregnancies that Dani instinctively tuned out.

"But the thing is," Mia cut into Rory's description of Jinna's latest cravings, "we left the flat on Doyle in a rush, and haven't been back, so Jinna's no notion about Gideon. Or the boat. Or anything."

"Well, there's a teleph in the other room," Sameen offered.

"We're not on the teleph," Mia told her before adding, with some heat, "we have to let her know what's what."

"If you're thinking of making a stop on the way to the airfield, there won't be time."

Everyone came up straight and turned to see Tariq, now dressed and slapping a pair of flight gloves against his coat, glaring at all and sundry.

"That was right quick," Rory huffed.

"Years of practice," Sameen told him.

"I've already radio'd Jacques," Tariq continued over the commentary. "We've enough crew aboard—and sober—to take off, but the lift window is narrow, which means we have to go straight to the airfield."

"But—"

"No need to worry," Sameen turned back to Mia. "I can deliver the updates to Jinna. It will give me something more to do than rattle about an empty house." She tossed that over her shoulder at Tariq, who Dani could see was already gearing up to object.

He settled back on his heels, visibly resigned.

"It'd be grand if you could," Rory said. "They're at 9 Doyle Street, likely in MacGuffin's, Jinna's tea shop-to-be."

"Brilliant!" Sameen lifted her tea in a toast. "I look forward to seeing it."

"I'm so relieved that's all settled," came Tariq's response. "Now we need only get to the air dock, raise the *Al-Djinn*, and find a way to track this missing boat of yours."

"We've a rickshaw waiting to take us," Rory said, moving for the door.

"And Elvis can track the boat," Mia promised, grabbing a fistful of dates as she rose.

Tariq looked at the dodger, then down at the draco, covered in pomegranate juice and delicately nibbling a bit of cheese. Then he turned to his wife.

"*Not* the morning I had planned," he told her.

"Consider it a plot twist," she replied. "Now, you lot go save the day. Oh, and Tariq?" She tipped her head back to grin at her husband, already at the door. "Try not to get shot, this time."

CHAPTER 22

THE SUNS WERE WELL UP BY THE TIME ISHAN HAMA STOOD outside of the building in which his son chose to live.

He was surprised to see a handful of window boxes on sills, with their colorful mix of flowers peeking over the broken cobbles of Jaffa Street.

A steady *whirring* had him looking further up to where the columns of windmills spun atop the roof, providing power to the building.

Tiago, he imagined, had a hand in getting those windmills working.

His son could be as innovative as he was stubborn.

Please, he thought, coming to the third-floor landing, *please let him be here.*

Here, because he had not been at the hospital, working through a second shift.

Had not, he'd learned on inquiring, even reported for the first shift.

It was then, as he'd stood in the doorway of the hospital, listening to the university clock chiming the hour, that he called the precinct, requesting a personal day.

If the lieutenant had a problem with it, she could take it up with him on his return.

But now, standing outside Tiago's flat, even before he rapped on the door, even before the long moments in which no one answered, his instincts told him the flat was empty.

He put a hand to the knob, found it unlocked.

Of course.

With a muttered curse, he opened the door and entered, one hand on his service shooter.

The first step in had him exhaling in relief, for, while there was no visible sign of his son, nor were there any signs of foul play.

A quick search of the place revealed a cup of tea on the handkerchief-sized kitchen table which, when Ishan touched it, proved cold.

The mattress Tiago called a bed was unmade, but Ishan had given up that particular battle long before his son entered university.

Procedure had him crouching to search under the mattress when a discreet tap at the door interrupted, and he returned to the main room to find company standing in the open door.

"Oh!" Cora Vin-Cielo's thin hands fluttered to her heart as he appeared. "Detective Sergeant, you gave me a start."

"Ishan, please," he said, recognizing Tiago's neighbor. "My sorrow for your loss," he added. "If I hadn't been on duty yesterday, I would have called."

"Such is the life of the copper," Cora said, understanding rising to mask the lingering grief. "Is your boy finally home?" As she spoke, she leaned to peer over his shoulder. "I came to ask him to dinner, and to thank him for his help with Vittorio."

"Finally?" Ishan latched on to that one word, moving forward so fast she gasped. "Forgive me, but Tiago—I can't find him. We were to meet earlier today, and he never arrived. Nor was he at the hospital, or the university."

"Oh! Oh. Well . . . " She paused, brow furrowing in thought. "It's possible he had a patient who needed tending. From his clinic, that is. Or perhaps he went out with his young lady?"

"He has a young lady?" Ishan asked. *And never mentioned her?*

"Not as he's said," Cora amended, waving her hand. "But I passed them on the stairs once or twice over the past few days. Lovely girl," she added with a smile, but sobered as she met Ishan's eyes. "I could be wrong, but, well . . . "

"It's no matter," he said; though of course it was a matter.

"Anyway," Cora said, brushing her hands over her worn trousers, "if you should see Tiago first, please tell him we would enjoy his company this evening. Or any evening."

"And if you should see him first, I hope you'll tell him I've been by," Ishan said. Then he added, "His young lady . . . could you describe her?"

"Jinna?" Ulf's voice boomed through the shop, almost causing Jinna to drop the sanding block she was using. "Mama is wanting to know if you want the spice rack over the stove, or the —Jinna?"

"I'm down here," Jinna called from where she knelt on the other side of the serving counter.

"Down where?" Ulf's shadow fell over Jinna, where she was sanding the counter's front. "Oh. Down there."

She looked up to see his brow scrunched in concern. She supposed she made a sight, all belly and hair, coated with a fine carpet of sawdust.

That dust brought on a sneeze, and the sneeze brought on a twinge in her lower back.

"I think, maybe, so much dust might be bad for the baby?" Ulf ventured.

"The dust won't hurt anything," she assured him, before another twinge in her spine told her that the dust might be harmless, but her back wasn't enjoying itself.

"Ulf!" Sonja called, rounding the counter. She had a rag tossed over her shoulder, her shirt sleeves rolled up, and her trouser knees were grimy. "I asked you to bring Jinna, and here you stand like poleaxed aurochs."

"It's not his fault," Jinna called, holding up a hand so Ulf could help her up and let out a little "Eep!" as he hauled her to her feet in one enthusiastic tug.

"Sorry!" He took her elbow while she grabbed at the countertop.

"Still not your fault," she said.

"His fault or no," Sonja said, "you should be sitting."

Jinna was more than ready to agree, but before she could respond, the door to the shop swung open. Ulf shifted his position to block all comers and Sonja eased up at Jinna's side, her expression wary.

"My, but you're a big one, aren't you?" Jinna heard a vaguely familiar voice say.

"I—yes?"

"Well, big fellow, I'm looking for Jinna Pride, or Sonja Ohmdahl," the newcomer continued. "Perhaps you know them?"

With a surprised twitch of her brows, Sonja patted Jinna's arm and moved around her son to face the speaker. "I am Sonja Ohmdahl," she said, her voice cool. "And this is my son, Ulf."

"Woof," was the newcomer's reply. "Kudos to you, Msr Ohmdahl."

Which was when Jinna's memory clicked, and she peeked around Ulf.

"Sameen," she greeted the other woman. They'd only met once, after the *Errant* returned from dealing with Galileo Kane, but Sameen was a memorable sort. "What brings you to the ninth district?" she asked. "Oh." She put a hand to her heart. "Please tell me you haven't lost someone, too."

"Quite the opposite, I'd think." The dark eyes locked on Jinna's. "Rory sent me," she said. "And Mia and Dani. And Elvis."

"Rory—Elvis? They sent you?" Feeling unusually slow, Jinna pressed a hand to her back. "Why?"

"I'm to tell you they're in pursuit of your missing people, and that they've engaged Tariq and the *Al-Djinn* to do it. All in all," Sameen added with a crooked grin, "I rather like their chances."

After bidding farewell to Cora, Ishan Hama's next destination was Tiago's clinic.

The clinic was another point of dispute between father and son, as Ishan believed those desperate enough to live in the wreckage of Lower Cadbury would also be desperate enough to take advantage of an idealistic young medical student.

At best, they would use him to feed an addiction, at worst—

Cutting short the speculation, he pulled his cycle to a stop in front of the little shop Tiago had co-opted.

It had once been a patisserie, he recalled, one the entire family used to visit.

Then Paolo died, and Ishan, finding himself unable to continue living in the place he and Paolo had been so happy, had taken their son and moved into a flat near the precinct.

It wasn't long after that move that the Adians had flown in from the west to decimate Lower Cadbury, including the building where Ishan and his family once lived.

But some buildings remained, among them the patisserie, where Ishan now spied a handful of people waiting.

"Oy there, DS," one of those people called out, hopping out of line.

Ishan took in the ragged infantry coat and the crutches, providing balance for the missing leg.

"Catriona." Ishan greeted his onetime neighbor as they met on the sidewalk. "What's all this?" he asked, glancing at the straggling line.

"It's clinic day," she said. "Figured that's why you were here, to visit your lad."

"I am looking for Tiago," Ishan confirmed. "But I wasn't sure of his . . . working days."

"They change some, depending on his lectures," Catriona admitted. "But normally, this term, he'd be here by now."

Ishan met Catriona's gaze, then both looked at the door. "Has anyone gone inside?" he asked.

"I haven't." Catriona glanced at the others, all of whom shook their heads or answered in the negative.

"You think we should look?" a woman holding a fussing toddler asked.

Rather than answer, Ishan headed to the door and peered through the grubby window.

There was no light, no sign of movement. He put one hand on the doorknob, found it unlocked.

"It's never locked," Catriona told him.

"Right." He looked at the mother, then her child. "Best stay out here," he warned.

But as he opened the door he knew, just as he'd known in Tiago's flat, the place was empty.

Still, he cleared the waiting area out front, where chairs reclaimed from any number of abandoned flats sat, waiting for occupants. He moved to the kitchen, which appeared to be Tiago's exam area, and found it empty as the rest, with only a makeshift cot and the pantry, which *was* locked.

"He keeps his supplies in there," Catriona said.

Ishan turned to see the veteran had followed him into the building.

"It's not much of a lock," Ishan pointed out.

"There's no one in LC would steal from Tiago," Catriona told him. "Only trouble he ever had was with old Wendell, and that Quinn fellow sorted him, didn't he?"

"Yes," Ishan murmured, "I suppose he did."

"You're worried," Catriona observed, her eyes sharp on Ishan.

He started to deny it, but there was no point. "I can't find him. Anywhere."

For a few moments, all was quiet.

Behind Catriona, several of the other patients had flowed into the shop, but they, too, said nothing.

Catriona chewed her lip, checked with her fellows before turning back. "So," she said, "how can we help?"

Of all the things she could have said, Ishan wondered why it was the simple offer of assistance that caught him by the throat.

"I think," he said at last, "if there were some who could stay here, in case Tiago arrives?"

"We can do that." The mother of the toddler said while a man, who appeared to be the boy's father, wrapped an arm around her shoulder, making them a unit.

"Thank you." Ishan turned to the others. "If there were patients too ill to come to—the clinic," he said, "might he tend them at home?"

Catriona nodded at that. "We should also hit A Fine Mess, in case a fight broke out, or someone drank too much."

"Martin's custom won't be too happy talking to a copper," another patient offered. "No offense meant," he added to Ishan.

"Might go easier if you were to have one of the Lower C folk along with you," an older woman agreed.

Catriona turned to Ishan. "What d'ya think, DS? Got room for a partner on that there ride?"

Ishan considered the woman, then her crutches.

"Never you worry about these," she said, reading his concerns. "Just mind the sharp turns."

"Good enough." He looked at the others. "I know no one's on the teleph here, but if anyone should find Tiago, please send word to the ninth precinct house. They'll be able to reach me."

Over the rumbles of assent and a determined, "He'll be found, guv," Ishan mounted his cycle and started the motor.

The engine's familiar hum was countered by the unusual judder of a passenger settling down on the pillion.

"Right, then," Catriona gave his shoulder a pat, "let's go find your boy."

CHAPTER 23

It didn't take long for the chill of their floating prison to seep into Gideon's limbs.

To combat the cold—and to seek out any weaknesses in the cage—he took to pacing the minuscule space.

Which was when he discovered the minute satisfaction of forcing Saeng to move out of his way every few steps.

After observing a few rounds of this dance, Rolf let out a bear-like sigh and squatted against the bulkhead, as far from the privy hole as he could manage.

Tiago crossed over to George, where he crouched to check the slumbering man's pulse before slumping to sit at his side, head tipped back against the bars, dark eyes fixed on the ceiling.

Wait, Gideon asked himself, *is it still called a ceiling if it's on a boat?*

His self appeared disinclined to answer, so Gideon spun, mentally and physically, onto another tangent, almost tripping over Saeng, who had folded himself in the center of the cell, legs crossed, hands balanced on his thighs, his un-confiscated coat spread out in a green circle around him.

Besides making a pretty picture, the coat took up additional space, restricting Gideon's route to a sort of rough star, with points in the four corners and the door of the cage.

He skipped the point that was the privy.

Each time he hit the cage door, he ran a hand over the lock.

If Mia were here—but no. The only thing worse than having Tiago to worry over would be if his apprentice were in this mess.

No, she was well out of it.

Her, and Dani . . . and Elvis.

Then the memory of how he'd left them sliced a fresh wound in his conscience, and he cursed, and walked another star-ish round.

At some point, he caught the soft rasp of a snore from Rolf, and an even softer murmur from Tiago's distant corner.

With nothing else going forward in his brain, he came to a halt midway through his route to study the young man.

"What is that?" he asked, watching the youth's lips move while his hand twitched in synch.

"What?" Tiago jerked back from wherever he'd been and focused on Gideon. "What is what?"

"That thing you were chanting." Gideon waved in his direction. "The thing about decapitating."

"Decapitating?" Tiago's alarm was immediately replaced by comprehension. "Capitate," he clarified. "It's one of the carpal bones. I was reciting the bones of the hand." He held up his left hand, knuckles facing Gideon. "I'd already done the feet."

"Good times."

Tiago's brows rose. "Were you aware that the hand has more bones than any other part of the human body?"

"I did not know that."

"Well. It does."

"Okay." His curiosity satisfied, Gideon started on his appointed rounds once more, but when he reached the cage door and turned, he saw Tiago had given up on his mantra and was still watching him.

Seeing him so, sitting with his hands hanging limp over the bent knees, eyes bereft of hope, Gideon doubled down on his determination to see the kid safe.

"I'm not a kid," Tiago said.

Gideon blinked. "Did I say that out loud?"

A twitch of Tiago's lip foreshadowed a smile that never arrived. "You had that look on your face, the same one Dad gets every time he tries to get me to move out of Lower Cadbury. 'No place for a kid like you,' he says. But I'm not a kid."

"No. You're not," Gideon agreed, turning his attention back to the lock. "So let's make sure you can get home and remind your dad of that."

"*How?*"

The question didn't come from Tiago, but Saeng.

Gideon grimaced.

"I'm working on it." He straightened and shoved his hands, which felt like blocks of ice, into his trouser pockets and started another loop.

"Must you keep stalking around like a caged animal?"

"It helps me think." Gideon stepped on the hem of Saeng's coat as he passed. "Oops."

"Some of us are capable of thinking without disturbing others."

"You're disturbing *me.*"

"*What did she ever see in you?*"

"What was that?" Gideon snapped at the other man.

Black eyes narrowed. "Nothing. And at least I don't need to stamp around like a spoiled child in order to come up with ideas."

"Yeah?" Gideon approached the door again. "And what

ideas have you come up with so far?" The silence spoke for itself. "That's what I thought."

"And what brilliant solutions have occurred to you while you've worn a groove in the deck?" Saeng challenged.

" . . . Nothing."

"I see."

Taking Saeng's comment as a challenge, Gideon again knelt before the lock.

From the left, Tiago sighed and Rolf grunted.

Another sound, possibly a snore, or a cough, or a snough, Gideon thought, emerged from the cell to the right as a prisoner rolled over.

"What do you hope to accomplish there?"

Gideon looked up to discover Saeng had risen to loom over him.

For whatever it was worth, his expression was more curious than combative.

"One second." He turned to the next cell to find Rolf had wakened. "Anyone have something I can use as picks? Something like, I don't know, a wire or tough thread?"

"You said this lock was unpick-able."

"Unpick-able for one person," Gideon corrected Saeng while Tiago and Rolf started going through their pockets, patting their coats, in search of anything that might do the needful. "Last I saw, you have two hands."

"Hands you will have to train," Saeng pointed out. "And Keepers only know how long that will take. And while you're looking for wires or string or the smogging moons, we are heading into the ocean, and away from any possibility of help."

"What makes you think we'll need help?"

"You, given you've asked for two extra hands." Saeng held up his own as he spoke.

Gideon sneered as he turned away with a sotto voce, "*What does she see in you?*"

"What was that? Never mind." Saeng waved off his own question. "But you heard Lekan. Even if we manage the door, we are still outnumbered and outgunned."

"Outnumbered, yes," Gideon agreed. "And, yeah, he's got that dart gun. But no way can twenty-five crewmen fit into one corridor, so no way we'd face them all at once. And while the dart-shooter and crossbows are a worry, a body can only chamber one dart or one bolt at a time. So, if we get this baby unlocked?" He jerked his thumb at the door. "It's just another stealth operation."

"Right. Of course. And how many soldiers are you willing to lose during your little operation?"

"Fine!" Gideon slammed his flat palms against the lock before rising and spinning to face the other man. "It's a crap idea."

"Now at least you're making sense."

"But it's better than sitting on my ass with the view there's no possible course of action."

"Is that so? Because, as I recall, you took exactly that view six years ago when you left Indani."

"I told you, we were *not* going to discuss that."

"And of course, everyone must do whatever Gideon Quinn says." Saeng's lip curled in a snarl. "Gideon Quinn, who'd rather martyr himself for a lie than tell the woman he supposedly loved the truth."

Gideon's fists clenched. "You have no idea what went down at Nasa, why I did what I did."

"Maybe not." Saeng settled into a fighting stance. "But I do know she's stronger than you ever gave her credit for."

"Listen to me, you f—"

"Found something."

Gideon and Saeng, fists at the ready, froze and turned to where Tiago stood next to a perplexed Rolf.

"*What?*" they asked as one.

"I said I found something." And the young man held up a small vial.

"Is that the—?" Gideon began, just before Saeng's fist slammed into his jaw.

Mia entered the *Al-Djinn*'s bridge with Elvis on her shoulder and Dani at her side, barely noticing the buzz of pre-flight chatter as her wide eyes tried to take in everything at once.

This wasn't her first time aboard an airship, having visited the *Errant* several times by now, but the *Al-Djinn*, she'd discovered, was half again as large as the light freighter Rory called home.

And it wasn't only the sheer size of the *Al-Djinn* that had her gaping.

Tariq's vessel was downright posh, with its honey-toned decks and gleaming allusteel fittings, and nary a plasma burn to be seen.

Entering the bridge, which smelled, oddly, of jasmine tea, Mia spied a railed command dais containing a chair and a side table.

"*Presumptuous much?*" Rory murmured as Tariq aimed for the dais.

Despite the derision, Rory seemed to appreciate all those shiny consoles with their gauges and levers, the nooks to right and left—or, no, port and starboard, she reminded herself—containing yet more consoles covered with more gauges and switches.

Forward of the dais, but behind the helm, there was a

narrow cut-out in the deck, circled by another rail. She supposed it was to keep anyone from falling in, but then, why have a hole in the middle of the bridge in the first place?

"That's the nav station," she heard Dani say, and turned to see her nodding towards the very hole Mia had wondered over. "You might have noticed on our way to the 'ship, the bubble under the gondola's nose?"

"Looked like a fancy fishbowl," Mia recalled.

"The fishbowl holds a telescope and navigation table that is projected to the helm, there," she pointed to a flat space between the pilot and copilot's chairs. "It also provides a good lookout from beneath, as the crow's nest—the bubble atop the envelope—gives a view above."

"What's our status?" Tariq asked the pilot, even as one of the crew stepped away from the helm and slid down the ladder into the bubble.

"Jacques reports engines warmed and ready," the woman replied. "And that he hopes you appreciate the minor miracle it took for him to prep and power all six with a scant hour's notice." As she spoke, she moved one long, burnished hand from the main wheel to flip two of the levers.

"I took the liberty of bribing the duty officer," the man in the radio nook announced, pulling his headset off one ear. "For the price of a case of Campbell's Best, Nike Flight has us cleared to launch whenever you give the word."

"Could be worse," Tariq decided, stepping up to the dais and laying a hand on the railing. "The word is given. Deraun," he said to the radio operator, "order the anchor lines released."

"Anchors released, aye," the ivory-haired Deraun replied, flipping the headset back into place, flicking a switch, then echoing the orders.

Moments later, the whole 'ship bobbed, followed by the odd sensation of Mia's feet pressing harder into the deck.

She felt the weight of a hand on her left shoulder, and she looked up to see, even through the shadows of worry, a flicker of excitement on Dani's face.

She grinned at the woman, and was rewarded by a like-minded smile before both she and Dani turned to the massive windows where Nike's airfield was falling away.

And it was the grandest thing Mia had ever seen, with those beams of sunslight slicing through the thickening clouds, the shadows and glitter of Nike's buildings; the silver-green of the Avon River beneath, and the gray-blue mass of the Oracle Ocean beyond.

Her heart gave a slow, heavy turn as, all of a sudden, the world she'd known—a world hemmed in by cobbles and buildings and agricenters and trams—shrank to the size of a patch on a quilt.

"Tariq." The pilot looked back. "Do we have a destination once we reach cruising altitude?"

"Not as such," Tariq said, glancing at Mia, who looked at Elvis, still latched to her shoulder.

"That's on you," she told the draco, ignoring the curious glances of the bridge crew. "Where do we find him?"

Elvis straightened from his hunched position, then launched himself across the bridge, earning several gasps from the crew as he lit at the front of the helm, fitting himself between the equipment panel and the vast, paned window.

Here he ruffled his wings once and then, with obvious deliberation, turned himself to the right, craning his neck towards the ocean.

"What does the draco say?" Tariq asked in a tone that didn't so much discourage mocking, Mia thought, as kill it in its sleep.

The helm appeared to agree, because she contemplated Elvis with care before speaking again. "He seems to be, ah, aiming, south by southwest," she said at last.

"South by southwest it is," Tariq said to the pilot. "And if anyone breathes even a word of this off the *Al-Djinn*, you will not enjoy my response."

"Aye to that," the helm replied, but Mia thought she heard the smile in her voice.

"What's out that way?" Mia asked.

"The ocean," the man at the radio said.

"And from the ocean, there are the Campbell Isles and the Doles," Rory added. "But those would be to the west."

"And Hollywood, if they go southwest," Dani tossed in.

"And Adia if one heads east upon reaching open waters," Tariq concluded. "Which is the direction a boat carrying abducted Nikeans would most likely be headed."

"I hate to be the soggy bottom," Deraun chimed in, "but even if this alleged boat sticks to the Apian approved sea routes, and there's no guarantee she will, there'll be more than a few sailing ships down there."

Mia, already on edge, deflated.

Until Rory gave the radio operator a grin.

"What?" Deraun asked, glaring at the *Errant*'s mechanic.

"It's just that, and I'm not telling tales out of the hive, but I was thinking, given your status in the trade, you lot run dark from time to time?"

Deraun's face closed. "I have no idea what you're—"

"I see your point." Tariq cut Deraun off in a way that made Mia think the radio operator really was a soggy bottom. "Keiko, and I still can't believe I'm saying this, do your best to follow the draco's lead. Virgil," he turned to the starboard nook, where another man stood over a slanted table covered with gauges, as well as a sort of fluid-y screen across which various blobs of light drifted.

"*Liquid-crystal radar,*" Dani whispered in Mia's ear.

"That LC display is the latest out of Tenjin," Rory added, "and right dear."

"And worth every ten-star," Tariq told him, before addressing Virgil. "You will keep an eye out for vessels in the draco's range, and you, Deraun, will report any vessels Virgil spies that are *not* broadcasting their ident codes."

Simultaneous "ayes" followed these orders. Keiko moved some levers and Mia gave a soft *"Whoop"* as the slow ascent shifted to a rapid climb, making her ears feel like something was pushing on them.

She stepped forward to better see the land below, and the river that split it, and the cloud shadows scattered over all, and thought how Gideon was down there, somewhere.

And then she thought how he'd smogging well better be alive, because she had some choice words to share, once they found him.

CHAPTER 24

MIGUEL GRABBED THE LATCH OF THE *YEMAYA*'S HOLD DOOR, steadying the pitcher of water he carried while, behind him, Galen carried the pot of lentils, and Xian three long loaves of bread.

As Miguel wrestled with the bar, Xian and Galen continued to discuss the potential earnings this run would bring.

"—still say Quinn will bring the highest bids," Xian maintained.

"You say that because he took Petris down without drawing blood," Galen told him. "But the bidders will only see a skinny man with attitude. Meki's second take," she decided, shifting her pot. "Young, educated, and gorgeous."

"Maybe," Xian said. "But only if there are enough ristos in the market for luxuries."

"It'll be the blonde aurochs from Stoli," Miguel finally put in his two cubes. "Muscle impresses more than skills or beauty, every time." As he spoke, he hauled open the hatch—and caught the unmistakable sounds of a fight in progress.

Automatically, he looked for the key to the cells, but it wasn't on its hook.

"Lekan used it last," Galen recalled.

"Get him," Miguel said, setting the water down as he drew his shock stick.

She spun for the ladder, lentils flying, while Xian dropped the bread to draw his sword.

Miguel took the ladder in two leaps, landing with a jarring *thud*. He inhaled the usual stench of unwashed bodies and old fish even as he homed in on the source of the tumult.

Gideon Quinn and Saeng Tenjin, going at it like dire wolves.

Miguel strode the rest of the way to their cell. "Break it the smog off," he snapped, rapping the bars with his shock stick.

In the next cell over, Galen's pretty youth and the Stoli aurochs also shouted, trying to reason with the two men.

Neither listened.

As Xian arrived, Quinn shoved Tenjin up against the bulkhead, his body not quite blocking the view of his fists pounding into the smaller man's torso.

"Gideon!" the youth shouted. "Stop! You're going to kill him!"

Miguel had to agree; it wasn't looking good for Tenjin.

And then, without warning, Tenjin raised his right hand to catch the left jab Quinn had just let fly.

Before Quinn could respond, Tenjin pushed the captured fist down, snapping his own left hand into the big fellow's face with a resounding *smack*.

While Tenjin's left hand dropped, his right released Quinn's and shot forward.

Quinn fell back, choking.

Throat strike, Miguel thought.

Now the young man was shouting at Tenjin, but the dark-haired colonel was no more receptive than Quinn.

Focused on his opponent, Tenjin caught Quinn's thrashing

fist and used it to haul him up before delivering a whip-fast double kick to the other man's gut.

When Quinn dropped to his knees, Tenjin swung around behind him, wrapping Quinn's neck in a chokehold while Miguel and Xian watched, unable to intervene.

Quinn's eyes glazed. His fingers clawed at the arm around his throat, then his fists thumped at whatever body parts were in reach, but nothing worked.

If they'd brought the fight even half a meter closer, Miguel might have dropped them with the shocker.

As it was, he could only watch as Saeng Tenjin deliberately, and with an expression of intense satisfaction, choked the life out of Gideon Quinn.

"Get out of the way." Lekan's voice had Miguel jumping to one side as his leader strode up to the door and inserted the Kairos key.

At his side, Galen raised her crossbow and aimed it through the bars.

Inside the cell, Gideon's struggles had gradually weakened, and the youth was the next thing to apoplectic as he watched the tall man's eyes dim, his lips go blue, his features slacken.

Miguel didn't think the *whirr* and *thunk* of the key had ever taken so long, but in time, it ran through the sequence.

Lekan drew his shooter as he pushed the door open. "Back off," the captain ordered, "or Galen will drop you where you stand."

Saeng, still staring at the man hanging from his grip, didn't move.

Lekan's hand raised, and Galen cocked her bow.

At the hollow sound of the arrow knocking, Tenjin's arms dropped.

He stepped away from his victim and watched with the rest as Quinn slumped, then fell face first to the deck.

"You were never good enough for her," Tenjin spat, his voice filled with a dark satisfaction.

"Step away," Lekan snapped, and Tenjin, raising his hands out to his sides, did as he was ordered.

Lekan gestured Miguel forward.

Flicking the shock stick off, he stowed the weapon and entered the cell. Dropping next to Gideon, he sought a pulse, though he knew he wouldn't find one. He met Lekan's gaze and shook his head. "He's dead, Boss."

"No." The youth clutched at the bars. "He can't be gone. He *can't.*" Then he shook, as if waking from some dream, and turned to glare at Tenjin. "Was it worth it?"

"Remove the body," Lekan ordered as he stepped out of the cage.

Galen maintained cover while Xian sheathed his sword and joined Miguel. Together they heaved the body over, then Miguel got hold of the shoulders and Xian took the legs. But as he backed out of the cell, his boot crunched on something and he paused to look.

"Why are you stopping? This guy's smogging heavy," Xian complained.

"Dead weight," Miguel muttered, and continued to back out of the cell.

As soon as they had the body clear, Lekan locked the cage.

"Are we going to dump him?" Xian asked over the *chunk* of the tumblers shooting back into place.

At the question, the Stolichnayan cursed, the kid made a choking sound, and even Tenjin appeared to jolt.

"Not yet," Lekan said. "Still too close to the Colonies. Keep him on ice until we're further out, then we can dispose of the remains."

Miguel grunted in agreement and continued his backwards shuffle to the stairs.

It took a great deal of effort to get the limp body up the steps, and in the end, Galen had to hand Lekan her bow so she could take one of the legs with Xian, but they made it through.

The last thing Miguel heard, as Lekan shut the door behind him, was a deep voice, heavy with Stolichnaya, uttering a single word . . .

"*Murderer.*"

CHAPTER 25

Ishan and Catriona did not find Tiago at A Fine Mess, though when asked, Martin Soong confirmed he'd seen a woman matching Cora's description of Tiago's young lady.

This would have been reassuring if Martin had not also confirmed the young lady in question had left the pub in the company of Rolf Ohmdahl.

With no joy to be found in the pub, Catriona offered the possibility of the Lower Cadbury market, where Tiago often visited patients unable or unwilling to come to the makeshift clinic. This reminded Ishan that one of Tiago's missing patients had been squatting at the market, and so to the market they went.

Once there, he let Catriona lead the way through the semi-enclosed warren. "Most of the locals will be out seeking their suppers," Catriona told him. "But the older folk don't venture out as much."

Ishan merely nodded, following as she swung her way to the market's center, where a steaming kettle hung over a carefully tended communal fire, and a small portion of Nike's displaced gathered over mismatched cups of tea to chat and read old newspapers.

And though they weren't above a bit of gossip with their old mate Catriona, not a one claimed to have seen any signs of Tiago since he'd come asking after George two days prior.

On leaving the market, Ishan glanced at Catriona. "I can take you home," he offered. "And then—" *And then what?* he asked himself. He could think of nowhere else to search, no one to question.

Even as he thought this, a shiver of motion had him turning, his hand on the weapon at his side.

"Oy then," the shiver said as it came to a sort of shuddering halt. "We ain't seen this much company in a bear dog's age as we 'ave this two-day."

"Company?" Ishan turned from the quivering pile of rags to Catriona, who shrugged.

"Folk what don't live 'ere," the mountain explained. "Busy, busy. Inna market. All along'er docks. Comin's and goings all the twenty-eight hours long."

"I see," Ishan said, blinking away tears inspired by the reeking mountain. "Was one of those folks a young man with a medical kit?"

The top of the mountain tilted closer.

Ishan held his breath.

"If you mean Tiago, just say so," it told him. "And sure, we seen 'im not two days past, when he come lookin' for George. But like we said to the tall one and the short one and the draco, George weren't home. Which is why we been out. Figure if Tiago and the tall one and the short one and the draco can be bothered to look for George, mebbe we should too."

George, Ishan thought. *Again.*

But the tall one, the short one, and the draco . . . well, that could mean only one thing.

Gideon Quinn was somehow involved.

"And have you had any luck finding George?" Catriona was asking.

"None. We figger mebbe he was on yon boat."

"Boat?" Ishan asked. "What boat?"

The heap sighed, fluttered some more, and the top of it aimed at Ishan to reveal two watery eyes. "Same one we told them others about, early this morning."

"Them?"

The rags shifted to Catriona. "The man, the woman, the short one, and the draco," it explained. "They was out t'the dock, they was, lookin' around for a body, same as you lot. An' we told them we saw their mate being put on the boat what was moored at the old dock, right? But the boat's gone now. Left afore Nemesis were full up, it did. But after the man, the woman, the short one, an' the draco goes off, we starts thinkin' mebbe George took sail on that boat, too."

"The boat is gone?" Ishan asked, turning to stare at the river.

"Didn't we just say?" The mountain shook all over. "You see any boats out there?"

"No," Ishan said, then met Catriona's gaze. "I have to talk to Quinn."

"Right. Good." She chewed over that for a second. "And Quinn would be?"

"He's a private facilitator."

"And what's that?"

"No one's sure, but since he seems to be facilitating this boat, I mean to find out what he knows." He turned back to his cycle, but Catriona remained where she was. "Are you coming?"

She hitched herself a bit higher on the crutches, looked at the river, then at the walking pile of rags.

"Maybe I'll stay here a spell, keep an eye on things; see if this boat comes back. Probably won't, but—"

"But best be safe," Ishan agreed. "Good thinking, that."

"Aye, well . . . " She shrugged, studied the river. "If it does come back, where will I find you?"

"Look for me at 9 Doyle Street, or the precinct." He climbed back onto his cycle. "And Catriona . . . " He waited for her to meet his gaze. "You did good work today," he said, and meant it. Getting information from the locals would have gone a deal harder if she hadn't been present, smoothing the way.

"Just want to find your boy," she said.

"I know. But still, you did good work." And with that, he started the engine, put the cycle into gear, and rode off to find out what Gideon Quinn was up to, this time, and what it had to do with Tiago.

Dani leaned a shoulder against the railing of Tariq's command dais and let her gaze flow over the quiet activity of the crew before her gaze slid back to the helm, where Elvis stretched to his full length on the forward console, his wings folded close and his tongue flicking.

It had been hours since they'd left the continent behind, and when Dani had led Mia to the port windows to show her the ocean.

At first, the girl had said nothing, but her breath escaped in a soft huff, fogging the glass of the circular port. "It's so big," she'd said at last. "And all those boats."

"Ships," Dani had corrected, looking down at the scatter of shapes moving along the western coast. "Sailing ships, but see," she'd added, pointing out and down. "Most of those are fishers, holding to the coast. The others are merchant or passenger ships, and they're sticking to the buoyed routes."

"You think the ones who took Gideon and Saeng won't stay on the routes?"

"Oh, they'll stay on the routes," Tariq had said, having appeared at Dani's side.

She'd let out her own huff of breath; the man made as much noise as fog.

"Those buoys aren't just for show," Tariq had continued to explain to Mia. "The keepers have radar equipment of their own, and only the keepers know where the sensors are planted. Should any vessels veer off their approved routes and into the marine preserves, it won't be long before they find themselves boarded by rangers."

"And if the crew involved don't have a good explanation for straying, it's impoundment for their boat and the courts for the crew," Dani picked up the narrative.

"Since it's unlikely our quarry are fools," Tariq continued, "they won't risk such a fate. They'll keep to the marked routes, either the Cousteau or Abdelghany Roads," he'd surmised, "given our heading is now south-southeast."

"To Adia," Dani murmured.

"Like you said," Mia had said, looking at Tariq, who hadn't appeared pleased that his assumptions were correct.

But as the hours passed, and they found no sign of the alleged slaver's ship, Dani began to wonder if they were simply on a wild draco chase.

She sighed and turned to see Mia was again peering out the port window while Rory leaned at her side, tapping a beat against his leg, while Tariq was pacing his bridge like a Tendo snow leopard. She assumed this was a habit, as none of the crew appeared discomfited by the tall, thin shadow pacing from station to station, occasionally pausing to read the gauges or tap a brief tattoo on the back of a chair before moving on again.

She had to admit, she hadn't expected this level of professionalism on a shadow trader's vessel.

Even Deraun, whom Dani expected wouldn't be invited to many crew picnics, went about his tasks with a quiet efficiency, maintaining communications with various stations aboard the 'ship and monitoring the external channels for any useful chatter.

On the opposite side of the bridge, Virgil focused on his screens, checking both air and water, watching not only for their target, but for any potential threats.

Not an idle job, as pirates were always a problem—*even for other pirates*, she thought—and then Elvis growled.

Dani turned to see him fluttering up, then dropping, then up again.

"I think—" Keiko began.

"Got something!" Virgil announced, waving one hand with excitement. "Deraun, there's a single vessel making for the Abdelghany Roads." As Dani spun his way, he rattled off the longitude and latitude of the vessel.

"Checking," Deraun replied, adjusting a dial while everyone on the bridge held their collective breath.

Even Elvis remained silent.

"Nothing," Deraun said at last. "No ident beacon sounding anywhere inside Virgil's range." He glanced up, easing the headphone off one ear. "They're running silent."

"That's them," Rory said.

"Or another smuggling vessel," Deraun countered.

"Not according to Elvis."

Everyone looked at the draco, who was again focused on the window, wings folding and unfolding.

Tariq stared at Elvis, then turned to radar. "What's our distance from the mark?"

"Range is three hundred ninety kilometers," Virgil replied. "Mark is making south, southeast at seventy-two knots."

"Keiko?" Tariq angled towards the helm and came up between the pilot and Elvis. "Time to intercept?"

"If they maintain current direction and speed, and we push the engines, we can reach them by fifteen-thirty hours." She glanced back, "The good news is, we'll still be in international waters."

"Why's that good?" Mia asked.

"We'll be breaking fewer laws," Rory told her.

"Oh."

"Continue to pursue the draco's choice," Tariq ordered. "But raise elevation five hundred meters. In case they're watching the skies," he added, glancing at Mia.

"Five hundred meters, aye," Keiko replied, hands shifting to the elevator controls.

"Is that too high to do a jump?" Mia asked.

"Yes, but we'd lower altitude on approach," Dani told her.

"Maybe not," Virgil cut in, and gestured to the edge of his screen while Tariq, followed by Dani, Mia, and Rory, crossed over.

"What is it?" Mia asked, slipping through the adults to peer at the shimmering bit of light at the top of Virgil's screen.

"A storm," Tariq said.

"A big storm," Rory agreed.

"A big storm moving in our direction," Virgil pointed out. "If we stick with our target, and they hold course for Domino, and that front maintains current course and speed . . ."

"All three will collide," Dani said.

"So, it's a kind of race, then," Mia offered.

"A race, aye." Rory ran his hand over his chin. "But who wins?"

"The storm," Tariq said bluntly. "At sea, the storm always wins."

Sameen sat opposite Jinna and Sonja in one of MacGuffin's's booths, polishing flatware while Freya and Ulf installed the benches for a third booth behind her.

While the task of cleaning forks was far from stimulating, Sameen understood it fulfilled the dual requirements of getting the tea shop prepared for opening and keeping Jinna and Sonja occupied.

As a woman accustomed to waiting for her beloved to return home, Sameen had a deep appreciation for mindless labor, and in fact possessed a set of scrupulously polished copper pots, thanks to Tariq's exploits.

Her eyes rose to where Sonja attacked some tarnish on an old spoon as if it were a Coalition battalion come to burn out Nike.

And right alongside Sonja's palpable distress, Jinna sat, her soft cloth slowly buffing a knife, her eyes taking on an inward cast, their gray depths as shadowed as the clouds gathering outside.

"I wish we could contact them," Jinna said.

Sameen looked at the young woman, now holding a butter knife that looked as if it might have been recovered from a 'shipwreck.

"Even if we could, what would they know, so soon?" Sonja set down her spoon, placing it in a pile of flatware with the same pattern. There were six such piles on the table, one for each of the flatware patterns in Jinna's motley collection.

Motley because, as Jinna explained, MacGuffin's's stock

came primarily from jumble sales, as well as a few of Gideon's clients.

As a result, almost nothing matched, but Jinna had made a theme out of necessity, using a hodgepodge of styles for everything from linens to lighting fixtures.

Sameen found it charming, and was particularly fond of the stools installed along the serving counter, which ranged from utilitarian spinning cushions to sleek Epsilon deco to rough-and-ready Fordian barstools.

"It doesn't feel soon," Jinna said, replying to Sonja's comment. "It feels—" But then her breath caught, and her cheek twitched, and she shrugged rather than complete the thought.

Sonja's eyes slid towards the mother-to-be, then over to Sameen, whose own eyebrow arched in acknowledgment.

"How close are you to opening?" Sameen asked, keeping her voice easy.

Jinna huffed out a breath that set a strand of hair, escaped from its braid, to fluttering. "We hoped within the fortnight, but now, well, I suppose it depends on whether I still have a partner."

"Of course you do." Sameen reached over to place her hand over Jinna's, noting as she did the clamminess of the younger woman's skin. "Everything I've heard of Gideon says he's tough, and tenacious, and not to be trifled with. And if your Rolf is anything like his siblings," she said to Sonja, "I can't imagine there's anyone capable of keeping him from getting home. And beyond all that," she added, "the party flying to their rescue is made up of a jumper, two dodgers, a draco, and my husband; and I can promise you both, Tariq is not a man to give up the chase."

"We may have to give up the chase," Tariq announced, rousing Mia from a half-doze.

"What?" she asked, straightening from the command chair into which she'd collapsed earlier and turning to see Tariq was studying the radar display over Virgil's shoulder. "No. *What?*" She scrubbed at her eyes and looked to where Elvis, still at the helm, was peering in the direction of a massive pile of clouds. "Cor!"

"Cor, indeed," Tariq said. "Those clouds are the leading edge of the storm."

"So?" Mia asked.

"So," Dani said, joining Rory at the rail of the dais, "keeping an airship steady in high winds is a challenge. Dropping line or ladder in the middle of heavy weather can also be difficult."

"And by 'difficult,' she means 'suicidal,'" Tariq clarified.

"So we go faster," Mia said. "Catch up with the wasps before they hit hard weather. We can do that, can't we? A great 'ship like this should be able to catch up with some old water-bound boat."

"Spoken like one who has never flown," Tariq observed. "We may be in the air, but we are still moving a great deal of mass, against the wind."

"I can get us a few extra knots," Rory offered. "If you and Jacques are willing to jigger the engines."

"No one is *jiggering* with the *Al-Djinn*'s engines."

Rory waved off Tariq's animosity. "'Tis merely a matter of boosting your crystal with a bit of juice from the liquid aluminium batteries."

"No," Tariq said.

"'Tis hardly a new idea," Rory pressed, undeterred. "The *York* had a hybrid engine system like yours, and many a time the captain found it needful to combine the L/A and crystal leads."

"It's doable," Keiko said, looking back from the helm. "I've flown other dual-powered vessels who used the work-around. It's doable," she repeated, glancing at her captain.

"You'd have to give us that boost fast," Virgil pointed out. "If we don't make speed—well—fast, it won't matter because the storm front is moving towards us at a greater speed than that ship is moving away."

Mia turned to Tariq. "We can always turn around later," she told him. "If you're scared."

"And if I were twelve, that might work," was his crushing reply.

"Pity," Rory said, angling so only Mia could see his wink. "Especially when you think how disappointed Izaldine will be when he learns his Da left Nike's first and only private facilitator to a fate worse than death."

"*Good one,*" Mia whispered.

"I never should have opened that door," was Tariq's response, but, before Mia could despair, he looked at Rory. "Engine access is on deck three. Jacques will meet you there."

"Aye, aye." Rory spun on a heel and raced off the bridge.

As Tariq made for the helm, Dani looked at Mia. "This better work," she said.

"It will," Mia determined, as the airship shuddered in the rising winds. "It has to."

CHAPTER 26

"Found something."

Several minutes before Miguel unlocked the hatch to discover two men fighting to the death, Gideon, ready to throw hands, swung to face Tiago.

"What?" he asked, at the same time as Saeng.

"I said I found something."

Gideon took a step towards Tiago to see him holding up a vial that, okay, looked familiar. "Is that—?" he began, then his head snapped left with Saeng's punch.

"Wait!" he held up both his hands in surrender. "Not fighting! See? No more punching."

Saeng, mid-swing, froze, looked at his hands, then shook his head and straightened. "Sorry."

Gideon worked his jaw. "Really?"

Saeng's lips twitched. "A little."

"Umm," Tiago said.

"Right." Gideon gave himself a full-body shake, hoping to disperse the adrenaline some, before striding over to where Tiago stood on the other side of the bars.

Once there, he jerked his chin at the young man's hand. "Let's see."

Tiago held up a flask, which was about the length and width of Gideon's thumb.

Inside the wax-sealed vial was a purplish liquid.

Which was when Gideon remembered, this was the same vial Tiago had shown him at the grieving for Vittorio Vin-Cielo, when he first asked Gideon to search for some missing patients.

Gideon looked up and met the youth's dark gaze. "Oh come, bitter conduct,'" he said, reaching for the bottle.

SAENG STOOD SILENTLY AT THE DOOR OF HIS CELL WHILE the previously drugged prisoners stirred towards wakefulness.

As for the non-drugged prisoners, not a one had uttered a sound since Rolf's bitter accusation of murder, now several minutes past.

During those minutes, Saeng had directed his breath back into a meditative pattern—to conserve energy, yes, but also to clear his mind.

In . . .

Out . . .

In . . .

Out . . .

In . . .

"I think they've gone," Tiago whispered.

Out.

Saeng turned to Tiago and Rolf. "I think you're right."

"Did it work?" Rolf asked, suspicion vibrating from his massive frame. "Or did you really—"

"It was not me," Saeng assured the young giant. "I *know* when I'm crushing a larynx."

"I imagine you do." Tiago appeared visibly ill.

"So." Rolf turned from one to the other. "Did it work?"

"If it didn't," Tiago said, staring at the deck where Gideon had fallen, "it will be me who murdered him."

"Not you." Saeng shook his head. "And not murder. If anything, it was suicide."

"Wrong quote, wrong scene," Tiago said as Saeng watched him pull the vial out of Gideon's reach."How many times do I have to tell you, this is not Romeo's poison. This is the—"

"The thing that mimics death. Yeah, yeah, I get it."

Then, surprising Saeng and Tiago both, Gideon shot his arm through the bars and snatched the bottle.

"Hey!" Tiago protested.

"What is in that bottle?" Rolf asked.

"A way out," Gideon said, folding the vial in his palm. "How long before they bring the food?" he asked Saeng, stepping away from Tiago's grasping hand.

"Ah." Saeng, blinked and turned to spy various bodies stirring in various cells. "Not long, I'd think." At Gideon's glare, he bared his teeth. "It's not as if I have a pocket watch on me."

"Fine. Great." The taller man started to pace, the same star-shaped path as before, Saeng noticed. "Okay, we're not sure on the timing, but they'll make some noise, right?" He paused and indicated the forward hatch. "We could hear Lekan when he was at the door. So . . . " But before Saeng could reply, Gideon turned again, this time to Tiago. "How long will it take for this stuff to . . . you know . . . do its thing?"

"I suppose it depends on who is directing the play, because, as I have already told you, I have never. Tested. It." Gideon's

lips pulled back in a snarl, and Tiago held his hands up in a calming gesture. "It should only take a few minutes. In theory."

"Five minutes? Ten?"

"If it works, which we don't know if it will," Tiago asserted, "it would be more like two."

"Two would be perfect."

"Perfect?" Tiago echoed.

"For what?" Rolf asked.

Gideon grinned. "For me to die."

And now Saeng spun to face the other man. "What?"

Tiago, feeling as ill as he had during the staged "murder," turned from Saeng's reassurance, just in time to see George stumbling to his feet.

"Hold up," Tiago told the veteran, crossing over to steady him. "Just lean on me and take some deep breaths. There," he soothed as George followed his instructions. "Yes. Like that."

As George's weight fell heavy on his shoulder, Tiago wondered if he could take any comfort in knowing he'd been right about the veteran.

George, at least, had not tried to kill himself.

"Tiago?" George's voice was thick as he focused on the young student. "Why are you here?" he asked, blinking owlishly. "Why am I here?" Then he frowned. "Where *is* here?"

"That is a very long story," Tiago told him.

"But one we hope will have a happy ending," Rolf assured.

Tiago, looking up to see Saeng's worried gaze, was not so sure.

Gideon contemplated the bottle in his hand as Saeng erupted.

"You're insane," Saeng told him. "And when I say that, I mean utterly, smogging, frothing mad."

"Thank you," Gideon replied, his own voice sounding distant in his ears.

"He's right," Tiago added. "It's too risky. We have no data—"

"Yes. I know. It's nuts," Gideon cut in, stalking to the cell door, where he looked towards the ladder. There he paused, opened his left hand and studied the vial, and wondered.

Had Juliet been afraid?

Or had she, in her youthful passion, been so determined to avoid what her people perceived as a sin that death was preferable?

Then he wondered about Dani, and their child, and if, in that darkest of hours, she'd felt the same seductive lure.

Gideon himself had never been overly concerned with sin, but he had, one dark day, been more than ready to die.

"Gideon?"

He glanced back, saw Saeng watching him, visibly concerned.

Saeng, who'd been there for Dani when Gideon had not.

From the forward ladder, they all heard the rattle of the latch working.

His eyes dropped to the vial.

"Listen," Tiago said, his voice sounding panicked. "That potion is an exercise. It's not even an experiment. It was never meant to be—"

Gideon closed his ears, popped the vial's wax seal, and downed the contents in one fast gulp. "Not horrible," he determined. "A little bitter, maybe."

Turning, he spied Tiago, his knuckles white on the bar, uttering a single, "No."

Gideon shook his head, not sure if he was swaying or the ship tossing.

His fingers twitched, and the bottle fell, breaking as it struck the deck.

"No," Saeng echoed Tiago's denial.

"Make it look good," Gideon said, throwing the first punch even as the door above swung open.

The *Yemaya* gave a wild pitch and Saeng clutched at the bars, adjusting his stance as the ship rose again.

"Storm is coming," Rolf said, eyeing the bulkhead as Tiago continued to comfort George.

A scuffle and a cough had Saeng turning to one of the other prisoners, coming back to life, and noted there were others stirring as well.

Stirring, and once more coming to terms with their circumstances.

He wondered how often they'd woken so, before Lekan's crew arrived with loaves and ladles, and the promise of fresh oblivion?

Not this time, he thought, and crossed over to the forward cell, where a woman was coming to life. "Forgive the intrusion," he said as she rolled onto her knees, "but there is something you need to know."

CHAPTER 27

While the *Yemaya* plowed onwards to Domino, Meki stared at the book her father had gifted her.

Usually, the book learning denied her for so long was as much an escape for Meki as fleeing the Adian coliseum.

But today, no matter how she tried, the geography text couldn't distract her from Tiago's shock as he spied her at Rolf's side—right before Xian struck him down in the street.

"Smogging, toxic Earth," she cursed, just as Galen shoved through the door to the berth they shared. "What is it?" she asked as Galen stood in the open door, her own expression blank. "Is something wrong? Don't tell me you drank some of the dosed water."

"No." Galen shook her head. "Nothing like that." She crossed to her bunk, her movements slow and creaky as an old auntie.

"Then what?" Meki asked.

Galen looked up, her eyes dark and unfathomable. "There was a fight," she said at last. "Down below."

"The prisoners?"

"One of them is dead." Galen paused. Swallowed. "It was—

a mess. And I dropped the rations, so I had to help Xian start up another—"

But Meki never heard what Galen helped Xian do because on the word "dead," she was already racing through the door.

She heard Galen calling after her, but didn't answer, didn't stop.

Not until she'd clattered down two more levels did Meki come to a halt, and that only long enough to unlatch the hold door, rattling the Kairos key on its hook as she threw herself down the stairs into the hold, where her eyes darted from cell to cell, down the port side and up the starboard until they landed on . . . "*Tiago.*" His name exploded in a breath.

He turned to face her, then stepped up to the bars. But his eyes no longer warmed, and his words may as well have been acid as he asked, "What are you doing here?"

"I thought you—I heard there was a death."

"There *was* a death."

And though he said it simply, even from where she stood, meters away in the dimly lit hold, she could see the way his throat worked, the way his expression became bleak.

It made her own breath catch, her own heart stutter, and so she crossed the deck before she could think better, to stand before him.

Once there, she tried to meet his gaze, but found herself staring at the line of his jaw, and the pulse, jumping, just beneath it.

"I'm sorry," she said.

"Why?"

With great effort, she shifted her gaze to the man who'd asked the question. *Wex's favor*, she reminded herself, meeting the dark-eyed gaze. "I hate to see unnecessary death," she said.

The colonel's brows arched. "You prefer only the necessary kind?"

A little sound, half laugh, half gasp, escaped from Tiago, and she turned back to face him, making herself look into his eyes as she said, "I tried to keep you out of it. I tried. You just—wouldn't stay away."

"Because if I had stayed away, this would all be so much better?" He gestured to the hold about him, and the cells, in which she now noticed the rest of the cargo had come awake.

Because, she recalled, the food hadn't been delivered.

The sedatives were wearing off.

With a shake of her head, she spun and raced for the ladder where, despite her best intentions, she turned back to discover every one of the prisoners staring at her.

Everyone but Tiago.

"Your rations will be down soon," she said, choking out the words before she raced the rest of the way up the stairs, through the door, and past Xian and Miguel, arriving with the promised rations.

"Oy, there!" Xian warned as he dodged to one side, but she didn't—couldn't—respond.

It was difficult, but she made it to the only room aboard guaranteed to be empty before the first sob escaped.

On the *Yemaya*'s bridge, Lekan held fast to the nav table as another wave slapped the ship, then looked up and over Dagne's shoulder to study the radar, where an ugly blot of light showed the storm towards which they sailed.

He had no doubt the *Yemaya* would weather it. She was a hardy vessel, and besides, the ship's turbines would collect several batteries' worth of power from the wind.

But the storm did mean they'd need to dispose of Quinn's

body closer to Colonial waters than he liked—he wouldn't put his people on deck in a tempest simply to unload a corpse.

And though Lekan didn't object to keeping Quinn aboard until they cleared the weather, many of the crew believed the presence of the dead on a seagoing vessel was bad luck, so he made the decision and stepped over to the radio, his gait rolling with the pitch of the deck.

Giving Dagne a nod, he flipped the toggle and hefted the mic as if he'd been working with such mech his entire life, when in fact he'd only learned how to work the radio after taking the *Yemaya*, scarcely two years ago.

At the rasp of static, he raised the mic to his lips. "Bridge to Miguel, come back."

He counted to five, then to ten, and was about to call out again when the mic clicked in his hand.

"Miguel here, Boss."

"Time to be rid of the dead weight," Lekan told him.

"Me n' Itu have got it." There was an audible huff, then Miguel continued, "You might want to talk to Meki."

"Meki?" Lekan said, then remembered he hadn't pressed the mic button, so he did and asked, "Why?"

"We passed her on our way to deliver the second round of rations." Even through the tinny filter of the radio, Miguel sounded uncomfortable. "She looked unhappy. I think she'd been in the hold, with the cargo."

Smogging toxic Earth, Lekan thought. "I'll speak with her," he said. "You get Quinn off the ship." He returned the mic to its hanger and just remembered to flip the toggle to "off" before turning to Dagne. "I'll be belowdecks."

"Kids, eh?" she said, not bothering to pretend she hadn't heard the conversation.

Since that didn't seem to require a response, Lekan didn't bother with one.

He did give the radar another glance before peering out at the increasing chop of the sea. "Do you want help up here?"

"Nah," she assured. "Me and the Oracle, we have an understanding. She don't sink me, I don't pollute her with my ugly face."

His eyes skimmed over the hunched back, the crooked nose, and the pale birthmark marring the warm brown skin, and felt the near occasion of a smile. "Ring through if you change your mind."

"Aye, aye, Cap'n."

Knowing she wouldn't ring, he started down the ladder, leaving Dagne to deal with one tempest while he sought his daughter to deal with another.

Miguel shut off the radio, hung it on its toggle, and made his way to the galley, where he'd last seen Itu.

Sure enough, the former gladiator was still in the galley, hunched over the pages of the book they'd found in Saeng Tenjin's coat.

"Oy! Itu!" Miguel called. "Time to do the needful."

The big man glanced up, then dipped his head in acknowledgment.

Then he put a small bit of fabric into the book, closed it with care, and slipped it into the inner pocket of his jacket.

With the book tucked away, he picked up his mug and drank down the remains of his tea.

At last he stood, and continued to stand, and then he stood a little more.

Even Miguel, by no means a small man, had to tilt his head up to see Itu's light brown eyes, which, as always, were focused elsewhere.

"Good book?" he asked as he turned back to the passage.

"The writing is a bit rushed, but I like the story," Itu replied, his rumble of a voice thoughtful. "This fellow shows up in Nike out of nowhere, see? And he's mad at some risto over something that happened during the war, but while he's trying to find the man he's mad at, he ends up helping a bunch of strangers, and making friends. I think it's a take on the Redeemed Ruffian trope. Whole thing's rough around the edges, but it fills the time."

"Uh-huh." Miguel, who hadn't been looking for a literary analysis, started up the midship ladder which led to a hatch built into the deck of the topside storage shed. He shoved the hatch open with a hollow *thunk,* then climbed up and into the middle of the shed.

Here, stacks of tarps, nets, racks of boathooks and hand torches were stored alongside the crossbows, swords, and fighting sticks added by Lekan's company.

Making room for Itu, Miguel breathed in the odors of hemp, ocean, the fust of old netting, and the fish those nets had caught. But not, he noted, the odors he usually associated with dead bodies.

Probably couldn't compete with the old fish, Miguel thought, and led the way to where he and Xian had left Quinn, wrapped in a bit of tarp.

He took a moment to grab hold of a weighted net from where it hung on the wall. Quinn may never get his tree in the forest of memory, but the ocean floor had a forest of its own.

As he started forward, the deck jerked beneath him.

To port, a rack of boathooks clacked.

Unnerved by the sound, he pushed past a stack of rowboats to where the tarp that had shrouded the body lay, twisted and tangled . . . and empty of Quinn.

"Bloody hells . . ." The curse slipped out with Miguel's breath, a ghostly fog in the ghost light.

Itu came up alongside him. "Did someone take him already?"

"Without Lekan's permission?" Miguel asked back, staring at the tangled bit of canvas. "No one would do that."

He took another step forward and eyeballed the tarp, as if the missing Quinn would reappear if he waited long enough.

He stomped on a lump of twisted fabric, then, unable to stop himself, crouched to lift the canvas and peer beneath.

Nothing.

Behind him, Itu let out a soft grunt, followed by a sigh.

"I know," Miguel replied, assuming the big man was eager to get back to his book. "I bet it's someone playing silly buggers." He dropped the canvas, hefted the netting, and turned back to where Itu waited. "We'll just take a look around and—" he began, but froze because Itu wasn't standing there anymore.

Itu was, in fact, lying unconscious on the deck, flat out under one of the rowboats stacked nearby.

A scraping sound to Miguel's left had his net-filled fist rising to strike as he turned to face—*smogging, swarming, toxic Earth!*—a towering, ice-eyed Gideon Quinn holding a boathook.

Miguel heard a little sound—half moan, half cry—and realized it came from himself, just before he recalled the net in his hand, and let it fly.

But Miguel was no fisherman, and Quinn shakily jerked to one side so the mass of weighted hemp barely caught him on the shoulder before slumping to the deck in a useless heap.

Quinn took a step forward, then another.

Miguel danced back, and back again, until he came up against a pokey, hard-edged object that rocked under his shoulder blade.

As Quinn took another shambling step, Miguel angled

around to nab whatever was poking his back and found himself in possession of a crossbow.

With his breath coming out in short, sharp gasps, he tried to pull one of the bolts from the attached quiver, but another dragging footstep, and another, had his hands fumbling, and he dropped the bolt with a clatter.

His eyes darted up to see Quinn, almost on him.

He turned to his right to spy one of the ship's cutlasses hanging, ready to hand.

With a snarl, he dropped the bow and grabbed the fresh weapon's hilt.

He didn't know if it was already slick, or the sweat of his hands made it so, but he didn't care. "A man dies once," he said, turning to face Quinn. "He can damned well die again."

Quinn, hearing the words, came to a halt.

His head tilted to study the sword Miguel hefted, then looked at the boathook in his hands.

As Miguel watched, Quinn opened those hands, and the staff dropped, bouncing on the deck.

For a moment—three panicked puffs from Miguel's point of view—they both focused on the staff, which idly rolled along with the pitch of the deck.

Then, as one, their eyes met.

Miguel, now facing an unarmed dead man, liked his chances.

He stepped forward, raising the blade, meaning to finish the job Saeng had started.

But it didn't matter what Miguel meant to do, because Quinn—no longer shambling, and with a glint in his eyes far more deadly than dead—leapt forward.

Before Miguel could respond to the motion, his sword arm was trapped against the wall by Quinn's frigid grip, and his head rang as Quinn's forward momentum slammed him against the bulkhead, so the bright tang of blood swam up to mix with the metallic taste of fear.

His breath wheezed and backed up in his lungs as Quinn's arm pressed against his windpipe.

More out of instinct than design, his right arm jerked, pushed, and tugged against the grip that held it fast. The fingers of his right hand numbed, and the sword fell with a *clang*. He clawed at the arm pressed to his throat, trying to make space for even the smallest trickle of air.

Dimly, he recalled this was how Quinn had died in the first place.

Maybe Quinn did, too, because the pressure eased ever so slightly, and a shadow crossed the blue ice of his eyes.

The not-a-corpse's body shuddered, and Miguel watched with fascination as Quinn's face quivered, and the pallor of death slid a shade closer to that of a living man.

Then the shadow in his eyes faded, and the ice returned, with an added spark of fury that had Miguel sucking as much air as he could.

But rather than press forward, Quinn's arm pulled away and his hands grabbed the lapels of Miguel's coat, hauling him close; so close Miguel could feel the very-much living breath as Quinn growled, "I *hate* this smogging play."

"M-M-Me too?" Miguel scraped out before Quinn, with the strength of fury, or death, or un-death, once again slammed him into the wall, where the quick explosion of pain in his head was followed by a soft and—given the alternatives—welcome darkness.

***

Gideon stood utterly still, holding Miguel by the collar like an oversized rag doll.

For several seconds he remained so, until the weight dragging on his arms had his hands opening, allowing the unconscious man to slide to the deck.

Gideon watched him for a moment, then he took a long, slow breath, and just as slowly released it.

He blinked and focused on his surroundings.

The deck listed wildly, and he stumbled, one hand catching at the nearest object, which he discovered was a boathook hanging on the wall, twin to the one he'd dropped.

The haft was slick with damp, and his fingers caught at a rough spot, where the wood had splintered.

Without thinking, he hauled the boathook down.

Inside his skull, images sparked, thoughts flared.

Elvis, shrieking on high.

Dani's eyes, filling with tears and rage and hurt.

A child that had never been.

Mia, lying pale and still.

Tiago, the bones of his face sharper than the worry in his eyes.

And the other one, the dark-haired enemy.

Flashes, of what was, what could be, what had never been, tumbled one over the other, crowding his thoughts, scraping at emotions bound in a thick sheet of canvas before being rudely woken in this dank place.

But through the flashes, and the sparks, and the flares, there came a single, spear-like thought—or more a *sense*—that there was something he was supposed to do.

He grimaced, gripped the boathook tighter, and again shuddered.

He looked at his hands, the knuckles white, the forearms covered with gooseflesh.

He turned towards the shed's aft door, but that didn't seem right, so he started forward, retracing the route Miguel and Itu had taken minutes before, soon coming upon the open hatch.

He peered through the opening, noted that it led to another, better-lit deck, and frowned.

Something teased at his scattershot memories . . .

A wave crashed against the side of the ship.

Then it struck him, and, with the satisfaction of knowing his purpose, Gideon angled the hook and descended the ladder.

Because at last, he'd remembered what he was supposed to do.

He had to kill Paris.

CHAPTER 28

BY THE TIME ISHAN REACHED DOYLE STREET, THE WINDS were heavy with the scent of rain, so he parked his cycle in the relatively dry alley between 9 and 11 Doyle.

As he came around the front of the shop, he noticed a small deer stepping through the woods of the park across the street, an elderly shopper exiting The Bitter Herb, and two younger folk stepping into Words, Words, Words; Sally's Mech Repairs appeared to be closed.

Ishan turned and entered the foyer of 9 Doyle and a welcoming warmth.

Voices filtered from inside the tea shop so, rather than climbing the stairs to Gideon's office, he turned into MacGuffin's, opening the interior door to the odors of polish and sawdust, and the savory scents of cooking.

A look over the dining area revealed no sign of Gideon, but he did see two out of three of the Ohmdahl triplets, plus their mother.

"Detective Sergeant," Sonja greeted him from the bench she was holding in place with Ulf, while Freya hammered at its base. "This is a surprise." As she spoke, she sent her offspring a look. "I hope you are not seeking my children."

"We have done nothing to earn a visit from the filth," Ulf told her over his sister's clunking hammer. "Lately."

"He is correct," Ishan assured Sonja. "I've had no reports of mischief." He expected she might have been relieved by his statement, but, if anything, the tension around her eyes intensified. "I apologize for causing you worry," he continued, hoping to soothe. "The fact is, I'm looking for—"

"—you've got a hit with that soup," a new voice broke in, drawing his attention to the kitchen arch, through which Jinna Pride and another woman were passing, "but it's the Spice Must Roll cookies that'll win Izaldine's heart."

"Mia's fond of them, too," Jinna said, and though her mouth tipped in a smile, Ishan noted that her eyes were as haunted as Sonja's. "Oh." She came to a halt as she noticed him. "Detective Sergeant."

"Ishan, please," he greeted the little mother with a touch to heart and forehead, honoring the new life she carried before turning to the woman at her side, who would have been tall, he thought, were she not leaning on a pair of crutches.

"This is Sameen, who's a friend of Rory's." Jinna introduced her companion while she worked her way around the counter in time for Ishan to see the mound of her belly moving in a most disturbing fashion.

"Yes. Well. A pleasure," he said, fixing his gaze on Sameen, but she was also watching Jinna.

"Did you need to speak to Gideon?" Jinna asked.

"Have you found Rolf?" Ulf's question barreled over Jinna's.

"Ulf." Sonja shook her head.

"The coppers weren't searching for Rolf," Freya told her brother.

Ishan turned back to Jinna. "Yes," he told her, "I do need to speak to Gideon." He then looked at Sonja, flanked by Ulf on one side and Freya—mallet still in hand—on the other.

And in all their eyes, he saw the fear he understood too well.

"Let me guess," he said, focusing on Sonja. "Rolf is missing?"

Her head dipped in acknowledgment. "Since last night."

Ishan returned his attention to Jinna. "And Gideon is—?"

"Not here," she admitted. "He went out on a case—missing persons," she clarified.

Which should have been a relief, but Ishan could tell there was more.

And he was right.

"Except we got word earlier from Rory and Mia that Gideon may also have been taken and—*Detective!*"

"*Tcha!*" Sonja clucked.

"Here, now," Sameen said.

They were all, he realized, converging on him, and against all reason, Jinna and Sameen appeared taller than the Ohmdahls.

Then he noticed the Ohmdahls, all three, were kneeling in front of him.

But why were they kneeling?

Then he blinked and realized that at some point during Jinna's explanation, his legs had given way, leaving him sitting on the floor.

"I thought he'd know," he said, his voice hollow.

"Know?"

"Where Tiago is." He looked at Sameen, who'd asked the question. "My son. It appears—that is, he seems to be—"

Sonja's head was shaking, and Jinna breathed a soft, "No."

"—missing," he concluded.

Jinna volunteered to make tea.

Detective—no, she corrected herself, *Ishan*—protested that she needn't trouble, but, as she told him, it was not only no trouble, but it was soon to be her business.

Besides, she needed the distraction, so she'd opted to hide in the kitchen while Sameen and Sonja explained to Ishan the rescue mission going forward.

She wondered if he'd believe it.

Not only the bit about Elvis, but that Tariq was nothing more than a freighter captain doing a favor for Rory. After all, Ishan Hama was nobody's fool, and freighter captains willing to swarm off after renegade slavers at the drop of a quarterstar were thin on the ground.

Still, however suspicious Ishan might be, he wanted his son back, possibly enough to let any oddities about the rescue itself slide.

Assuming said rescue was a success.

"Nope," she said, setting cups on a tray, "not going there."

Instead, she measured tea into the pot, poured the boiling water, and assembled her tray. She'd only just lifted it when a wave of pain rose to swamp her, but practice—and a history of handling live explosives—kept the tray steady in her hands. Once the wave passed, she pasted what she hoped was an expression of optimism on her face and headed out to join the others.

"Elvis," Ishan was saying as Jinna entered the room. "The draco."

"Yes," Sameen replied.

He was sitting at the newest booth, the one Freya had only just completed, with Sameen and Sonja opposite, while Ulf and Freya leaned against the counter.

"And your husband has taken his vessel out in search of these missing persons, using Elvis as his guide?"

"Sounds mad, I know," Sameen agreed with her crooked smile. "But if you'd seen the little fellow, I think you'd have been convinced as well."

"No one would need Tariq, or Elvis, or Gideon, if the coppers would call a person missing before eighty-four hours pass," Freya opined darkly.

"Freya," Sonja began.

"No, she's right," Ishan said. "Here, let me help you," he added, rising to take the tray from a noticeably wan Jinna. "She is right," he said again, setting the tray in front of Sonja with the lightest clatter. "It is a foolish rule, a holdover from the bad old days of Earth. But try as we might, the Avonian parliament seems determined to keep it on the rolls."

"Even if the filth—sorry," Sameen said to Ishan. "Even if the police weren't bound by ancient idiocies, there's no certainty they'd have been able to uncover whoever disappeared your sons."

"Gideon seemed to think they were taking people who wouldn't be missed," Jinna said, rubbing her back.

"You should be sitting," Sonja told her.

"No, it's fine, I'm just—"

Then the door opened, and everyone turned eagerly to the front of the shop, only to settle back in disappointment as they saw it was not Tiago or Rolf or Gideon, but rather two women.

One was petite, with close-cropped black hair, dressed with an elegant simplicity that Ishan knew only the wealthy could afford.

The woman at her side was antithetically tall, blonde and

fair, and dressed in a uniform Ishan recognized as belonging to Black Chiral Security.

Seeing that uniform set his teeth on edge as, unlike Gideon's private facilitation—a small enterprise intended to help those in need—Black Chiral was a massive organization that sold themselves to whomever wanted a private police force.

"I'm sorry," Jinna said to the two newcomers as Ishan ranged himself at her side. "We're not open for business yet."

"Oh," the shorter woman said. "No. That is, we didn't come for tea. We came looking for . . . " She glanced at her companion. "What was his name again?"

"Quinn," the blonde said, her eyes cool as they skimmed over the rest of MacGuffin's's occupants. "Gideon Quinn."

"Yes, that's it. Forgive me," the shorter woman said. "But this is all—you see, my nephew's wife gave me this address when she came looking for Saeng, and—"

"You're Saeng's aunt," Jinna declared. "Yuko Tenjin," she added, for the benefit of the others. "Dani mentioned you."

"Yes." Yuko's expression shifted slightly, though Ishan wouldn't call it a smile.

"She didn't mention you," the blonde said to Jinna.

"Skellig," Yuko warned. "Indani said—*hoped*—that if Saeng didn't join her here, Msr. Quinn would be of some use finding him. But I haven't heard from her, or Saeng, since yesterday." She raised her hands in a helpless gesture. "I don't want to send a tel-gram to Saeng's mother until I know more. I don't want to have to send one at all," she added.

"Of course," Jinna began, then she paused and made a soft sound, and Ishan turned to see her expression had gone—odd.

"Umm," she said.

"Oh," Yuko added. "Oh, my."

Ishan, hearing another sound, a wet sound, turned his attention to the puddle forming at Jinna's feet.

"Ah," was Sameen's comment.

"Time to get you to the midwife," Sonja said.

"I don't—" Jinna began, then clutched at Ishan's hand so hard, he felt bones meet. "No way am I getting in a rickshaw," she said between her teeth.

"Skellig?" Yuko asked.

"Not part of the training," the blonde replied.

"Get Tomaz," Jinna said as Ulf, Sonja, and Freya converged.

"Who?" Yuko asked.

"Where?" Sameen added.

"Bookstore. Words, Words, Words."

"You want a bookseller to deliver your baby?" Ishan asked.

"He was a medic in the Corps," Jinna said, then spat out a curse she'd probably learned while in the Corps, herself.

"Freya, find Tomaz," Sonja snapped. "Ulf, we are taking Jinna to her room."

"Yes, Mama," the two said in unison.

Impressed, Ishan watched Freya race for the door while Ulf, without so much as a huff of effort, swept the laboring woman into his arms.

"Woof," was Sameen's opinion. Then she shook herself. "I'll go after Freya, in case this Tomaz needs extra convincing."

She swung towards the door at the same time a yank at his arm brought Ishan's attention back to Jinna.

"Maybe you should be letting go of DS Hama's hand?" Ulf said with a surprising gentleness.

"Oh, but . . . "

"I will be right behind you," Ishan promised.

"Come along, then," Sonja said, leading the way to the foyer.

Ulf, carrying Jinna, followed while Ishan trailed after, passing the confounded Yuko and Skellig on the way.

"We'll clean up," Yuko assured.

"We will?" Skellig asked, but by then the door was closing behind Ishan, so he didn't hear Yuko's response.

Some minutes later, Wex Jihan slipped into Gideon Quinn's office.

He'd meant to come in earlier, while some sort of meeting went forward in the tea shop, but the sudden emergence of two women had him ducking back into the alley.

As he watched, the taller woman held open the door to the bookshop for the one on crutches, then, mere moments later, both emerged in the company of a colorfully dressed man carrying a medical satchel.

Yanking the hood of his coat closer, Wex ventured into the street, walking with the brisk stride of one trying to beat the rain as he passed the trio close enough to hear that Jinna Pride had gone into labor.

He continued to the end of the block, counted to one hundred, and then returned to 9 Doyle. Finding the foyer empty, he slipped past the door to MacGuffin's and up the stairs to Quinn's office, which was fortuitously unlocked.

As soon as he entered, he began to search the place, starting with a desk that had seen far better days, all the while accompanied by the sounds of a new life emerging from the upstairs flat.

Fifteen minutes later, he was forced to admit defeat and eased the office door open. Once certain the path was clear, he slipped down the stairs, pausing midway to confirm there were no witnesses to his presence, before heading out to the street.

Once outside, he turned towards Cornwell, where he passed another man heading up Doyle. There was an air of excitement about the fellow, as if every step he took led to some sort of prize.

On reaching Cornwell, Wex turned to see the man pausing in front of 9 Doyle before straightening his coat and diving in.

Busy place, Wex thought, and continued around the corner.

As Wex slipped down the stairs from Gideon's flat, Sameen swung from MacGuffin's kitchen to view the dining area.

At Freya's newly constructed booth, Yuko sat staring into her tea while Commander Skellig stood, ever vigilant, at its side.

Freya and Ulf were perched on stools at the counter, along with Kinu, one of the two women who ran The Bitter Herb. She and her spouse, Maria, had joined the party a few minutes after seeing Tomaz speed by.

Maria, for her part, was tending the soup Jinna had set to simmering before things got exciting.

Every so often, a blistering curse would drift from above, leading everyone to look up, but when no further sounds emerged, they all returned to whatever form of waiting they'd chosen.

"I didn't think this would take so long," Skellig observed.

"From the level of swearing, I'd say we're close to having a baby," Sameen told her, coming up at her side. "When my son was born, my language became quite creative around crowning."

"I didn't know you had a child," Skellig commented.

"No reason you should," Sameen replied easily.

"No, of course not. Only I can't help thinking you seem familiar," the blonde explained.

Sameen smiled. "I have that kind of face."

Before Skellig could reply, the door opened.

Once again, those anxious for news of loved ones came on point.

And once again, they fell back in disappointment.

"Can we help you?" Sameen took the lead as the man, a striking fellow of middle height, entered.

"Maybe?" He stepped further into the shop and offered a smile that went all the way to his lively brown eyes. "One of my actors told me I could find Gideon Quinn at this address."

"Actors?" Freya echoed.

"Msr Quinn's not here at present," Sameen told him.

"He is on a case," Freya added.

"Would you be wanting to leave him a message?" Ulf asked.

"I suppose I should. My name's Horatio. Horatio Alva. I'm the manager of The Queen's Rogues," he added grandly.

"And is that supposed to mean something to us?" Yuko asked.

"Only if you've a craving for the most scintillating of theatrical experiences," an undaunted Horatio replied.

"Queen's Rogues," Kinu echoed before snapping her fingers. "That's the company Tomaz's beau belongs to."

"Tomaz is one of our biggest fans," Horatio confirmed. "That's how I learned Gideon was here. We're old friends and —" He cut himself off as a fresh burst of cursing echoed down the stairs. "Ahh—"

"Not to be worrying," Ulf assured him.

"That is only Gideon's business partner," Freya added.

That had Horatio's eyebrows shooting up. "What kind of business is he in?"

"The partner in question is in labor," Sameen explained. "You know, having a baby?"

"Oh. Ah. Well." Horatio again looked up. "I suppose I'll just leave her . . . you . . . her, to it, then."

He shuffled backwards, in the direction of the door.

"Did you not wish to leave a message for Gideon?" Freya asked.

"Right! *Right, right, right!*" Horatio came to a halt, then frowned, then patted at his coat until he pulled out a sheet of printed card stock. "Yes!" he exclaimed, waving it like a flag before also drawing out a pen and, coming to the counter, dashed off a note. He capped the pen, waved the card a moment to dry the ink, then held it out to Sameen. "If you'd please give him this," he said, then seemed finally to notice the crutches. "Ah. Sorry."

"No worries," she said as he spun and offered the card to Freya, just as another shriek rang from above.

"You know? I really should go now," Horatio said, eying the ceiling. "It's almost call time, and . . . " Another shout split the air. "Anyway, be sure to pass that note on to Gideon." As he spoke, Horatio backed out of the shop, delivering a final, "And my compliments to the new mother!"

Then he fled.

"Wow," Kinu said as the door swung closed.

"He is like one of those winds that spins over the Allianza plains," Ulf offered.

"This Quinn person has such interesting friends," Skellig noted.

CHAPTER 29

Tiago couldn't stop moving.

He knew he wasn't alone in his concerns; he knew the others were also worried.

Not only Saeng and Rolf, but the other prisoners, who were now awake and fully aware of their situation.

But Tiago imagined everyone else's worries centered on: *What if it didn't work?*

His worries, however, were running on an endless loop of: *Have I killed a man?*

"You have done nothing wrong."

At Saeng's quiet assertion, Tiago came to a halt mid-cell and turned to where the other man stood watching, his hands clasped behind his back.

Nothing in his posture showed unease.

"I gave him that potion."

"No." Saeng's head shook. "He stole that potion from you, and then he took it, without a single thought to the conse-quences."

"But you went along with him," Rolf observed from where

he leaned against the bulkhead next to George. "You did a very good job of playing murderer."

"He left me little choice." Saeng's eyes slid Rolf's way. "He left none of us any choice. It's how he operates. It is how he has *always* operated, but as much as it irritates—and against all reason—how he operates works."

"*Worked*," Tiago corrected. "Past tense." He let his gaze shift to Rolf, then to the hulking figures of the other prisoners, all awake, all waiting for the salvation Saeng had promised them. "We have to face facts. If he were going to wake at all, he would have, by now. If he hasn't, or they've already disposed of him—"

Here he cut himself off.

It was not a pleasant sensation, hoping his friend had died before he drowned.

While Tiago wrestled with his conscience belowdecks, Xian descended the port stairs, nibbling an olive pie left over from the crew dinner.

It was his turn to collect the cargo's meal trays, a task he relished only slightly more than tending the bact tanks, as the hold smelled almost as bad.

Since he didn't want the stench of the hold to ruin the taste of the pie, he popped the last savory bite in his mouth as he reached the deck landing and stepped through the open door to the short corridor.

At the same moment, another figure appeared in the starboard door and, seeing that figure, Xian had cause to be grateful he'd already swallowed that last bit of pastry, or else he'd surely have choked.

As it stood, he still had to quell a rush of bowel-churning

terror before his instincts—and legs—kicked in and he rushed at the other man, drawing his sword as he went.

Saeng wished he could argue with Tiago's dire conclusion.

More, and despite his prior assertions of Quinn's success-to-insanity ratio, he'd been battling similar fears since Miguel and Xian dragged Gideon from the cell.

Now, as Tiago continued to pace, and the other prisoners began to murmur their concerns, he suddenly pictured Indani, alone in Nike and, thinking of her, swore he would forgive every one of Gideon's insane acts, so long as the man survived his latest dance with madness.

Just as that thought sparked, he heard a cry drift down from the upper deck.

The soft sound of distress was immediately followed by a much less soft *crack*, which was in its turn followed by the screech of metal, and the *thunk* of the hold door slamming open. Next came a slithering series of *thuds* which, on looking, he found to be caused by Xian, now sprawled at the foot of the stairs.

Saeng's eyes slid up, past the stunned Xian, to the top of those stairs to find a tall, rangy figure wearing the long coat of the Colonial infantry.

The figure held a short sword in one hand, the Kairos quad-mech key in the other, and a boathook crooked under his arm.

While Rolf and Tiago and half a dozen people he didn't know whooped with joy and slapped one another on the backs, Saeng's lips turned up in a genuine smile. "And all is forgiven."

Meki stood alone, arms wrapped around herself, staring at nothing in the dark of the processing room.

It was the only untouched relic of the *Yemaya*'s former life as a fishing boat.

Unlike the rest of the ship, it hadn't been repurposed, being little more than a vast, empty space, gritty with salt crystals and stinking of catches past.

Meki had taken to coming here when she needed to be alone.

The stench didn't bother her; compared to the business her father had chosen, the life of a free fisher seemed pristine by comparison.

"I will never understand why you come here."

Lekan's voice shoved its way into her thoughts. "It's quiet," she said, giving her face a quick scrub with her shirtsleeve.

"It stinks."

"So did the cages. So does the hold."

"Meki, we've talked about this before."

"No." Shaking her head, she turned to look at her father. "*You've* talked. It is always you talking."

"And when has anyone disagreed with my words?"

"How would they?" Her hand waved at the surrounding ship. "How *could* they? You are the mighty Olalekan, the man who freed them from their chains. If you were to order the crew to make war on the Dole Islands, to hijack a crystal shipment from Stolichnaya, to sail upriver to the Amazons, they would do it, or die trying."

Lekan lifted one shoulder in a shrug. "I can't control their beliefs."

"No, but you *do* control their actions," she countered. "And in the end, how wide is the river between owning a body, and owning a soul?"

"This has nothing to do with—"

"You've convinced an entire crew of former slaves to go into the slave trade!"

"They're not all slaves," he pointed out.

"No, some are pirates." She huffed out a breath that fogged the air before continuing. "I could understand, almost, if you had us hunting in the Coalition, hunting the people who kept us in chains, but you don't."

"No. I don't."

"Because it's easier here? Because no one in the Colonies expects it to happen?"

"Because no one in the Colonies cares it *is* happening." The answer came out in a growl. "Happening every day, to thousands . . . and they . . . don't . . . care."

"We don't know—"

"They did *nothing*!"

She froze.

Her father seldom raised his voice. He seldom needed to.

"They did nothing," he echoed himself.

"I don't understand. Who did nothing?"

Rather than answer, he turned and walked to the door he'd left open. "We're heading into some weather," he said as he reached the sill. "Be ready to report to the bridge if Dagne sounds the alarm."

"She never sounds the alarm," Meki said, but he was already closing the door, leaving her in the quiet, and the dark.

Gideon, with some fumbling, got Lekan's pricey key into the lock of the cell he'd shared with Saeng.

He knew it was sheer luck the key was kept on the hold door —and having found it there reminded him he maybe should have accounted for the locks before he'd swilled down Tiago's Juliet juice.

No doubt Saeng would remind him of that at some point.

But for now, he fumbled the key into place and flipped the toggle that activated the mech that tripped the tumblers that, eventually, opened the swarming door.

As soon as the lock clicked, Saeng pushed the door open. "You're mad," he said. "And thank you."

Gideon met the dark eyes and his memories tripped back to those moments after he'd woken, when he stood over Miguel's concussed body and images shot through his brain.

Elvis, Mia . . . Dani . . . Juliet . . . Mercutio . . .

"Paris."

Saying the name aloud, he hefted the sword, raised the boathook high, and took a step towards Saeng. "Paris dies at the end."

Saeng's amusement flickered.

"I think," Tiago said, "we may have a problem."

Gideon froze, grinned at Tiago. "Nah," he said. "I'm just messing with him." Then he tossed the boathook to Saeng, who caught it in one hand while Gideon retrieved the key and proceeded to unlock Tiago, Rolf, and George's cell.

"Mad," Saeng repeated.

"As an arctic bear in Nasa," Rolf agreed.

"Says the man who tried to grow Chicken Tolstoy," Gideon muttered.

"What?" Tiago asked.

"Rolf can explain later," Gideon said, yanking the unlocked door open. "Here," he passed the key to Tiago, who took it and moved to Lupe's cell.

Meanwhile, Gideon turned to Saeng and Rolf. "Things are still a little muddy," he said, pointing to his head. "I'm pretty sure I took out four of theirs. But it might have been three of theirs and a mop."

"Must be a side effect of the potion," Tiago noted, moving on to the next cage. "If you could describe what you felt, your physical and mental responses, both before, and on waking?"

"Not in this or any other lifetime," Gideon replied.

"But—"

"So, we have anywhere from twenty-one to twenty-three of the enemy remaining." Saeng turned the conversation back on point.

"Yes." Gideon turned from a disappointed Tiago. "About that many."

Xian, still at the foot of the steps, groaned.

"May I?" Rolf asked.

"Be my guest," Gideon said.

Rolf strode past Gideon, crouched down, and waited for the man's eyes to open. "Hello!" he said brightly, then delivered a jab that had Xian's head snapping so hard, it bounced off the deck.

Gideon looked at Saeng. "Ready to check my maths?"

Saeng considered the question, then his lip twitched. "A moment," he said, and angled the boathook, bracing it on the deck.

Before Gideon could ask what he was doing, Saeng's boot came down on the staff, about a third of the way up. When it snapped, he lowered the new end to the deck, kicked again, breaking what remained in half, so now there were two fighting sticks and a hook.

He kept the hook, retrieved the sticks from the deck, and held them up. "Short division," he said to Gideon.

"Show-off," Gideon replied.

Saeng ignored him and held the third stick out to Rolf. "Can you use this?"

"I can," Rolf said. "I can also use these." He held up his hands.

Gideon jerked his chin at George.

Saeng looked at the veteran.

"I can handle it."

Saeng tossed the last stick his way.

George caught it, gave it a testing flip and a couple of swipes.

"You're on protection duty," Gideon pointed the short sword at the veteran. "And don't forget to lock this one up," he continued, giving Xian nudge.

He looked at the other members of his advance team.

Rolf grinned hugely and, at Gideon's gesture, thumped up the stairs.

Saeng offered Tiago a tap to the heart, shifted the hook so he'd have a weapon in each hand, and followed Rolf.

Gideon waited for Saeng to get halfway up before he set foot on the lowest tread, then he looked back to see George and a big kid from one of the other cells dragging Xian into a cage of his own. "Get the rest out," he told Tiago, "but don't follow us up until you get the signal."

"What signal?"

"You'll know it when you hear it," Gideon said, and then he climbed up after the others to find Rolf looming to port and Saeng lurking to starboard.

"What are you waiting for?" Gideon asked, giving the sword he'd stolen a testing flip. It was one of the shorter, thicker blades favored by the Adian military, and he found he liked the weight.

"We thought you'd have a suggestion on which direction to take," Saeng said as Gideon gave the blade another flip, misjudged the timing, and dropped the sword to the deck with a spine-shrinking clatter.

"I meant to do that," Gideon said.

"Plan?" Saeng prompted as Gideon retrieved the sword.

"I figured we'd clear the boat—"

"Ship."

"We clear it, deck by deck, until we get to the bridge."

Saeng waited. "That's it?" he asked when Gideon finished. "That's the entire plan?"

"There may be a few details I haven't worked out yet."

"Forgive my saying, but your plan is looking much like my Chicken Tolstoy."

"Supposing we make it to the bridge," Saeng asked, "what then?"

"Then we turn this boat—"

"Ship."

"Whatever. We get to the bridge, turn this tub around, and head back to Colonial waters."

"Right. Of course. And do you know anything about sailing this *tub*?"

"Don't you?"

"Knowing the specs of a ship isn't the same as having piloted one."

Gideon scratched his chin. "Can't be harder than piloting an airship."

"You crashed that airship."

"I keep telling you people, it wasn't a crash, it was an aggressive landing, and besides that, there's—"

Saeng held up a cautioning hand as footsteps clattered from the port stairwell.

Both men looked at Rolf, who grinned and dashed up the stairs.

A moment later, a soft yelp, followed by a series of meaty thuds, filtered back.

Gideon turned back to Saeng, "As I was saying," he said, again, "there's a lot less to crash into in the middle of an ocean."

"*Keepers preserve us,*" Saeng muttered as another set of footsteps emerged from the starboard ladder.

Both men moved, but Saeng moved faster.

Gideon, a few steps behind, got an impression of a round head and round body, and eyes that became even more round on discovering one of the prisoners blocking his path.

Then Saeng got down to business, shooting the butt of his cannibalized boathook into the man's gut before snapping up to strike the bulbous chin.

Gideon guessed Saeng wanted to make extra-special sure his opponent was out, because he finished by whipping the second stick around for a strike to the temple.

Still holding both sticks, Saeng wrapped his arms as far around the man as they'd go and, grunting with the effort, eased him to the deck.

Gideon watched the process with a bemused expression. "Worried he'll hurt himself with the fall?"

Saeng straightened. "I didn't want to risk the excess noise."

From Rolf's stairwell, a small shriek emerged, bouncing off the bulkheads in a frantic echo.

"I think that airship's flown," Gideon said, then placed a hand to the nearest slice of wall as the boat chose that moment to heave up, then down. "Time to go."

Trusting Saeng to follow, he headed to the port stairwell.

He came up short where Rolf was slamming a fist into the face of a musclebound man with scars on top of his scars.

Gideon studied the crewman, whose head was lolling and eyes glazed, then at Rolf. "If you're done playing?"

Rolf considered the slack figure. "I think we are finished."

The *Yemaya* tipped up as she struck another wave, pitching mightily.

Distantly, they heard a crash of thunder.

"Storm," Saeng observed.

"Woof," Rolf said, his eyes going as glassy as his limp opponent's.

Gideon eyed him warily. "Tell me you're not seasick."

"I am not seasick," he agreed, going a bit green.

The boat heaved again.

"Ah, maybe a little."

"We should move," Saeng suggested, and suiting action to word, slid past Rolf and up the stairs.

"I've heard hitting people cures seasickness," Gideon said, giving Rolf a bracing *thwack* on the back before racing up the steps.

Rolf didn't look convinced, but then the semiconscious sailor chose that moment to groan and Rolf tossed a casual fist into the man's face, sending him the rest of the way to unconsciousness, and beamed. "Ha! It works," he said to Gideon.

"Great," Gideon said, not a little surprised, himself. "Now," he added, gesturing to the stairs, "let's go find you some more anti-nausea medicine."

CHAPTER 30

Down in the hold, Tiago waited with George and the other prisoners.

And waited.

And waited.

Eventually, he looked at George. "I don't think there's going to be a signal."

George scratched his stubbled cheek. "You may be right."

"In that case, maybe we should go? Do you think it's been long enough?"

George raised a shoulder. "No knowing." He thought for a moment. "If they've cleared the road, no reason not to go. If they haven't, might be they could use support. I'd say it's your call, Doc," he said, dipping a chin in the direction of the rest of the escapees. "Can they make it?"

Tiago hesitated; this was the first time anyone had deferred to his authority, and it was unnerving. So unnerving, he nearly put the decision back onto George's shoulders, but at the last, turned to assess the rest of their company.

Most were clear-eyed and eager to move, but two required a

quick administration of pressure to their five-kilometer points before he felt confident in their ability to walk on their own.

"Ready?" George asked.

Tiago positioned himself at the rear; he wanted no one left behind. "As we'll ever be."

"That's the spirit, Doc," George said, and led the way up the stairs.

Gideon, Saeng, and Rolf came to a halt at the top of the stairs connecting the fourth and third decks, where a closed door blocked any further progress.

"What's on the other side?" Rolf asked.

"More doors," Gideon said. "I didn't stop to see the sights."

"You must have stopped somewhere, if only to retrieve your coat," Saeng noted.

Gideon ran his hand over the fabric of his left sleeve, briefly mourned the loss of Lulu. "I guess I did. I wonder where—*the mop*." He snapped his fingers, grinned. "It wasn't a mop, it was a crewman. With long hair. He had my coat. I got it back."

"Yay?" Rolf said.

"Double yay. It means I took out four of theirs."

"Congratulations." Saeng put his hand on the latch, tested. "It's not locked."

Rolf peered over Gideon's head. "Who goes first?"

Gideon held up a fist. "Wanna play Wasp, Keeper, Draco?"

"Seriously?" Saeng asked.

"You got a better idea?"

In answer, Saeng rolled his eyes, opened the door, and stepped through just as another door, midway along the corridor, opened with a puff of steam.

Out of the steam came one of the *Yemaya*'s crewmen, wearing nothing but a towel.

Saeng, wearing a feral grin, attacked.

"So," Rolf said, looking from the flurry of sticks and kicks erupting a few meters away, "who goes second?"

Gideon would have answered, except that's when a towel flew in his face.

"Ack!" He threw the towel at Rolf and dove into the corridor, in time to meet another member of the crew emerging from the showers.

Rolf shrugged, dropped the towel, and waded in to join them.

A deck and a half below the battle, Tiago stood midway up the ladder, holding the shoulders of another escapee, who said his name was Sean, waiting out the bout of illness that had taken the man between one step and the next.

"Sorry, Doc," Sean said. "Came on me all sudden, like."

"Could be the drugs," Tiago told him.

"Like enough. But it's true the boat's rocking is doing me stomach no favors."

As if in agreement, the stairs under their feet rose, tipped, then dropped rather dramatically.

"Ah—"

"No worries, Doc," Sean said. "Naught much left to heave now, anyway."

"I suppose not," Tiago agreed with a glance at the earlier remains. "We should catch up to the others," he said, and the two started toward the door through which the rest of their party had passed several minutes ago.

As Sean pushed open the door, Tiago heard a voice calling his name.

Meki's voice.

"Tiago . . . Wait," she called, and helpless not to, he turned to see her racing up the steps.

"Doc?" Sean, still at the door, looked over his shoulder.

"It's all right," Tiago said. "Tell George I'll follow."

The man didn't move right off, but once Meki was closer—close enough to see she wasn't armed, Tiago suspected—the door swung closed.

As Rolf followed Gideon down a corridor to the next stairwell, another door opened.

As Gideon was closest, he solved the problem in a very Gideon-like fashion, grabbing the emerging enemy by the collar and bashing his head into the door two or three times before tossing the stunned man back into his room and closing the door.

Not as elegant as Saeng, but still efficient.

"Which way now?" Rolf asked Gideon.

"Ahhh—"

"Didn't you come from the top deck?" Saeng asked him, tossing his remaining stick from his left hand to his right—he'd had to abandon the boat hook when it became lodged in one of the crew quarter's doors.

"As I believe I said earlier, things were muddy. What with all that coming back from being dead."

"Mostly dead," Rolf offered.

"Wrong story," Saeng corrected, studying their surroundings. "We want the bridge. Helm," he mused aloud. "That will be aft." He turned to the right.

"No, wait." Gideon held up the sword; still unbloodied, Rolf noted. So far, Gideon's strikes had been with the hilt, or his fists. "Forward. We go forward." He turned to their left.

"The helm will be in an aft tower."

"I know. I mean, I don't *know*, but there's another way," Gideon said, his brows furrowed. "There was a shed."

"Storage unit," Saeng speculated, eyes narrowed in thought. "That would be on the top deck, maybe fifty meters from the tower."

"With the storm, the main deck will likely be less crowded than the tower," Gideon offered.

"So . . . " Rolf looked from one man to the other. "Which way?"

Saeng and Gideon held each other's gazes.

At last, Saeng let out a breath. "Forward."

Gideon gave a short nod, and as one they turned towards the fore of the ship with Saeng leading, Rolf in the center, and Gideon at his seven.

As they passed more rows of doors, one opened to Rolf's right.

Without a thought, he plowed a fist into the emerging face, shoved the slumping figure back, slammed the door, and kept walking.

He heard Gideon's low whistle of appreciation and felt a pleasant warmth.

This was a bad situation, no arguing, but there was also no arguing that here, in this moment, Rolf felt more right in his skin than he had since leaving the Corps.

Tiago faced Meki. "Where's your crew?" he asked. "Unless you mean to recapture all of us on your own."

"I don't want to recapture you," she said, her voice breathless, but firm. "Not any of you."

Tiago checked the ridiculous surge of glee that wanted to erupt at Meki's declaration. "Then what *do* you want?"

"I don't know." Her head gave the tiniest shake. "I only know I don't want you, or anyone else, to suffer. I don't . . . I don't want *this*," she added, slicing her arm at the surrounding ship.

Tiago let out a slow breath. "It's a start." He met her gaze. "Will you help us?"

"You don't know what you're asking." Now she looked away. "He's my father."

"Your father is a—he's a very bad man."

"No." Again she met his gaze. "What he is, is a man who has done bad things."

His hands rose, then fell. "What is the difference?"

Something—regret, pity, perhaps even anger—stirred in her eyes. "I hope you never have to find out."

"Meki—"

"Your friends are waiting." She took another step closer, close enough to place her palm to his cheek, as she had the last time she shared his bed.

Then her hand dropped, like a petal from a dying flower. "I can't help you."

"*Won't* help us," he countered.

"Won't," she agreed, as if too weary to argue the point. "But I won't stop you, either. Go. And . . . Tiago . . . ?"

He'd already turned, and, not wanting her to see what burned in his eyes, he didn't look back as he asked, "What?"

"Nothing. Never mind. Just . . . go."

He didn't respond, but strode through the door to see Sean and the others were no longer visible.

Faced with the barren corridor, he turned back, but the

stairs were also empty, and so he stood, staring at the barren stairwell for some time before he heard footsteps—probably Sean coming back to fetch him—and turned to catch up with his companions.

Saeng followed Rolf and Gideon through the chill, damp shed until Gideon came to a halt.

Easing closer, he saw a giant of a crewman flat out on the deck, his legs and half of his torso sticking out from beneath an upside-down rowboat.

"Your work?" Saeng asked, crouching next to the man.

"Possibly?" Gideon angled his head to peer at the man's face. "He looks kind of familiar."

Saeng shook his head. "How many times did you hit him?"

Now Gideon leaned closer, supposedly to better view the contusions rising on and around the stricken man's forehead. "I don't know, but I think I'd remember doing something like that."

"Should he not be waking?" Rolf asked.

Saeng placed a hand beneath the stubbled jaw. "Pulse is steady," he reported. "His breathing is easy, I don't—"

The giant let out a roar and Saeng sprang to his feet, hefting the fighting stick.

Then he, Gideon, and Rolf all watched as the man sat straight up, smacked his head into the hull of the overhanging boat, and once again fell back to the deck in a stupor.

"That explains a lot," Gideon said.

"Maybe we should move him away from the boat?" Rolf suggested.

"I suppose we should," Gideon admitted.

"Hardly fair to leave him to bash his own brains out," Saeng agreed.

It wasn't easy, even with Rolf assisting, but they soon had the fellow snoozing in a concussion-free zone.

Continuing on, they passed a tangled net on the deck, and a crossbow, its string broken, tilted against the wall of the shed.

"I think there was another guy, here," Gideon said, staring at the crossbow.

"Not anymore," Saeng observed.

All three turned aft, where, even in the dim overheads, they could spy the tipped-over crates and scattered bits of hooks, oars, and other paraphernalia kept in the shed.

"Guess he went that way," Gideon said.

"And likely raised the alarm," Saeng added.

"So we must assume the enemy is waiting on deck, where greater numbers are more advantageous than in corridors below," Rolf added.

Both Saeng and Gideon turned and stared.

"That would be a reasonable assumption," Saeng said after a beat. "We've dealt with eleven, so far. Which leaves fourteen standing."

"Fifteen, since this guy's mobile," Gideon pointed to the broken crossbow. "And Lekan has his shooter. *And* I'd bet we're dealing with at least one crossbow in the lot, assuming they don't mind losing their profits."

All three stood silent for several seconds. Then the deck tossed up, then fell, and a flash of lightning illuminated the shed.

"Did you see that?" Gideon asked the others, looking around.

"Yes." Rolf placed a hand over his stomach. "Weather is getting worse.

"No, not that. I mean, yes that, but—"

"The lightning," Saeng explained to Rolf. "How is it we saw the lightning?"

They all turned their eyes upward, where they found a skylight set in the shed's low roof.

After studying it a moment, Saeng turned his attention to Gideon, whose eyes were alight with a disconcerting sort of glee as he asked, "Anyone else thinking what I'm thinking?"

Saeng let out a sigh. "As much as I hate to admit it, I believe I am."

CHAPTER 31

ON THE EXPOSED DECK OF THE *YEMAYA*, MIGUEL IGNORED the icy spits that proclaimed they'd met the leading edge of the storm.

Dagne had already pulled in the solar sails, so only the turbines powered the ship forward, the twin columns spearing fore and aft, and adding their deep thrum to the crashing waves and gusting winds.

Lightning forked through the sky to the east, followed many seconds later by the rumble of thunder.

"Do we know how many got out of the cells?" Shari, at Miguel's right, checked the draw on her bow as she spoke.

"No idea," Miguel replied. "But orders are to preserve as many as possible. Boss doesn't want to waste the trip."

"Except for Quinn," Shari said, nocking an arrow. She and Daehan were the best shots, and Daehan was posted to starboard.

"Except for Quinn," Miguel agreed, patting the crysto-plas rifle in his hands.

It was the only one aboard, and seldom used, since dead cargo earned no rubiks.

But Quinn, according to Lekan, was no longer cargo.

What he was, was trou—

"Eyes up," Petris, at Miguel's left, announced. The big man held an axe in one hand, and Quinn's fancy baton in the other.

The shed's aft door was opening, and a shadow loomed within.

"Forward hatch it is." Miguel raised the rifle but held his fire. The battery had enough power for two, maybe three shots at best, and he wanted to be sure of his target.

So as the shadow moved through the door, Shari and Daehan loosed their bolts.

Behind the bulk of the rowboat that he used as a shield, Rolf's arms shook with the percussive *thunks* and noted the point of the crossbow bolt that had penetrated the bow . . . at chest height.

"Good aim," he said, to no one in particular.

He waited for three heartbeats, and was not disappointed when another arrow struck, lower than the first.

Then came the sound of a mad *whoop*.

Gideon, he thought, and with an answering roar of his own, shoved the rest of the way out of the door, using the boat as a battering ram to plough through anybody that dared try to stop him.

The moment the two crossbows fired, Gideon was moving across the roof of the shed.

The surge of a timely wave gave him a boost as he let loose a howl and jumped from the roof to land on the starboard deck, where one of the enemy was posted.

The jump, the wave, and the slick footing sent both Gideon and the enemy crewman up against the rail, where Gideon threw an elbow into the man's throat and the hilt of his sword to the temple.

As the man dropped, Gideon turned to find his next target.

***

"Fan out!" Miguel ordered as Shari nocked another bolt. "Look for the others."

A hiss of air moving counter to the wind touched his cheek, and he felt, more than heard, the meaty thunk to his right.

Miguel turned to see Shari dropping her crossbow to clutch at the bolt piercing her shoulder.

***

As soon as his bolt struck the enemy at Miguel's side, Saeng moved.

Still holding the crossbow he'd found on a hook in the shed, he jumped to the port side of the deck, aiming for the nearest body.

Swinging out with the bow as he flew, he felt the concussion of wood to skull all the way up his right arm.

While his first target dropped, he spun to catch an incoming blade in the curve of the crossbow. A quick twist of the bow sent the sword flying overboard, just as the *Yemaya* crested another wave.

Saeng moved with the ship, softening his knees as he brought the bow-entangled crewman close enough to jab two fingers under her jaw.

She fell, and he turned to face the next.

The frigid rain mixed with the warm blood running down the side of Gideon's face as he brought the hilt of Xian's sword to the temple of yet another crewman.

When no one else came at him, he looked around to discover he was momentarily in the clear, but found Rolf was holding off five of Lekan's people with an oar.

With a mad yell, Gideon half-ran, half-slid into one of Rolf's attackers, striking him in the spine with his shoulder.

"Didn't your mama teach you to share?" he asked, kicking the groaning enemy aside and taking a position at Rolf's back.

"Gideon!" Rolf thrust the oar into the belly of another crewman. "Good to see you."

Before Gideon could respond, a body slid across the deck from port, followed by a dripping-haired Saeng, who now had a cutlass along with the broken stick he'd managed to hang onto.

"Now we are all here," Rolf said, "we can have some fun."

"I'd settle for getting to that bridge," Saeng told him. He followed this statement by slapping an incoming sword to one side with the cutlass before using the stick to bash the enemy across the cheek. The crack of wood to bone rivaled the next clap of thunder. "But a little fun wouldn't go amiss," he concluded.

"Keep talking like that, I might forget myself and start to like you," Gideon told Saeng.

"Not to worry," Saeng replied. "I will never like you."

That had Gideon laughing, and then the three soldiers angled, back to back to back, to face the oncoming members of Lekan's crew.

Wind tore at their limbs and rain stung their eyes while, singly or in pairs, the enemy stepped in to attack.

But as Gideon soon discovered, however great their fighting skills, the enemy fought as individuals; likely because they'd been trained for single combat, for the entertainment of the masses.

Fighting as a unit, trusting the ones at your back, was a whole other apiary; so when Rolf's oar missed an incoming blade, Saeng's sword was there to block it.

If Saeng's back was open because he was catching a sword meant for Rolf, Gideon's blade forced the enemy away from Saeng and into the returning arc of Rolf's oar.

And so it went, with the three soldiers fighting as six, and Lekan's people falling back, regrouping, and falling back again.

But they wouldn't be able to keep this up forever.

Arms would eventually tire, and one sword would sneak in, and then another.

Even as he thought this, a wave surged over the deck of the boat—ship—*whatever*, almost sweeping him from his feet.

It was then, as he grabbed Rolf's shoulder for balance, he noted they'd pushed half a deck closer to the bridge tower.

He turned to point this out to Saeng, but he was engaged with Galen, while Rolf bashed at two more crewmen.

Gideon, with no ready targets, scanned the aft deck for signs of archers and found none.

Nor could he find any sign of Lekan.

What was the sneaky bastard planning this time? "No kids to shoot here," he muttered.

"What?" Saeng asked, flipping Galen's weapon out of her hands.

"Nothing," Gideon replied as another wave swept over the deck. "Is it me, or is the weather getting worse?"

"It's not just you," someone said from Gideon's left.

Except Rolf and Saeng were both to his right.

Uh-oh.

Spinning, he raised the cutlass to block the incoming axe, and recognized its wielder.

"Bruiser Two!" he shouted as his blade bit into the axe's haft, halting the blow. "Long time no pound."

"My name . . . is . . . *Petris*," the bruiser ground out between clenched teeth as he brought a slim, silver column around to strike Gideon in the right shoulder.

"Lulu?" Gideon, his right arm numb from the strike, identified his baton, then ducked as the axe swiped over his head with a whistle.

"No, *Petris*," Petris insisted, bringing both axe and baton around to Gideon's left.

"Not you," Gideon yelled, parrying both weapons with the one short blade. "The—smog it, never mind." He held the parry, stomped on Petris's instep, then shot his elbow to the big guy's nose, sending him stumbling back a hitch before he came swinging in with an overhead cut with both weapons that had Gideon diving towards the starboard rail.

He came to his feet only to be slapped back by a wave cresting the bow.

At the same time, the *Yemaya* pitched to port so sharply, he lost both his footing *and* his sword.

The sword was swept across the bow and into the sea while Gideon skidded to a halt on his knees and looked up to see Petris raising his axe.

And suddenly, there was Saeng, sliding between the two men, blocking the killing blow with his sword.

While Gideon struggled to his feet, Saeng grabbed the axe haft, swept it down in an arc, then continued the swooping motion until he slammed the hilt of his sword into Petris's temple, dropping him to the deck.

"Thanks," Gideon said, grabbing Lulu as she fell from Petris's limp fingers.

"Don't mention it," Saeng replied. "Seriously, don't ever mention it."

"Listen—" Gideon began, but stopped as another body appeared from behind Saeng, the serrated, scythe-like weapon she held already slicing down towards Saeng's unprotected back.

Gideon shouldered Saeng to one side as he snatched Petris's fallen axe and threw it with all the skill of a man who'd never thrown an axe in his life.

But luck, or more likely the weather, was with him, because the *Yemaya* heaved up just as he made the throw, so the axe—that would have flown harmlessly past the pale-haired woman—instead slammed haft-first into her forehead, and she, too, thudded to the deck.

Gideon and Saeng stared at the prone, dazed figure.

"Thank you," Saeng said eventually.

Gideon looked up. "I cannot believe that worked."

"The others are here!" Rolf's shout drew both men's attention to where George was leading the rest of the escaped prisoners from the shed in a rush to engage the remaining *Yemaya* crew.

"If you can cover me," Saeng called as they moved to join their party, "I will make for the bridge."

"Or you could cover me," Gideon countered, "and *I* could make for the bridge."

"Again, you *crashed* that airship," Saeng reminded him. "And I'd as soon not—" He froze mid-sentence, staring over Gideon's shoulder, causing Gideon to turn to the top of the shed, where yet another of the enemy forces rose.

Lightning flashed behind the figure, sparking Gideon's memory.

Dark hair, panicked eyes, his hands on a thick throat.

It was the other man from the shed.

The one, Gideon now recalled, that he had come close to killing.

And that man had a crysto-plas rifle aimed at Gideon's chest.

CHAPTER 32

GIDEON HEARD SAENG'S HISSED, "MIGUEL," FELT THE TUG of Saeng's hand pulling him from the line of fire, even as Miguel's finger tightened on the trigger.

But instead of the sick explosion of plasma Gideon expected, there came a loud *hiss-thud* as a slender shape dropped from above to land squarely on Miguel's shoulders, causing the slaver's shot to flare harmlessly over the starboard bow.

With Saeng staring at his side, Gideon watched the prodigious jumper straighten, taking the precaution of kicking Miguel's rifle off the roof before looking at the two men she'd saved.

"Indani?" Saeng sputtered at the same time Gideon said, "Dani?"

Then another figure thudded to the deck, and another to starboard, and another amidship, all armed with shooters and rifles of their own.

From above, a deep hum underscored the rising tempest, and the life-and-death struggles on the *Yemaya*'s deck stuttered to a halt as an airship lowered from the clouds to hover above the contested vessel.

Gideon gaped at the airship, then turned as the whip of a man who'd landed amidship put a burst of plasma into the leg of the nearest sword-bearing crewman.

Over the pained howls, Gideon looked at Dani. "Good timing."

While Tariq and his people worked with the escapees to contain the slaver's crew, Dani muscled the unconscious Miguel from the roof and into the waiting hands of a large red-headed youth and a man in a ragged Corps coat.

As soon as they'd hauled him off to where the rest of the crew was corralled, she detached from her line and hopped to the deck, landing just in time to hear Gideon complaining.

"I don't know if I'm impressed or disappointed," he said to a big fellow, the spitting image of Ulf, but with long hair.

"How so?" the man, who she presumed to be Rolf, asked.

"I don't know." Gideon shrugged and looked over the deck. "Just feels anticlimactic, is all."

"Only you would view a timely rescue as a disappointment," Saeng commented. "I'd say Tiago's potion addled your brain, but, seeing as you started out a few drones shy of a hive . . ."

"Says the man born with a stick up his—"

"Gentlemen," she cut in, "we're on something of a timetable here." Then her thoughts caught up with her hearing and she said, "What potion?"

All three men froze.

"It was his idea," Saeng and Rolf both said, pointing at

Gideon, who cleared his throat and turned his attention to the continued activity on deck.

Dani figured she'd find out everything later, but for now, Saeng was looking at her in a way that made her skin hum.

"You lost your ring," she said, indicating his left hand.

"Your boots are ruined," he pointed out, gesturing to the stiff and muddied blue suede boots.

Their eyes met.

"Some honeymoon," she said.

"I'll make it up to you."

"Wait," Gideon said, and she turned to see him scanning the deck. "Where's—"

"Tiago," Rolf rumbled.

"Lekan," Gideon announced at the same time.

Dani and Saeng both followed their gazes to the aft tower, where the man who'd shot Mia was stepping out of the door to the bridge.

Before him, with a knife at his throat, was a young man, his dark hair whipping in the wind.

In a breath, she had her rifle at her shoulder.

"I wouldn't," Lekan's voice boomed across the deck before his gaze snapped to starboard, where Tariq was moving towards him. "Any of you move in a way I don't like, and the boy dies."

"I'm not a—"

"That might matter," Tariq cut through the denial, his own shooter to hand, "if I cared about the boy."

"And who's that guy?" Gideon asked.

"Tariq," Dani murmured, still sighting on Lekan.

"Maybe you don't care about him," Lekan said to Tariq. "But I imagine each of you cares about your own skins." Saying this, he raised his right hand high enough for everyone on deck to see the crystal-det grenade he held. "I've removed the pin," he announced. "Shoot me now, and everyone on board goes up in a flash of plasma."

***

"Boss?"

"Lekan?"

"What on toxic Earth?"

"I'd say we all value our skins," Gideon called over the crew's exclamations. "Do you value yours?"

"I value my freedom," Lekan said. "And a man does not have to be breathing to be free."

"Great," Gideon murmured as, to port, the *Yemaya* crew shifted uncertainly.

But not a one spoke.

Not until—

"Papa?"

Gideon turned to see a young woman shooting through the door of the shed, followed by the giant who'd been concussing himself on the boat, now looking only slightly dazed.

Tariq gestured to his people, and the *Al-Djinn* crew stood down, allowing the pair to join Dani, Saeng, and Gideon mid-deck.

Gideon saw Tiago jerk at the sight of her, and the blade at his throat jerked too, and a dark line dripped from under the blade.

The woman's breath sobbed out.

"Easy." Gideon snatched her by the arm.

"Keep your bloody Colonial hands off my daughter," Lekan snapped.

"Sure," Gideon replied, waving Lulu. "As soon as you get your crazy Adian hands off my—doctor. *Work with me*," he whispered in the woman's—Meki's—ear. "How about this?" he called to Lekan. "You let the doc go, I let your kid go, you put the pin back in the boomer and we part ways. Everyone lives. Everyone's happy."

"Or," Lekan countered, "you release my daughter and return to your cells. These invaders climb to their airship, and I don't slice the boy's throat." He flashed a glance at Tariq, "But the pin stays out until your airship withdraws."

"I don't see that happening," Gideon said.

Lekan grinned. "I do."

Gideon's eyes narrowed. "And why is that?"

"Because you're not willing to kill my daughter. And *that* one?" He jerked his chin at Tariq, "He's not willing to die for any of you."

"That is true," Tariq said, but his eyes remained fixed on Lekan.

Or, more, Gideon thought, on the grenade in Lekan's hand.

"All right. Fine. You got me." Gideon released Meki. "I'm not going to hurt your kid. But that leaves the pressing question: are *you* going to? Because I can promise you I am not going back to that cell."

"Nor I," Tiago said, his voice clear and strong, his eyes on Meki.

"Nor I!" Saeng called out, before muttering, "*I hope you know what you're doing.*"

"*Almost never,*" he muttered back as Rolf, and then George, and then the entire cadre of escapees declared that they would not return to the hold.

"So you see," Gideon said as he collapsed Lulu and stowed her in his pocket, "there's no going back from here. But you can go forward. You'd be going without us," he indicated the other escapees, "but it's still forward."

Lekan didn't answer.

"Papa?" Meki called. "Please, let him—let *them* go."

"I can't." Lekan's expression softened when he addressed her, and the blade in his hand eased away from Tiago's throat. "I *can't.*"

"Why?"

"Because they have to pay!" Lekan's voice cracked as he responded to his daughter's plea. He let out a shuddering breath and continued, "Because they left us in the cages, and your mother and brother died for it. They *have* to *pay,*" he said again.

"I don't remember that." She frowned, stepped forward again. "I don't remember."

"You were only a little thing when they came," Lekan said, his eyes sliding from his daughter to Saeng, then Gideon. "The Colonials made a strike at Domino, air and infantry swarming the skies, filling the streets. The assault was so swift, the coliseum guards fled without a thought to the fighters locked inside."

As Lekan spoke, his eyes were on Meki, so when the next wave slapped the side of the *Yemaya*, spraying all and sundry, Gideon slid another step closer.

"Those of us in the upper cells were able to watch the invading Colonials as they passed the coliseum," Lekan continued, shaking off the water. "Marching, fighting—dying—often so close, we could see the light fading in their eyes.

"And we called out." He turned his eyes, a dark accusation, in Gideon's direction. "All of us, locked in those cells, abandoned by the Adian guards; we called out to the Colonial soldiers, begging them to free us, promising we'd fight for them —*die* for them—if they would just let us out. But none of them did." His lips twisted in a snarl at the memory. "Instead they marched, and fought, and bled, and died, and we watched; until the Adians shot down one of their airships, and it crashed into the coliseum, where the anterrium cells blew."

Gideon heard Meki let out a soft gasp, but didn't look away from Lekan, who was looking at his daughter.

"Half the gladiators in the coliseum died in that crash," Lekan continued. "Buried under the rubble or frozen by the gas —they died in the cells, because not a single Colonial soldier saw fit to set them loose."

"That's how mother and Okun died?" Meki asked. "They were killed in that battle?"

"It was the anterrium that did it," he told her. "It swept through the cells, frosting everything it touched, including a body's lungs, if they happened to breathe it in. I had you shielded beneath me, and your mother was on the other side of our cell, holding Okun under the cot." Tiago let out a soft hiss as Lekan continued, "We held our breath. They didn't."

For a time, after Lekan's story ended, the only sounds were the slap of waves, the splash of rain, the thrum of the turbines, and the guttural roar of thunder.

Then Gideon broke the silence. "That's a rough story all right," he agreed, "But, as my apprentice would say, 'boo swarming hoo.'"

"Gideon!" Dani snapped.

"Keepers in the apiary," Saeng muttered.

"And now we die," Rolf intoned.

"*What?*" Lekan asked.

Gideon ignored the protests rising behind him, riding his own anger two steps closer to the enemy. "To be clear," he said to the shocked Lekan, "you're pissed at the world because you lost people? Who hasn't?" he demanded. "It was a war. People died."

"Soldiers." Lekan's expression shifted from shock to contempt. "You signed on to bleed."

"Wrong." Gideon's voice flattened. "I signed on to kill the people who killed my friends."

"And these friends? Were they enslaved? Trapped by their own people and left to suffer by an indifferent enemy?"

"No. They were kids. Forgotten by their own people, so when the Adians bombed them to oblivion, I was the only one left to remember Yribe was allergic to strawberries, and Aaya carried a piece of green flannel with her all the time, and Maurian had nightmares about her parents being taken by the same people who put you in a cage."

As he spoke, he took another step forward. "And that's just me. The kid?" Gideon's eyes shot to Tiago, who watched him with a clear, calm gaze. "He lost his father. So did that one." He jerked a chin in Rolf's direction. "Hells, I'd bet hard starbucks there's not a soul on this boat—"

"Ship," he heard Saeng's automatic correction.

"—who hasn't suffered a loss? Maybe big, maybe small, but a loss. No one got out of that war unbloodied. No one."

Lekan shook his head, but the hand holding the grenade lowered.

Gideon's eyes shifted to Tiago before dipping his chin the merest fraction.

Then Gideon thanked the First Landers as Tiago took the cue, his left hand shooting up and his fingers digging into a pressure point on Lekan's arm, causing the knife hand to go lax and the blade to fall with a clatter.

Tiago fell with it, landing on his hands and knees before throwing himself into a stumbling-rolling maneuver that put him well out of Lekan's reach.

All this Gideon noticed in the periphery because, even as Tiago's hand was rising, Gideon was leaping across the scant space between himself and the slaver, spanning the distance in time to catch the grenade Lekan dropped in the half-second between losing the knife and Tiago's escape.

Later, Gideon would wonder if the boomer had fallen by

accident, or if it had been the deliberate act of a man so eaten by hate that he would sacrifice what he had to avenge what he'd lost.

For now, however, he was occupied with the sphere of death slapping into his outstretched hand as he fell flat out on the deck.

Before he even tasted the blood from the tongue he'd bit on landing, he was rising to his knees and pivoting to starboard, winding up to throw the grenade out into the ocean.

Then the *Yemaya* jerked and more spray shot across the deck, and following that spray came Lekan, kicking Gideon in the ribs and then wrapping his trunk of an arm around Gideon's neck.

And though he heard the rush of boots on wood, felt the lessening of pressure as the mass of bodies pulled the slaver off his back, Gideon's eyes were locked on the grenade.

The grenade which, in the midst of Lekan's attack, had fallen, and was now rolling across the deck.

CHAPTER 33

Gideon was counting down as he watched the grenade's progress.

He knew the Corps' standard delay on a boomer was twenty-eight seconds, and twelve of those had passed while multiple hands hauled Lekan off of Gideon.

Three more seconds passed while he struggled to his feet.

In those few seconds, Gideon heard the scuffle around Lekan, a soft sob from Meki, a murmur of reassurance from Tiago.

Dani's voice snapped an order. A blade whistled and clanged—probably Saeng dealing with one of Lekan's diehard loyalists.

Well, they'll be dying hard now, Gideon thought, realizing in that moment that no one else saw the boomer.

Engaged in their own battles, reunions, or rebellions, they had no idea Gideon had lost the grenade.

What was the count, again?

Six . . .

He managed a single, crooked, step.

Five . . .

Another step, reaching out, knowing he'd never make it.

Four . . .

The *Yemaya* lurched over a wave, and then Tariq swept into Gideon's vision, snatched the grenade and, in that same fluid motion, pitched the boomer over the starboard bow.

Gideon looked from Tariq to the storm-tossed ocean, then back to Tariq.

"I never take my eye off the ball," Tariq told him.

"Good thing." Gideon staggered to his side, where both stood and stared at the gray-green chop of the ocean.

"Is it me, or is there a distinct lack of boom?" Gideon asked.

"Not just you."

"Maybe it was a dud?"

"Or Lekan was bluffing," Tariq replied.

Before Gideon could respond, a deep, submarine roar rose from the waters to compete with the nearing thunder.

Seconds later, a massive wave swelled in a circle, rocking the *Yemaya* further.

"So, not a dud," Gideon concluded.

"And not bluffing."

As one, the two men turned to see the rest of the players gaping at the ocean, only now realizing how close they'd come to death.

Together they strode to where Rolf, along with the man Gideon had last seen beating himself senseless on a rowboat, pinned a furious Lekan to the deck.

"Gideon, this is Itu," Rolf said, his left arm lying across Lekan's shoulders like a bar.

Gideon studied the big guy. "How are you feeling?"

"I have a little headache," the man replied, his eyes focused a bit to Gideon's left. "But all in all, happy to be alive."

"I hear you," Gideon said, and glanced to port to see Dani and George holding Galen and Petris at bay.

The other escaped prisoners held the remaining *Yemaya* crew in front of the shed.

He continued to scan the deck and found Tiago and Meki communing in front of the bridge tower.

And Saeng was—

"Smog it!" He spun, gave the ship another scan. "Where's Saeng?"

"Who?" Tariq asked, then his expression cleared. "Right, the husband."

"Who are you again? Never mind. *Saeng!*" Gideon called out, "I swear to Earth, if you've gotten yourself tossed overboard—"

"I'm right here."

Everyone but Lekan turned towards the bridge as the man himself emerged in the company of a short woman with a white birthmark, gray hair, and curved spine, who surveyed the scene before her with a grimace. "Well, ain't this a smogging mess?"

One of Tariq's people led the woman to her crewmates, and Saeng joined Gideon. "You were worried about me," he said.

"I was worried about what Dani would do to me if anything happened to you."

Saeng's lips twitched. "You were worried."

"Whatever," Gideon replied. "Meanwhile, do we have a plan to get this circus home?"

As he spoke, a ladder dropped from above, the rungs clacking as they unfolded, the bottom few striking the deck with a heavy clatter about half a meter from where Gideon and Saeng stood.

Both turned to Tariq, who offered a small shrug.

"Nice," Gideon said. "Okay, let's get the crew locked up. We can leave some loose to release the others once we're in the clear."

"Wait." Saeng raised his stolen sword. "You mean to leave them here? Free?"

"You got a better idea?"

"We drop anchor and radio the nearest authorities."

"And who are the nearest authorities?" Gideon asked, not of Saeng, but Tariq.

"I am aware of one Keeper station in the Sarasa Archipelago, but they wouldn't interfere."

"So, no law to speak of," Gideon summed it up.

"Which means they get away with their crimes," Saeng protested.

"They did just lose their cargo," Tariq pointed out, then frowned. "Which reminds me . . ."

As Gideon and Saeng watched, he turned to Lekan, standing now, but still held fast by Rolf and Itu.

"Pardon me." Tariq pulled Lekan's coat open, confiscated the dart shooter and, after a brief search, the cartridge of spare darts. "I don't suppose you care to say where you found this little toy?" he asked, pocketing the cartridge.

Lekan's glare was his only answer.

"I thought not." Tariq turned to face the others. "Now we can go."

"We'll be leaving them to hunt again," Saeng said to Gideon.

"I know," Gideon told him. "But from where I'm standing, we have two choices. Either we let them go . . . or we don't."

Saeng looked at Gideon, then at Dani, then Itu and, lastly, at Tiago, who had Meki wrapped in his arms.

Only Gideon was close enough to hear the curse that preceded a reluctant, "We go."

"I'm so relieved," Tariq remarked, making Gideon believe he may have met his match in snark.

Rather than dwell on that disturbing possibility, he worked

with George and the rest of the liberated Colonials in herding the *Yemaya* crew, saving Lekan, Itu, and Meki, down to the cells.

It went quickly, as none of the crew put up much fuss.

Once assured the crew was secure, Gideon turned to Rolf. "Give us some space," he said, glancing at Lekan.

"You are sure?"

"The fight's done," Gideon assured. "For now."

At that, Lekan's eyes narrowed, and his lips twitched.

Rolf and Itu stepped away.

Gideon faced Lekan. "So, are you going to continue hunting?"

"Why wouldn't I?" Lekan asked back.

Gideon shook his head. "Is selling people really that lucrative?"

Lekan's fists clenched and Gideon braced for impact, but those fists remained at Lekan's side. "It was never the money. I do what I do to make the Colonials understand what is happening in Adia."

"Right. Sure. Except the Adian slave trade would get more attention if you took people who might be missed. But you didn't do that." He gestured to the last of the escapees, carefully ascending the ladder to the *Al-Djinn*, where crew members waited to pull them in to safety. "You said it yourself. You hunt the invisible people; the homeless, the immigrants, veterans who'd fallen through the cracks. People the system forgot. Which tells me you don't want to spread the news of what's happening in Adia. You just want Colonials to suffer the way you suffered, as many as possible, for as long as possible, until they die. The way your wife and son died."

At that, Lekan smiled, and leaned in to Gideon. "I wanted to kill the people who killed my friends."

"Good one." For a moment, Gideon held Lekan's gaze.

"Since it appears you and I understand each other so well, you won't have any trouble understanding this." He moved closer, speaking so only Lekan could hear. "We're letting you live. Live and take your fine boat—sorry, *ship*—anywhere you like. But— and let's be crystal clear on this 'but'—if you ever dock in Nike again, the *Yemaya* will be shy one captain, and Meki will be an orphan."

They both glanced at the young woman, then locked eyes again.

"I think she deserves better," Gideon said. "Don't you?"

Lekan's answer was a sneer.

Knowing it was the only response he'd get, Gideon turned away to discover most of the prisoners had made their ascent to the *Al-Djinn*.

Dani and Tariq, the two aeronauts still aboard, were both at the ladder, both watching the skies with visible nerves.

Of the escapees, there remained only Rolf, Saeng, Tiago, and himself, and Tiago was still communing with Meki.

"Romeo! Juliet!" Gideon's shout had Tiago turning to see him jerking a thumb at the ladder. "Time to go!"

"Romeo?" Meki echoed Gideon's call.

Tiago shook his head. "I'll explain later."

But when he stepped towards the ladder, her hands slipped from his. He turned to see her looking at her father. "Meki?"

Her head dipped, then she met his gaze. "Tiago," she began.

"No." He shook his head, seeing the farewell in her eyes. "No."

"He needs me," she said, her voice thickening. "My father needs me."

"Tiago!" Gideon's voice boomed across the deck. "We. Have. Got. To. Go!"

Both Tiago and Meki turned to the ladder where Rolf was taking his first, careful steps and Gideon was pointing to the lightning playing over a wall of black clouds.

"He's right," Meki said. "The storm won't wait. You have to leave."

"I—" he began.

"*Tiago!*"

Tiago cursed, and with a pained jerk, he spun and strode to where the others waited.

"You're up," Gideon told him as he neared, pointing to where Dani scrambled lightly in Rolf's ponderous wake.

Tiago, saying nothing, put his hands on the cold rungs.

"You will have to hold tight," Saeng told him.

"I understand."

"Saeng will be right behind you," Gideon said.

"I will?"

"Unless you're up for a round of Wasp, Keeper, Draco."

The snarky byplay sounded so normal, even after so short a time, Tiago felt a choked laugh emerge.

"You gonna be okay?" The query came from Gideon.

"I'll live." But as he spoke, his gaze turned again to Meki.

She was with her father, his arm over her shoulders, both watching their former captives climb to freedom.

Turning, he grasped the rung and, for the first time in his life, climbed a drop ladder to an airship.

In the middle of the ocean.

In high winds.

Later, he would have cause to thank his broken heart for distracting him from the sheer terror of that act.

For now, he simply hurt.

"A hard blow for the boy," Saeng said to Gideon as he watched Tiago climb.

"He's not a boy," Gideon said, and, after a beat, met Saeng's gaze. "He'll be okay."

"If you don't mind," Tariq cut in from where he stood staring to the east, "I'd like to take flight before that lightning gets any closer."

Gideon grimaced, but, with Tariq's aid, anchored the ladder and Saeng began to climb.

The winds were indeed becoming interesting, but this wasn't Saeng's first extraction, and soon enough he reached the open hatch, where the hands of the *Al-Djinn* crew were waiting to pull him aboard to join the other escapees scattered through the jump bay.

Some he saw receiving blankets from a young girl in a rust-colored jacket. Others were being tended by a pleasantly round woman with silver hair and laugh lines in a face the same complexion as Indani's.

Even as he thought of her, she was there.

Like his, her hair—that long, glorious fall of ink—was dripping with rain, and there were shadows under the eyes he'd lost himself in, so many years ago.

"You're late," she said, her brow quirking.

"My apologies for worrying you."

"Who said I was worried?"

He said nothing, only looked at her.

And then she was in his arms, and her lips were on his and—

"Wait!" He pulled away as something flapped past. "Is that a *draco*? That's a draco," he said, turning to his wife's laughing eyes.

"Wait until you hear how that draco saved your life," she told him.

***

Gideon was barely inside the *Al-Djinn* before Elvis descended, landing on one shoulder, then bounding to the other.

"Hey. *Hey*! It's okay." Gideon moved away from the hatch while, with every step, the hissing, fluttering draco gave him what for. "It's okay. I'm okay. I'm sorry."

Elvis gave a poignant croon and commenced nuzzling Gideon's cheek and nibbling his hair. "You're going to make me pay for this for a while, aren't you?"

The little growl, low in the draco's throat, may as well have been a resounding, "*You think?*"

Gideon sighed, then turned to study the new digs.

In moments, he found Tiago crouching next to one of the rescued prisoners.

A rumble from aft had him looking to where Rolf and George were laughing over steaming mugs.

Lupe slipped by Gideon with a mug of her own, and Gideon caught the odor of strong black tea.

Following her path, his eyes came to rest on Dani and Saeng.

They stood together, hands linked, foreheads touching, eyes closed, oblivious of the surrounding bustle.

Watching them, something in Gideon's chest fluttered, sighed, and slipped away.

Before he could fully register the absence, he heard a light thump of boots, followed by the pleased greetings of several voices.

Turning, he spied Tariq striding from the jump door to the

port bulkhead, where he lifted the mic from the radio affixed there.

"Tariq here. All aboard and ready to fly," he snapped as the crew hauled in the ladder. "Get us above the weather and set a course for Nike." A tinny response came from the other end, then Tariq returned the mic to its hook and surveyed the tumult of his jump bay. "Best hang on to something," he announced as his crew locked the jump door in place. "The climb is like to be steep."

A series of "Ayes," "*Yahoos!*" and "*Thank yous!*" exploded throughout the bay.

While they did, Gideon, with Elvis grumbling on his shoulder, crossed the deck, which, yes, tilted quite suddenly, to join Tariq. "Thanks for the save."

"No need to thank me." The captain's fingers brushed Lekan's dart shooter, stuffed into his belt. "I've been paid."

"About that—"

Gideon turned to find Saeng, his arm slung over Dani's shoulders, leaning forward against the thirty-degree angle of the deck.

At his side, Tariq squared off, at ease with the 'ship's ascent. "You have an issue?"

"That shooter belongs in a secure place."

"And I will see it placed in one." Tariq flicked a glance Dani's way.

"I'll explain the situation," she told him.

"Then if you will excuse me, I must return to the bridge. There is food, and more tea in the galley," he called back over his shoulder. "Just ask one of the crew to escort you."

Saeng took a step after Tariq, but Dani's hand on his chest stopped him.

"*Delbar-am,*" he told her, covering her hand with his. "That weapon belongs in military hands."

"That weapon was the price of your rescue," she told him. "Tariq kept up his end of the bargain, and so will I."

Gideon saw Saeng's visible struggle and Dani's firmly set chin.

Then both turned to him.

He held up his hands, palm out. "Don't look at me. I have no hive in this meadow and hey, didn't Tariq say something about food?" With a vague wave, he started aft.

"Quinn . . ."

"Gideon . . ."

But Gideon was already halfway to the mid-deck ladder when he spied a familiar figure, one much smaller than all the others.

"*Mia?*" He changed direction to join her. "I didn't know you were here."

"No reason you should." Her shoulder rose in a patented Mia shrug, but, before he could say anything, she darted around him and up the ladder, slithering past Rory, who was on his way down.

"Oy!" Rory grabbed the rail as Mia dashed past, then turned in time to block Gideon before he could follow her.

Gideon's eyes dropped to the hand Rory had slapped against his chest, then met the younger man's steady brown gaze. "You don't want to be getting in my way."

"Truer words," Rory admitted. "But before you go swarming after the lass, you might take a minute to ken why she's sae stung."

"Say again?"

Rory sighed. "Learn why she's angry."

"Oh," Gideon said, then frowned. "Why *is* she angry?"

"I can't believe you have to ask." Dani's voice rose from behind.

He turned to discover both she and Saeng had arrived.

"Colonel Tenjin," Rory nodded at Saeng. "Good t'see you, again."

"And you, Msr McCabe," Saeng responded.

"You two know each other?" Gideon asked. "No, never mind; one mystery at a time," he grumbled, before focusing on Dani. "Why is she angry?"

Dani's mouth opened, then closed, then opened again. "She's angry because you *left*."

Oh, he thought. "Listen—" he began.

"No." She cut him off. "You listen to me." She stepped up, and up again, until she was close enough to poke him in the chest as she continued. "You have a chance to make a place for yourself. A chance at a family, and *yes*, I *know* that word makes every nerve in your body go off like an air-raid siren, but trust me . . . " And here she poked him again in emphasis. "This is a good thing—if you're willing to stick. But if you're not—if you *can't*—then at least have the decency to do the needful now, and leave before you hurt anyone else."

"You're right."

"Because if you can't make a commitment one way or the—" She stopped, and her eyes narrowed. "What did you say?"

"I said you're right," he repeated himself. "Or I was wrong. Or both."

Her breath huffed out, and she tipped her chin up at the same stubborn angle she'd just displayed for Saeng. "Wrong how?" she asked. "I just want to make sure we agree on where you've erred."

But Gideon shook his head. "Not the time."

She opened her mouth.

"Because it's Mia I should apologize to, first." He managed a smile. "See? I can be taught."

"Maybe." The stubborn tilt eased. A little. "But I think you should give yourself some time, Gideon, to be sure. Whatever choice you make, you have to be certain it's one you can live with, because Mia—all of them waiting on Doyle Street—deserve that certainty." Then she surprised him by pressing her hand to his cheek. "And so do you."

For a moment they stood so, her looking into his eyes as if searching for something.

Whatever she found must have satisfied her, because she dropped her hand and turned to Saeng, who looked at her as if she were a gift he didn't deserve.

Gideon knew exactly how he felt.

As the couple wandered off to commune over whatever couples communed over after near-fatal battles, Gideon turned to where Rory still stood on the ladder above him. "Can I go now?"

He didn't move. "She thought you were dead." The mechanic's brown eyes, usually so lively, were cold and unforgiving.

"Right." Gideon cleared his throat. "So . . . I should give her some space?"

"And then some."

Gideon sighed. "So, maybe I could help Tiago with the others?"

"I think that'd be for the best."

Gideon pivoted, headed back to the hold and assisted Tiago and Liliane—who served as the *Al-Djinn*'s medic—in treating the other escaped prisoners.

And once they'd seen to everyone else, Tiago turned on Gideon, insisting his injuries be treated as well.

"You could use an acupuncture treatment," Tiago added, already swabbing antiseptic over a gash on Gideon's jaw.

"I don't need—oww!"

"To assist with your recovery from the potion," Tiago added.

"We did the same for the prisoners who'd been taking Lekan's drugs the longest."

Both men glanced at the cots filling the hold, all occupied with escaped prisoners, many of whom were now sleeping naturally for the first time in days. "Doesn't seem to be any room," Gideon noted.

"You can come up to the medbay," Liliane offered.

Gideon responded with a noncommittal grunt.

It wasn't that he objected to the practice, but if the treatment put him to sleep, he was pretty sure he'd dream, and after the past few hours, he didn't care to think what dreams may come.

But then he met Tiago's eyes, hollow with loss, and the head-shake of "No" became a nod of "Yes," and Gideon and Tiago—and Elvis—followed Lilian out of the hold and up two decks to the medbay where, and despite his reservations, Gideon was asleep before Tiago inserted the third needle.

CHAPTER 34

GIDEON WOKE TO FIND ELVIS AT HIS SIDE, TIAGO GONE, and a strange sense he'd forgotten something.

He blinked at the foot of the cot and spied his clothes—now clean, mended, and folded.

Since Gideon had been stuck full of needles and wearing those clothes when he'd fallen asleep, he looked at the pile, then peeked under the blanket, then shook his head and grabbed his coat, which his instincts told him was involved with whatever he'd forgotten.

A quick search revealed his baton, collapsed and tucked into an ammo pocket, for which Gideon was grateful.

But finding Lulu didn't settle that forgetful sensation, so he kept searching the coat until he hit the inner pocket holding the envelope Dani had brought; the envelope containing a copy of Nour Tabak's letter.

He'd just began to pull the envelope from the pocket when Liliane bustled in, bearing two steaming mugs.

"Ah, you're up. Best be moving," she prompted, setting one of the mugs on the stand next to Gideon's cot. "We're just now anchoring."

"Right," Gideon said and, with some relief, slid the envelope back into its hiding place. He could think about that later. Or possibly never. "Thanks," he said to Liliane, setting the coat aside and reaching for the briefs.

Since the medic remained, sipping her tea, he sighed, doffed the blanket, and got dressed.

Her lips pursed as he drew on his shirt.

"You don't mind me saying, you look a right mess," she said.

He buttoned the shirt over the assortment of scars. "I've been told the ladies like them."

The snort of a laugh that followed was heartening. "Next time I'm stitching up the captain, I'll remind him of that. Though he only has eyes for Sameen."

Who Sameen was, Gideon was left to wonder, because Liliane was waving at him. "Get on with you then, before that wee slip of a ghost comes haunting the room again."

Gideon, reaching for his boots, froze. "Ghost?"

But Liliane was staring at the cot. "What's wrong with your draco?"

Gideon followed her gaze to where Elvis was standing on the mattress, wings outspread, stepping from foot to foot to foot to foot.

"Ah." Gideon grimaced and looked up. "He needs to use the little draco's room." He shrugged at Liliane's gaping expression. "Got a spare bedpan?"

"Keepers preserve us," she said, but she found a bedpan.

***

By the time Gideon and Elvis reached the cargo bay, the *Al-Djinn* was secure, and the gangplank lowered.

The odor of damp swept in on a gust as he joined Mia, Rolf,

Rory, Saeng, Dani, and a red-bearded fellow, whom Rory introduced as Jacques, the *Al-Djinn*'s mechanic.

While Jacques greeted Gideon with a thick Mooseheadian, "Meetcha," Mia slid behind Rolf and out of Gideon's view.

But he recalled Liliane's comment about the slight ghost and held on to that as he looked at the others. "So, do we have a plan? Or are we going to stand around staring awkwardly at each other for the rest of the night?"

"You are welcome to stand and stare as much as you like, as long as it's not on my 'ship."

Gideon and the rest of the party turned to see Tariq descending the stairs, his black coat billowing behind him.

"Nice entrance," he muttered to Rory.

"I think he practices," Rory muttered back.

"Boss." Jacques moved out of the pack to greet his captain. "Simon got'cher a lorry off the main dock. Says it's ours until sunrise. Gotta be back in its slot by then."

"Give Simon my thanks, and some of the Campbell's Best," Tariq replied.

"You got it." Jacques jerked a thumb over his shoulder. "She's right outside."

Without hesitation, Tariq started for the gangplank.

The rest of the odd party remained still for a second before Mia trotted after the *Al-Djinn*'s enigmatic captain.

Rolf followed Mia, then Rory followed Rolf.

Tiago looked at Gideon, who shrugged, and both stepped up to join Jacques, while Dani and Saeng brought up the rear.

"Are we allowed to ask where we're going?" Gideon looked at Jacques.

"Can't think why not," the mechanic replied, scratching his shrub of a beard. "Boss wants to see his wife."

"Okay, but—"

"It's all right," Dani said from behind. "Sameen told us she'd be waiting at MacGuffin's."

"Gotta say," Jacques told Gideon with a sideways glance, "you're looking a lot less like the walking dead than when you boarded."

"Technically, he is the walking dead," Saeng piped up, offering Gideon a thin smile when he glared over his shoulder.

"No," Tiago snapped, also glaring at Saeng. "He is not. His heart rate and respiration were considerably slowed, but at no time was he ever actually dead."

"Umm," Jacques said.

"Let me explain." And as Tiago launched into a detailed account of the link between an Ancient Earth tragedy, a pharmacology course, and a mad facilitator, Gideon fell back to join Dani and Saeng.

"I still can't believe you took that potion," Dani said as Tiago's explanation filtered back.

"It wasn't that crazy of an idea," Gideon commented.

"Yes, it was," Saeng countered as they stepped out onto the gangplank. "Especially since you drank it before knowing Lekan would leave that quad-mech key where you could easily find it."

"Ever consider just taking the win?" Gideon asked as Saeng, predictably, made a fuss over that one little detail.

"Probably as often as you've considered the consequences of your actions," Saeng replied.

The two men halted midway to the tarmac and turned to glare at one another.

"Anyone not on this lorry in two shakes of a draco's tail is walking!" Jacques called out from where he was already climbing into the driver's seat.

"You heard the man," Dani said, slipping between the two and heading for the rear of the lorry.

Gideon and Saeng held their position a beat longer, then, as one, turned to race after her.

As the lorry rattled out of the airfield, Tiago listened to Rory and Dani describe how Elvis had tracked him to the docks, and thence to the *Yemaya*.

"Hail to the king." Gideon stroked the draco curled half under his coat before the lorry hit a pothole, and the conversation faltered as everyone focused on keeping their seats.

Unfortunately, the silence also allowed Tiago's mind to wander back to Meki, and how they'd first met outside the old market; how he'd woken with her at his side, asleep with her hand over his heart, and how her hands had slipped from his, when she stepped away from him on the *Yemaya*.

My father needs me . . .

"A little help?"

"What?" Tiago blinked and dragged himself to the present, where he realized they'd come to a halt and Rory was working the latch on his side of the lorry's gate. "Oh. Yes. Sorry."

With a yank, he unhooked his latch, and the gate dropped open, slamming against the fender with a resounding *clang*.

Both men jumped to the rain-slick street, then moved away from the bed, making room for the others.

The rain which had followed them from the ocean was falling in mean spits and Mia, from a distance, shouted for everyone "to hurry the smog up," which Jacques followed with, "Who's MacGuffin?"

At which point the door to 9 Doyle opened, and from the column of light spilled Freya and Ulf Ohmdahl.

Behind them came a woman on crutches who Tiago didn't know, but, judging from the ensuing embrace, Tariq did.

Last of all came a harried-looking Ishan Hama, stripped down to his shirtsleeves and sidearm, and flipping a towel over one shoulder.

"Dad?" Tiago's jaw dropped. "What are you doing here?"

And then Ishan was standing before him, his dark eyes glaring through the spitting rain. "You missed our breakfast."

"I . . . That is . . . Something came up?" Tiago offered.

"I assume this something was of vast importance?"

"It—" Tiago began, but that was all he got out, because this was when his father reached out and pulled him in close, thumping his back.

A heartbeat later, Ishan pushed him away again before framing Tiago's face, as he'd done when he was a little boy before saying simply, "It would have killed me to lose you."

"I'm sorry," Tiago said before throwing his arms around Ishan, pulling him close and discovering, as he did, that his heart may not be whole, but at least it was home . . . and his father needed him.

Gideon, with Elvis latched to his pauldron, slipped out of the lorry's bed only to step back against it because the street was crammed with reuniting families.

"What's happening out there?"

At Saeng's question, Gideon peered under the tarp. "Some folks are happy to see each other," he explained. "This may take a while," he added as an unfamiliar voice rose from the sidewalk.

"It appears you've returned to me without a burn, bolt, or bruise," the voice was saying, and Gideon turned to see a dark-haired woman addressing Tariq. "Who are you and what have you done with my partner?"

"I may have a bruise or two," Tariq offered.

"Never mind how he got near to being vaporized by a madman with a plasma grenade," Jacques said as he joined the pair, seemingly oblivious to his captain's glower.

"Ah, that sounds much more like him," the woman affirmed, then laughed as Tariq swept her, crutches and all, into his arms. "Husband," she said, her voice no longer laughing.

"Wife," he murmured, lowering his lips to hers.

Gideon looked away.

"For the love of the First Landers, why are you all standing in the wet?" Sonja Ohmdahl—small, brisk, and efficient as ever —called from the open door.

"Maybe it won't take so long," Gideon called back to Dani and Saeng as, with a cluck here and wave there, the triplets' mother got the milling crowd outside MacGuffin's to mill their way in.

Tariq was first through the doors, his arms now full of his wife.

Mia slipped in after, not once looking at Gideon.

I'll fix it, he promised himself.

You'd better, his self whispered back.

Rory, along with the triplets, followed Mia.

Since a glance at Tiago and Ishan told Gideon they needed a minute or two more, he trailed the big three into 9 Doyle, with Dani and Saeng splashing in behind him.

He came up short in the door of MacGuffin's, finding the dining area as crowded as the outside.

Then Dani's husky laugh filled the air behind him, and Gideon strode further into the morass of humanity to make room for Dani and her husband.

See? I can even think of the word "husband" without choking, he told himself.

Yes, you've clearly grown, his self replied.

"I can hear that sarcasm," he muttered.

"What?"

"Ah." Gideon hitched to a stop in front of Sonja and her threesome. "Nothing. Just, you know, talking to Elvis."

Elvis, who'd been flapping his wings dry, flicked his tongue at the lie.

"You owe your draco many tins of mackerel," Sonja said, beaming at Elvis, who sat back on his haunches, the better to accept her appreciation.

"Has anyone any towels?" Saeng asked as a shifting of bodies towards the shop's front revealed Tiago and Ishan entering, arms slung over each other's shoulders and dripping onto the tile. Then a petite woman, dressed in a rich fabric the color of ripe plums, came out of the kitchen.

"Aunt Yuko?" Saeng said, pushing through the crowds to meet the woman.

"Your wife told me you were to meet her here, yesterday," Yuko said, inclining her head to Dani before her eyes returned to Saeng. "And when the morning brought no news, I had to come." Her hand rose, then dropped. "I had to know."

There was another woman accompanying Yuko, Gideon noted. But where Yuko was petite and willowy, this one was tall and solidly muscled, and the blonde braid she wore contrasted sharply with the jet of her uniform.

"Black Chiral," Dani murmured as Yuko introduced Commander Skellig as the head of Tenjin's security team.

"Nice to meet you," Gideon said to Skellig, then turned away. "About those towels?"

"I wish there were any towels remaining," Sonja called from where she was surrounded by her children. "But we have used them all."

"*All?*" And now Mia appeared at Sonja's side. "We had a good four dozen in the shop, never mind the lot up in the flats."

Which Gideon knew to be true, as the towels had been his payment for facilitating a labor issue on behalf of the weavers of Neith Street.

"Was there a spill?" Rolf asked his mother.

"It'd have to be a pretty big spill," Mia said, and for the first time since he'd seen her on the *Al-Djinn*, looked at Gideon, her eyes worried.

As one, they turned to scan the shop, Gideon counting heads as he did, and found one missing. "Where . . . " he began.

"Where is . . . " Mia said at the same time.

"Where on toxic Earth is Jinna?" Rory demanded, bursting from the kitchen.

"Ah." Sonja turned to Ishan, who wordlessly returned to the lobby door and pulled it open.

In the new silence, a faint, infant wail slid down from above.

"That happened," Tariq's wife said with a grin.

"Huh," Gideon said, and looked at Rory, who was staring at Ishan.

Then the wail increased and Rory took off, weaving through the crowded shop and sliding past Ishan, grasping the doorsill as he made a sharp spin towards the stairs.

Mia turned to follow, but Gideon put a hand on her shoulder, ignoring her draco-like hiss as he looked at Sonja. "Is she—? Are they—?"

"Were there any complications during the delivery?" Tiago asked.

"Everyone is fine," Sonja promised.

"Tomaz, knows his way around a delivery room," Ishan added. "Jinna is well, but tired. And ravenous."

"So we came down to fetch her some dinner," Sonja picked up the narrative, but she was already talking to Gideon's back as, on hearing the first pronouncement of "fine," he'd released

Mia, who'd raced for the door, and by "ravenous" he was on her heels, Elvis taking to wing over his head.

As Gideon swept past he heard Tiago's, "I should—" and Ishan's "Go," and then the quick steps of Tiago following him out of the tea shop.

By the time Gideon, with Tiago at his heels, reached the second floor, the cry had softened to a breathy whine.

By the time he reached the third, it had ceased altogether.

The door to the flat was open, so Gideon followed Elvis to Jinna's bedroom, where he almost walked into Mia, who'd come to a halt just inside, while Rory was already on his knees next to the bed.

Elvis came to rest on the headboard and, from the opposite side of the room, Tomaz looked on. The bookseller-slash-midwife's eyeliner was smudged, but he still managed to appear fashionably smug as he dropped a towel into a full basket at the foot of the bed.

"Gideon, Mia." Jinna, propped up on what Gideon believed to be every pillow in the place, smiled. She was, as Ishan had noted, visibly exhausted, but at the same time her gray eyes shone. "This is Nasila," she said, looking at the babe, who was busily nursing and oblivious to anything but her hunger. "Nasila . . . this is Gideon and Mia—and Elvis," she added at the croon from above. "They're another part of your family."

She looked up again, and this time at Rory, who, after a heartbeat, tore his eyes from the tiny, pinkish-brown Nasila to meet her gaze.

"*Delbar-am,*" he said.

The look the two young people shared had Gideon almost backing out of the room when Nasila unlatched and smacked her heart-shaped lips.

"She's nursing well," Tiago observed from behind Gideon.

"Tiago! Thank the keepers, a real doctor," Tomaz exclaimed.

"Not real, yet," Tiago reminded him.

"More real than me, darling. Here," Tomaz tossed Tiago a bottle before hefting the full basket. "Get the rest of these people de-germed while I get the laundry going and see what's keeping dinner."

"Oh, please," Jinna said, as the big man left. "I could eat a mammoth."

"You'll want fluids too," Tiago told her, already pouring the antiseptic salve over Rory and Mia's out-held hands.

The room took on the ambiance of a eucalyptus grove, but Gideon accepted his share of the lotion and disinfected himself thoroughly before joining Mia on the far side of the bed to get a closer view at the creature bundled in a soft green blanket he knew Jinna could not possibly have knitted.

Eyes of a blue he suspected would lighten to Jinna's gray blinked at the new world around her, and the cap of black hair had already begun to curl.

He didn't think she looked confused, as some said infants did. She appeared to him to know exactly where she was, and what she expected of those around her.

And if, for a heartbeat, his thoughts gave Nasila darker eyes that would become a deep brown, and hair that would grow straight as rain, there was no one to see those thoughts, or to sense the ache when they faded. And once they had, he was able to focus on the tiny face before him, who had Jinna's eyes, and Jinna's lips making a little O, while the cleft in the baby's chin, like the dark hair, must have come from her biological father.

"I wish Liam were here," Rory said, one finger gently touching Nasila's chin, as if his thoughts had followed Gideon's observations. "He wanted this baby so much. He'd have been over the moons."

"I know," Jinna agreed, one hand rising to cover his, so they were all connected, Jinna, Rory, and the baby. "I named her for his mother."

"A grand choice," Rory said, his voice thick. "He loved his mum."

No one said a thing about Liam's father, who was currently doing time in the Barrens, while the grandchild he'd meant to abduct lay safe in her mother's arms.

"I won't ask if anything hurts," Tiago said, crouching next to Rory to study both mother and child, "but does anything feel off? Did Tomaz—"

"He followed all the protocols we learned in the prenatal classes," Jinna told him.

"That's fine then," Tiago said with a smile, but Gideon suspected there would be a detailed exam in both Nasila's and Jinna's immediate futures. "For now, why don't I find you some chamomile tea to go with that dinner?" Tiago rose, laid a hand on first Jinna's, then Nasila's heads. "Blessings to you both." Then he rose and stepped away, sending Gideon a look that said, clear as words, to keep the visit short.

Mia, meanwhile, leaned over the bed, entranced by the baby. "She's wee," she said, glancing at Jinna. "I didn't think she'd be so small."

"I *know*," Jinna agreed, beaming at the scrunched-up face and waving fists.

Rory held his hand out to the baby, and Gideon half expected him to burst when Nasila grasped at his finger.

"Really wee," Mia echoed her earlier statement, then looked at Jinna to ask, "what took up the rest of the space?"

Jinna's brow arched, almost in tandem with the baby's. "Do you really want to know?"

Gideon thought of the towels. "I bet you don't."

Which was when, for the first time since they'd entered the bedroom, Mia appeared to recall she was angry with him.

"I'll go help Tiago with that tea," she said to Jinna before giving the baby one last fascinated study and leaving the room, not once looking in Gideon's direction.

"What was that about?" Jinna asked.

"I messed things up," Gideon admitted, staring at the door.

"He really did," Rory agreed.

"Then you'd better go fix it," Jinna said. Nasila gurgled, but Gideon doubted the infant had any real opinion on the matter.

"You heard the mum; best get to it," Rory chimed in.

Gideon refrained from curling his lip, but he did click for Elvis.

Elvis, eyes fixated on Nasila, didn't budge.

"Seriously?" Gideon said to the draco. "Listen, I'm going to need all the help I can get. I promise, you can obsess over the baby later."

Elvis released a long-suffering croon, then flapped up and over to Gideon."Thanks so much," he said, then offered a last salute to Jinna as he left the room.

Once they'd gone, Jinna turned to Rory, "No one's ever called me 'mum' before." And then, "No one's called me their *delbar-am* before, either."

"You'd best get used to both," he told her, sliding in to deliver one of the kisses he'd waited long and long to deliver.

"Rory?" she asked as he eased back to once again ogle over the baby.

"Mmm?"

"Why are you so wet?"

CHAPTER 35

GIDEON TURNED FIRST FOR THE KITCHEN, WHERE HE found Tiago putting a kettle on for the promised tea.

He gave the student an awkward wave, then checked Mia's bedroom and, failing to find her there, continued into the living room, which was also empty.

Here he paused and considered the possibility of her going to his office, or down to join the party in MacGuffin's.

Then he thought of her mood, walked out of the door, and looked up at the attic hatch, where the pull rope was swinging.

He took hold of the rope's knotted end, but as he did an idea sparked, sending him down the stairs to his office, Elvis clutching the pauldron for dear life.

As he burst through the unlocked door, Elvis debarked in favor of the desk while Gideon continued to the back room, where he grabbed hold of the tool satchel and, after a bit of a search, one of his latest facilitation payments.

As he headed back, Elvis, rather than joining his person, sat up on his haunches, flapped his wings, and hissed. "What?" Gideon asked, but even as he did, looked down and saw that the lower desk drawer, the one with the naked screw, was open.

With a grimace, Gideon added that oddity to his growing list of things to think about later, and headed back up to the third floor.

Once there, he yanked the attic hatch open, stepping aside as the attached ladder unfolded with a wooden creak, then climbed up.

The moment his head emerged under the pitched ceiling, he felt the bite of night air and the damp of rain.

Elvis let out a soft hoot, but remained on Gideon's shoulder while he climbed the rest of the way up to see Mia seated on the dormer bench.

She'd folded her legs under her chin, and was staring out the open window.

She'd pulled her hood up so he couldn't see her face, which Gideon didn't mind because that meant she couldn't see *his* face as he recalled Dani easing Mia's limp figure through that small opening, after she'd been struck by Lekan's dart.

Gideon gave himself a shake and climbed the rest of the way up the ladder. Ducking to avoid the roof beams, he crossed to where she sat, dragging a small barrel he passed along with him, scraping the floor the entire way.

Once he reached the window, he set the satchel on the floor and took a seat on the barrel.

Elvis hopped from Gideon's shoulder to the bench, where Mia reached out a hand to stroke him.

It was the first time she'd moved since Gideon entered the attic. "So," he ventured, "I guess you're not too happy with me."

The nearest shoulder hitched in response.

"Right." He took in a breath of rain and dust, released it, then took another before he heard himself say, "I don't remember my family. My birth family."

Okay, where did that come from? He asked himself.

Just go with it, his self replied.

He went with it. "There are little things," he continued as she remained silent. "Crumbs of memories. The whisper of a woman's voice. The smell of those cinnamon and sugar cookies . . . you know, the soft ones Jinna rolls in balls?"

"The Spice Must Roll cookies," Mia said, still staring out the window. "Jinna makes 'em proper."

"Yeah, she does," Gideon agreed. "I can remember that smell. That, and shadows of people-like shapes, but the truth is, I don't remember much of anything before Martine. She figured the Midasian fever got them, my parents," he continued. "But I'll never be sure, because I can't remember them; but I remember Martine." As he spoke, he also turned to look outside, into the dark and the wet. "Martine, and the rest of the dodgers. Yribe, Viv, Maurian, and Aaya, who was maybe five when an Adian plasma strike took all them."

The bench creaked as Mia shifted.

"That was my second family," he told her. "And when I signed on to the Corps, I wasn't thinking of ever having another. Of ever caring enough to have another. Hells, I didn't think I'd live long enough for it to matter. But I did . . . and I lost them, too."

Now he felt her turn, so he did as well, to see her studying him. "Excepting you didn't lose Dani," she said.

"You're right," he agreed. "I didn't lose her. I pushed her away, as hard and as far as I could. To keep her safe; I told myself I was doing it to keep her safe, and I was." Here he paused, and his eyes slid to the window, and back. "I was trying to protect her, but pushing her away protected me, too."

"How?"

"Because no one could be taken from me if I had no one left to take. Except, it turns out, I lost someone, anyway."

"The baby," Mia said, and at his start explained, "Dani told me. After you ran off. She also said she figured learning about the baby was why you ran off."

"She's smart that way," he murmured. "And being as she is, and I'm not, when she told me what happened with—told me what happened, and I realized I'd left her to face that alone, the only thing I could think to do was to find Saeng. To find him, and to bring him back to her."

"Except you did it alone." Mia's voice shook. "You went out on a job by yourself . . . without me . . . without even *saying*."

"I did," he admitted. "And I was wrong. No question about it. But the thing is, I wasn't thinking right or wrong. I wasn't thinking much at all, because I was afraid."

"No swarming way," she said, jerking upright.

"Terrified," he affirmed, leaning forward so his elbows rested on his knees, hands clasped between as he held her gaze. "Four families," he said, including the one he and Dani might have made. "That's a lot of people to lose in one lifetime. And when I saw that dart hit you? When I saw you fall? I was sure I'd lost another one. So when I went looking for Saeng by myself, I wasn't thinking of leaving my partner out of the job . . . I was thinking of keeping the last family I will ever have from getting hurt."

"But it did hurt," she told him after a beat. "Being left behind hurts."

"Yes." He looked to the window, then back. "I know."

For a moment, they were both silent. "Would you have come back?" she asked at last. "I mean, if you'd found Saeng on your own, and we hadn't had to come after you?"

"If you listen to Saeng, even if we'd gotten control of the *Yemaya*, I'd have crashed it into something and we'd all have drowned."

"If you'd managed it all on your own," she repeated, refusing to be diverted. "Would you have come back?"

"I don't know." It was a risk, but Gideon figured she deserved the truth. "But if I hadn't come back, it would have been the biggest mistake I'd ever made. And I think we both know that's saying something."

Elvis let out a little croon, and Gideon reached over, stroking a finger between the ridges on his head.

"If you . . . " Mia's voice quivered, but she gave herself a shake and swung so her legs dropped over the sides of the seat before she angled to face him. "If you could go back and change things, would you? Would you make it so you didn't send Dani away? So you could have been together and had your baby and all that?"

There was a held breath, during which Gideon revisited the dream of himself, and Dani, and the dark-eyed infant, then the breath released. "Here's the thing," he began, letting himself discover the answer as he spoke, "even if I had told Dani about General Rand, and she somehow managed to keep me out of the Barrens, we can't be sure how things would have turned out with . . . we can't be sure. Maybe she would have been fine, and everything would be crystal and comb. Maybe Dani and I would have had a chance; that's a lot of maybes," he pointed out. "But let's say all those maybes worked out. If I hadn't gone to the Barrens, I never would have met Elvis." A rustle of wings indicated a bit of preening at that. "Add to that, if I hadn't gone to the Barrens, Dani and Saeng wouldn't have pushed the investigation into Odile, so Celia might still be causing trouble. I wouldn't have been in prison, so I wouldn't have needed to come to Nike—and you'd never have saved me from drowning. Probably, you'd still be with Ellison."

She made a face at that, but he saw her following the dance. "And Jinna'd be locked up in Killian Del's house so he could take Nasila. Tiago would still be payin' protection to Wendell, and the Ohmdahl triplets . . . " Here she paused, her brows knitting.

"Would still be causing Ishan no end of paperwork?" he guessed.

She grimaced. "Probably. But what about Dani?" Now Mia hitched up her legs to cross them as she leaned forward. "You and her were, *you know*, and now she and Saeng are, *you know*."

"Yes. I know." Then he leaned forward too. "But—and don't ever tell Saeng I said this—I think that's for the best, too."

Her brows rose so high, they hid under her hair. "Really?"

"Really."

Now her eyes narrowed. "That must've been some potion Tiago gave you."

"You have no idea. And you never will," he added, even as the question formed in her eyes.

She sighed and straightened. "That's what Tiago said you'd say."

"He asked you to have a go?"

"He asked everyone on the *Al-Djinn*."

"Gotta admire his dedication," Gideon said while icy fingers that had nothing to do with the weather danced up his spine. He shook it off and focused on his partner. "So, we still have an airship's worth of people downstairs."

She considered that. "I guess they're kind of our guests."

"Kind of," he agreed. "And we need to deal with them at some point, but first, I thought we should put this up."

As he spoke, he opened the tool satchel, withdrew the gleaming brass plaque he'd retrieved from the spare room, and held it up so she could see the inscription.

GIDEON QUINN & ASSOCIATE

PRIVATE FACILITATION

Rates Negotiable - Inquire Within

Mia eyed the sign and, for the first time since he'd come up, the too-adult face shimmered away to reveal the naked hope of the girl she still was.

Then her brow wrinkled, and she looked outside, then back. "You know it's raining out, right?"

"And you know we just got home from fighting our way off a slaver's ship in the middle of a storm, right?"

"Good point." She reached out, plucked the sign from his fingers, and hopped off the bench.

Elvis flapped up and came to roost on her shoulder and together they headed for the hatch.

Gideon grabbed his satchel and rose to follow, but a breeze gusted through the open window and he spun on his heel and returned to the window to pull it closed, making sure to latch it securely. He turned to see Mia standing half in and half out of the hatch, watching. "Don't want any damp rot in our place," he explained, reminding her of the many warnings she and Jinna had given him over the months.

Her grin flashed bright as sunsrise, then she clambered down the ladder.

And Gideon, thinking of families—and of old letters and open desks—shot one last glance at the locked window, and followed.

EPILOGUE

OVER AN HOUR AFTER GIDEON FOLLOWED MIA INTO THE attic, Commander Skellig waited for the door to her office at Tenjin R&D to close behind a subdued Wex Jihan before turning to the bottle of plum wine on the shelf behind her desk.

Outside, the wind was whipping through the orchard and lightning scythed across the windows, illuminating Skellig's desk as the door to her office opened to reveal a new guest.

She grabbed a second glass.

Her guest looked at the glasses, then at Skellig. "I sense bad news."

"It isn't good," Skellig agreed, setting the glasses down to pour the wine. She allowed herself a moment to enjoy the fruity perfume before continuing. "Jihan searched Quinn's office, but there was no sign of Saeng's copy of the letter."

Her guest took one of the cups. "That may no longer be a problem."

"Oh?"

"There was some talk of a new weapon in enemy hands; it's the kind of thing Special Operations enjoys investigating. We can always count on the military to focus on weapons over people."

Skellig chose not to comment on that.

"Though it would be best to keep an eye on Quinn," her guest added, sipping her wine, "in case he proves to be a problem."

"I'll make arrangements," Skellig said, then glanced at her desk, on which sat the copy of Nour Tabak's letter Skellig had made during Saeng Tenjin's visit, the previous day. "And what about Amaya Hidalgo's husband?" she asked, tapping the fragment of a name on the page.

"What about him? The man is a convicted criminal, a monster in the eyes of his peers. Even if he dared speak of Amaya's research, no one would listen."

Skellig didn't argue. In fact, she said nothing, until her guest huffed out a breath. "I swear, I can *hear* you thinking. What is it?"

"Nothing I haven't already told you." Skellig swirled the wine in her cup. "Only that all this would have been simpler if you'd let me kill Saeng in the first place."

"Simpler, yes," her guest agreed. "But you know how it is." Yuko Tenjin looked out into the rain-swept orchard. "He's family."

Gideon Quinn, Mia, and the gang will return, along with the Errant *crew in* **Fortune's Lost.**

ORPHAN, DODGER, SOLDIER, SPY
A GIDEON QUINN ONE SHOT

Ducati, Midas
Coalition States
June 23, 1440 After Landing

Colonel Gideon Quinn shoved, dodged, and slipped through the thronging Ducati marketplace.

Ahead of him, Sergeant Nbo Mulowa and Corpsman Bert "Walsie" Walsingham also pushed through the crowds.

As he followed his team, Gideon caught the scents of unfamiliar spices and rich, meaty smoke from the food stalls. Passing a textile merchant, the back of his hand brushed up against the nubby silks favored by Midasian ristos and his feet thudded unevenly over the convex pavers Midasians used on their streets.

Voices bartered, argued, and chatted in the Midasian dialect that sounded to Gideon like an offshoot of Colonial Avonian.

In theory, that similarity should have made it easy for the three Colonial soldiers to blend in.

In fact, the difference was so subtle that only Nbo could

grasp it with any consistency. This meant she got to wear the uniform of a Midasian commandant, and do all the talking, while Gideon and Walsie wore the simple black fatigues of the lower ranks and spoke as little as possible.

Between the counterfeit uniforms and Nbo's ease with the vernacular, the trio had easily infiltrated Fort Ducati, not an hour past.

Once in the fort, Nbo and Walsie distracted the duty officers with the ruse of an internal audit.

That left Gideon—falling back on his past as a dodger—to search for the lab where, according to Special Operations, a new and less-likely to explode plasma cannon was under development.

Originally, Gideon had had low expectations for the operation; in his experience, intel from Spec Ops was often more buzz than honey. However, soon after clearing the research wing with warnings of a crystal refiner in a nearby lab going critical, he was surprised to discover the frame of an actual cannon.

Not only the frame, but blueprints, metallurgy samples, and a handful of lenses, all of which fit handily into the map tube he carried.

He was tempted to explore some of the other labs, but it wouldn't be long before the scientists he'd ousted noticed the lack of a catastrophic explosion, so he slipped out of the lab.

He'd just exited the fort's research facility when the first shouts began.

Gideon put on a look of concern and even pointed the emerging security forces towards the labs as he passed.

By the time he rejoined Nbo and Walsie, the entire fort was on high alert. Nbo, who'd been snapping orders at the locals, announced she would order the gates closed and departed with Gideon and Walsie at her heels.

To her credit, Nbo did order the gates closed, but not until after their small company was outside.

Leaving the sentries under the impression she meant to reconnoiter the nearest civilian neighborhood, Nbo led Gideon and Walsie away from the fort and into Ducati's main streets.

By now, Gideon figured they'd put about a kilometer between themselves and the fort.

"I hear eight metros per length of allusteel," an auctioneer called as he passed by. "Eight metros, do I hear twelve? Twelve to the Sister's Bruhl. Planning another of your land yachts, ladies? How about fifteen, fifteen metros..."

The practiced wheedle faded into the rest of the market's tumult while Gideon put all pushed on, trailing Nbo through a wind-tree grove, past a rickshaw repair shop, and thence across a large open space where the traveling merchants penned their animals.

About two stalls later, the sergeant took a sharp left between two stalls.

Gideon followed, moving as casually as he could, passing between the stalls and into a cleft separating two stone and mortar shops.

"Did you see that?" Bertie asked in a low hiss as he laid his crossbow on the ground. "Did you *see* that? They have bald mammoths here." He glanced back at the market, where he'd spied mammals in question. "Little, bald mammoths."

"Those are elephants," Nbo told him, unbuckling her sword belt while keeping watch over the opposite side of their passage.

"Right." Walsie started unbuttoning his jacket. "Only, what are elephants?"

"Little, bald mammoths," Gideon said, his eyes on the narrow sliver of market visible as he unslung the map tube. "Now shut it and get changed."

"Copy that, sir," Walsie said, peeling off his shirt. Once it was off, he pulled the sleeves inside-out and shook it so that the extra fabric tucked within came loose. When he put the garment on again, he was wearing an unstructured emerald-green tunic. Gideon thought the color was a bit much, but it was certainly a change from the crisp, black uniform shirt he'd been wearing.

"Do you think we're clear?" Nbo asked, shrugging out of her own jacket to reveal a sleeveless under-blouse of dull gold.

"Not sure," Gideon replied as he unbuttoned his own shirt. "Better hurry."

At his side, Walsie had literally ripped away his fatigue pants to reveal a pair of flowing dark green trousers, then pulled his regulation pack inside-out as well, so it became a well-worn standard shopping tote, into which Gideon deposited the blueprints, samples, and lenses he'd stolen.

Walsie then took his former trousers—designed by Corpsman Siska, whose mother was a tailor—and stuffed them into the tote.

Nbo's uniform pants followed, leaving her in a trim brown jacket several shades lighter than her skin, and darker brown leggings tucked into the calf-length boots, and she was covering her close-cropped hair with a brightly patterned dhuku.

As she knotted the fabric around her head, Walsie tossed his crossbow and Nbo's sword into a nearby recycler.

Gideon started to pull off his own shirt, but then he heard the telltale sound of shouts, curses, crashes, and the thud of multiple boots rising from the market.

Very close by in the market.

All three Colonial soldiers froze.

"That don't sound good," Walsie said.

"No," Gideon agreed, "it doesn't." As he spoke, he started re-buttoning his shirt.

"Sir?" Nbo, resplendent in silk, stepped up.

"Time for Plan B," he told her.

"We don't have a Plan B, sir."

In the market, the sound of a small, bald mammoth trumpeting told him how close the enemy was.

"Actually, there is, but Command preferred I not share it." As he spoke, Gideon grabbed the tote and handed it to Nbo. "Take this and get back to the rendezvous," he ordered.

"But what about you, Colonel?" Walsie asked.

"I'm going to draw the enemy away," he explained, recapping the tube and slinging it over his shoulder.

His two subordinates shared a glance. "Due respect, sir, but that is a terrible plan. For you," Nbo said.

"Yes, I know. It's also an order," he told her. Behind him, he heard Walsie's boots shuffle over the pavers. "Command and Spec Ops both figured there was no chance we'd get away this without a sacrifice play."

"But—"

"Listen," he said, pointing to the market. "What you're hearing is the entire Ducati base swarming the market, looking for their stuff. And this is Midas, which means they will not stop looking. Ever. Which is why I'm going to make sure they have something to look for, while you two get those plans out of here.

She wanted to argue—he could see it in her eyes—but he could also see she knew he was right. "Yes, sir."

"Get gone," he said, jerking his chin towards the opposite side of the small passage and turning to head back into the market. "If I'm not at the rendezvous by 2800 hours, you get the company back to the regiment."

"But Colonel..." Walsie began, only to be shushed by Nbo.

She might disagree, but she knew her job.

Just like Gideon knew his.

Right now, his job was to play a game of net the queen . . . with himself as the queen.

Midasian soldiers were already swarming the market when Gideon emerged, pockets of black uniforms scything through the colorful civilians like hyperactive blots of ink.

Individual blots rummaged through stalls while others, in groups of three or four, shoved their way into the permanent stores around the market's edge.

Gideon joined in, poking through bins of produce and peering into storefronts near the alley where he'd split from his team, hoping the real Midasian soldiers would figure the sector was covered and move on.

Most of them did, and Gideon was just thinking he might make that rendezvous when the clanking rumble filled the air, foretelling the imminent arrival of a military crawler.

Time to go, Gideon told himself.

Ya think?, his self replied.

Gideon turned to jog after another band of searches, meaning to split off as soon as they hit the residential block on the far side of the market.

Which might have worked, if not for the fact that, even as he swung onto the cobbles, an elephant from the paddock decided to unload a trunk full of water on the passersby.

One of those passing turned out to be a child who, as Gideon watched, shrieked and dashed away, waving their hands in a manner Gideon had seen from Specialist Juster's daughter, who was exceptionally sensitive to things like, say, unexpected sprays of water.

None of which would have been an issue, except the kid was running into the path of the oncoming crawler.

He didn't hesitate, didn't even think, and even as the child's parents were realizing little Navi or Veria was missing, Gideon was diving into the street, grabbing the frenetic kid and carrying them out of the way of the oncoming crawler.

On the far side of the road, he set the child down and, as the transport rumbled on, asked, "Are you okay?"

Wide dark eyes fixed on his for a heartbeat, before shifting a little to the left and being followed by the faintest of nods.

"Yuening!" one of the kid's adults came swooping in, still dripping.

Gideon straightened and stepped back, then back again, but there was a crowd around the kid now, hemming him in with pats on the shoulders, along with a few murmurs of surprise that one of the "black shirts" would put themselves out for a civilian.

"You know better than to run off like that," the man said, running his hands over Yuening's shoulders and arms, as if to assure himself the child was whole.

"It was cold," Yuening replied, his gaze averted from his father's.

"I know," the man said, his voice softening as a woman and another man slipped in to crouch next to Yuening. "Thank you," the man who, from his looks, was Yuening's father, said to Gideon.

Gideon waved it off, realizing it was well past time to scarp. "It was nothing," he said, doing his best to match the other man's accent.

"I don't know about that," yet another voice emerged from the crowd, and Gideon turned to see a Midasian officer—a lieutenant, from the rank tabs—standing at the edge of the gathered circle.

Already the civilians were melting away, like salt in the rain, leaving the man in black staring at Gideon. "That was a brave stunt," the lieutenant continued, his dark eyes fixed on Gideon's. "You're not from the fort," he added.

Keep the answers short, Gideon thought. "No, sir," he said, noting that the wall of civilians had shifted, so there was now an opening.

The lieutenant's brow arched. "And this is where you tell me your name and battalion."

"Okay," Gideon said, then turned and fled through the gap created by the civilians. He thought he saw Yuening wave, but the crowd closed up behind him, cutting off his view of the child and the suspicious lieutenant, who was shouting for troops to "Follow that private!"

Gideon spared a single look over his shoulder to where the officer was pushing free of the helpful civilians, then started to run, heading in the opposite direction from the one Nbo would be taking.

By the time the Midasian soldiers caught up with him, Gideon had seen more of Ducati than he'd ever hoped, including a too-close encounter with an Illyrian beaver in one of the city's green zones.

The three-meter-long mammal was impressive, but its teeth were genuinely terrifying. Then there was the tail, which Gideon barely avoided as he pivoted away from the beaver's habitat and out to the city's southern wall, where two of the enemy squads flanked him.

As the Midasians closed in, Gideon looked over the wall at the Toyota River, tumbling wildly at the base of the sharp, stony slope, then at the approaching soldiers.

Not the best odds.

He looked at the river again and then, with one swift move,

pulled the leather tube from his shoulder and, as the shouts erupted from both sides, drew his arm back and cast it out like a spear.

There was, he had to admit, a small glow of satisfaction as he watched the tube arc up and out, and then inevitably down, to splash in the rushing waters of the Toyota, where it bobbed and tumbled a few times before disappearing in the tumultuous stream.

That glow lasted just long enough for the first Midasian to reach him, at which point it was replaced with the much less satisfying thud of a sword hilt to the back of his skull.

When he woke up, the situation was measurably worse.

Rather than the bright, colorful city, Gideon found himself inside a dark cell that smelled of damp, sawdust, and a little of rusted iron.

It was also, since he lacked both shirt and boots, quite cold.

They had left him with his pants, for which he supposed he should be grateful.

He'd have been more grateful if he wasn't hanging from the ceiling by his shackled wrists.

Gideon took in what he could of the room. As his eyes adjusted to the dimness—the only light came from a lone solar panel—he could see it was larger than he'd first thought.

In front of him, an allusteel door stood closed. Against the wall to his left squatted a rough-hewn table, stained and covered with an assortment of tools that looked as if they'd be at home on a carpenter's belt.

Given the location, and despite the sawdust scattered over the floor, Gideon doubted those tools saw any actual carpentry.

"You are new."

The sound of a voice from somewhere behind him made Gideon's breath hitch. He tried to peer behind him, but the positioning of his arms made such a move impossible. However, the rattling of chains accompanying the voice told him the unseen speaker was also a prisoner.

"Sorry," the voice continued, deep and raspy. "I probably shouldn't be talking, but I've been alone in here for...a long time."

"I'm sorry to hear that," he said.

"Not as sorry as I am."

The response was so dry, Gideon's breath huffed out in an almost laugh.

But only almost because, not only was the situation not funny, an unfortunate side effect of having one's arms strung up over one's head was that it made breathing difficult.

"Dare I ask why you're here?" the voice asked.

"You can ask," Gideon said.

"But you won't answer...nor should you," the voice reasoned. "You don't know me, can't even look at me. I could be one of them, trying to earn your trust."

Since everything the voice said was true, Gideon opted not to comment.

"Your accent," the unseen speaker continued, as if passing the time over a cuppa, "from Ford, if I am not mistaken?"

"And you're a Midasian," Gideon offered, without confirming the supposition.

"True for you," the voice replied with the hint of a smile under the rasp.

A moment of silence passed before Gideon ventured a question of his own. "So, why would the Midasian army lock up one of their own?"

"I am not one of their own. I am a civilian—a scientist."

"Okay, so why would the Midasian army lock up a scientist?"

"Because I published a theory they don't like."

Gideon glanced at the table and the not-carpentry tools. "I guess not," he said, then asked, "What kind of theory?"

"A study on non-human sapience."

"Like dolphins? Or dracos?"

"Not exactly," the voice said with a hacking sound that he took for a laugh, one that ceased abruptly as the lock in the allus-teel door snicked and the door itself swung open to reveal a man wearing the ubiquitous black of the Midasian armed forces. The only thing breaking up the monotony were the silver sabers on his collar, marking the man who'd entered as a Major of Infantry.

He was holding a pair of boots and a uniform shirt.

"You're awake," the major said to Gideon.

Since that was obvious, Gideon opted not to respond.

"I wonder," the officer continued, "if you understand how large a hornet's nest you've stirred up?" He held up the shirt he'd brought in. "A Colonial soldier, out of uniform behind enemy lines?" He clicked his tongue like a disapproving teacher and set the shirt and boots on the table. "That alone is a hanging offense."

"What makes you think I'm some smogging soldier?" Gideon asked.

"Aren't you?"

"Hells no," Gideon replied. "A thief? Yeah, well, ya got me there, but I ain't inclined to risk my neck for no Colonial High an' Mighties."

"Is that so?"

"Very so."

The major seemed to consider that. "And yet, when cornered, your first act was not to return the stolen property in your possession, even though doing so might save your highly valued neck, but to throw said property into the Toyota."

"One thing you learn on the streets," Gideon said with a vocal shrug, "never get caught with the goods. A lot harder to make charges stick with no evidence."

"In the Colonies, perhaps," the major nodded. "You'll find, here in Midas, we have a stricter view of criminal justice."

Gideon looked up at the shackles, then down at the enemy officer. "I've noticed."

The man studied Gideon for a moment. His eyes were dark pits in a face that, in this light, appeared chalky, with cheekbones so defined it was almost like having a conversation with a skull. His dark hair formed widow's peak, and the pale lips turned up in a permanent, and somewhat reptilian, smile.

He wasn't overly tall, and his slenderness made him appear less than threatening, until he began rolling up his sleeves and Gideon observed the line of muscles in his forearms—the sort of muscles that might be built up in the not-a-carpenter trade.

"Dr. Tabak," the man said, tucking his sleeve into place.

A resigned-sounding "Major Revin" came from behind Gideon.

"I wonder if you've had time to reconsider your position?"

"Every day you ask," the voice—Tabak—replied. "And still, my answer does not change. I will not recant my findings. My theory is sound."

"Even knowing every copy of your thesis has been destroyed? That your laboratory, research, every bit of data, every scribbled lie, no longer exists?"

"Even knowing," Tabak said. "My research may be gone, but Fortune has other scientists, and they will make the same connection as I. It will not be ignored forever. The truth will out."

It? Gideon thought.

"The truth," Revin said, "is what we make it."

Which just confirmed Gideon's private view of Midas as the Mwahaha Mad Villain capital of Fortune.

Sure, he despised the Adian pillage-and-burn approach to warfare but the southern coalition state had nothing on Midas for sheer, Earth-minded arrogance.

Right now the Earth-minded Coal-fart in the room was setting Gideon's clothing on the table before picking up the saw.

Tabak's breath shuddered out in a whimper, and Gideon was pretty sure he made an unhappy sound himself.

Thankfully, Revin put the saw down and picked up an item that had been hiding beneath it, which turned out to be a shock stick. Thumbing the stick to active, he turned to face the two prisoners. "Now, who goes first?"

Neither Gideon nor Tabak replied.

"I recall hearing of a game they played on Earth," Revin offered, leaving the table and crossing to Gideon's left. "A choosing game called 'Eeny, teeny, tiny toe...' Ridiculous, I know, but I find it helps one decide when faced with two equally attractive options."

Gideon kept his eyes forward; looking wouldn't change any outcome.

"Let's try it now, shall we?" the Midasian continued. "Eeny... teeny... tiny..."

Gideon didn't hear the "toe," but he felt it as the shock stick came to rest against his spine, causing him to buck wildly while crystal-charged electricity shot through his system.

"See?" Revin asked. "Now, wasn't that simple?"

For obvious reasons, Gideon didn't answer.

"That was only a taste of what will follow," the interrogator explained, circling Gideon, "if you choose not to tell me what you did with those plans."

"Your people saw...what I did with 'em," Gideon muttered.

"My people observed you throwing a document tube in the river," Revin agreed. "But that's hardly proof, and I don't believe you would have destroyed something of so great a value…"

"I would," Gideon asserted, meeting the dark pits of Revin's eyes, "if I were the soldier you say I am."

"Perhaps," Revin allowed with a nod. "Or perhaps you hid them somewhere in the market. Perhaps you handed them off to an accomplice. Either way," he said, "I expect to learn the truth, in time."

To which Gideon probably wouldn't have responded, even if Revin hadn't jammed the shock stick into his ribs.

The shock stick got a decent workout as Revin alternated between the two prisoners, allowing each sufficient recovery time that, by the time he returned, they'd be able to fully appreciate the experience.

When basic electrocution palled, Revin pulled out a packet of needles, proving himself an expert in the less medicinal forms of acupuncture, and when that failed to produce any satisfactory results from either party, he moved on to the lash.

Tabak ceased responding soon after—Gideon assumed the boffin had lost consciousness.

Gideon lasted a little longer, but when he woke, he found Revin waiting to start again, and again…and again.

And between the needles and the brands and the lash—but so far, thank the Keepers, no saw—he asked Gideon questions.

"Who are you?"

"What is your rank?"

"Where are you from?"

"What is your regiment?"

"Where are your accomplices?"

"What did you do with the plans?"

"Who is your commander?"

"What is your mother's name?"

That last earned a broken laugh from the orphaned Gideon, who had only a mother-shaped space where her memory should have been.

Unfortunately, the laugh led to a cough that continued for some time, during which Revin turned back to the boffin, who he asked to name any other scientists who shared in the controversial study.

Gideon felt bad for the doc, who'd been here longer and, from the sounds Tabak made, wasn't becoming numb to the process.

He lost count of how many times he blacked out.

After one particularly inventive session, he woke to discover Revin was no longer in the cell.

He also noticed that the breathing behind him had become much more labored.

"Hey," he croaked, before clearing his throat and trying again. "Tabak...you with me?"

He heard a slow exhalation—the sort he'd heard too often around the battlefield—and experienced a moment of inexplicable panic for the stranger.

"Here," the husky voice emerged at last. It sounded, to Gideon, both thick and hollow at once, like an echo trying to escape an earth-clogged crevasse. "I am just... tired. And thirsty."

Gideon could relate. His mouth was dry as the Barrens, his lips cracked and every ligament screaming for relief.

"How long have you—" he began, but cut himself off. "I'm sorry..."

"Never sorrow," Tabak's response was a sigh. "But I could not say. Time, in here, has little meaning."

Maybe not for the doctor, but it had some for Gideon, who held no illusions about his ability to remain silent. At some point, assuming he survived Revin's attentions, he'd start talking.

His job now was to do the needful and hold on until he was sure Nbo and Walsie got those plans to safety.

Closing his eyes, he tried to do the math.

The rendezvous point was a good three hours out of Ducati, if one stuck to the roads. Which they might not, so that'd add a couple hours.

Assuming they made it to the rendezvous, the company would still wait until 2800 hours for Gideon to return and, once he didn't, set sail under cover of night. If all went well from there, he expected them to reach the Epsilon border in another nine to twelve hours.

And once his company was safe in Colonial territory, Gideon could sing like an Amazonian phoenix and no one would suffer from it, because the second he was reported MIA, every codeword and radio frequency, every operation he'd been read in on, would be burned, changed or scrubbed.

The 12th Company, known throughout the 63rd Regiment as Quinn's Dirty Dozen, would get a new CO and it'd be as if Colonel Gideon Quinn never existed.

But he had to stay quiet until they were clear and, as Tabak pointed out, time in the cell was subjective. He had no clue how many hours had passed since his capture. Five? Eight? Thirteen?

And how much longer—

The telltale snick of the door's lock broke into his thoughts and he tried not to acknowledge the icy dread that coiled in his gut at that sound.

With a faint creak, the allusteel door opened.

Gideon tried to brace himself.

Then a thickset individual in a Midasian sergeant's uniform entered the room, followed by a woman wearing the bars of a commandant.

Gideon blinked, then blinked again.

"Sir?" Nbo stepped closer, squinting in the dim light. "Are you—" But the question went unfinished as her eyes adjusted to the dark, and she saw how he'd been spending his time. "We'll have you down in a moment," she promised, her voice brisk and a few degrees colder than the air in the room.

"Okay," Gideon said as Walsie approached with a key the size of his palm, then he grunted and started looking for a ladder, because no one was tall enough to reach the cuffs.

In the end, he and Nbo had to drag the table over to Gideon, where Nbo climbed on top, hissing as she kicked some of Revin's tools aside. In seconds, she had the shackles unlocked.

Gideon, after spending untold hours hanging like a side of aurochs, dropped into Walsie's waiting arms like... well...like a side of aurochs.

"Thanks," he said as his body erupted in fresh spates of wasp stings. "Except, why are you here? Because I remember ordering you both to not be here. Was I somehow unclear?"

"No, sir, you were perfectly clear," Nbo said, climbing down from the table and grabbing Gideon's shirt and boots from where they lay next to the shock stick. "And we did follow them."

"We made the rendezvous," Walsie assured. "Delivered the package neat as you please—but then I remembered the Corps motto."

"The Corps motto," Gideon echoed.

"Leave no one behind," Walsie confirmed, as if Gideon, who'd been part of the Corps since his sixteenth year—or maybe fifteenth, as he wasn't a hundred percent on his birthdate—had never heard it. "And I mentioned it to Sarge," he nodded towards Nbo.

"And at that point," Nbo picked up the narrative, "as ranking officer, I ordered the rest of the company on to Epsilon while Walsie and I returned for you, as the Corps motto overrides individual orders."

"It does, does it?" Gideon asked as Walsie attempted to rub the life back into his arms.

"Yes sir. At least the stupid ones."

"Stupid ones?"

"Yes, sir."

Gideon sighed, then let out a strangled noise as Walsie's vigorous massage struck a needle Revin had left in place.

"Sorry, sir," Walsie hissed, and, with far more delicacy than the corpsman had ever shown before, removed the offending item while sweat beaded on Gideon's skin and black spots danced in front of his eyes.

Something tightened over his shoulder—Nbo's hand, gripping him. "Are you all right, sir?"

"Good... I'm...good," he lied.

She nodded, first to him, then to Walsie. "We should get you dressed. We haven't much—"

"Wait," Gideon's voice cracked as he remembered. "We can't go."

"Colonel—"

"I mean, we can't go without the doctor. Tabak?" Still cradled in Corpsman Walsingham's arms, he tried to angle his head to where his partner-in-suffering was located, but he couldn't see more than the legs stretched out from the wall, bare and battered and rail thin.

"Colonel, we can't—"

"Doc?" he prompted. "You still with me?" He looked back

to see Nbo and Walsie sharing a glance. "I know Tabak's a Midasian, but—"

"It isn't that, Colonel."

"Then what?"

"It's—"

"It's that she's dead," Walsie cut in, his voice barely more than a growl.

"What?" Gideon's body instinctively rolled up and out of the corpsman's arms so he was on his knees and facing the other prisoner. "No," he said, dimly aware he was shaking with pain or shock or—something else. "That's not...that can't be right." His head slipped sideways because there was no light in the staring brown eyes, no hint of life anywhere in the thin body chained to a wall in the dark of a stone cell.

"Sir?" Nbo's hand came to rest on his shoulder. "We have to go."

"Yes," he said, blinking hard. "Except—"

"Yes, sir?"

"I didn't know she was a she." Gideon's own hand, thick and barely responsive, reached out to rest against the bloodied foot. "I didn't know. I didn't know...anything."

"You know her name," Nbo told him. "You know what happened here. But, Colonel, if we don't leave now, no one else ever will."

His head dipped in a nod, but still he didn't move, just knelt, his body trembling uncontrollably until Nbo gestured to Walsie and the two of them somehow got Gideon dressed.

By the time Nbo had the shirt buttoned, he was functional enough to stand, and once standing he looked down on the doctor, a woman who'd made a discovery about non-Human sapience—and been killed for it.

Then he realized he had never told her his name.

She'd died at the hands of a sadist, in the company of a stranger.

"Colonel?"

Nbo's query broke through the fog of remorse."Moving. Right."

Nbo, radiating brisk efficiency, moved to the door. "It's two hours 'til dawn with a skeleton guard, so we should be well out off base before anyone notices you gone."

———

Nbo was right about the guards.

The hours between 2800 and sunrise were the dead hours on most every base, and Ducati was no exception.

Sentries were stationed on the outer doors but no one patrolled the empty halls, so the way was clear and Gideon able to lean on Walsie all the way through the ward and into the admin area before they came upon an office with the door open and the light on.

After so many hours in the dim, Gideon's eyes teared upon seeing it.

Then someone from inside called out in a familiar voice, "Sergeant Simmons?"

Gideon came to a jerking halt as the adrenaline he'd thought long-spent rushed through every limb.

"It's about time," the voice continued. "I'm perishing for want of that tea."

The fog lifted from Gideon's eyes. He pushed away from Walsie and started towards the office, fueled by the memory of another unseen voice.

Behind him he heard Nbo hiss and felt Walsie's hand on his arm, but he ignored the one and shook off the other, continuing on until he stood inside the office, which was not only warmly lit but comfortably furnished with an ebony desk, upholstered divan, and shelves of books.

It smelled, Gideon thought, of oranges.

And sitting behind the desk, facing the door, sat Major Revin, staring down at a report.

"Just put it anywhere, Simmons," Revin ordered, not bothering to look up.

Nbo came up behind Gideon, didn't speak.

"Simmons?" Revin finally looked up.

"Colonel Quinn?" Nbo murmured.

"Wait outside," Gideon told her as Revin came slowly to his feet. "This won't take long."

It didn't, and when he stepped out of the office, the fuel that pushed him into it was all but spent and his body with it, so that both Nbo and Walsie had to half-carry him to the detention ward's main doors, where they left him propped while they dealt with the guards who, from the twinned *thuds* Gideon heard, wouldn't be waking for a long time.

But they would wake up, which was more than could be said for Dr. Tabak...or Major Revin.

Gideon had left the interrogator slumped over his desk, his head at an angle that would leave no doubt as to how he died.

The rest of the escape proceeded without incident, or Gideon assumed it did, because he passed out the second Nbo bundled him into the staff car Walsie hijacked.

But in his dreams, his mind's ear kept replaying Tabak's hollow voice, declaring, "It will not be ignored forever. The truth will out."

And even in his dreams, he wondered what, precisely, would not be ignored.

What truth had Tabak discovered, but never seen emerge?

Then he heard her voice again, so close she might have been whispering in his ear as she said, "You'll see…"

"See what?" he asked back, but the question woke him.

His eyes opened, and he found himself stretched out on the lower bunk in a small compartment, listening to the rhythmic sluice of water in a wheel.

Everything still hurt, but the worst bits were padded by various forms of bandaging.

Nbo appeared at his side, emerging from the shadow, where he expected she'd been keeping watch.

"Where are we?" he asked, his voice rough as Tabak's.

"On the Toyota, about a hundred kilometers west of Ducati," she explained, perching on the edge of the cot. "We booked passage on a riverboat flying keeper colors." She pointedly did not say it was a Keeper boat, which told Gideon they were likely in the company of smugglers. "We reached Colonial territory about an hour ago. We're in the clear."

Gideon nodded, then sipped the herb-laced broth she offered, then looked up into the warm, brown eyes. "It wasn't a stupid order," he told her.

Her head dipped in the barest hint of a nod. "I know."

"Thank you," he said.

"You're welcome."

"But don't do it again."

"Wouldn't dream of it."

"I'm not kidding, Sarge—Nbo," his voice lowered, no longer colonel to sergeant but friend to friend. "Candace needs her mother."

"Candace knows her mother is a soldier," Nbo replied. "And she'd likely never forgive me if I let anything happen to Uncle Gijin," she continued, using her daughter's pronunciation of his name. "You should get some more rest," she continued. "You'll need your strength for the After-Action report."

He wanted to keep arguing, to remind her of little things like chain of command, but even as she spoke his eyes began to drift closed and he was soon asleep.

This time, no dreams followed.

Want more time on Fortune?
Follow our Outrageous Crew on Ream for free to access more shorts, as well as complete novels, new outrageous stories, and our Crew community.
Scan the QR code below to begin reading!

https://reamstories.com/outrageouscrew

ACKNOWLEDGMENTS

Profound gratitude to Dr. King and Dr. Wong respectively, for keeping me both sane and healthy enough to finish the book, and Kelley McKinnon, Fortune's other founder, must take a bow for her plot input and her dramaturgical support.

Thanks always to the Wombats (ask Lori), Lori Drake and Cameron Coral, for the morning writing/editing sessions, as well as Lori Diederich and Youness Elh for making the Fortune Chronicles readable and pretty, respectively. Further applause for C.K. Brown for taking on the mantle of Sensitivity Reader.

Thanks, always to the family, both blood and chosen, and thanks to Kelley the Younger for discovering our forever home.

ABOUT THE AUTHOR

As a lifelong fan of complex characters and outrageous worlds, I lean on my history in theatre, fight choreography, and parenting to create immersive adventures, engaging characters, and unlikely partnerships (because I pretty much live for oddballs teaming up against a bad system).

I can also be found hanging out at Ream Stories, growing more outrageous adventures featuring flawed heroes, chosen families, and all the snark you care to entertain.*

*__True story:__ In first grade, my youngest turned in a daily journal entry featuring the opening phrase, "Sometimes, my mommy can be sarcastic."**

**I've never felt more seen.